BY CALLIE BATES

The Waking Land
The Memory of Fire
The Soul of Power

The Soul of Power

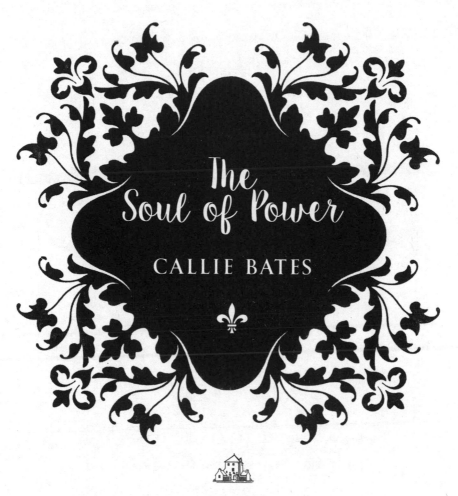

The Soul of Power

CALLIE BATES

DEL REY
NEW YORK

Published in the United States by Del Rey, an imprint of Random House,
a division of Penguin Random House LLC, New York.

DEL REY and the HOUSE colophon are registered trademarks of
Penguin Random House LLC.

The map by Laura Hartman Maestro was originally published in *The Waking Land* by
Callie Bates (New York: Del Rey, 2017).

LIBRARY OF CONGRESS CATALOGING-IN-PUBLICATION DATA
Names: Bates, Callie, author.
Title: The soul of power / Callie Bates.
Description: New York: Del Rey, [2019] | Series: The waking land; 3
Identifiers: LCCN 2018059132 | ISBN 9780399177446 (hardback) |
ISBN 9780399177453 (ebook)
Subjects: | BISAC: FICTION / Fantasy / Epic. | FICTION / Coming of Age. |
GSAFD: Fantasy fiction.
Classification: LCC PS3602.A8555 S68 2019 | DDC 813/.6—dc23
LC record available at https://lccn.loc.gov/2018059132

Printed in the United States of America on acid-free paper

randomhousebooks.com

246897531

First Edition

Book design by Diane Hobbing

To Nan

Western
Isles

THE TAIL RIDGE
(Bal an-Dracan)

Dalriada

Altan

CAERIS

Taich-na
Ivaugh

Barrody

Dearbann

Threve

Lake
Harbor

TINAN

Cerid Aven

The Ard River

Portmason

EREN

Ganz

Oise

Laon

Roquelle

Gulf
of
Eren

Great Ocean

EMPIRE of
PALADIS

Tarican
Strait

Middle
Sea

BAEDON

Illustrated map by Laura Hartman Maestro ©2016

The Soul of Power

PROLOGUE

The soldiers came early that morning. I woke in the chill before dawn to my mother's touch on my arm. "Sophy, get up. Put on your boots."

I rubbed my eyes. I wanted to go back to sleep. I was tired of running and being cold and hungry—though at first, when we had slipped out of our rooms in Barrody in the middle of the night, it had seemed like an adventure. The king of Eren's soldiers had not seemed like a real threat. I thought we'd go home to my grandmother with stories about our escapades, but we only kept running—and somehow more than a year passed. Food grew thin; my clothes did, too. Now I dreamed of real beds and a fire that actually kept me warm. I longed for my friends and the home I once had; those memories haunted me every day.

Ma stroked the hair back from my forehead. "Sweet girl, get up. I have a job for you."

I squinted open one eye. A job for *me*? I was almost eight and I was dying to prove myself as bold a rebel as my mother. All the same, I pretended nonchalance. "How much do I get paid?"

She managed the flicker of a smile, ghostly in the half-dark. "I need you to take a message to Duke Ruadan."

I bolted upright with a squeal. *"Me?"*

"Shh." Ma reached into the pocket of her waistcoat. She pressed a cool, hard object into my hand. Its metal chain trailed between my fingers; I felt instinctively for the clasp.

"I'm supposed to take him Pa's locket?"

My mother did not speak. She took my head in her hands and kissed me, once—resoundingly—on the forehead. Then she hugged me tight. I felt her heart pounding against my ear. The stifled noise in her throat. I knew then that whatever Ma wanted, it would not be an adventure. I knew it would leave an ache in the space beneath my breastbone—an ache I knew too well, by now.

"You're a strong girl, Sophy." Ma's voice was rough, huskier than usual. "Promise me you'll take this to the duke. You'll go all the way to Cerid Aven and not look back."

"How am I going to find you after?" I couldn't help the thin plea in my voice.

She paused. "I'll come after you."

"You promise?"

"Yes, sweetheart. I promise."

I hugged her tighter, and for a moment she returned my clasp. Then she pulled out of my arms, clambering down the ladder to the barn below, her boot heels ringing on the wood.

I swallowed hard and draped the necklace over my head. I had never worn it before, despite numerous pleas, and I marveled at how it settled into the hollow of my chest. A steadying weight, like my mother's touch—or my father's. The locket held a piece of his hair, a ruddy gold, tied up with a black ribbon. I knew, because I'd harassed my mother into showing it to me any number of times, since she refused to offer me his name or any further details about him. "I'll tell you when you're older," she'd say, and I'd roll my eyes and groan—not that it ever made any difference.

But now I was taking his locket to the duke—which must mean there was a secret message inside. Maybe the duke knew my father, and he was going to take me to him.

I put on my boots. I was already sleeping in my clothes—the same ones I'd been wearing for several months, since that woman in the hill town gave me the hand-me-downs that had once belonged to her son. The trousers were starting to get tight around my hips, but the coat sleeves still dangled, dirty, over my hands.

Beneath me, in the lower part of the barn, a cow lowed, and the whispers of our rebel friends filtered through the dark. I clambered down the ladder, warming to the idea of carrying the locket. I was going to prove myself worthy. Then they wouldn't sing songs only about Mag Dunbarron, but about her daughter, Sophy, too.

And maybe someone would give me a new change of clothes.

My mother and the other rebels were gathered in a circle toward the front of the barn. They'd opened the doors and fog seeped in, purling around their shoulders. They'd been talking quietly, but stopped as I approached.

"Ready to head out, Sophy?" Jock asked. His voice strained over the words.

They must all be afraid of sending me alone to Cerid Aven, where the duke lived. In truth, I was scared, too, but I wasn't about to let anyone see it—especially not my mother, who was the bravest person in the world. I widened my stance. "Of course I am!"

Something flickered in his eyes, but I couldn't see what it was in the dimness. "Goodbye, then," he said. He kissed my forehead.

"Be careful, Sophy." That was Ethna. She, too, kissed my forehead.

The other rebels came forward one by one to kiss me and say goodbye—a dozen people with cold hands and sad eyes. My initial flush of pride began to shrink into something cold and scared. Maybe I wasn't being sent to be brave, but I didn't know why else I'd be sent away.

At last the goodbyes were done, and Ma led me out of the barn, into the fog, my hand tight in hers.

The last of my bravery slipped away. "I wish you could come with me," I whispered.

I heard her swallow. "I'll come after you, sweetheart. I promised, didn't I?"

We were silent, then, as we approached the edge of town, where small gaps showed through the wooden walls. The fog hid the soldiers' lights from us, but I smelled the smoke from their campfires, and heard an eerie jingle, like a horse's harness.

Ma paused beside the wall, her fingernails digging into my shoulder. "Once you reach the edge of camp, there's a path marked by a stone cairn. Follow it to the next cairn, and the next, and the next. You should reach Cerid Aven tomorrow, or the day after. You have hardtack?"

I nodded, waiting for her to give me a lecture about drinking only clean water. But she only said, "You'll make it."

I don't know if she really believed it, or only hoped.

"But how—" I began.

A creak sounded on the other side of the wall, shivering into the dark air. My heart surged. Ma hugged me tight—so tight I heard the sharp inhale and exhale of her breathing. She whispered, "Are you ready to be brave?"

The question she always asked me. The answer was always yes.

Although the truth was usually no.

"Yes," I whispered, even though fear tumbled liquid and hot through my limbs.

Something crunched on the other side of the wall, and I shuddered. There was a soft tap on the wood. My head jerked up, and my mother breathed against my cheek. "Go!"

I didn't want to go. I clung to her until she peeled my arms off and nudged me to the ground. My lips were trembling. Tears gathered in my eyes, but I had to be brave. My mother demanded it, and I couldn't let her down.

I crawled through the gap in the wall.

Rough hands grasped my wrists. The gap was low; I tasted dirt in my mouth. A man, little more than a silhouette in the fog, pulled me onto my feet. I caught the motion as he put a finger to his lips. Gestured to something behind him.

I stepped over to it, still shaking, numb with the shock of actually leaving my mother. My fingers met cold metal. A wheelbarrow. The man's hands closed on my waist, and I sucked in a panicked breath as he boosted me up. My shoe hit the metal with a resounding *ping*, bell-like in the fog. I jumped but the man didn't startle.

He settled me down in the bottom of the wheelbarrow, and I

curled there with my knees tucked up to my chin. The man squeezed my shoulders, as if to reassure me. Then he unfurled a nubby blanket and threw it over me, and I was breathing hard in stuffy darkness, my heartbeat a crimson drum in my ears. I never got a good look at the man's face.

Several heavy objects settled on top of me. I smelled the pungent, sweet odor of new-cut wood. So he was pretending to gather fuel for their fires. The wheelbarrow tipped, jamming my feet below the rest of me, and we began to move.

At first I couldn't hear anything over the creaking wheels and the fear pulsing in my blood. Then there was a voice—in Ereni!— and white terror erupted through me, so bright I almost wet my too-tight trousers. But the man didn't stop. More voices passed overhead, a din of Ereni, and I shook in the bottom of the wheelbarrow, wondering if one of them belonged to the Butcher of Novarre.

The man kept on, and the voices faded. My chin jolted against my knees as we bumped over rough ground. Then suddenly I was lowered. The barrow stopped. The weights came off me, and the man ripped the blanket away.

He leaned over me. "You have two minutes. There's a trail at the base of the ridge. Get out and go!"

Then he was gone. I sat up in time to glimpse his retreating back.

I hauled myself out of the wheelbarrow, my legs shaking and buckling. I was going to be spotted by the Butcher of Novarre; I could feel it in my bones. I would be shot.

I forced myself to look around. The man had told me I had minutes, and I needed them. I wanted to live.

I was in a clearing beneath a forested ridge. A rock cairn marked the path between two trees. I forced my wobbling legs into motion and ran to the rock cairn that marked the narrow track. I charged uphill over roots and stones, my lungs burning. Near the top of the ridge, another cairn marked a turn deep into the woods. I looked back one last time, but I'd gone so far I could barely even see the

Ereni camp. Only the faint whiff of smoke reminded me of what I'd left behind—that, and the locket pressing against my chest.

MY MOTHER HAD trained me well. I could walk all day, with only short stops for water and a bite of hardtack. I'd learned to manage without much food. Even through a haze of exhaustion and fear, I knew how to keep going. At night, I knew not to light a fire but to make myself a bed out of dry pine needles.

I lay awake all night, all the same, touching my chest where the locket covered the empty hollow in my heart. Wondering why Ma had sent me away. Feeling small in the hugeness of the dark woods. I whispered words to comfort myself. The old poem about Wildegarde, the first steward of the land, and Aline, the queen of Caeris.

From the mountains beyond the moon, nursed by dragons, Wildegarde came—down to the court of Queen Aline. The queen did not know what to make of such a woman, her hands and legs covered in leaves as a tree is. She said, "Who are you? Why have you come?" and Wildegarde answered, "I am the breath of the mountains, the whisper of the waters, the swift passing of a bird, the hollows within the hills. I have come for you. I have come so we can make a song together."

I must be brave, I told myself. *Brave, like Aline. Like the queens of old.*

By dawn, I was ready to go again. The path clung to shadowy forests, only occasionally crossing farm fields and nearing towns, and I took care that no one noticed me. A second night passed much the same as the first, though exhaustion forced me to sleep. I began to wonder if I'd missed a turn; if I wasn't really headed for Cerid Aven but to Eren and all the dangers that lurked in the south.

When I ran out of hardtack around noon, I started to cry. Why had Ma sent me out like this? I wasn't brave. I was just a scared little girl, with aching feet and an empty stomach.

But scared as I was, I was still Mag Dunbarron's daughter. I made myself stop crying and walked on, passing the rocky shoulder of a high limestone hill that jutted far overhead. The forest had turned to a woods full of enormous old oaks, their trunks five times my size. I'd lost track of the rock cairns, and the path I was on seemed well trampled. I should get off it, find somewhere more secure. Except where was I supposed to go? I was so lost, and so frightened.

The edge of a pale-gray building came into sight ahead.

I slowed, my heart thudding in my hollow chest. The path had brought me here, but was this Cerid Aven, as my mother had promised? And how would I know? It wasn't as if there were a big sign out front, proclaiming my destination. Yet I had clearly arrived at a wealthy person's mansion. The building stretched into a series of fine, many-paned windows, and sculpted gardens cupped it, studied and elegant. If Duke Ruadan lived anywhere, it must be here.

I edged closer. There was a woman out in the gardens. She wore a blue coat over a pale-yellow gown, and her hair was piled up in a dark, lustrous mound atop her head, the way I remembered ladies in the city doing theirs. She was humming, patting her hand against her thigh in rhythm. Even though she was making music, something about her seemed unaccountably sad.

I tried not to make a sound, but she must have felt my gaze on her back. She turned and saw me.

For a moment, we both stared at each other, frozen.

"Who are you?" she demanded. The edge of an accent warmed her voice, and though it wasn't Ereni, I didn't know what it was. Maybe I had wandered off the very edge of the map.

"Is this Cerid Aven?" I asked, my voice high-pitched. If it wasn't, I'd run. I could run faster than this woman in her fine gown, I knew it.

"You're a girl," she said, and the sadness in her intensified. She held out her hand. "What are you doing out here, child?"

I asked my question again. "Is this Cerid Aven?"

She nodded.

Relief burst through me in huge, cartwheeling warmth. I actually swayed and almost fell onto my knees. The woman started toward me, her face worried. But I had a job to do. "I have a message for Duke Ruadan."

"A message? But you're barely . . ." She shook her head. "Caerisians." She took my arm, and I let her, because her touch was gentle and she looked so worried, the way my mother had looked when I'd fallen on that rock and sprained my ankle once. "I can take you to Ruadan. I'm his wife, Teofila."

"Oh," I said. That explained the accent—she came from Baedon, across the narrow strait. It also explained why she was sad. The king had taken away her daughter Elanna, who was only a little younger than me. "My name is Sophy Dunbarron."

As we went inside, I glimpsed my face in the windowpane. It was thin, with huge, staring eyes. My hair hung in dirty ropes beneath my hat. I looked like a beggar. A vagrant.

Teofila led me over fine carpets, past statues and paintings, calling out to well-dressed servants to bring tea and food and the duke. She took me to a big room full of cozy furniture the same yellow as her skirt and stood me in front of the fire. I had never felt anything so glorious. I thought I was going to melt into a puddle there on Duke Ruadan's soft wool rug.

Then I opened my eyes and a tall, sharp-eyed man was coming into the room. He gave Teofila a questioning look.

"This is Sophy," she said. "She—"

I widened my stance. I'd come all this way, and I had one job. I lifted my chin and addressed Duke Ruadan myself. "I have a message for you from Mag Dunbarron."

Ruadan looked startled. He exchanged a glance with Teofila. "Mag? Are you her daughter? Where is she?"

Duke Ruadan knew my mother by name? I wanted to melt again, though at the same time nothing seemed more natural. My mother was a force of nature; the queen of the rebels. Of course the duke who'd tried to lead a rebellion knew her. "She was in the village of Marose a few days ago."

"Marose," Ruadan repeated. Again, his gaze flicked to his wife.

I reached for my locket and pulled it over my head. "This is for you."

Wordlessly, he opened the locket. But only the single, inch-long strand of red-gold hair slipped from it, still bound tightly with a black ribbon. It fell to the carpet at my feet.

I stared at it. There was no message. No carefully folded paper with a secret missive from my mother. "It's my father's," I said.

Teofila crouched beside me. She handed the hair to Ruadan, and touched my cheek. "Sophy, are you sure your mother was in Marose?"

I nodded. I couldn't escape the feeling I'd been cheated.

She drew in a breath. Ruadan was watching us, but Teofila didn't take her eyes off me. "It's just that we've had some terrible news from Marose this morning. The Butcher of Novarre had the town surrounded."

"I know! I had to escape in a wheelbarrow."

Teofila gripped my hands. "So you were there when it burned?"

My mouth dropped open. The hope that had been fluttering in me stilled and died. I whispered, "Burned?"

"Yes." She held me harder, but did not spare me the truth. "Your mother must have sent you to safety. The whole village was burned to the ground, along with everyone in it. I'm sorry. I'm so, so sorry."

Air whined in my ears. I was more numb than I had been when I climbed from the wheelbarrow. I couldn't comprehend it. Everyone, dead? The rebels, the villagers? *The cows?*

The duke crouched beside Teofila. He reached out, touching his fingers to my chin. I looked up at him, and I knew then that he'd known my mother, because there was winter in his eyes the way there was winter in my heart. But there was also something else. Hope.

"You don't have a message," he said. "*You* are the message."

Teofila looked at him sharply.

"She's the future of Caeris," he told her. "Sophy," he said to me, with an urgency I didn't understand, "did Mag ever tell you who your father was?"

I shook my head.

The duke gripped my shoulder. He held the locket out to me. "This hair belongs to Euan Dromahair, the rightful king of Caeris. He's your natural father, Sophy."

I glanced uncertainly at Teofila. Her lips were pressed together, but she nodded at me. It wasn't entirely reassuring. My father, the man who should be king? It didn't make sense. And yet, knowing my mother, I believed it.

"And if he doesn't come to Caeris to claim his throne," the duke continued, "or if his son doesn't, do you know who will?"

"Who?" I whispered.

Ruadan Valtai looked into my eyes, searchingly, as if he were trying to find the backbone of a queen. "You."

And I knew then that I must be brave, alone.

CHAPTER ONE

Ruadan is gone now, executed on the steps of the Tower in Laon, and all I am left with, in the cold light of dawn, is memories. And a creeping doubt about whether I can possibly become the queen he raised me to be.

There's a soft noise outside my tent. The mountain women who form my queen's guard shift on the other side of the flap but don't seem alarmed, so I guess who it must be.

I throw on my riding habit and step out just as Elanna goes by, a slight figure bundled in an overlarge greatcoat, curls of chestnut hair escaping over its worn collar. As usual, she seems oblivious to my presence. I follow her out into the gray-green dawn. Light softens the rough tents that make up our run-down camp above the river Ard, near a town called Tavistock. Across the wide, rocky water, mingling with the fog, smoke drifts from the Tinani camp where King Alfred's troops are waking to begin their latest offensive. They should have no idea that the Butcher of Novarre is here, along with Elanna and myself—or at least, I hope they don't. The Butcher keeps claiming our ranks are littered with spies loyal to the Ereni nobles who fled the kingdom after our rebellion, and who now have the ears of King Alfred of Tinan. I've heard no rumors that they wish to reinstate Loyce Eyrlai, so maybe they're simply working against us out of spite. Given the narrow-minded thinking of some of my ministers, I wouldn't be surprised.

The guards on the edge of camp acknowledge El, but—as

usual—no one seems to take much notice of me. Despite my greater height and brilliant red coat, the people only have eyes for their *Caveadear.* I might as well be invisible.

We leave the guards behind, though. El doesn't want anyone to witness her weakness.

At the top of the bluff, overlooking the river, she pauses, and I step up beside her. Softly, I say, "Can I help?"

She casts me a tight, skeptical look. She's been angry with me ever since I encouraged Jahan to go to Ida and argue our case before the emperor of Paladis, but now she simply seems condescending. "No, Sophy. There's nothing you can do."

I swallow down a pulse of frustration. As if she needs to remind me, again, that she possesses sorcery and I don't. That she is the real leader of Eren and Caeris, the one they truly respect, and I am not. That *she* is Ruadan's real daughter, and I am merely the one he replaced her with. As soon as she returned to Caeris, our rebellion and our lives became all about her. She is the *Caveadear,* the steward of the land, the future of Eren and Caeris. She's the hope of the kingdom, the symbol of magic reemerging throughout the world.

I am the backup. A would-be Aline to her earth-shaking Wildegarde. The second choice—the girl who took her father's throne when her dead half brother could not, and whose father has never once acknowledged her existence. Who took the throne, in some ways, because she knew her mother would expect it, encourage it, if she still lived.

I'm not proud of how I feel. I remind myself that I love El like a sister. But like a sister, I wish she would learn how to share. And take me seriously.

She's already descending the steep trail down to the river—a spot she picked out yesterday, when the Butcher insisted a display of her magic would put the terror of the gods into the Tinani and destroy their current offensive.

I'm more worried about it destroying El.

There's a scrape behind me. Rhia Knoll hops up through the fog, alert despite the tiredness pinching her eyes. I can feel my own exhaustion mirroring hers. As usual, a frown puckers her black eyebrows, belying her delicate features. She tugs the collar of her dark-blue coat up to her ears. The wind is sweeping down from the north, bringing the coldness of the still-snowcapped mountains in the Tail Ridge, though we're in the north of Eren, several days' travel from the peaks.

Rhia peers toward the foggy river. "Is she down there?"

I gesture with my chin. El has reached a rocky shelf above the water. She's just visible through the fog, her old greatcoat rendering her shapeless.

Even though she frustrates me, I'm worried about her. Rhia and I might be tired, but Elanna's exhaustion seems so deep it runs into the marrow of her bones—and into the land itself. The Butcher wanted her to perform this feat of magic at high noon, for the world to see, as if she could merely snap her fingers and burst the dam upstream that will flood the Ard. And perhaps, in the days after she woke the land, she could. Now, though, her magic is tired and so is she. I'm afraid she won't be able to swamp the Tinani camp, and if we have to fight this battle with guns and men and horses, we're going to lose. Tinan's being supplied by the empire of Paladis; they have more manpower and more guns. And it's not been our forces that have stopped the Tinani crossing the river, despite the Butcher's attempts to impress his superior generalship upon everyone. Elanna's the one who has stopped them, time and again.

She needs help. A respite. Something. Yet I'm too afraid to suggest she rest. We all are.

"Are you feeling better?" Rhia asks me.

I inadvertently touch my fingertips to my stomach, then stuff my hands into the pockets of my coat. "I don't know what you mean."

She eyes me. "Don't be cagey with me, Dunbarron. You looked green all last month. Father thought someone was poisoning you."

"Oh, that." I attempt nonchalance. "Something I picked up in Laon—stomach sickness. Everyone had it."

Rhia raises an eyebrow but shrugs. I slowly release my breath. Rhia remained on the border the last time I went to the capital, so how would she know I'm lying? Besides, for all I know, people have been ill; it's that time of year.

All the same, the temptation to tell her the truth presses against the back of my throat. We're alone on the bluff—or as alone as we're going to get—and the weight of this secret is pulling me down. I feel the need to confess like a hand between my shoulder blades. But I know what Rhia Knoll will say. She'll tell me I'm being a fool in more ways than one. There's only one solution for this problem, and Rhia won't have any trouble telling me what it is.

Am I being a fool?

Of course I am. I know it, but I have no other choice. At least, not one that will let me sleep at night. Ruadan used to say that we are defined by the decisions we make, and that the larger the choice, the more we must face it head-on, clear-eyed. I made this choice; I can't pretend, even to myself, that it was an accident.

But sometimes I wish Ruadan had said something else. That we are more than the sum of our decisions.

I fold my arms, unable to confess, and neither of us says much. The fog's beginning to burn away as Elanna sits motionless on the shelf below us, giving no indication she's aware of our presence. The cold seeps into my bones.

"Queen Sophy!"

I turn. A runner is coming up the hillside from our camp. "You have a visitor," he pants.

I look past him, toward the rough, fraying tents the Butcher insisted on using, trying to disguise the fact that not only is he here, but El, Rhia, and I are, too. Our intelligence intercepted the Tinani plan to cross here, north of Tavistock, and now we can only hope that information was accurate. I wonder if the two new arrivals who have appeared outside the command tent—two men, from the looks of it, on black horses, though I can't make out their faces from here—have anything to do with that. The Butcher's come out to greet them; I recognize his bandy-legged silhouette.

"There'll be hot coffee down there," Rhia says. She's been obsessed with the stuff since she first had it in Laon a few months ago. Now, true to form, she charges off toward camp. The messenger hesitates between her and me.

I glance down the slope, toward El. She's still unmoving. To all appearances, she's unaware that we're even up here.

With a sigh, I follow the messenger and Rhia toward the command tent.

The men have gone inside by the time I arrive, along with Rhia, who's standing in front of a silver coffeepot with a look of sweet bliss on her usually ornery face. "Here, Sophy." She thrusts a cup at me. "It'll do you wonders."

One of the new arrivals swings around: a wiry dark-haired young man in a coat of green Caerisian wool. "Soph! I mean . . . Your Majesty," he corrects himself, doubling over into a low bow.

I smile down at the top of his head. "Alistar." For once, his hair isn't in spikes, but lies flat in soft brown waves. My fingers twitch.

He looks up at me, with a grin on his narrow mischievous face, and his eyes spark in a familiar way. "You look well."

I claim the cup of coffee from Rhia and smirk at him over the rim. But then out the corner of my eye, I catch sight of the Butcher's disapproving scowl and sigh. Some people—Rhia, for instance—don't care that Alistar and I are together, but I know from past conversations that the Butcher considers my relationship with Alistar a disgrace to my crown. Maybe this is just because he hates to see other people having feelings, not to mention affection, but enough other people seem to agree with him that I've become self-conscious. I can already feel the weight of his stare.

I give Alistar a stern glance. "What are you doing here?" I ask, striving to sound businesslike and not as if his knowing smile is unraveling me. "I thought you were evacuating the people from Tavistock."

It's the other new arrival who speaks, his light voice Ereni-accented. "I'm afraid I interrupted Master Connell's work." He bows. "Your Majesty."

I finally look beyond Alistar and startle. His companion is a young man with cropped auburn hair and a fox's clever face. Philippe Manceau, the minister of public works.

"Lord Philippe," I say, and though I know my tone is starved of warmth, I can't change it. "What are *you* doing here?"

Again, he bows—an insistence on etiquette that sets my teeth on edge. "The ministers wished me to observe the *Caveadear*'s use of magic in person. I prevailed on Master Connell to guide me here."

"I was coming this way anyhow," Alistar says gruffly. I can tell the *Master Connell*ing is putting his back up.

I study Philippe Manceau, the Count of Lylan. He's the only man in the tent—in the entire camp—not in uniform or at least wearing a sash to show his allegiance to Eren and Caeris. Instead he's in dark, somber colors, like a banker who's gotten lost on his way to examine an investment. I don't need to ask which ministers decided, independently, that they needed to send a representative to check up on me. The Ereni are always doing things like this, to quietly remind me that, as far as they're concerned, I'm still on probation.

Philippe gestures toward the river. "Who can resist an opportunity to see the steward of the land in action?"

"I can think of a few," I remark. Half of the people in my Ereni cabinet openly distrust magic—and, by extension, Elanna. They were elected, so I can't simply throw them out, but we all know they bought those votes. We may have brought elections to Eren, but even though most commoners seem to approve of my rule, the wealthy still control their lands—and, thus, many people's choices.

And some of those nobles are still angry that we overthrew the Eyrlais. Philippe, I suspect, is one of them, though he's never said anything overtly against me.

The Butcher of Novarre intervenes. "You'll see, Lord Philippe. If all goes according to plan, the Tinani will no longer pose much of a threat to Eren at all."

"Let us pray to the gods that this is the case," Philippe says.

"Who needs gods when we have the *Caveadear*?" Rhia says.

She's drunk a second cup of coffee and seems to be vibrating slightly.

I exchange a glance with Alistar. "Let's go down to the river."

DOWN BY THE shore, Elanna raises her arms. We all fall silent, watching her. She looks so small down there. A hush lifts from her, so strange and tremulous even I can feel it. My skin itches. I rub the back of my neck. I may not be a sorceress, but sometimes—often, lately—my body reacts when magic is performed nearby.

Philippe turns his head toward me, and I force myself still. At least Rhia and Alistar are also here. A loud clatter echoes from the Tinani camp, then all falls into silence like an indrawn breath. It extends and extends. The sunlight glimmers on the water. The weight of it tugs through the reeds along the shore. On the other side, some Tinani have come down and are staring across at us, gesturing.

Pressure pulses behind my eyelids. There's a rushing in my ears. I stumble, my body flushing with heat, my head swimming and my stomach churning—

Philippe catches me against his arm. "Are you ill?"

"I—"

Water erupts down the river. A surge of it, swelling and overflowing the reeds on the banks. Shouts rise from the Tinani camp. They're on a curve, and the river is naturally pouring into their camp—but I can hardly hear them over the roaring in my ears. My coat seems to be strangling me. I fling out a hand—someone grasps it—but I'm blinded, my ears filled with a sweep of verdant sound— a kind of music that rises, trembling, through the layers and fissures of the land, caught on the current of the great black river. It splits through the earth's inertia, a driving green force that transforms everything in its wake. I'm shaking, dizzy—

My knees fetch up against a rock. An arm cups my back. Alistar is hugging me to his chest; his face blurs, and then my eyes focus. His eyebrows are pinched. With worry?

"You're ill, Soph," he says.

I shake my head. "I'm fine."

I've never *felt* Elanna's magic before. Not like that. I've *seen* it, and felt the tremble of tree roots skimming the earth, but I've never *heard* it in my own body, as if it were a part of me. As if it were a song so powerful, it mingled with my very blood.

I'm still light-headed. Rhia and Philippe are hovering anxiously behind Alistar's shoulders. When Rhia says, "Put your head between your knees," I do.

Or at least I try. My stomach bulks up, in my way. I jerk back, glancing down at the overlarge twill waistcoat—once Ruadan's, for he was taller than me—that I've been wearing for weeks over my increasingly muddy riding skirt. Its plain brown buttons seem to stare back at me, innocent.

Alistar crouches beside me. "Sophy, breathe. It's all right. What happened?"

"I'm fine. Don't let anyone else see."

"No one's watching but us. Are you all right? Should I call a doctor?"

"No—"

Above us, Rhia tenses. She screams. *"Elanna!"*

I lift my head, but another wave of nausea rolls through me. This shouldn't be happening. The nausea left me weeks ago. All the same, my stomach feels as if it's doubling over on itself. I press my hands to my cheeks. My face feels cold and clammy.

"Where's El?" I manage.

Philippe has also tensed, rocking up onto his toes. He shouts. *"Caveadear!"*

Rhia sprints away, leaping over the lip of rock onto the narrow path. I force myself upright. Alistar's leaning forward, past Philippe. He sucks in a breath. Swears. Whatever he sees galvanizes him, too. "Elanna!" He leaps up, then pauses. He points at me. "Stay here, Soph."

He charges down the steep trail, Philippe at his heels. I crawl forward on my hands and knees. The nausea is passing. My ears are clearing.

A bell rings over the water—a quivering, grasping sound.

Witch hunters. My whole body jolts with sudden, white fear. They found us—they found El. I stare across the water, willing them to come into view. But the fog, rather than clearing, is gathering more densely over the river. I can only just make out movement on the opposite bank.

There's a noise below me—a grunt. I look down, and I see her. I see *them.*

Below me, a man is running down along the bank's edge. He wears simple, dark clothes—they're wet, I realize, as if he got caught in the flooding water. Another man hurries behind him. My heart turns over. These aren't our men; they must be Tinani. But how did they even *get* here over the flooding river?

Unless they knew El was going to be here. They could have crossed over, somewhere upstream where the river narrows, before dawn.

Or they could have been here much longer. They could have been put into place long before we arrived; they could have been waiting for this moment. And the intelligence the Butcher intercepted, about the Tinani being here . . .

The first man jumps over a rock. He's almost reached her. *"El!"* I scream. Alistar and Philippe are still too high up. Rhia has had to slow on the steep bank, still more than a man's height above El. One of the assailants reaches for El's arm—she dodges him, but the other is coming up, and—

She slips. The rushing water catches her. She's swept off her feet. Her hat falls off. Black water billows up her greatcoat.

Then the water sweeps Elanna under. Downstream.

The men race after her along the bank. Behind them, Rhia takes a flying leap and dives into the water after El.

I'm running. Running after Alistar and Philippe, down to the shore. "El!" I scream.

The land loves her. She can control the flood and where the river's sweeping her. Can't she?

Downstream, her head pops back up, wet and sleek as a seal. The current is driving her toward the opposite bank. She thrashes, but it makes no difference. She doesn't know how to swim. Rhia seems to—she's making headway toward El, at any rate—but now the roaring river's caught them both. They're sweeping away from us at impossible speed.

And the assailants are still running along the bank—downstream to the ford, no doubt. Shouts echo from the opposite bank, still shrouded in fog, over the roaring water. We're all being followed.

Ahead, Alistar's flinging off his coat as he runs. Philippe pumps his arms. I manage not to trip on the rock scree. "Downstream!" I shout as I barrel between the men. "Go downstream!"

We're all running together now, along the marshy shore, my feet catching in pockets of mud and moss-slimed rocks. El's and Rhia's heads flash above the black water. The next moment, El disappears again. Rhia shouts, for all the good that does. The two men have vanished around the curve in the river.

We charge through the marsh, past drowning trees, onto a rock spit of land jutting into the river. Water surges over my shoes, drenching my stockings, weighing down my skirts and the heavy wool of my coat.

An arm reaches out of the water far ahead of us, just visible through the dense fog, on the opposite bank. El's head follows. She drags herself up through the muck, a small, distant figure. Rhia swirls past her with an echoing cry, thrashing toward the shore.

"I'm going after them." Alistar tugs off his boots.

"So am I," Philippe begins.

There's a shout behind us—the Butcher charging through the trees toward us, shouting for us to stay back. He points toward the opposite bank.

I turn, squinting. The fog is still too thick, but again I hear shouts.

I'm defenseless. Weaponless. The queen of Eren and Caeris, standing bareheaded on the riverbank.

And the *Caveadear* and the daughter of the warden of the mountains are trapped in enemy territory.

But I was the girl who slipped under the Butcher's nose.

Alistar's already splashing deep into the water. He knows how to swim; we used to challenge each other to see who could hold their breath longest in the clear, cold pool beneath the Sentry Rock at Cerid Aven. He flings himself forward with sure strokes.

On the opposite bank, El's clambered up, staggering as she vanishes through the fog into marsh grass. She seems to be heading for Rhia, who's also made it to shore, though much farther downstream.

The fog, rather than lifting, drifts more thickly from the river. Elanna's disappeared completely into it now. As I watch, it swallows Alistar, too. Maybe it's El's doing—to hide us, to save herself.

The thought galvanizes me. I grab Philippe's elbow; he's hesitant to get in the water. Maybe he can't swim. "This way!" I say. We run along the bank, staggering over downed trees and the long grass hiding soft, watery holes. Mist gathers around our ankles, growing thicker and thicker over the river. We are swaddled in white. There's little noise but my breathing in my ears and the rush of Philippe's and my footsteps. Behind and to our right, soft whistles fly through the woods—the Butcher and his men communicating our location. He must be heading for the ford half a mile downstream, and so are El, Alistar, and Rhia.

And the men who sneaked onto the bank.

The Butcher may be able to deal with them—if Philippe and I can distract the Tinani, even for just a few minutes.

"We need a diversion," I tell Philippe between gasps for breath. "We need to make them think El went the opposite way."

What would my mother do? What *did* she do, when I was a child?

The fog twines thick around us. White, muffling. Disorienting, even on land, but especially on water.

"How far can you throw?" I ask Philippe.

"A rock?" He fishes one out of the shallows. His silhouette is melting into the fog; his breath billows, white.

He turns and with his whole body, throws the rock back upstream. It splashes loudly.

I nod. "Another. Farther, if you can."

He tries again. This one makes a smaller splash, closer to shore. The fog chokes the water, so thick now I've no idea where Alistar is, much less Elanna and Rhia.

Philippe throws another rock, and I crouch and do the same, making as much racket as we can. My arm starts to ache. Philippe looks at me, ghostly in the gloom. "It's not—"

"Shh," I whisper.

A voice echoes across the river. A Tinani voice. I know enough Tinani—the language is closely related to Caerisian and Ereni—to pick out the words *here* and *watch* and *nothing*.

"Come on," I breathe in Philippe's ear, tugging him back upstream. I fumble for another rock and throw it, farther up.

The Tinani go silent, then their voices rumble again.

We throw more rocks. A Tinani soldier barks an order, somewhere nearby.

The fog has fully swallowed us now. Moisture condenses, cold on my face. I crouch, listening hard, gripping Philippe's arm to still him. The Tinani voices are drawing away from us—upstream.

By silent consent, Philippe and I rise and begin to make our way back downstream along the marshy riverbank. The trip seems to take longer than it should. In the white, it's impossible to see our soldiers, but my ears catch a murmur of voices. There's a sharp whistle.

"It's me," I say as the soldiers appear through the fog.

"Milady." They relax their guard. We've arrived at the ford, as far as I can tell; the ground has firmed to solid sand.

The Butcher pushes through the throng of soldiers. "We thought we'd lost you two."

"We were diverting the Tinani," I say. "But Alistar crossed the river."

The Butcher swears. He looks drawn. Cross. "So we've three to find. Do I have a volunteer to take a party across?"

"No," I blurt out, before I think better of contradicting Gilbert Moriens in front of his men. Tension thickens the foggy air. "I mean, let's wait a little longer. If we've successfully drawn the Tinani off, El and the others can cross back here. We don't want to draw more attention. You know Alistar and Rhia can handle most anything. I don't want to put anyone else at risk unnecessarily . . ."

I'm babbling, but my point must have been taken because Lord Gilbert gives a curt nod. The men relax fractionally.

"We wait here," the Butcher says.

Philippe touches my arm. "I'll escort you back to camp, my lady."

"I'm staying to wait for my friends. You can go back."

He holds my gaze. I don't look away. It's as if he wants to communicate something—as if he really does want me to go with him—and while this makes me wonder, I also don't entirely trust him.

At last, he sighs. "Fine. We stay here."

There wasn't a *we,* but I let this go. I stamp my feet to keep warm and blow on my hands. The fog gathers around us—a cold and inescapable embrace. I listen and listen, but I hear nothing. Nothing but the men around me breathing and sighing, shifting their feet. They must be as exhausted as I feel. My back aches. I try to beat back the worry creeping through me. If we lose El—Rhia—if we lose Alistar . . .

A sound.

A bell, ringing.

"Damn the gods," Philippe whispers.

The witch hunters have followed us downstream—or maybe they were waiting here all along. A shudder runs through me.

Another bell rings. A shout goes up. Across the river, a woman screams. I startle forward instinctively.

"Henri, Laurence, take your men and go!" the Butcher barks.

I start to move past him, but he grabs my arm. "Your Majesty, you have to *stay here.*"

I gather my breath to shout at him, except he's right. If it's an ambush, we can't afford to lose El, Rhia, Alistar, *and* me. Someone has to stay here.

And it has to be me.

Angry tears burn my eyes, but I hold myself back. The Butcher gives me an approving look; I want to smack him. El has an admirable tolerance for the man, but I can never even look at him without remembering his past—what he did not only to me, but to so many others in Caeris and Eren alike. It galls me that he has the nerve to act superior—because while he may be a good tactician, he has never been an exemplary man.

We wait. The Butcher on my left, Philippe on my right. The fog muffles their faces and I start to panic. What if Alistar's dead or captured? And I never told him?

Finally, a grunt carries over the water. Feet splash. I suck in my breath. A man's voice—in Ereni. Our people.

They come into view—their faces weary, their bodies silhouettes in the fog. As I stare, they part. Alistar staggers forward, carrying Rhia's limp body. Alistar's face is haggard. And Rhia . . .

Alistar sees me, and relief eases his face. "Sophy!"

"Where's El?" I whisper.

He shakes his head. Droops close to me, so I smell his sweat and the brackish water, and I see Rhia's eyelids twitching as she fumbles toward consciousness.

"They took her, Soph," he says. "The witch hunters. They have Elanna."

CHAPTER TWO

I stare at him. Around us, I'm all too aware of the soldiers whispering and the stillness of the Butcher and Philippe watching me. All of them are waiting for my reaction, but I can't find any words. My breath has gone shallow in my throat. Someone must have betrayed us—that, or the Tinani fed the Butcher's informant misinformation. Either way, our intelligence is compromised, and Elanna . . .

It seems impossible that they took her. While we were just standing here—at my command. But I see the truth of it in Alistar's eyes.

Rhia flails alert, gasping. Her face is white with pain. "I have to go after El," she chokes out.

"Those brutes cracked you on the head, Knoll!" Alistar exclaims.

Rhia draws breath to protest, but I interrupt. "You will stay right where you are." I'm not about to lose her to the Tinani's machinations, too. "I won't let you go traipsing around Tinan with a broken arm and a concussion."

Her eyes narrow, but her voice is weak. "I'll break *your* arm, you tyrant!"

"Send for a doctor!" I order the guards at large. This is one thing I know how to handle. "Rhia, sit down right there."

Philippe shrugs out of his coat, laying it on the ground for Rhia. She swears but drops down on it, hissing through her teeth and clutching her arm, tears leaking from her squeezed-shut eyes. She grips my hand with her good one. "I lost her, Soph. I couldn't save her."

"It's all right," I whisper, though it isn't. My fingers are turning numb in her grasp, but this seems like the punishment I deserve for a trap I somehow failed to see. The Tinani have been trying for weeks—months—to capture Elanna; of course they would turn to subterfuge. And none of us saw it, or even guessed. It galls me.

"I thought we evaded them." Rhia's panting. "They came out of nowhere."

Above us, the men are talking in low voices, Alistar and the Butcher and Philippe, their gazes darting toward me and away.

"Are you sure they took her?" I ask.

Rhia's eyes glint with tears. "They put a *sack* over her head. Yes, I'm sure."

I flinch. "We should go after them—"

"No. Too many. Not sure where they were taking her. Men everywhere. I . . . they struck me down. Must've thought I was dead. Alistar dragged me out—unconscious, like a damned coward."

I glance up to see if Alistar's listening. His gaze flickers to me. A tightening of his mouth. Coldness runs over me. What have they been talking about?

The doctor arrives in a bluster of tired grumbling, carrying a heavy leather bag. I'm ordered out of the way, and I move back to stand beside Alistar while Rhia swears at the physician through her teeth.

"Majesty." The Butcher steps in front of me. "We need to speak privately."

I let him guide me off to the side, Philippe and Alistar trailing us into the modest cover of some shrubs.

"We need to decide how we will handle Lady Elanna's disappearance," the Butcher begins.

I can't seem to catch my breath. It's not enough to know El's gone. I don't have the luxury to come to grips with the fact, or to bury myself beneath guilt. I haven't only lost my friend, my would-be sister, I've tumbled into a political disaster.

Philippe says, "I really think this can wait, Lord Gilbert."

But the Butcher isn't about to give in to anything as human as grief or shock. "This must be contained at once. Tell them she's escaped south to torment the Tinani troops. Make that Knoll woman keep silent."

There's a moment of silence as Philippe, Alistar, and I absorb his words.

"You want us to lie?" I say. "You want us to pretend El hasn't been captured?"

Philippe shakes his head. "Word's going to cross the river. The Tinani know. They'll make sure our people do, too."

"I think we should hear Lord Gilbert out," Alistar says unexpectedly.

I stare at him. He lifts one shoulder, an awkward shrug.

"Very well," I say slowly. "Tell us, Lord Gilbert, why we should lie to our people."

The Butcher returns my stare. "You must quell your impulse to be overly moralistic, Your Majesty. This is a far graver matter than the black-and-white dichotomy of ethics makes it appear. A *lie* is sometimes necessary, if one wants to keep one's throne—and one's kingdom."

Cold runs down my arms. "Are you threatening me?"

Beside me, Alistar and Philippe have both tensed.

"*I* am not threatening you," the Butcher retorts. "But there are others in this kingdom—powerful people—who would gladly see you removed from the throne and replaced by an Ereni monarch. The *Caveadear*'s power has so far protected you. Without her, you are in far greater danger."

I wish it didn't make me so angry to hear El credited single-handedly with popularity *and* power. "Most people support us—"

"That may be, but those who would depose you have power. Or they did."

He means the nobles who lost control when we claimed the freedom of not only Caeris, but Eren, too. Aristocrats who have gone to earth on their estates, and a few who have clung on in Laon. Some who are even in my cabinet.

Like Philippe Manceau, who stands beside me, breathing tightly.

"If you don't see the danger you're in," the Butcher is saying, "you're being a fool. We don't yet know who betrayed us today, or who was discovered and duped. This plot could go deeper. It could be part of a larger whole."

My eyes sting. "The people elected us—elected *me*. They deserve the truth."

The Butcher raises an eyebrow. "What do you think the people will do with the truth? They see the Tinani on the border. They know it's only a matter of time before the black ships of Paladis arrive by sea, and the navy of Baedon as well. The Tinani, we might be able to fight. But I am a realistic man, madam, and I tell you that without the *Caveadear*'s power, we are in serious danger."

I swallow hard.

"The people know it, too," the Butcher continues remorselessly. "If you tell them Lady Elanna has been captured, that we may have been betrayed from within, they'll panic. We'll have riots in the streets. Deserters in my army. More lives lost, in all likelihood, than if we keep silent."

I stare at him. He looks back, not giving an inch. It galls me that we fought our rebellion for the sake of the common people, and this man has such little faith in them that he refuses to tell them the truth.

"The people aren't stupid," I say tightly. "When Elanna doesn't appear, when there's no land magic, they'll figure it out. And then they'll know we lied to them. Just like Antoine Eyrlai." I look hard at him. "We can't simply put them down. We won't burn their villages or force them to submit."

The Butcher purses his lips, but I don't know whether he understands my reference to Marose and my mother's death. He's burned more than one village, after all. "How popular do you think you are, Queen Sophy?"

"I . . ." I hesitate, sensing a trap.

"Popular enough that when you tell the truth, the people won't think you weak? Foolish?" He coughs delicately. "Incompetent?"

My eyes are stinging. In Caeris, with the memory of Ruadan's fondness for me, with the loyalty to my family, perhaps people would follow me no matter what. But in Eren . . .

Yet Ruadan used to say that lies were abhorrent, especially the ones used by the Eyrlais to hoodwink the people. He used to say, *If you do anything, Sophy, tell the people the truth. Preferably the truth they want to hear. If people trust you, they will follow you anywhere. And if you fail their trust, even once, you should never expect to have it again.*

"Then I must do everything to appear powerful," I say to the Butcher of Novarre. "But I won't lie."

He utters an exasperated sigh. "Think longer and harder about this, Your Majesty. I, for one, do not want to lose everything we've fought for."

"You could simply switch sides again," I retort. "Not much loss there."

The Butcher stares at me, his nostrils flaring, but I don't back down. Now, at last, I think I glimpse him, the man who ordered the village of Marose to be burned to the ground. I feel strangely vindicated, as if he's proven to me that he still is the monster I always believed him to be.

Philippe intervenes. "Lord Gilbert, with all due respect, I agree with the queen on this. Take a day or two perhaps to shore up support, but she needs to tell the truth. Otherwise the people will never have reason to trust her. She must set herself apart from the Eyrlais."

I eye him. "Didn't you swear fealty to the Eyrlais?"

"I did, madam, but with little choice in the matter."

"Those who want Sophy deposed will use this to their advantage," the Butcher warns Philippe.

"They'll use her deceit even more." Philippe pauses. "Do you think they're not in communication with Tinan? Do you think they don't have spies *in the royal guard*? We have to act before they can, unless we want them to tell this story for us. And you can be sure they won't paint a flattering picture of Her Majesty."

I watch him speak, his shoulders back, addressing the Butcher with the confidence of an equal or even superior. It's confusing. Philippe Manceau has no reason to like or help me; the Ereni royalists in my cabinet adore him. Yet what he's saying seems perfectly reasonable—even wise. And after what happened today, I wouldn't be surprised if there *are* spies within my guard—not my inner circle of mountain women, of course, but among the Ereni I inherited from Loyce.

"Fine." The Butcher spreads his hands, and I can't ignore the sting that it's Philippe's counsel that swayed him, not mine. "Tell the truth."

I nod. "I'll address the camp now."

"No," he says.

I feel my muscles tense further. Does this man have to fight me on *every* move?

"We need to investigate this ruse further," he says, and I am aware of how he carefully does not look at Philippe. "I suspect my informant in Tinan may have been discovered—indeed, more than one of them, since I had two sources corroborate the Tinani movements."

His informant—not ours. Even in his language, the Butcher constantly reminds me that he's the one with the power here.

"You don't suspect them of duplicity?" I, too, carefully don't look at Philippe. "Or anyone else?"

"It's possible," the Butcher acknowledges. "That's why I wish to keep the matter quiet for now."

"Then I'll cover for you. Pretend nothing is wrong, while you work on your investigation."

"With respect, no, Your Majesty. You need to leave," he says, gruffly this time. "Immediately. We can't afford to lose you as well. We don't know who is working against us, and what additional plans they may have. I'll double your guard on the road back."

It's logical. And yet I hesitate, purely on principle, because he's annoyed me so much.

"Sophy," Alistar says, the first time he's spoken in a while. "He's right. We have to keep you safe."

I look at Philippe, who nods. "We'll return to Laon now," he says.

I release a sigh. They're right, of course. I need to return to Laon and meet with the ministers, then make a public statement about Elanna's capture. And if she's arrived in Laon as she wrote to me she would, I need to be the first person to tell Teofila that her daughter has been taken hostage once again, the same way she was when she was five, by the former king of Eren. Only this, somehow, is infinitely worse.

I swallow hard. "Very well."

The others begin to move away, toward Rhia—presently arguing with the camp doctor—but Alistar doesn't move.

"One more thing," he says. "I'm going after El."

We all go very still. At last, in a tight voice, I whisper, "What did you say?"

He's addressing all of us, but his eyes are on me. "I'll take a party of Hounds, no more than five. We'll disguise ourselves in Tinani colors; we know the language well enough to blend in. We need to see where they're taking her, Sophy."

A frantic pressure is clawing up my chest. There's a sudden flutter in my stomach, as delicate as a bird, and terror spikes through me. I put my hand to the buttons of my waistcoat. Is it nerves, or is this what a child feels like? But it's already gone, if it ever was there, and I'm left with hollow fear and Alistar's eyes on mine. "What if they capture or kill *you*? It's too much of a risk."

"I'll be careful," he says, again to me, not the others. His gaze doesn't leave mine. "You know the Hounds and I will move like ghosts in the night. The Tinani won't even know we're there. If there's the slightest chance we can get El back . . ."

I can't speak. I'm aware of my ragged breathing; the thump of my own heartbeat.

Unexpectedly, Philippe Manceau decides to offer his opinion. "It's a good idea. You might—"

"I wasn't asking you," Alistar says evenly. "I was talking to the queen."

There's a silence. Philippe and the Butcher are exchanging a glance. I close my eyes to shut them all out. They'll think I'm hesitating because I don't want to lose my lover, and they're right, but it's more than that. It's the secret I haven't told him, the truth that both thrills and frightens me. I have to tell him, but I can't, not before he leaves. He has to go. If there's any chance we can save El, we must try.

I look at him. It's hard to speak the words, but I do. "Then of course you must go."

ALISTAR AND I trek back to camp through the dissipating fog, my hand tucked around his elbow. Rhia has already been carted off by the doctor; she seems likely to survive, since she's spent the last twenty minutes subjecting the poor man to a string of blistering commentary. A light rain has begun to fall, dampening our faces. Guards tramp through the brambles ahead of us, their racket enough to warn away any would-be assassins. I sigh. It exhausts me, being constantly surrounded. But at least Alistar and I have this moment together. At least I can feel his warmth for a few minutes, without guilt, before he leaves for Tinan. The thought makes me breathless again.

"I don't trust him," he mutters.

I nod. "You know he was there when my mother died."

"Not Lord Gilbert—that Philippe. I don't know what to make of him. He's polite. We even had a pleasant ride here together. But he knows things we don't about the other Ereni. Who to trust in your cabinet, and who not to. He's too damned polite to say any of it directly, so I can't decide what he really thinks about anything."

"Well, he *is* a courtier." Yet I wonder about Philippe, too. The last thing I expected him to do was counsel me to tell the truth, or to help me try to save El. Even the most consummate actor couldn't fake so much. Could he?

"You know . . ." Alistar pauses. "The Butcher might be right."

"Alistar!" I'm genuinely shocked. "I can't believe you would say that."

His head lowers. "Of course you *should* tell the people. It's what we fought for. But he's right about the panic. People are going to be terrified."

"We're so helpless without El." I can't stop the anger from burning into my voice. "As if we have no power of our own!"

"It's not only that. She's the uniting factor, not us. Without her, we're just Caerisian overlords in Eren, the same way the Eyrlais were Ereni overlords in Caeris."

"You're simplifying things. We have plenty of support in Eren. Victoire, Count Hilarion—half the ministers support me . . . The common people *want* us."

"But the people who *don't* want us are powerful."

I press my lips together. He's right.

"And there are more of them—more Ereni than Caerisians . . ."

"That's why I have to get back to Laon. I'll take charge of the situation. I'll show them we can be powerful without Elanna."

He puts his hand over mine. "I know you don't want me to go into Tinani territory. But—"

"I know," I interrupt him. "Rhia's out of commission. You need to go."

"I wish I could send her and be the one who stays here to guard you."

My mouth tugs into a sad smile, though I don't believe him for a moment. Alistar Connell wants to be where the action is, not stuffed in coaches and tramping along palace corridors. Teasingly, I say, "Then I'd have to appoint you captain of my guards, and *that* would mortally offend Rhia. I value my life."

He strokes his knuckle down my cheek, quick, subtle. A flash of warmth. "I'll come straight to you when I return."

"I should hope so," I say, and then I wince. For the thousandth time, I remind myself that what Alistar and I have is only a dalliance. The ministers have been pressing me to marry, and the last person they'll approve of is this bold, brash Caerisian man. So I say what must be said. "But if the Butcher needs you here on the border instead, you and your Hounds should stay here. I'd rather you protect Eren and Caeris now, so we can be together in the future."

"That's my Sophy," he says, and I hear the sad smile in his voice. "Always practical."

"But not always very much fun."

"Oh, you can be *quite* fun . . ." The peaks of the camp tents come into view ahead of us, and Alistar's hand slides down my wrist. "Straight back to Laon, is that it? Perhaps I should come into your tent. Review . . . plans."

A familiar spark flares through me. Drily, I say, "No one would notice that at all, especially when you're supposed to be leaving for Tinan."

He heaves a dramatic sigh. "My darling, *practical* Sophy. I suppose you're right."

"I am," I say firmly, but at the same time my pulse is fluttering high in my throat. I should let him close to me. I should take the risk, and tell him the truth.

Footsteps scuff the path behind us. I startle back from Alistar's warmth. Philippe is coming toward us, his shoulders bowed.

Alistar sighs again. "I suppose I should see which of the men are willing to go."

If there were any time to tell him, it's now—before I lose him across the Tinani border, or he loses me to the machinations in Laon. Yet as we approach the camp, I feel the nerve seeping away from me, leaving a cold ache in its place. I can't burden him with this before he leaves, and there is no practical way to tell him even if I wanted to. A thicket of mountain women surrounds my tent. The whole damned camp has ears.

There's a sudden shout from the outskirts of camp. I stiffen, grabbing Alistar's arm harder, but then there's a ululating shout. Alistar's Hounds of Urseach have found someone—a man on horseback, who thunders ahead of them into camp, his brilliantly woven cloak flapping behind him.

"Ingram Knoll!" I call. He wasn't due to arrive until this afternoon.

But he doesn't hear me; he's seen Rhia being carted into the infirmary and is swinging off his horse. "What's happened?" he's demanding of the doctors.

I should go after him, but the tent flap has fallen closed behind him, and fear and worry are already twining too close to my heart. I approach my tent instead, releasing Alistar's arm, though more than anything I want to take him into the tent with me, grab his chin, and kiss him. Bury my hands in his hair.

I just let my fingers linger for a moment on his elbow before letting go. He sighs.

I face the mountain women. "You heard the news." It isn't a question, and they don't even bother to nod. "I'm sorry," I say. "I'm terribly sorry."

"We've sent for a coach," one says, "on the Butcher's orders. It isn't safe for you to remain here."

No, I suppose it isn't—though who wants to kidnap me? I'm no sorceress whose magic can change the face and fabric of the world. I'm just a girl who seized her father's crown, and kept it when he neither came to claim it nor even returned her letters. No wonder some people whisper that I'm little more than a pretender. All the gods, how am I going to survive without El? How are any of us?

Going into the tent, I wash my face in a basin of cold water, then pin my hair back up. I know I should be taking better care of myself. Sleeping, for instance. Eating regular meals. Bathing. I smell of sweat and river water—not the odor the Ereni are used to, in their queens.

I should see a midwife, but who would I trust not to tell my secrets to the world?

I go out, brushing my fingers again over Alistar's elbow. He follows me with his eyes.

The Butcher's waiting for me outside the command tent, his

boots muddy from the river. The unyielding lines of his face give nothing away, not even his frustration with me or his fear of what may happen. He nods at a black coach waiting on the edge of camp, the horses already buckled into their traces.

"Your conveyance, madam," he says.

An aide brings me a stale sausage roll and a cup of the bitter coffee Rhia likes so much. As if the scent summoned her, Rhia herself stumbles out of the infirmary, a sling trailing from her arm. The doctor's shouting after her and her father is on her heels, trying to argue with her. She ignores them both.

"I'm coming with you."

She's swaying on her feet. I can just imagine the doctor told her to stay right here; Ingram Knoll has folded his arms, giving her a stern stare, but I'm not about to leave her behind. I need someone at my side I can trust implicitly. "Good," I say.

The Butcher frowns. "Lady Rhia, you're injured."

Rhia rolls her eyes. *Lady Rhia?* she mouths at me.

I choke down a laugh. "I need her, Lord Gilbert, even with her injuries. She's the captain of my queen's guard. Besides, with her father here helping you, I need someone to represent the warden of the mountains."

"I see." But his mouth pinches primly. He probably thinks Rhia's a bad influence—too rash and opinionated to actually be much help in consolidating power in Laon. He might even be right. But I happen to know Rhia scares the daylights out of my more hidebound ministers—even with a concussion. She'll be plenty useful.

Besides, fierce as she is, she's wounded. If I take her with me, I can keep an eye on her.

I'm not about to insult her by mentioning this, however, so I just give the Butcher a significant look. He sighs and glances at Ingram Knoll. Rhia's father just gives a short shake of his head. He's far too much a mountain lord for the Butcher's taste, with his weathered, flinty gaze and colorfully embroidered waistcoat, his thick silvered hair unfashionably long. Yet he's proven himself a competent army captain—one would have to be, to keep the fractious mountain lords in order—and he and the Butcher have forged a reluctant respect.

I say to Rhia, "Let the poor doctor finish wrapping you up."

She glowers. "I'm not a sausage." But she goes back into the tent, her father trailing after her.

"Shall I send an outrider ahead?" the Butcher asks.

"No. We don't want the news to spread uncontrolled." I pause. I want to tell him that he should trust me, that I'm not a foolish, callow girl. That Ruadan raised me to think like a leader, to put the people first. But I don't know how to say it, so in the end I simply nod to him. He nods back. Feeling just as young and callow as I claim I'm not, I retreat to the coach.

Alistar follows me. At the coach door, I turn to him. We have the barest modicum of privacy; the tents block us, thankfully, from the Butcher's eyes, and no one else seems to be looking, though I suppose they always are.

"Keep an eye on her," he says, jerking his chin at Rhia, who's shouting from the infirmary, trying to convince the Butcher to send his coffeepot with us.

"I will." I put my hand to his chest, and he immediately covers it with his own. "Be safe, Alistar. Don't do anything too bold, or rash, or—or stupid—"

He laughs. "Don't be myself, you mean?"

"You're not stupid." I lean closer. "You're more than a warrior."

A muscle jumps in his jaw. "Tell that to my sister, Oonagh. Or the Butcher."

"I don't need to tell them—they know it. Oonagh might be the head of your family, but she needs you. She relies on you." I grip the front of his coat, and he finally looks at me, his black brows a heavy line. I know every inch of his face, but still I drink the sight of him in, as if it can steady me. "I need you to come back from Tinan. There's something I need to talk to you about."

His green-flecked eyes sharpen at that, but before he can ask, I lean into him and press the lightest kiss on his lips. He sighs, and so do I. I wish I could melt against him, but of course that would be unqueenly. Lifting my chin, I glance around. No one seems to have taken much notice. The mountain women are studiously looking the other way. I pull Alistar's face down to mine and kiss him deeper. He puts his hand between my shoulder blades, pulls me close. His mouth is warm, tender, fierce. Even here, he somehow tastes of Caeris—the spice of whiskey, the tang of forested air.

"Be safe," I tell him, a little breathless.

His gaze caresses my face. "You, too, Soph."

I climb into the coach, and someone coughs. I startle violently, grabbing for a weapon—but as usual, I'm unarmed.

There's a person sitting on the bench seat.

"I didn't mean to scare you," Philippe Manceau says with forced politeness. "Especially as you and Lord Alistar were . . . engaged."

My cheeks heat. My dalliance with Alistar may be an open secret—or, let's face it, a blatant source of gossip—but even so, I'm not keen on having one of my ministers watching us undetected, a few feet away. Thank all the gods I didn't tell Alistar what I needed to talk to him about.

I drop onto the seat opposite him, pretending I don't see Alistar walk away. Pretending his going to Tinan, into such danger, doesn't hurt like a splinter lodged in my skin. "Coming back already? You've hardly seen anything of the border."

"I've seen enough. After all, the Ard isn't going anywhere."

He sounds positively cross, and I hide a smile.

"Have you decided what you'll tell the ministers?" he asks abruptly.

I feel my jaw clench. "There will be plenty of time for that en route to the capital."

"Ah. I thought Lady Rhia might—what do you say?—shift us there."

I shake my head, surprised by the vehemence of my own protectiveness toward Rhia. In Caeris, she knows the folds in the land, which bend space and dissolve the distance between two places, like the pattern of her own palms, but here in Eren it seems more of a struggle for her, even on a good day. "She's too weak. She—"

Rhia herself interrupts me, clambering in awkwardly with her sling. She glowers at Philippe and settles beside me. She smells of coffee and medicinal herbs, and her eyes seem brighter than usual. She hates leaving her father, I know; they're very close, and he's in as much danger as Alistar.

"You shouldn't be traveling anywhere," Philippe notes. "You're white as a sheet."

Rhia turns her bandaged shoulder toward him and says to me, "The Butcher wouldn't give me the coffeepot."

"Well, I don't know how you'd have kept it from spilling."

"I suppose," she says begrudgingly.

As the coach rocks into motion, she slides back, resting her head against the coach wall and closing her eyes. I find a lap blanket squashed behind my back and drape it over her knees. The doctor gave her a small tincture of laudanum for the pain, and she's already asleep, her mouth open, a deep frown between her brows. She's hurting more than she let on.

"We can stay tonight at my family's estate," Philippe says quietly. "It's on the way to Laon."

I nod, albeit reluctantly. Since Rhia's in no shape to shift the land, I suppose it's better to rely on Philippe's hospitality than to take over an inn.

Our coach trundles slowly through the day. Philippe and I run out of topics of conversation quickly enough, and I'm left with the thoughts milling in my head. I can't believe they took El. How on earth am I supposed to get her back? How am I supposed to rule without her?

If the world discovers the truth about what's growing inside me, I won't be allowed to rule anything. Not for the first time, I wish my father had answered even one of my letters—and more than that, that he'd come here to help us. I don't know why he's lingering at the imperial court in Paladis, or what he's waiting for. Maybe he never truly intended to come. But I can't shake the feeling that if he were here, all this might be easier.

Wouldn't it? My dead half brother, Finn, never spoke highly of

Euan Dromahair, and my mother never spoke of him at all. He's still the king across the sea, though. People would rally to his name.

Only they're stuck with me for now.

This is what my mother would have wanted—isn't it? Mag Dunbarron wouldn't have hesitated to place her daughter on the throne. Sometimes I think she gave her life for this: so that her daughter might someday be able to wear the crown. I just wish I felt more worthy of it.

I close my eyes, putting one hand protectively over my stomach. The slightest twinge meets my touch. I feel myself go very still. Did I imagine it, the way I imagined that flutter earlier? Perhaps it's simply my guts roiling after everything that's happened today. But other women say they feel their children move in their wombs. Once, one of the ladies visiting us at Cerid Aven was with child, and she let us put our hands on her swollen stomach to feel the baby kicking. I remember laughing as the sharp movement met my hand. Could it be, finally?

Yet fear comes chasing on the heels of my excitement. I'm going back to the city, where I will no longer be able to hide my growing belly beneath a man's waistcoat and overcoat; where I won't only be among the incurious eyes of my queen's guards; where the maids will wonder why I'm complaining of my stays, and grow wise to the reason why my clothes no longer fit me. Maybe I should have done something about this weeks ago, when the nausea grew almost unbearable and tiredness dogged me everywhere, when I realized what had happened, when the creeping sense of the consequences started to shorten my breath. But I didn't. I don't know what I could have done, in truth.

Maybe I should have forced the issue with Alistar; I should have told him. The weight of this secret drags on me like shackles.

My eyes itch with tears. I let one or two leak out, when I'm certain Philippe can't see them. They give me no more comfort than the child growing silently in my womb.

CHAPTER THREE

The clatter of wheels on cobblestones startles me awake. The day has worn past noon. On the other side of the coach, Philippe squints sleepily at me. Rhia's snoring.

I push myself upright. We're passing through a pretty little village of honey-colored stone, with early flowers in the window boxes despite the hard winter. I sigh. It reminds me of the town outside Cerid Aven. All villages, I suppose, look much the same from the outside. There's comfort in a place so small—especially on the road back to Laon. I've never really liked cities, though I suppose I've never spent much time in them until the last few months, except for my early years in Barrody. But when you flee a place in the dead of night because Ereni soldiers have come to arrest your mother—and you have to leave your failing grandmother in the care of a family friend, only to find out months later that she died without you—well, it doesn't instill much fondness.

"You look pensive," Philippe observes.

I shake my head. "Not at all. I could live my whole life in a place like this."

He raises his eyebrows. "Could you really? When Ruadan Valtai raised you to be queen?"

He's watching for my reply, his eyes attentive. I wish he'd stop *noticing* so much about me. "That's not what he raised me for," I say briskly.

"Really? What, then? He gave you a royal education."

And a royal sense of responsibility, I reflect. Maybe Philippe's right, curse him anyway. I'd never shirk my duties.

Yet this still looks like a place I could call home. Maybe I'd be a lace-maker, sitting up high in one of the houses overlooking the little rushing river and the little honey-colored town. Alistar could make furniture, or something. He could build us a wide bed to put in our honey-colored house, and we would eat brown bread and have babies and—

There's a shout, somewhere ahead in the line of soldiers. The coach sways to a stop, throwing Rhia and me back against our seats. Philippe has to brace himself against my knee. He moves away with a quick apology. Grasping the latch, he pushes the door open and hops out.

I follow on his heels. The spring ground is soft underfoot, and I stagger a little after sitting for so long. Rhia leans out behind me, looking wan. "What's going on?"

"I don't know." I look around at the train of royal guards dismounting from their horses. We've stopped on the edge of the honey-colored town, where the buildings yield to rolling green hills stubbled with last year's wheat. Sheep eye us skeptically from the other side of a mossy stone wall. It's so bucolic it hardly seems real.

Philippe has already pushed toward the guards. "What happened?"

The note of alarm in his voice troubles me. I stride over to where he's standing at the front of the coach, the men fanning out around him.

"There's been an incident, my lord," one of the men is saying. He glances at me but doesn't acknowledge me. My gut clenches. He's got an Ereni accent. "A man . . . a refugee, from what the farmer said. He's in the left-hand field."

"Tell us what happened," I say, asserting myself as firmly as I can. But the guard only glances at me before addressing Philippe again, as if it were he who asked the question.

It's maddening. I'm the queen. I want to tell the man I'm more like him than Philippe is. I've marched across this land—granted, running from people like him. But still, unlike Philippe, I know what it's like to be poor. I know what it's like for your stomach to be empty, and your clothes ragged, and for no one to know your name.

And I know what it's like to be ignored by the people I'm most like. The awkwardness of the servants in Cerid Aven, the awe-struck whispers that I was the daughter of Mag Dunbarron, the pitying glances, the tactful kindnesses, mixed with the rumors that my mother had lied about my parentage, the jealousy that some-one as common as me was raised up to be Ruadan Valtai's ward. How the Caerisian nobles who occasionally visited treated me, once they learned the secret of my father's identity, both as some-thing special and as something other. Only Alistar didn't pay atten-tion to all that. He wasn't interested in how Ruadan was grooming me to be a backup heir; he was interested in *me*. For myself.

"The farmer doesn't know where it came from," the guard is saying. "It appeared overnight."

"*It?*" I echo.

This time, the man does look at me. He swallows, glances at Philippe, then gestures behind him.

I stare across the backs of the horses, into the farm field. A tall, old oak rises there, gnarled from age.

And from its lower branches, a body swings.

Bile rises in my throat. I gag, clamping a hand over my mouth. In my womb, there's a sharp, hard sensation. Like a jab. I startle, my hands falling instinctively to cover my stomach. This time, it must be the child. It's as if it's reacting to my own horror.

Because they didn't only hang this man. They cut off his hands. His feet. Bloody stumps.

Without a word, Philippe marches toward the hanging corpse. I follow, swallowing down the sour taste of bile, and the jittery awareness of my child's first likely movement. We cut in front of the horses, to where a cluster of guards stand on our side of the stone wall, staring at the tree. A farmer stands on the other side of the wall, shaking his head, gesturing.

I don't hear what he's saying. I can see the man better now. They didn't only hang him, and they didn't only mutilate his hands. The black heads of nails have been driven through his eyes and mouth.

I'm going to throw up.

I can't throw up.

I'm going to scream.

I can't scream.

I manage a gasping word: *"Why?"*

The crowd parts, giving me a sudden view of the farmer and an even better look at the corpse.

"The nails?" the farmer says in a country accent. "I reckon they did that so he couldn't come back from the dead."

"What?" I say shakily.

"It's in all the old stories," he says. "The only way to keep a sorcerer dead is to dismember him and drive nails through his eyes so he can't see to work a spell, and through his mouth—"

"Enough," I interrupt. I'm panting. Shaking. Covered in sweat. "Take that poor man down from there. Now. *Go!*"

The guards hesitate, staring from me to the farmers.

"You heard her," Philippe says.

Now they scurry off, opening the gate and approaching the tree, while the farmers look on, somewhat bemused.

Philippe touches my arm. "Are you all right?" he whispers.

"I'm fine." But he can feel me trembling, and we both know I'm not. I train my gaze on the farmer. "Who did this?"

The farmer shrugs. "We don't know, lady. Got up this morning and found him swaying there. When I got a look at the body, I realized it had to be a sorcerer. One of them refugees. A few have passed through from Tinan. Nobody recognizes this fellow, though."

"Why do you think he's in your field, then?" Philippe says.

"Your guess is as good as mine."

Pressure whines in my ears. I watch the guards cut the man down from the tree—the abrupt sagging of the body, the mutters and grimaces of the men handling the mutilated corpse.

A sorcerer nobody recognizes. A body that just happens to turn up on the road I'm taking to Laon.

Cold prickles all the way up my arms and dives down between my breasts. "Philippe." I gesture him back toward the coach, with a quick apology to the farmer for interrupting him. I grab Philippe's lapel and pull him toward me. "Who knew we were coming this way?"

He blinks. "This is the main route to Laon from Tavistock . . ." I watch the comprehension dawn on his face. His lips part. "You don't think—"

"It's a threat? Since I've welcomed the sorcerers to Laon? I don't know; I'm not sure what to think." Of course, it's equally occurred to me that Philippe could be behind this—as much as he could, in theory, be behind the trap the Tinani sprang this morning. After all, he is a common factor. I watch him carefully. His shock seems genuine, but there could be other reasons for that. "Either way, we need to get to the bottom of what happened here."

He scrubs at his jaw, and I realize he's not only shocked, he's shaken. "Maybe . . ." He clears his throat. "Maybe we interrogate the villagers."

"No!" Now I'm the one who's shocked. "The farmer stated their innocence. It's a sure way to turn them against us."

"But someone local must have done it."

I shake my head. "We don't know that, especially when that man claims not. We can't threaten our own people—or make them feel as if they're being threatened."

Philippe lets out a breath. He's frowning down the road behind me, toward the village. He turns toward the farmer. "What's the name of this place?"

"Ichou."

"Whose lands are these?"

"They've belonged to the Rambauds these last five hundred years, though with the new queen, we're looking to change that." The farmer gazes keenly at me. No one's told him who I am, but he must have guessed. He glances back at Philippe. "You'd be the

Manceau heir, wouldn't you, now? Your lands start just ten miles yonder. In case you haven't walked them."

Philippe freezes. I watch the muscles tighten in his jaw.

The guards have set the dead man down in the grass. Quietly, I say to Philippe, "I think our work here is done." To the farmer, I add, "We'll see about giving you the opportunity to own your own lands. I'm Sophy Dunbarron, and I intend to do right by the people of Eren."

THE CORPSE HAS yellow hair and pale skin, though I have to resolutely look away from the ruin of his face. His clothes—tattered, rent—are serviceable wool and linen. Heavy. A guardsman fishes a handful of coins from the dead man's trouser pocket. All small, foreign change.

Whoever killed him wasn't interested in money, or they'd have stolen it. The thought frightens me. There's a Tinani coin stamped with the likeness of King Alfred, and two small ones bearing the profile of a Czar of the Ismae. He must have come all the way from the Ismae to die like this. He must have thought, once he was well beyond the Ard, that he was home safe in Eren. He must have stopped being careful.

Who found him? Who did this?

"Your Majesty," Philippe murmurs. His fingers tentatively brush my elbow.

I come back to myself with a start. Tears are rolling, cold, off my chin. The weight of grief has filled me up, so full I'm sinking beneath it.

I didn't used to be like this, so emotional. Now it sometimes seems like I can't hold back a single feeling. I need to be showing the guards my strength, and instead I feel so helpless.

The guards are staring, though most of them pretend not to. I wipe my face with the back of my wrist.

"We should all be mourning him," I say, just loud enough for everyone to hear. "This is a failure of our kingdom. To kill the very people we've sworn to protect."

There's a silence around me, uncomfortable. Only the farmer takes off his hat and cradles it against his chest.

I grimace. If Elanna were here, if she said something like this, they might listen, but I know in my bones the only thing the Ereni guards are hearing is my Caerisian accent—and the only thing my Caerisian guards are hearing is my commitment to serve someone other than themselves. Many Ereni think letting more sorcerers into their kingdom is lunacy—they're willing to accept the existence of Elanna, because she sort of belongs to them, but other magic workers? They don't know them or trust them. The Caerisians, on the other hand, think we should shut down trade and seal the borders off with magic. Even if it were possible to do such a thing, we'd all be at one another's throats in a matter of days.

And by now, some of them have probably figured out that El's been captured.

"What if he was a bad sorcerer?" an Ereni guard whispers to his companion, just loud enough for me to hear.

I whirl on him. "No one deserves a death like this. *No one.*"

The man stares in surprise. Then his gaze narrows—into resentment.

I look around at the others, ignoring him. I meet all the eyes I can. Some flinch away; most stare back at me, by turns thoughtful, worried, and scared. "I will not tolerate this in Eren and Caeris. If anyone knows something about what happened here, or hears whispers about something that might happen elsewhere, you must tell us at once." I turn to the farmer. "Rest assured, we will get to the bottom of this. I don't want you or your neighbors to fear."

I expect the man's face to reflect his distrust of magic and all Caerisians. Instead he bows.

"If you can, milady, we'd be forever grateful."

I don't miss the warning, but even so, there's a kindness in his face when he straightens. I want to take him back to Laon and sit down with him to tea and have him tell me all the things I could do better, to make all the Ereni look at me the way he does.

That would, however, be its own kind of inconsiderate, so I just say, "Master Farmer, if you ever come to Laon, find me. I would be curious to hear your thoughts on the future of our country."

He leans back in surprise, then unexpectedly smiles. "Aye, I'll do that, Your Majesty."

"I hope you do." I nod to him, and to the others say, "I want a thorough search performed. See if the culprits left any evidence. Write down the condition under which we found the body, and all evidence of this man's identity. We'll see if any of the other refugees in Laon know him, or of him. Master Farmer, I'm sorry to burden you with his burial."

"I'll see it done right," the older man replies.

I reach across the stone wall and press his hand, and he looks at me with his faded eyes, deeply, as if he really sees me. I turn back to the coach, before the tears can start again.

CHAPTER FOUR

The man's ruined face haunts me as we jolt toward Philippe's family home. As the farmer said, it's not much farther down the road, perhaps fifteen miles. I look at Philippe, but he won't meet my eyes.

Thick rage is building in my throat. I want to shake him; I want to shout at him and demand he confess what he knows.

But I know that's not the way to pull the truth from someone.

Besides, Rhia seems tired and confused. She didn't even get out of the coach when we stopped, and seemed not to fully understand the explanation we gave about the murdered sorcerer. She's dozing now. The last thing she needs is a shouting match.

So I chew on my lip and bide my time. Soon enough we pull up the long drive to the Manceau country house. It's just as grand as I imagined, stately and made of the same honey-colored brick as the village we just left. Carven lions flank the doors, and three stories of black windows stare us down. I glare back. I'm in no mood to be intimidated by Philippe's family wealth.

I help Rhia from the coach. Philippe tries to assist, but even groggy and exhausted, Rhia glares at him. Still, she leans on my arm, which tells me all I need to know about her state; Rhia Knoll would never consent to aid if she were in full self-possession.

Philippe leads us into the house. It's colder within than under the chilly breeze outside, and gloomy as well. Philippe has to ring the bell twice before a startled butler emerges from a back door. "My lord! We did not expect anyone. Please accept my deepest apologies . . ."

"The house should be ready at all times," Philippe says with thinly disguised irritation. "See that guest chambers are made ready for Queen Sophy and Lady Rhia, and rooms for Her Majesty's retinue. We'll need a full supper for everyone."

The butler gulps and hastily bows to me. "Majesty."

"It's quite all right," I say, annoyed by Philippe's rudeness. "Please make up my chamber last. My friend here needs rest and warmth first. Don't put yourselves to too much trouble with supper, either. Something simple will be perfect."

Philippe looks at me, his cheeks visibly flushed even in the dim light. He probably thinks *I'm* rude ordering his servants about. But after what happened this afternoon, he has no business being angry with me.

"Perhaps Her Majesty would take tea in the sitting room," he says, though judging by his tone it's not exactly a suggestion. "Your guards can escort Lady Rhia upstairs."

I'm reluctant to let Rhia out of my sight, but I'm equally reluctant about Philippe. Of the two, he's the one I need information from. So, patting Rhia's shoulder, I release her into the care of the guardswomen and follow Philippe into the sitting room. It's grand and formal, with thick carpets and a gilded fireplace, which the butler makes a quick business of building a fire in. I pace over to a window. Even though the house is cold, the grounds outside are well kept, complete with a topiary garden and some statues of nymphs.

"My mother's doing." Philippe, joining me at the window, nods at the nymphs. "She says it civilizes the place."

Makes it more Paladisan, he means. I look at him. His profile is strong, his shoulders tense.

Quietly, I say, "Someone knew I'd be coming that way. That sorcerer was a message for me, not that poor farmer."

"Coincidences happen." He turns brusquely from the window.

"It must have been someone local. The death was like the ones in the old stories."

"I'm not sure I'm keen on these stories."

"Don't you have them in Caeris? How to kill a sorcerer?"

My mouth twists. "We like to keep our sorcerers alive."

He casts me a skeptical look. "Not all of your sorcerers can have been good people. You must have had to put a few down."

"Nonsense," I say, but I think of Halmoen, the court sorcerer to an old Caerisian queen. They say he fought battles with creatures made of nightmares. Someone did kill him—and if the stories can be believed, they had to do it more than once. "Well, sometimes. But those aren't the stories we like to tell."

"Maybe not where you grew up, but I'll wager they did elsewhere. My nurse was full of such things."

"The Ereni have always been more tied to Paladis. And then when the empire invaded, they told those stories to suppress our magic . . ."

"Many of the stories come from the Paladisan conquerors, it's true. But not all." He paces toward the fireplace, back to me. "Here in the Low Hills, we have memories just as long as you Caerisians. This used to be wild country. Sorcerers would hide high up in the hills to escape the witch hunters the Paladisans brought with them. Some of them caused trouble."

I frown. It's hard to imagine these bucolic hills overrun with fleeing sorcerers, two hundred odd years ago, but I suppose they might have been. It's a good place to avoid the crown, if you can't flee as far north as Caeris.

It's also a good place to foster a rebellion.

A tap at the door interrupts my thoughts. It's a maid, in a tidy apron, carrying a tray of tea and cake. My stomach growls. The nausea of a few weeks ago may have subsided, but now it seems I'm always hungry. I descend on the sofa beside the now-crackling fire and claim a plate holding a dainty slice of cake. I spoon the delicate sponge into my mouth. It tastes like heaven. And it's gone in three bites.

Do I really care what Philippe Manceau thinks of my appetite? I smirk and help myself to a larger serving of cake.

"They should have brought more food," he says, though he hasn't even touched the cake. (More for me, I suppose.) Instead he sits there, jiggling his knee and holding his teacup without drinking from it.

I wolf down the rest of my second slice, then pause while I consider how quickly I can safely eat the rest of the cake. "Did the people here support our bid for the throne?"

Philippe's gaze snaps to me. Slowly, he says, "Some did, I suppose. It's a long way from Laon."

I cover my skepticism with a swallow of tea. The farmer made it perfectly clear that the locals take an interest in what happens in the capital, whether the nobility believe it or not.

"So," I say. "These Rambauds. Tell me about them."

Philippe hesitates, running a hand along the back of his neck.

"You must know them well," I prompt him. "They're your neighbors."

"Yes," he agrees, still reluctant. "They're cousins of the Eyrlais, and of my family as well. Their lands extend from our border to the Ard, and well south."

So their lands abut the border with Tinan. "They must be wealthy," I note. "We passed a good number of prosperous farms."

Philippe has an aristocrat's disdain for money talk; his chin lifts. "They would be, I suppose, by any measure."

I let my glance wander around the elaborate room.

"Excuse me." Philippe gets to his feet. "I need to see the butler about—about supper. You stay here and enjoy the cake."

There's nothing I would prefer more, but the minute he leaves, I jump to my feet and follow him, easing the door open. Two mountain women stand guard outside it. They must be exhausted after the long journey today, but their hardened faces don't show it.

I start to ask them where Philippe went, but one simply points. I smile at her and hurry off, past the butler's door, into the depths of the house. The corridor takes me past a silent dining room and two darkened salons before ending at a quiet door on the right. Philippe's voice murmurs within. I step as close as I dare. The open door reveals bookshelves full of matching leather tomes. I listen hard.

". . . Anything from my mother?" Philippe is demanding. "Letters, orders for money . . ."

Another man replies. The butler, from the sound of it. "She did have funds withdrawn from the bank, almost a month ago now. I'm sorry, sir, I don't know more."

"Did she leave any sort of instructions? Anything she ordered to be kept secret?"

"Not at all, sir." The butler sounds scandalized. "The last we heard from her was the day she and Duchess Rambaud passed through on their way to Tinan."

"Did the *duchess* leave any instructions?" Philippe asks.

"What are you saying, sir?" the butler exclaims. "If you'll pardon my saying so, it sounds as if you're accusing my staff of something we did not do."

"Of course not. I do apologize." Philippe pauses. "It was only Duchess Hermine with Mother, was it? Not the duke himself?"

"No, sir, only Duchess Hermine and the children. She said they were going to meet Duke Rambaud in Tinan."

"I suppose Duke Aristide had already taken shelter with King Alfred," Philippe says, but he seems to be talking to himself. He sighs loudly. "Assemble the staff, would you, before supper? I would like to know more details about my mother's time here."

"Sir, I would not permit any member of my staff to—"

"I know. But you know what my mother's like."

The butler simply says, "Yes, sir."

I bolt back to the nearest deserted salon just before the butler emerges from the study. I stuff myself behind the door, peering through the slit into the corridor. The butler passes me. I wait. And wait. Finally Philippe emerges, taking brisk strides down the hall. I slip out behind him. He left behind the faint odor of brandy, a note above the dust and the chill.

Whatever else he's hiding, I have the feeling Philippe Manceau does not care for his mother.

RHIA'S ALERT WHEN I knock on her bedchamber door an hour later, lying on a sofa in front of the fireplace. She grimaces at me. She's clutching a hot-water flask to her head. "I'm not myself. A Knoll should never be caught lying down!"

I laugh, coming into the room, but the truth is her weakness has worried me, and beneath the bluster, I can see she's scared herself. She fiddles with the hot-water flask.

I settle down in a wingback chair across from her. Climbing the short flight of stairs up to this room left me more winded than usual, but I've had a light meal in the bedchamber that belongs to Philippe's mother, and I feel decidedly more human.

"Did you get anything to eat?" I ask Rhia.

"A maid brought in some soup. I wasn't very hungry."

Rhia, not hungry? This, too, is unlike her. "Did you eat it?"

"Oh, yes. I never turn down a meal."

I smile, somewhat reassured, and lean back in the chair, closing my eyes. It feels indecently comfortable and for the first time in weeks, with only Rhia beside me, I feel almost like my old self. Not that Rhia is always an easy presence, but she's Caerisian, and a mountain woman besides. You always know where you stand with Rhia Knoll.

She eyes me. "So you had a chat with Manceau."

"He told me about his mother—and then I overheard him talking to his butler after. It seems his mother fled to Tinan with some other disgruntled nobles—including Rambaud's wife."

Rhia gives a low whistle. "That explains a lot."

"It explains why the nobles were so eager to have Philippe elected to council." I pause. "The butler claims no one's heard from Philippe's mother since she left, but she's withdrawn funds. If she's done that, she might be in touch with someone here—and she might be involved in the sorcerer's death. I think Philippe suspects her, along with the Rambauds."

"Well, if she ran off to Tinan, she probably loathes sorcerers." Rhia considers. "And us."

"Probably. Philippe asked the butler if his mother had left any instructions behind."

Rhia arches a brow. "So you didn't just overhear them; you were listening in on their conversation! Look at Goody-Goody Dunbarron, eavesdropping."

I offer her a prim smile. "Merely listening to the voices of my subjects."

"Ha! Well, did you confront him on it?"

"No, not yet. I don't want him to clam up. I'm playing it out."

She toys with the fringe on her throw. "The ministers keep bothering you to marry. Isn't Manceau one of their prime candidates?"

"He seems to be," I allow, though the ministers haven't named him outright—and I'm not sure I trust him enough to even consider it. I've spent the past few weeks trying to forget how my last visit to Laon ended, with the ministers informing me that a bastard queen would look more legitimate if she were married. And how I snapped back at them that I wasn't a heifer for them to breed to the highest bidder. And how the minister of agriculture grumbled, *She'd be a lot more tolerable if she were.*

Getting along so well, my cabinet and I. I realize I'm grinding my back teeth together just at the thought of talking to them again.

"You could just ask him," Rhia says. "About the marriage, and about his mother and the murder."

"I could." But I won't. Not yet.

"It's what El would do. She'd demand answers."

"That's why she wouldn't get any." I pause. "Wouldn't you demand answers, too?"

But Rhia Knoll, normally as irascible as a knife, hesitates, fingering the hot-water flask. At last she says, "I'm starting to wonder if the way you do things isn't better. It's a lot more tedious, don't get me wrong. But they still don't trust us, Sophy, the Ereni. Or the ministers and nobles, at least. The common people stand behind our cause, for the most part, and I like them well enough. But when you feel as if someone's sneaking up on your back, sometimes the best thing to do is draw them closer before you spring."

"I suppose."

"And . . ." She worries at the flask. "My father's on the front. If anything happens to him, I might get elected to replace him. I might become the warden of the mountains."

I look at her, with her delicate-seeming face and wisping black hair and forearms strong enough to crush a man's skull. "Do you want that?"

"Did you want to be queen?" she counters.

I don't know how to answer that. Of course I felt I'd be better at ruling than Finn, my half brother, whom I wanted so much to like but found myself unbelievably exasperated with. But I was thinking like a child, I realize now, as if ruling a kingdom is the same as writing an essay on history or taking an oral exam—something where the definitions of skill and quality are clear-cut and where you're rewarded after. There aren't any rewards here, not really. And there isn't simple or universal approval, just because I claimed the throne and Ruadan educated me well.

Yet I will never give it up.

Rhia seems to see some of this pass over my face, because she says, "That's what I thought."

I sigh. "I miss Elanna."

"Me, too." She laughs. "Though I never thought I'd admit it!"

"She does make things easier; everyone's scared of her power."

"The terrifying *Caveadear*."

I return Rhia's smile, but inside I'm fighting with my own unease. For months, I've struggled with gaining the same instant respect El commands, and now I'm beginning to wonder if half that respect came from the simple fear that she'd bury someone in the earth if they annoyed her. Of course, she's just and merciful and compassionate as well. But being terrifying helps, too.

Rhia yawns.

I rise. "I'll let you get some rest."

But though I go to bed myself, I lie awake for a long time, staring up into the dark canopy of Philippe's mother's bed. Seeing the face of the murdered sorcerer, and El being swept away across the water. Wondering whom I can trust.

CHAPTER FIVE

Philippe is subdued in the carriage the next morning—clearly preoccupied, as when I ask him a question, it takes several long moments to receive an answer. Rhia has fallen asleep, her head pillowed against the window. She must have taken more laudanum; I don't know how else she'd sleep with the carriage chattering over potholes. Beyond her, the blue imprint of low hills rises up on the horizon, above the farmland. We're approaching the river Sasralie, which flows through Laon.

I look at Philippe. His chin is at his fist—but Rhia is asleep, and I sense an opportunity before we arrive in Laon and I'm overwhelmed with the telling of El's capture.

"What's on your mind?" I ask.

He blinks. Then he sits up straight, shaking out his shoulders. "I apologize. I've been lost in thought about . . . about that refugee."

He's obviously lying, but I decide to nod and take it at face value. "I've heard complaints about letting the sorcerers into Eren, but never thought anyone would stoop as low as murder." I pause. Innocently, I say, "But I wanted to ask after your mother. I don't think I've met her."

"You wouldn't have." His eyes narrow a bit, but he says, "She followed Loyce Eyrlai to Tinan."

I do my best to look shocked. Maybe I am, a little; I didn't think he'd come right out and say it. "She left you behind?"

"I didn't exactly volunteer to follow her into self-imposed exile," he says sharply. "If she wants to live out her life at Alfred's court, so be it."

"And you haven't seen her since," I muse.

"No." He looks at me. "We disagreed on the matter of her departure."

"I suppose she wanted you to go with her."

He drums his fingers on his knee. "In fact, no. We both agreed it would be better if I remained here." Drily, he says, "It's one of the few things we did agree on."

I study him, wondering how much they disagreed on our new regime. "What did you do during the rebellion?"

This time, he looks away. "The old king had sent me out to Denare to quell dissent. It was where your friend the Count of Ganz kept one of his secret printing presses. I . . . My job was to burn it."

"And you did?"

His silence is answer enough.

I stare down at my hands, twisted together in my lap. In my mind's eye, I can't help seeing that printing press going up in flames. Such a petty gesture. I can't imagine ever ordering such a thing.

Yet if there were dissidents in the kingdom fighting against me, endangering my people . . . what would I not do?

At last, he clears his throat. "I suppose it's trite, but we've all done things we're ashamed of, have we not? My mother raised me to believe I must obey a royal command, or I would be a traitor and treated as such. But I believed your rebels might win, and I'm glad that you did."

"Thank you," I say.

He laughs hollowly. "For what?"

"You told me the truth. It's not an easy thing to do."

His eyebrows lift, and he changes the subject. "To be even more honest, my lady, we may never be able to charge anyone with the murder of that refugee. But I promise I will help you get to the bottom of why it was done, and try to prevent it from happening again."

"Well," I say, "I suppose that's as much as anyone can ask for."

An awkward silence falls between us. The carriage has turned onto the royal road going west. I glance out at the hills we're passing on the left, and the river Sasralie gleaming to the right. Ahead, one hill rises higher than the rest, its hardscrabble rock dominating a shallow valley. A town perches on top of the hill, its walls and roofs winking in the sunlight.

Philippe cranes his neck around, following my gaze. "That's Montclair."

"Whose land is this?" I ask.

"It's the people's own." When I look at him questioningly, he explains, "It used to belong to a noble family, but they fell from power under Antoine Eyrlai's father, and the town council sued for independent governance. They won."

I look up at the high walls. "So they didn't need Caeris to liberate them."

"They didn't think so." He pauses. "The mayor is great friends with Aristide Rambaud. The town's always enjoyed Rambaud protection. Until, well, recently."

"I see." And I do, for this feels like a warning. I remind myself that the Duke of Essez is safely ensconced in Tinan with Philippe's mother, tormenting King Alfred. But all the same, as the carriage rolls past the high hill town, I shiver.

LAON ARRIVES TOO soon on the horizon. I shrink a little as we pass through the high, pale-gray gates, shadowed under the late-afternoon sun. I've never been entirely comfortable in this city, and now I'm trying to resign myself to the fact that I won't be able to make a public announcement until tomorrow morning. It means waiting to meet with the ministers, as well.

I suppose this is as good a test of Philippe's trustworthiness as any. If word of El's capture gets out ahead of tomorrow morning, I'll know who did it. Although Philippe Manceau doesn't exactly strike me as that much of a fool.

We rattle through the streets, our coach and retinue largely ignored by the people going about their day. I look out at women carrying baskets filled with flowers over their arms, and men in simple coats and thick hats, two young fellows carrying a ladder and laughing. Bitterness worms into the back of my mouth. If only I could be one of them again, on the streets where I used to belong, a woman of the people as my mother raised me to be, not the king's daughter and backup heir Ruadan molded me into. If only I could run.

If only my father had come here when Finn died, the way he was supposed to. Then I wouldn't have to manage this fractious kingdom on my own.

The fine glass windowpane separates me from the common run of the world, the same way it has for the last thirteen years. And guilt swamps me. My mother and Ruadan and Finn are all dead. Wanting to run feels like failing them.

Philippe's watching me. I pretend not to see him, yet I can't forget his presence. I find myself talking to Ruadan in my mind, the way I have ever since he died. *Should I trust him?*

But of course, no answer comes.

"You'll summon the ministers to council, yes?" I say to Philippe. "First thing in the morning?"

He frowns a little and begins to speak, then seems to think better of it. "You're wise. It's a large secret to keep overnight."

I nod. "We don't want to force them to remain silent."

The coach tramples through the streets to the palace, situated on a low rise with a view over rooftops to the river, and to the Hill of the Imperishable to the southwest. We pass through the wrought-iron gates tipped with gilt, into the wide cream-colored arms of the palace. I disembark and head for the sweeping stairs, acutely conscious of my dirty hair and the mud still crusted onto my coat. I am not the sort of queen this place was built for. Some days, I still can't believe Elanna grew up here. It's such a cold place, despite the bright painted ceilings. Chill always seems to leach off the walls.

Charlot Bain, the steward who appointed himself the head of my household in Laon with such little fuss that I couldn't object, is waiting in the colonnade at the top of the steps. He's an impossibly tidy man invariably attired in a fawn-colored coat and trousers, so perfectly groomed that I always find myself searching him for a stray unshaven whisker, or a crease in his impeccable neckcloth. As usual, there's nothing. He's serene, unflappable: the model facto-tum. "Your Majesty! We didn't expect you for some time."

I give him a brittle smile. "If I announce my return, it's harder to tell if my ministers have been behaving themselves."

"You'll be so pleased to know Lady Teofila arrived this morn-ing. She's in the music room."

A hand seems to grip my throat. "Teofila's arrived?"

"Yes, my lady, ready to translate for the refugees."

I knew Teofila was bound for Laon, and Elanna's capture is one secret I can't keep till morning. Truthfully, in some ways, it would have been easier to tell the ministers we lost her first.

"Thank you," I manage. With a start, I remember the others. Rhia's looking wan as she climbs from the coach. I begin, "Do you—"

"No." She waves me ahead. "Go tell her."

The cowardly part of me would gladly help Rhia up to her chambers, and spend perhaps an hour fussing over her. But Teofila has been like a mother to me—more a mother, for more years, than my own ever was. I need to tell her what happened, even if it breaks her heart.

I tug my waistcoat habitually down, and freeze. Teofila is like a mother to me, indeed—and if anyone recognizes my condition, it is bound to be her. She'll probably take one look at me and . . .

It's a horrible thought, but at least this news about Elanna may distract her until I can think what to tell her, how to present it. I'll have to do a good job of acquitting myself. I can already see how she'll look at me.

I remember to nod to Philippe.

"Tomorrow, my lady," he says, and bows before departing across the courtyard to his townhouse.

On shaky legs, I walk into the palace. No one knew I was coming, so there isn't anyone waiting to greet me. That's a relief, at least. The foyer, as always, seems to swallow me up: a vast white room with a soaring ceiling and an enormous inlaid clock whose hands make precise, vaguely disapproving ticks. I climb stiffly up the carpeted stairs. Charlot told me Teofila was in the music room, but I'd have known it anyway because notes from a clavichord dance through the walls and down the steps.

There's a faint, disorienting flutter in my stomach. The child, again, or my own nerves. Perhaps the baby likes the sound. At least one of us is looking forward to this.

As I draw closer, I find the door of the salon open. Teofila sits at the clavichord, tinkering with some high notes, her dark silvered hair tumbling over the back of a pale-blue gown. Hugh stands at her side, a self-possessed figure in Caerisian tweed, thumbing through a musical score. The sight strikes me in the chest, and I have to stop there in the doorway. It takes me back to childhood, to the instinctive comfort I found in the warmth of Teofila's presence and the bright effusiveness of her music.

Hugh was always there, too. But he was Ruadan's friend, and while he and Teofila were always cordial, they never seemed particularly close. Now they are near each other, murmuring over the music, and Ruadan is gone, and my chest has turned soft and hollow. Ruadan in so many ways made us what we are—he made it seem possible to launch a rebellion to depose a king and to bring back the old magic. Sometimes I wonder if Elanna's sorcery returning after all this time sprang not from the whim of the gods, but from the force of Ruadan's belief. He was determined that his daughter would be a *Caveadear* like the ones of old, like Wildegarde herself, and so she was.

And now they're both gone.

A small choked noise escapes my throat, and both Hugh and Teofila turn. He smiles. She jumps up from the clavichord and throws open her arms. "Sophy!"

Tears pulse behind my eyes, but I choke them back as ruthlessly as I can. This isn't about me. I won't have Teofila comfort me like a child.

"What is it?" She's come to me, hugging me close—too close. I pull back, afraid she's already sensed the roundness of my belly even through layers of wool and skirts. But she doesn't fully let me go. Her arms are warm and she smells of roses and spice. Her chin is delicate—just like Elanna's. "What's wrong?"

But despite my effort of control, I find I still can't speak. I shouldn't even be holding Teofila like this, as if I have a daughter's right to her love. Because I lost Elanna, her real daughter. How can I tell Teofila that El has been taken from her, again?

"Sophy, come sit here." She guides me over to a settee. I scrub a hand over my cheeks. They're dry, thank the gods.

Behind us, Hugh closes the door, but he doesn't leave. He comes over to a nearby chair and sits, his hands clasped between his knees, his level brown eyes feathered with new lines. This is the man who taught me the history of Eren and Caeris, the stories of the great kings and queens, the rhetoric of Paladisan orators; who filled my ears with philosophy and poetry. Ruadan might have taught me about governance, but Hugh gave me a queen's education.

And Teofila gave me music. When I was thirteen or so, I used to get terribly nervous performing in front of guests. She always told me the same thing. *Chin up, shoulders back. Tell the nerves to respectfully leave you be. Remember this isn't about you. It's about the music.*

But this isn't about me—it's about Elanna, and Teofila, and the future of our kingdom.

So I raise my chin and pull my shoulders back and draw in a breath. "I have terrible news to share with you both. I am so sorry." And I tell them. As I talk, Teofila's hands close over mine, gripping harder and harder, and when I finish she's still holding me, but there's an emptiness in her eyes.

Hugh clears his throat. He looks as stricken as she does. "They'll have taken her to Paladis, then. To the emperor."

I nod. "To the Ochuroma."

Teofila slowly balls her hands into fists and presses them against her forehead. She breathes through clenched teeth. "So who are we sending to get her back? I'm not going to sit here and—and *pray* again!"

Hugh looks at me over the top of Teofila's head. He doesn't say anything; he doesn't need to. We both know that sending someone to rescue Elanna from the Ochuroma prison would be a suicide mission.

Teofila knows it, too. She brings her fists to her mouth and silently screams into them.

"Jahan's there," I say. "He went back."

Teofila's head snaps up. They both stare at me, and so I explain where Jahan has gone, and why. "Alistar has gone into Tinan as well," I add, "on the chance they aren't taking her to Paladis. He and his Hounds will find out all they can."

If the Tinani don't capture them, too. I swallow hard.

"All right." Teofila's still got her fists locked at her mouth. "Maybe it will be all right."

But frantic energy still hums off her, a high pulsing note that seems to hit between my eyebrows. I rub at the spot. I want to touch Teofila but don't quite dare.

Hugh sinks lower in his chair. "You plan to tell the people, I assume?"

"Yes, though the Butcher counseled me not."

Hugh snorts but manages to withhold his opinion on Lord Gilbert.

"I'll tell the ministers first thing in the morning." I am suddenly weary down to the depths of my stomach. I want to go up to my rooms, take a bath, dismiss my maids, and finally let myself cry alone, in peace. "Then I'll make a statement to the people."

Teofila says suddenly, "If she's going to die, I just want to see her one last time. That's all. Why isn't there anything I can do but pray? I believe in the gods, but sometimes belief isn't enough."

Hugh and I exchange a glance. I place my hand tentatively on Teofila's shoulder. I don't know what to say. Teofila has already lost her husband—though we all feel the ache, and sometimes I wonder if I miss him more than she does. But to lose both him and El . . . it will be impossible to bear.

Yet Teofila is the strongest woman I know. If anyone can endure it, it's her.

"I'm sorry," I whisper. "I'm so sorry."

She looks at me now. Touches my cheek. "Oh, Sophy. You look done in. Why don't you go rest before supper? You've had a long journey here."

"But you—"

"I'll be all right. I have Hugh here with me. And I . . ." She shakes her head. "Go, sweet girl. It's all right."

It's hard not to feel I've been dismissed like a child while the adults talk. I kiss her cheek and rise all the same. Give Hugh a brief embrace. He kisses the top of my head, a fatherly gesture. Ruadan never did anything like that. Ruadan was all fire and ideas and plans and doing. It—among other things—drove Teofila mad.

Now it's a struggle not to feel that she's pushing me away, the way she pushed Ruadan away after Elanna was captured.

I make my way to the door. Turn the knob. Glance back over my shoulder. Hugh's taken my place on the settee, grasping Teofila's hand. Their heads are close together.

I go out before my heart can crack further.

I WALK BLINDLY through the palace, entirely missing the entrance to my own apartments. My feet take me down a set of stairs and down a long corridor to a set of glass doors, their panes gently fogged with warmth. I step inside. The greenhouse is warm and humid. Trees, shrubs, flowers seem to proliferate from every surface, a sweet-smelling greenery.

I've come instinctively to Elanna's favorite place. The late-afternoon light slants, buttery and gold, through the white-framed windows; long shadows stretch over the palace lawns.

The greenhouse appears deserted; Guerin Jacquard, the royal botanist and Elanna's old friend, does not emerge with his usual preoccupied air. So I sink down onto a stool beside the potting table. I feel as though a fist has been driven into my gut. I can't stop seeing Teofila's face, her silent scream. It was terrible enough knowing I'd failed Eren and Caeris. But it's far worse knowing that I've failed her, too.

"Your Majesty?"

It's a man's diffident voice. I startle.

Someone is approaching through the plants; he evidently followed me into the greenhouse. "I do apologize for tracking you down like this," he's saying, "but it's the perfect opportunity for us to talk."

I rise, blinking away my preoccupation. "High Priest Granpier."

"My lady." Armael Granpier, the high priest of the temple to Aera, bows and straightens with a smile. He's a small, twinkling, middle-aged man with thinning hair and robust good humor undiminished by the trials of the last months. The people elected him minister of religious affairs, and since the first refugee sorcerers began to arrive in Eren, he's taken it upon himself to house and feed them at the temple. He dresses plainly in a robe of dark-blue broadcloth; the long white tunic beneath it and the narrow cloth fillet banding his head mark him as a priest.

I manage a smile in return. "You found me with remarkable alacrity."

"Indeed, Your Majesty, as luck or the Good Goddess would have it! I had word that your retinue passed by and rushed up here." He glances swiftly around the greenhouse. "It seems we are alone."

"I'm glad you did." I pause, unsure how to deliver my news, which may upset Granpier even more than the others on account of his work with the foreign sorcerers. "How are the refugees faring?"

"As it happens, that is why I've come to you. I wondered if you might accompany me to the temple." He lowers his voice. "I find myself at a crisis point. Our accommodations are overflowing. Food has grown scarce. I will continue to take in all who come to me, but their quality of life is rapidly decreasing. As we both know . . ." He sighs. "This is not a topic that my fellow ministers find particularly moving."

"I'm terribly sorry to hear it." Though it's nothing less than what I expected—the last time I was in Laon, Granpier warned me that he was running out of space. "I think you don't give the other ministers enough credit. Juleane Brazeur and Lord Faure are keen to put the refugees to work."

"That is, in fact, the other reason why I came." He looks at me, serious. "Two refugees have come forward to volunteer on the front."

Two sorcerers are willing to fight for us? I glance around the space Elanna once inhabited, swallowing back the hope that pulses in my throat. This could make the difference on the front. It could be what saves us from Tinan and Paladis.

"I'll come with you," I say. "Let's go now. As it happens, I have some news for you, too."

CHAPTER SIX

My back protests at the idea of getting into a carriage again, so Granpier and I walk the short distance to the temple, a retinue of palace guards trailing after us as dusk begins to settle over the city. While we walk, I tell him about the murdered refugee.

"You believe it a threat?" he says. "Not a murder out of fear and ignorance?"

"Perhaps both. But the farmer didn't know anything about the dead man; none of the villagers seemed to. It was on land that belongs to the Rambauds."

"The . . ." Granpier casts a surreptitious glance around the street. "My lady, I think it would be wise for us to wait and speak of this privately."

I nod. His alarm is reassuring, in a way; obviously I didn't make up the potential danger. I change the subject, projecting my voice just a little. "It's a lovely evening, isn't it?"

"That it is." He positively beams. "Spring at last!"

It *is* lovely. The air holds a hopeful smell, and even in the lavender dusk, Laon's wide avenues are brighter and cleaner than those of Barrody. The people, who aren't accustomed to seeing queens tramp on foot through the city, take no notice of me or High Priest Granpier, but have great interest in the guards—all men, since I ordered my mountain women to rest. Girls flick their skirts at them, and lads call out, "How can I get a hat like that?" One of the guards self-consciously straightens his decorative helmet with its white-plumed crest.

Our route takes us toward the river; the temple lies at the heart of the city, not in the aristocratic neighborhood surrounding the palace. The streets narrow, and soon the domed roof emerges through the sea of sharply angled slate. Granpier, who's kept up a comfortable chatter, tells me that the Paladisans built the temple during their brief rule, basing it on the great old buildings of Ida—and even going so far as to import marble from Vedelos. I suppose they thought a more beautiful edifice would assist with their conquest, but they pulled out of Eren before the temple was even finished, leaving their language and their gods behind, along with a fair number of colonists. This is why the Ereni language borrows so much from Idaean, Granpier tells me: centuries of rapport.

"Or blind subservience," I suggest.

He chortles. "Perhaps. Yet I think the Paladisans had much to offer, in their way. Where would we be without their culture, their philosophers . . ."

"Largely Idaean," I note; Ruadan educated me well in the frustrations of other conquered peoples.

It is a curious question, though. Eren and Caeris separated into different kingdoms centuries before the Paladisan conquest; and while Caeris clutched tight the old ways and beliefs, Eren was always leaning south toward Ida and the great cities on the Two Seas, incorporating language and beliefs even before the conquest. Maybe, in that way, the Ereni have been more forward thinking than we've ever been.

The temple is certainly a building of Paladisan splendor, its white walls glowing in the twilight, and its façade dominated by a massive colonnade, each pillar capital carved with leafy abandon. They never built the arcade that was supposed to dominate the square, but the area around the temple still has a certain pristine look, albeit filled with doves and pigeons who scatter as we walk. Two square wings emerge from either side of the temple's central dome. Granpier gestures to one on the right-hand side.

"That wing has always been reserved for the poor or any who needed sanctuary. But now we've people sleeping in the main temple, and in the administrative rooms on the other side . . . The novices are trying to make the best of it, but you can tell it discomfits them."

"A good learning experience?"

"Yes, certainly. Many of them are learning Idaean—and the true nature of charity." He winks. "Come inside."

A novice is standing in the vestibule, shifting from foot to foot; she's obviously been waiting for High Priest Granpier, for she rushes up to him the moment we top the steps. Her red hair is bound back by a fillet, like Granpier's, and she wears a simple cream-colored robe knotted at the waist with a length of green cloth. Tasseled wooden prayer beads hang from her left wrist. With her open, rounded face, she appears younger than I have ever felt. I still find the novices strange. In Caeris, a young man or woman might offer several years to a temple before marriage, but most of them still live at home and attend school or university at the same time. Priests and priestesses likewise live among the community; our town midwife at Cerid Aven also led ceremonies at the temple. But Granpier's novices come to him after school, and some of them have taken vows like his, that wed them to the priesthood for life.

"We don't have enough barley for supper," the girl is saying, "and the carrots have run out, and Desmond says—"

"A moment, Felicité." Granpier holds up a hand with a smile, and the girl whooshes out a breath. She must be about my own age, and even though I've been crowned for several months, it's strange still when he gestures to me deferentially. "First, greet our guest: my friend Sophy Dunbarron."

I'm so glad he didn't call me *the queen* that I smile, too.

The girl blinks rapidly. She makes a sort of bow, and I nod back.

Granpier turns to me. "Many of our patrons have been unable to give money these last months, and some refuse now that we're taking in the refugees."

We enter the temple. I've only been here once before, at my coronation. The coffered dome seems to float overhead, an oculus shedding light into the room. There is a reflecting pool, mirroring in perfect stillness the simple statue of the goddess Aera—herself a Paladisan import, though they claim she's like the Caerisian goddess Anu. The statue is another item the original builders ran out of money for; instead of marble and gilt, she's carved of old, blackened wood. A blue cloak swaths her carven shoulders, a gift women in the city make for her every year.

"Go find Demetra and Ciril," Granpier tells the novice. He gestures to the far side of the chamber. "As you see, quarters have grown so crowded that some are choosing to sleep out here."

Looking past Aera, I notice them now. People sitting on bedrolls against the far wall, talking; parents crouched beside children, playing games with cards and dice. Several faces have lifted toward us, curious, but there's a kind of hollowness to their eyes that tells the truth of what they've endured to get here.

A lump swells in my throat. My mother and I once took refuge in a temple, though only for one night, because not even temples were safe from the crown's soldiers. It was a simple wooden building, and I remember falling asleep with the glow of candlelight washing the beatific face of the goddess Anu.

Granpier leads me over to the refugees. They regard us doubtfully.

I step forward, holding my hands open, as if this gesture of welcome can extend to all of them. It's at moments like this that I feel like I'm playacting at being queen. Who am I to welcome these people to Eren, a land where one of their own has already been murdered by unknown hands? Yet now it's more important than ever that I do greet them. Ruadan used to instruct me to say hello to everyone I met with as much genuine warmth as I could. *People don't ever remember the words you say, but they remember how you made them feel when you said them.*

"I'm Sophy," I say, first in Ereni and again in my fumbling, self-conscious Idaean. "Know that you are very welcome here. We intend to do everything we can to help you."

Some of them still look confused and wary, though others nod guardedly. High Priest Granpier leans forward and says, in much better Idaean than mine, "This is Sophy, the queen of Eren. She's been on the front and has only just returned to Laon, and this is one of the first places she came."

A few faces soften at that, but not all. I suppose I wouldn't trust so easily, either—especially if they have any idea their fellow refugees are being killed on Ereni lands. I twist my fingers together. I'm not going to tell them about the murdered sorcerer, not yet. "I'm sorry you've had to flee your homelands," I tell them all. "I promise I am doing everything in my power to ensure you don't still have to live in fear."

A woman steps forward. She's about Teofila's age, dressed in a ragged gown that must once have been fine, and there's pity in her eyes. She seems to see how young I am, how much I'm struggling. "We are making our home here, as best we can," she says.

"Please," I say to her, "tell me how you came to be here, if you're willing."

They exchange reluctant glances, but all the same the woman begins to speak. "We come from Omira. The provinces in the west of Paladis." She tells a story of generations of her family hiding their magic, of an aunt carted off to the Ochuroma and a cousin drowned in his own backyard in a fit of local justice, when people blamed him for a bad harvest. She says it seemed like their family was cursed. But then they heard about the rebellion in Eren, and the *Caveadear* waking the land and declaring our nation a safe haven for sorcery. Her sister's children were just growing into the first stirrings of magic. They thought they could bring the children to a place where they wouldn't have to hide. Where they wouldn't always have to fear death. Where they might at last shake their curse.

"So we bought a cart," she says. "We left behind everything we couldn't carry, except for the dog." It lies snuggled against one of the children, watching me with bright eyes. "We walked all the way to Tinan, and across Tinan. And then we realized soldiers were patrolling the border—looking for people like us." She glances back at her family. "A fisherman took pity on us. He said we could take his boat across the Ard, for a fee. So we gave him everything we had—the rings my mother had given me. My husband's fine coat. The last of our food."

Her daughter says, "There were almost too many of us for the boat—eleven people. My brothers and I had to swim behind. But we made it."

"They walked all the way here," High Priest Granpier says softly. "Almost starving."

The refugee woman says robustly, "We could have drowned, like the people who have come to Eren across the Tarican Strait. The patrols could have found us. But none of that happened. We're here, together. We have food at last. Blankets." She gestures to the bedrolls. "But all our belongings are in Tinan. We do not speak Ereni. The Ereni don't trust us. We don't know where to go."

I'm aware that the novice has joined us along with two new people, but I don't turn to them quite yet.

"What did you do, in Omira?" I ask. "You must have skills we can use here."

She nods. "I am a dyer. My brother and his son are carpenters."

"We should find employment for you, then, and real beds. You've slept on the ground long enough."

She smiles, but it tells me she doesn't quite believe me.

I *will* find a solution—even if I have to take on my entire cabinet to do it. I nod at her with all the confidence I can muster. "Thank you for telling me your story." I glance at everyone else. "I should like to hear *all* of your stories, and what your skills are, and how I can help you now that you are here. I am so glad you've come."

High Priest Granpier coughs delicately, and I turn to him and the novice with the two new arrivals, a man and a woman. The man is older, with graying hair and a thick neck, a certainty about him, and the woman a few years older than me, perhaps thirty, her black hair gathered into a sleek knot. She stands quite still, her hands clasped before her, her long, capable fingers locked around each other.

"My lady, this is Ciril Thorley and Demetra Megades."

They both incline their heads.

I offer them a smile. "I'm Sophy Dunbarron."

"They both wish to volunteer their services at the front," Granpier says in Ereni, and again in Idaean, then Tinani.

I look the two of them over, wondering if there's any chance I can get my more traditionalist ministers to accept even one of them, much less both. Of course, the radicals will want me to recruit everyone, even the children, even the people who have been sleeping on the floor and crossed the strait in a rowboat. The traditionalist ministers will definitely find Ciril threatening, while Demetra is so tranquil looking they would probably not take her all that seriously.

"We are, of course, grateful that you want to help," I say in Ereni, which Granpier translates into Idaean. "Though we would never demand it of anyone. Can you tell me what skills you have, and how you might help?"

Ciril nods. His hands, I notice, are also thick and square, corded with veins, and his nose has been broken more than once. There's something about him that might unnerve even witch hunters. To my surprise, he answers me in accented Ereni. "I will make it rain on our enemies day and night. I will strike them down with lightning. Make them perish in floods."

"You're Tinani," I say, my thoughts ticking. This fellow's magic sounds similar to Elanna's. If he can restrain himself from wantonly killing everyone in Tinan—his own people!—he might be able to use some of her same tactics on the front.

He inclines his head. "Yes, I come from Darchon."

That's Tinan's capital, and our frequent trade probably explains how he knows Ereni. I study him, uncertain. I don't know this man. Do I really dare to entrust him with the truth about Elanna's capture, and the defense of our kingdom? "You would fight for us against your own people?"

He meets my gaze levelly. "I would fight for justice for people like me."

I suppose that's fair enough. I turn to Demetra. She's tall, almost my height, with winged eyebrows and an aquiline nose, olive skin, and her shoulders are broad and capable. She wears an elegant striped gown, its skirts somewhat crumpled; a white cloth is draped absently over her arm. "And you?"

"I'm a midwife," she says, tugging at the white cloth, and I sense tension underneath her placid exterior. "I come from Ida. I've healed many women and babies, though they did not know it. I thought if I can do so for women in childbirth, I could do the same for men at the front. I have three children of my own. I don't wish to see them beaten down and forced to hide like me."

She glances at the other refugees as she says it, as if willing them to step forward and declare their willingness to fight. But none of them do.

"We can certainly use your skills," I say, trying to hide my disappointment. Of course a healer will be a tremendous asset, but she won't be able to approximate El's abilities. Which leaves Ciril, unless someone else comes forward.

"Did you bring your children here?" I ask Demetra.

She nods. "They're with their grandmother. But my husband . . ." She looks away. "He had to stay in Ida."

So she's Idaean, then. I look at Ciril. "And you? Did you come with family?"

His face draws closed. "My family is gone. I came alone."

I find myself wondering what became of the family—maybe he struck them with lightning because they offended him. But I force my face and tone to remain pleasant. "We will certainly find a use for your help, but I must consult with the ministers first. In the meantime, High Priest Granpier, if we could complete our tour of your facilities? Then I'll know what we need to supply, and for whom."

*

IN THE EASTERN wing, the refugees' beds are packed tightly together, occupied by children with hollowed eyes. Though the floor
is clean and incense smokes nearby, an undeniable odor clings to
the large rooms. "Most of these people don't have a change of
clothes among them," High Priest Granpier murmurs. Delicately,
he adds, "They are keeping the place, and themselves, as clean as
they can."

"Ah." I wince, as much out of shared shame for the refugees as
for the stench. I cannot imagine the difficulty of trying to maintain
one's dignity in a situation like this.

A man comes up to us. In broken, insistent Ereni, he says, "We
are not here to make trouble. We are here to live."

I press his hand. "I will do everything I can to help you, I promise it."

At the end of the corridor is a small washing chamber, its walls
hung with ragged towels and a forgotten stuffed animal. With a
swift glance to make sure we're unfollowed, Granpier takes my
elbow and pulls me through the washing chamber and out a back
door into a narrow courtyard. Wooden privies occupy the far wall.
To our left, a gate leads to what must be the temple's garden. Granpier stops beside the compost heap. I do my best not to inhale.

Granpier grimaces. "We're finding that our accommodations
for . . . refuse . . . are somewhat inadequate."

"We'll find another solution," I promise him.

"I hope that we can." He pauses. "My lady, I think the news of
the dead refugee would come better from me than from you. Let
me make inquiries."

It feels like the coward's way out, but at the same time I can't
face any more of their despair. "Tell them we will do everything in
our power to dispense justice and discover the culprit."

"That is why I brought us out here." His gaze grows keen. "You
said it happened on Rambaud land?"

"Yes. The farmer—"

Someone calls Granpier's name from inside the bathing chamber. With a hiss of exasperation, he opens the garden gate and shoos me through it. The bushes are drab and brown, only a hint of green shoots pressing up through the earth; the garden is empty. He pulls me all the way through to a small potting shed, its walls sheltering us from the garden and, in turn, from the city itself.

I turn to Granpier. "What do you know about the Rambauds?"

"They're an old family. A powerful one. Wealthy—they've donated much to the temple, as well as to many other causes. One might say that, where privilege doesn't open doors for them, they buy their way into what they want." He pauses. "I—and many others—expected Aristide Rambaud, the duke, to remain in Laon after your victory. It would have been in keeping with his nature to procure a seat on your council, and make himself a thorn in your side until he got what he wanted. But he hasn't."

I'm shaking my head. "I didn't even know about him until yesterday. Only the name, of course."

"I thought perhaps he'd gone to Tinan, with his wife. Perhaps he has. But . . ." Granpier looks at me. "My lady, you need to know that Aristide Rambaud has not been seen since you deposed Loyce Eyrlai. He was in Tinan until a few weeks ago, and now . . . my contacts have lost sight of him. Powerful men like the Duke of Essez don't simply disappear."

I swallow. "Then where—"

The gate thumps behind us. "There you are, High Priest!" It's the red-haired novice Felicité and, behind her, a man shouldering through into the garden.

"Your Majesty. High Priest Granpier." He bows, lowering the handkerchief from his nose with a look of distaste. "I heard you had returned, my lady. I wanted to bring you my regards."

"I hope you've been well, Lord Devalle." I manage a smile at Nicolas Devalle, the minister of finance. He is a sleek sort of man, with smooth hair and shrewd eyes, his clothes tailored without being gaudy, his buckled shoes always polished to a high shine. "High Priest Granpier is just showing me how tight the housing has become for the refugees. I wonder if there's another place that might have room for them."

Lord Devalle looks thoughtful. "Perhaps there is. Indeed, it might be a wise move. There are those, you know, who wish you would aid Laon's own poor. They call the foreigners nothing but leeches on our resources."

"I merely offer help where it's most needed," Granpier says serenely.

As always, I wonder whether Devalle's gossip is, in fact, his own handiwork. He has reason to be disgruntled with me—he owns a fleet of merchant ships, and our lack of trade has severely impacted his income. However, he insists that his place on the council makes him uniquely poised to bolster Eren's floundering economy, and that indeed, he sees it as an opportunity rather than a disappointment. It all gives me a headache.

"That is, of course, your prerogative," Devalle says to High Priest Granpier, with the faintest quirk of his eyebrow, the gentlest implication that Granpier's prerogatives might, in fact, be suspect. He turns to me. "You have, of course, seen the letter from His Imperial Majesty."

"I've only been in Laon a few hours." A cold finger slithers down the back of my neck. A letter from the emperor of Paladis isn't likely to contain pleasantries. "I shall read it directly when I return to the palace."

He bows. "Pray permit me to offer counsel when you do. You may find his language somewhat alarming. But I am certain there are ways to accede to his demands."

"Oh," I say with the brightest smile I can muster, "have you read it, then?"

Lord Devalle doesn't miss a beat. Humbly, he says, "In your absence, Your Majesty, I thought it prudent that someone find out what the emperor had to say."

"You didn't think to forward this message on to me?" I say, sharply now. "When did it arrive?"

"Why, I couldn't imagine Your Majesty would agree to his demands!" he exclaims. "Especially now that we are a haven for dread sorcery. You would never remove the *Caveadear* from her post and let witch hunters into the country, now would you?"

"Naturally, no," I say.

Devalle looks at Granpier with a sigh. "The emperor promises such swift retribution against those who defy his laws. It's a trifle distressing, as well as tiresome."

I bite my cheek in an effort to control my growing anger. "Our laws are not his. Emperor Alakaseus doesn't govern our country, and he has no right to impose his justice upon us."

"Not at all," Devalle says soothingly. "None of us expect you to grovel before him."

I glance at Granpier, who gives me a warning look. As usual with Devalle, I feel the thread of the conversation slipping out of my control. He means that I *should* grovel—that I have no choice— I'm sure of it. Yet his manner is entirely at odds with this message.

"That's fortunate," I manage. "Because I have pledged to protect sorcerers, no matter the emperor's threats."

No matter that El has been taken, I think bleakly. What would Nicolas Devalle say if he knew?

He spreads his hands. "Perhaps you would permit me to write to Emperor Alakaseus on your behalf. I lived in Ida for a time in my youth, and made my bow at Aexione. Even attended some of the parties. I spoke privately with the emperor once. He may remember me."

And by extension, he's implying that his Idaean is better than mine. It probably is.

I think of Elanna, hauled away by witch hunters. The Tinani gathered on the border, and the ships the queen of Baedon has reportedly promised the emperor when he mounts his attack against us. This is not something I want Devalle arranging for me.

"I'm sure the emperor and I can reach an agreement," I say. We will have to. Without El, we stand no chance against him.

Devalle inclines his head. "As you wish. I am sure you know the best way to word it carefully, in order to prevent war."

"Indeed," I say flatly.

"On another note, Your Majesty, I brought a . . . friend." He gestures to the temple proper. "He's waiting for us."

My shoulders tighten instinctively, but Devalle is already moving toward the temple, clearly expecting both of us to follow. I sigh and go after him.

"This man arrived in Laon this morning," he tells us confidentially, stepping through the temple's back doors and into the kitchen. "He wanted to speak to Your Majesty and, alas, in your absence, I had to fulfill the need instead. He'll be so glad to see you."

"Mmm," I say.

The man in question is waiting for us in an antechamber, twisting his brown hat in his hands. He's stocky, middle-aged, and to judge by the mud stains on his rumpled coat and trousers, just in from the country. Amid the brilliant tiles, he looks rather shabby—probably not much different from me, I think ruefully. He bows practically double when he sees me.

"Your Majesty!"

I smile and gesture him up, trying to ignore Devalle and Granpier watching from behind me. "What can I do for you?"

"I have come to beg a boon from you." His gaze flickers to Granpier. "I've come to ask that you stop valuing the sorcerer refugees more than your own people."

I blink and bite back a frustrated sigh. Naturally this is the kind of person Devalle would *just happen* to pick up from the palace. "The refugees are harming no one. They have no other place to go where they don't have to live in fear."

"You don't understand," he says, his brow wrinkling. "They're making it worse. It needs to stop."

"They're making *what* worse?"

"The magic!" he bursts out. "Maybe you city folk don't feel it, but in the country, we do. Ever since the *Caveadear* woke the land, the stone circles have been whispering. *Things* have been happening, strange things. The snow around my sister-in-law's house melted while the rest of the village stayed covered, and a few days later, she lit a fire with only the touch of her fingers."

I'm staring. Other people have been feeling Elanna's magic—not just me?

"There's too much magic in Eren," he says, before I can reply. "That must be it. Too many sorcerers."

"So you blame the *Caveadear* for your sister-in-law's sudden ability?" I say carefully. "And the refugees for . . . bringing more magic into the kingdom?"

He nods vigorously. "There's another town up in the hills, where a woman woke one morning and claimed she saw spirits moving through the streets! She claimed they were passing her arcane knowledge about the stars and the magic that lives in the heart of each living thing. She started neglecting her husband. Her children." He shakes his head. "They had to lock her up."

My throat closes in such revulsion I struggle to speak. "They *locked her up*?"

"Yes, but she escaped by crawling through the earth, don't ask me how. They caught her and put her in a house with a good stone floor."

"And has she escaped from that?" I ask, dreading the answer.

"Not yet." He twists his hat in his hands. "Please, Your Majesty, if you stop the magic, perhaps she'll come back to her right mind."

Stop the magic? How on earth does he think I can do that?

"Has it occurred to any of you and your friends," I say tightly, "that perhaps she *is* in her right mind? That this is her true nature?"

"Can't be," he says with appalling confidence. "She was never like this before."

I try another tack. "Sorcery isn't evil—that's a lie the Paladisans taught us. What she's doing isn't wrong."

"She was never crazy before," he says stubbornly. "But she's mad now."

I breathe out through my nose and remind myself that Granpier and Devalle are watching us closely. I can't simply tell this man that *he's* the crazy one, for advocating that this woman be locked up because she can see ghosts who are apparently teaching her sorcery.

"With respect," I say, "it sounds to me like she might not be crazy. Perhaps you simply haven't taken the time to understand what's happening to her."

"You're not listening, my lady! She never used to be like this."

I study him. His face is closed, stubborn; he doesn't seem deliberately cruel, but rather aggressively ignorant. He doesn't want to entertain the idea that either of these women had magic all along, and if he won't listen to them, he's certainly not going to listen to me—another woman who supports sorcery.

It makes my hands clench with anger—and yet maybe there's a way to help the women. "What villages did you say these were?"

"Tristere and Fontaine," he replies, looking much more satisfied now that I seem to be listening to him.

"Thank you. I'll send someone to investigate the stone circles in your area, and speak with the woman. And the villagers as well, of course."

He beams. "Thank you, lady!"

I manage a smile in return. I'm not sure who I'll send, but I'll make sure they talk to the villagers—before they break that poor woman out of her prison.

I turn to find Devalle staring at me. When I lift an eyebrow, he merely bows.

CHAPTER SEVEN

Granpier arranges for a coach to take me back to the palace, as the evening has now turned full dark. Lord Devalle has, thankfully, taken it upon himself to escort our villager friend to his lodgings.

"I'll send down some food stores," I tell Granpier as I clamber into the carriage, its swaying lantern-light dancing across my vision. "And extra blankets."

He clasps my hand in gratitude, yet hesitates. "I truly value your generosity, Majesty. Yet as Lord Devalle pointed out, we must both not neglect our own people . . . The winter has been hard on many."

He nods toward the beggars who have begun to gather beneath the lanterns on the temple steps, ready to enter for the evening meal promised them by Granpier's ministry. Their faces are no less hardened and careworn than those of the refugees. A cold fist grips my stomach. That could have been me, if Ruadan hadn't taken me in—a motherless girl living on nothing but her wits.

Sometimes it seems like nothing I do could ever be enough to ease this heartache. I bid Granpier farewell and climb into the coach. For once, I'm alone, unescorted—without even Rhia—and for a moment, the silence feels a balm. And yet I keep seeing the refugees, their paltry beds, their sunken cheeks, their grief. If I find a way to feed and house and clothe them, the ministers will protest that I'm caring for foreigners before my own people. But who could look at them and not be moved?

The coach draws up before the palace, its windows ablaze with candlelight despite my instructions not to waste the tallow. I disembark with a sigh, pausing in the courtyard to look up at the bulk of it. Most of the palace is crisp and white-gray even in the evening shadows, but there's a section off to the east made of old dark bricks that blend into the night. No lights shine in its windows.

I go inside. I find Charlot in the lesser drawing room, instructing some footmen on polishing the silver. He bows, and the footmen immediately go to attention. "Your Majesty?"

"I apologize for interrupting," I say, and gesture for him to follow me into the corridor. Once we're away from the listening ears, I turn to him. "Did a letter arrive for me from the emperor of Paladis?"

He winces. "I apologize, my lady. Lord Devalle's people intercepted it before I could send it on to you. He returned it, however. It's waiting on the desk in your study. This way."

"Thank you." We climb the back stairs, and I glance down the long corridor to a distant door, heavily locked. "The old part of the palace—the east wing. Does anyone live over there?"

"Not at all, my lady. The late king Antoine planned to renovate it in style with the rest of the palace, but after the hunting lodge at Oise . . ." He coughs discreetly. "He ran out of funds. The wing is still full of old furniture. An absolute mess of cobwebs and dust and broken windows. I can arrange a tour if you like, but . . ."

"Yes," I say. "I would like that."

He manages to look both acquiescent and mildly appalled. "Very well. Tomorrow morning, perhaps?"

"It may have to be afternoon," I say. "I am planning a speech to the people tomorrow—about midmorning. Could you see the word spread?"

"Of course, Your Majesty. We will see a suitable crowd assembled. Will you need anything?"

But I'm distracted by a door opening at the top of the stairs. Teofila is emerging from her room, bundled in a heavy coat. "No,

Charlot. I'll simply speak from the balcony. Thank you for seeing to it."

He bows, but I'm already hurrying after Teofila.

SHE DOESN'T LOOK at me; only barely seems to register my presence. She's got a lit lantern in one hand, a bundle of dried flowers in the other, and her coat is buttoned up to the throat. I ask where she's going, but still she doesn't answer.

"Let's stay here," I say. "I'll order supper."

She just shakes her head. There's something brittle and wild about her. Her hair is flying loose from its knot in wild brown curls. I never realized before how much she looks like Elanna.

Guilt and grief settle in my chest, heavy as stones.

Wherever she's going, I'm coming with her. I button up my coat with a sigh. So much for that bath I was hoping to get, and the emperor's letter.

Teofila leads us out of the palace. Darkness has swallowed up the city streets. We've emerged through a side door—the palace has so many entrances and exits, I don't know half of them—and out into a quiet street. Beyond the bare trees, a shoulder of rock and grass rises. The Hill of the Imperishable, with its ring of stones. Elanna's favorite place in Laon, aside from the greenhouse.

But Teofila doesn't make for the path leading up to the tall, eerie stones. Instead we turn left and make our way north, passing the fine terraced houses of the nobility. I am entirely lost, but she doesn't seem in the mood to speak.

Then the houses peter away, and we're on a rough, muddy track climbing onto a high ridge of rock that arches like a spine over the city. Suddenly I know where we are. "The Spring Caves?" I say aloud.

Teofila doesn't answer. We've reached the height of the ridge, and the city glows below us, the warm ambience of its lanterns and lamps interrupted by the black curl of the Sasralie. I pause for a long moment, the wind tugging at my hair. This is the first time I have ever thought Laon beautiful.

"Come," Teofila says, just that one word.

She's making for the hollow in the ridge—the black mouth of the Spring Caves. Even I, the resident Caerisian, know the people of Laon have used these caves for centuries to hide, to survive. Hundreds of people supposedly packed in here during the Paladisan invasion—a haven right under the conquerors' noses.

But what on earth does Teofila want with this place?

My shoulders have tensed, but I follow her into the cave. It's fronted by large, flat rocks; a trickle of water mutters between them. Teofila is ahead of me, the lantern's light a startling gold in the darkness. I only have to duck briefly, to enter.

Then the ceiling rises. Teofila straightens, and so do I. We're standing in a vast shadowed cave, its roof soaring high, cobbled from old river stones. In the cave's center, black water purls from beneath a small raised stone. The rocks are littered with objects—necklaces, shriveled flowers, cups and bowls. A small statue sits next to the stones—a woman with her hands on her swollen stomach. I instinctively touch my own.

"What is this place?" I whisper, though I know a holy spring when I see one. There's one at Cerid Aven, too, at the base of the Sentry Rock. Teofila took me there after my first bleeding, and I washed my hands three times in the cold water while we prayed to the lady of the springs, and I left behind a necklace made of red beads. But the spring at Cerid Aven is a comfortable place—a soothing one. Not like this.

Teofila has crouched before the spring, and I follow suit, understanding what the flowers are for now. I hand them to her, and she sets them beside the goddess's statue. Then she props her chin on her fists and squints at the water. She goes very still. She doesn't speak, yet a humming sound resonates from her, forceful and yellow. I wonder if it's the sound of her prayers. Then I shake my head. I can't hear that, not really.

I study the black water, too. It's cool in here but not cold, and there is a lingering smell of the resin other women have burned. I wonder who still comes here, when the Paladisans tried so hard to stamp out the old gods and drive our worship aboveground and indoors. I rest my hand on my stomach, looking at the water. For the first time in days—perhaps months—my mind finally quiets.

It's so soft at first I think I'm imagining it. A dark, pulsating hum that spikes over and over into a high, frenzied note. Instinctively, I turn away, but the sound isn't coming from anything audible. Instead it seems to be humming through the very air into my skin. Pouring itself, dark and crimson as a wound, into my mind.

"Do you hear that?" I whisper.

Teofila just grunts. She's crouched even lower, whispering. Straining.

A prickle runs up my back, not entirely unrelated to the water dampening my face and clothes. "What are you doing?"

"I'm trying . . ." She draws in a breath. ". . . to work magic."

"You—"

I stop. Something is happening. A pressure is building inside my body, the way it did when Elanna flooded the Ard. My breath goes shallow.

Because this feels like a flood. And I realize the sound I heard isn't simply permeating the air. It's pulsing off Teofila in waves like heat, an endless, burning repetition. For a moment, I don't just feel it or hear it; I see it, too—a momentary crimson glow. I blink and the color fades, lingering only at the corners of my vision. But still there. Still red.

She sits back with a long, tired sigh and rubs her head. "I thought, with the magic coming back . . ."

"Didn't you feel it?" I can't believe she doesn't sense the magic she attempted. The air is still humming.

"There's . . . something." She frowns and doesn't continue, and I realize that she must sense it but be unable to do anything with it.

She can't use it to save Elanna, or even, simply, to see her.

I start toward her. The sound is still pulsing from her, though I hear it more faintly now that we're talking. "Teofila . . ."

But she doesn't respond to my tone of voice, or to my outstretched hand. With a grunt, she pushes herself to her feet. Her face is colored by a grief I can't mitigate. Tiredly, she says, "Let's go back."

I AVOID THE emperor's letter, though I know it does me no good. I busy myself settling Teofila in her rooms and ordering supper for her, but when I try to eat with her, she just says, "You're still in your traveling clothes, Sophy! You should have a bath and go to bed."

It's clear she wants to be alone. There's an ache about her, so deep it bows her shoulders. At another time, I might put my arm around her shoulders, play her some music, send for hot chocolate. But this time the hurt is too great to be soothed by such small comforts. This time, it's my fault, too. I have never failed Teofila this profoundly before.

So I leave her, even though tears sting my eyes, and make my way back to my chambers.

My maid, Fiona, greets me when I enter. "Miss Sophy!"

I smile. "Hello, Fi." She's known me for years, ever since Teofila decided it was time for me to have my own maid when I was fourteen. She comes from the town outside Cerid Aven, serving the Valtais the way her family has for generations. She has a quick smile and an efficient touch, though as always there's something distant about her kindness. I have never forgotten she's the servant and I the lady, especially now that I'm queen. It always leaves a bitter taste in my mouth.

"I have a hot bath for you," she says briskly, "and a change of clothes as well. I must say, you smell of the front."

"You mean of mud and sweat?"

Her eyes crinkle. She's gotten herself a new dress, I notice; an Ereni style, white and crisp with embroidered blue posies. Her hairstyle has changed, too—no braids anymore, but a tidy bun beneath a lace cap. At least her freckles are still Caerisian, and the look in her eyes. "I turned all the palace servants out. I figured you could do with a Caerisian welcome."

"Thank you," I say, truly grateful. I almost took Fiona with me to the border, but she herself told me it would be more useful to keep her here, someone I trust in the palace. Even though I agreed, it still made me feel somehow pushed aside, the same way I used to when she told me it was unseemly for Duke Ruadan's ward to attend the village dances when I was fifteen and wanted nothing more than a gaggle of female friends, a pretty dress, laughter and flirtation with the village boys.

Going into the bedchamber, I close the door. A copper tub awaits me before the blazing fireplace. I unbutton my waistcoat with a groan, and untie the layers of skirts beneath it, and finally shuck off my chemise and stockings. Naked, I run my hands over the firm dome of my stomach, looking down at the reality of my body for the first time in weeks. Fiona has guaranteed me privacy, and I have to trust that no one will barge in and discover my secret. Yet my thoughts skitter, anxious, against one another. How on earth am I to conceal the child now? Fiona will suspect in a trice—none of my gowns will fit. I might be able to let out the skirts, but the over-dresses won't close. I could change my style, but that would look even more suspicious . . . unless I used the right approach.

Ruadan used to say that with a smile and enough confidence, one could get away with anything. I suppose it's time to put that to the test—though I doubt my adopted father ever had to worry about the shape of his own body betraying him.

Shaking my head, I clamber with a happy shiver into the steaming tub. In the other room, Fiona summons another servant and orders food brought up. I lay, covering my stomach with my hands. Weariness seems to unspool from my limbs. Every day, I've been fighting this persistent tiredness, and now I can finally relinquish to it.

A small sideways sensation, like a slither in my stomach, startles me. The baby's moved again—in an entirely new way. A smile is sliding up around my lips, despite everything.

With a sigh, I wash out my hair, then climb from the tub and into a chemise, soft robe, and slippers. My whole skin seems to relax at the sensation of clean linen. The robe is thick enough that it doesn't reveal my silhouette, but I still spend minutes in front of the mirror, worriedly adjusting the belt. The finished look certainly isn't my most attractive, but it hides my condition.

In the bedroom, Fiona has set out supper by the fireplace. "Fi," I begin, and she looks up inquiringly. A smile and confidence, I remind myself. "I'd like to have my gowns made over—a new style for a new regime."

Fiona raises her eyebrows but to her credit only looks moderately astonished. I have never expressed much interest in fashion before.

"Something like the old queens used to wear," I say. "A more . . . natural fit. Loose, with a shawl—"

She claps her hands together. "Like Queen Aline! You know, in the old tapestry where she's standing with the mountain lion, in that blue gown."

"Yes . . ." I used to adore that tapestry in the house at Cerid Aven, though I was always more excited by the mountain lion—and, if I'm honest, Aline's crown—than her dress.

"We can modify your morning gown," Fiona says decisively. "Oh, it will be easy! And to think of you setting a new standard"—something, her tone suggests, she had never before imagined—"*everyone* will be talking of it."

I just smile. As long as they're talking of my gown and not my pregnant belly, I'll be content. "I hate to ask this of you since it's so late, but . . . by tomorrow morning?"

Her eyes narrow, and I sense her hesitation. But then she says, "You need to make a statement, don't you, before the ministers in the morning? I'll see to it. I'll wake up the modiste if I have to."

"Oh, you shouldn't," I protest instinctively.

"Nonsense! You're the queen. Every once in a while," she declares, "you must take advantage of that privilege."

I nod weakly and settle into the chair where the supper dishes have been set out. A heavy, folded letter leans against the tray.

Fiona nods at it on her way to the dressing room. "From the emperor of Paladis. Charlot sent it over from your study." She marches off with almost as much enthusiasm as she had the day we claimed freedom for Caeris.

I sigh. There's no more point in delay. I pick up the missive. The seal, of course, is already broken, the wax threaded with cracks.

This isn't going to be pleasant. I open it anyway.

The handwriting contains grandiose flourishes. My eyes struggle over the Idaean.

To Sophy Dunbarron, who styles herself Queen of Eren—

"I was elected," I mutter. There is a great deal of fluff, but eventually the emperor gets down to the heart of the matter:

Eren's support of a criminal sorcerer forces us to consider action against her. Unless you renounce the witch Elanna Valtai and cooperate with our imperial witch hunters cleansing your kingdom, Eren will make itself an enemy of our great and illustrious empire, and both you and the witch will be treated as such.

His Imperial Majesty,
Alakaseus Saranon, emperor of Paladis

I set the letter down and close my eyes. It takes all my control not to fling the cursed thing into the fire. The missive arrived last week; he must have known about the plans to capture Elanna long before he sent this, and hoped they would succeed. There's no point in fooling myself. I've been outmaneuvered. I don't have any other cards to play.

"Sophy?"

I look up. Fiona's back, the morning gown tucked over her arm. She touches the back of my hand, real kindness in her eyes. "He's quite harsh," she says, "but he isn't a Caerisian. He doesn't know what real strength is made of."

I utter a sour laugh. I might have known Fiona would have read the letter, too. I almost tell her what happened to Elanna. Almost confess how desperate our situation really is. But no matter if I once told her about my hopeless crushes and my dreams for the future, no matter how much I wanted her to be the older sister I never had, no matter that now, suddenly, when I'm feeling broken and failed, she is acting the part—it doesn't make me feel better, strangely. Only more incompetent.

So I simply say, "I hope you're right."

CHAPTER EIGHT

I startle from an uneasy sleep. It's just after dawn. Pale light seeps through the shutters, illuminating a figure standing before the fire. I startle, clutching the bedclothes to my chin.

"Sorry," Rhia says, "but you need to get up."

"All the gods, Rhia!" I breathe out, shaking off my nerves. "You must be feeling better."

"Mmm." She doesn't precisely agree. "Couldn't sleep any longer. I met a messenger in the hall. He came from the Butcher, with news. The Tinani have retreated from the ford at Tavistock."

I blink. "Retreated?"

"That's what he said. I asked him a couple of times, too, but he seems sharp enough to have gotten it right."

If the Tinani have retreated . . . The room's cold, and I tug a robe over my shoulders, thinking. Rhia plops down on the end of the bed, smothering a yawn.

"They'll attack elsewhere," I begin, hesitantly.

Rhia pushes her toes against the bedpost. "That's the other bit of news. Alistar and the Hounds sent word that the army is being dispersed along the border to strengthen defenses. And Count Hilarion smuggled word from court that King Alfred is recalling the remaining forces to the capital."

"That makes no sense. We're sitting ducks."

She sniffs. "Don't give us away too easily! We're better than that."

Whatever the Tinani are doing, it's undeniable that this gives me an advantage today—both in the cabinet room and when I speak before the people. A great thread of tension unwinds from my shoulders. I dig the heels of my hands into my eyes.

Then I remember the emperor's missive.

"Elanna?" I ask, dreading the answer. "Did Alistar—?"

Rhia just shakes her head. "They didn't catch the witch hunters who took her. They had already smuggled her onto a ship bound for Paladis, by the time Alistar caught them up."

I bite my lower lip. It's nothing more than I expected, yet the confirmation sits like a stone in my gut. And King Alfred's activity makes little sense. Unless, now that the emperor of Paladis has Elanna, things have changed. Maybe Emperor Alakaseus has withdrawn his support from Tinan, since El was his true objective all along. Paladis used Tinan, and now that Alakaseus got what he wanted, they're abandoning Alfred.

Time, I suppose, will tell. I climb out of bed, then pause. Rhia didn't actually say that Alistar and the Hounds returned to camp. "Is Alistar still in Tinan?"

She doesn't quite meet my eyes. "It sounds as if he's gone farther inland, to meet with Count Hilarion."

"That's good," I allow, "if it can be done safely." Count Hilarion of Ganz has been functioning as our ambassador in the Tinani court these last months—but with the violence on the border, we haven't been able to communicate easily with him. If Alistar can meet up with him, it *is* a good thing, though I'd rather he would come back to Eren without risking his skin on yet another mission.

There's a tap on the doorframe, and Fiona comes in carrying a bundle of white cloth—my morning gown. Her eyes are pouched with tiredness, but she's wearing a smile. "Your Majesty, the gown you requested. I daresay the modiste was as excited as I!"

Rhia looks a bit ill. "Isn't it too early in the morning for fashion?"

"Thank you, Fi. And please be sure to pass my deep gratitude on to the modiste." I take the gown, holding it up. It's as simple as I hoped—an easy style that I can slip over my head. I shoo the other two out of the room, despite Fiona's protests that she can assist me. I tie on two layers of petticoats, then tug the dress on. The modiste altered the gown so it fits—by apparent divine intervention, with a drawstring!—at my natural waist. I tie on a pretty coral sash; with the petticoats, and some tugging and tucking, my rounded stomach vanishes under layers of frothy voile. Just to be safe, I wrap a patterned shawl around my shoulders, arranging it so the ends drape loosely over my front.

Fiona looks dismayed when I come out. "The shawl ruins the line!"

"I'm too chilled without it," I say promptly, and smile. Rhia harrumphs from the table by the fire. I turn to her. "Come on, Rhia. Let's have breakfast. The ministers will be waiting."

THEY ARE WAITING, though they don't all look particularly thrilled to see me when I walk in with Rhia at my side. Of course, the hour might have something to do with it; I can't imagine Lord Faure getting out of bed much before noon. Good thing I had the foresight to serve tea and coffee, along with two platters of butter pastries warm from the oven. One man thanks me with a grunt. None of them seem to take much notice of my clothes; I suppose it's too early.

Soon the clock chimes the hour. I push back my chair and stand, just as High Priest Granpier enters. The two refugees follow him, and the other ministers burst into whispers, openly staring. I step over; someone needs to greet them civilly.

I clasp Demetra's hands. She looks tired this morning and has made an obvious effort to look her best: Her hair is wrapped in a scarf, her striped gown spotless, free of wrinkles.

"Thank you for coming," I say. I nod at Ciril.

He says in bold Ereni, "We must take our stand against those who would harm us, Queen Sophy."

The ministers murmur quite a bit more at that, and Victoire

Madoc, Elanna's friend, looks over at me with narrowed eyes. They all heard Ciril's Tinani accent, of course. I keep my expression neutral, though I can sense Lord Devalle muttering a question to Philippe.

"Please seat yourselves," I tell the sorcerers, gesturing to two chairs set up against the wall. They sit, and I turn back to the twenty or so people watching me.

"Well, Majesty?" the minister of agriculture pipes up. "The *Caveadear* is still tromping around on the border, I trust? Is there a reason for hauling us all out of our beds first thing in the morning?"

I look at him. He's a friend of Devalle's, a nobleman from a long and, in his case, less-than-wealthy lineage. This is the irony of people like this: They cling to their elaborate rules of etiquette and are scandalized when you break them, but when it suits them to forget a ritualized custom like letting the queen speak first in cabinet meetings, they pretend they've done nothing whatever wrong.

I gesture for the footmen to close the doors. "I trust you went to bed all the earlier, Lord Marchmont, knowing I had scheduled this meeting." I address them all: "What I must share with you is a sensitive matter. I trust those who met with me yesterday will appreciate the fact that I kept it secret until now." I glance at Devalle and Granpier, who both stare back at me, puzzled.

I look down the long, polished table. It's packed with mostly men and a few women. Philippe, about halfway down, appears subdued. He gives me a small nod.

I didn't catch a breath of rumor about El's disappearance. Of course, it's hard to credit him with trustworthiness based on that alone. Nevertheless, I nod back. Several of the others note our exchange; for some reason, Devalle's mouth quirks in amusement. I stifle a sigh. The ministers' constant machinations exhaust me.

I glance at the Caerisians, who make a small contingent to my right: Hugh, Rhia, and Teofila. Teofila's mind seems elsewhere, and she hasn't touched her cup of tea. I don't think she heard a word I said. I'm glad to have her here, all the same.

The rest are Ereni. With the exception of Victoire Madoc, with her glossy black hair and bright eyes, and Juleane Brazeur, the minister of commerce, who wears the finest blue coat among us, they're all nobles. When we allowed the Ereni to elect their own ministers, the nobles responded by blackmailing their servants and tenants into voting for them—or at any rate, some of them did. I suspect some of the others simply got elected thanks to the ease of familiarity. As always, I have to remind myself that just because they have titles and perfect manners and costly clothes, they aren't all wicked people. Though it is tempting to think so.

"I'm afraid I have terrible news," I say, "and at the same time, extremely good news."

"The good first!" Juleane Brazeur calls out, to general applause. She's a bit older than Teofila—a solid, pragmatic woman with short-cropped hair who has supported my more enterprising measures. She's in trade and popular among the common people for her generous philanthropic donations.

I smile reflexively. "Happy to oblige. I received word this morning that the Tinani have withdrawn from the ford at Tavistock. According to the Butcher's intelligence, they are in fact either reassigning the majority of their troops to fortify the border, with no aggressive action to be taken, or recalling them to the capital."

Juleane Brazeur looks surprised and pleased, and several others cheer.

I can't even force a smile. Through a tight throat, I say, "I suspect we haven't seen the last of them. It's unclear to me why they have retreated, except that they got something they wanted."

I wait. The ministers go quiet, watching me.

"They took Elanna," I say. "With the help of witch hunters. They abducted her just after she flooded the Ard."

There's a moment of stunned silence.

"They're taking her to Paladis?" Juleane Brazeur says. The others are staring at one another. Most of them look the way they should. Terrified. Victoire has risen out of her seat, bracing herself on the table. She's not a minister—rather a self-appointed representative of the people, for whom she's always gathering digests of palace news—but I have no doubt she argued her way in here successfully, on account of her friendship with Elanna. I can't meet her eyes. I should have told her yesterday. I didn't even think about her.

"Let's remember the good news," I say, and they quiet again, though this time they're communicating with one another in little glances and worried looks. "Tinan has—for the moment—withdrawn. We have an opportunity to enact a plan."

"What about Elanna?" Victoire bursts out. "Do you plan to just let her rot in the Ochuroma?"

I control my urge to cower in the face of her anger. "Jahan returned to Ida, just before El was captured. If anyone can save her from that fate, it will be him. I've sent Alistar and the Hounds to track them into Tinan, but we can't risk anyone else. I won't let any of us end up in the Ochuroma with her." I look at them all. "I will do everything in my power to persuade the emperor to spare her life. I will write to him and . . ." My mouth goes dry. ". . . I will plead."

Victoire folds her arms, her nostrils still flared, but the others murmur hesitant agreement.

Quietly, Devalle says, "What of the emperor's letter? Do you think he will withdraw his threat, now that he's captured the *Caveadear*?"

"Only a fool would doubt Emperor Alakaseus's intention to conquer our kingdom once again," I say heavily. "Undoubtedly he is already planning to use Elanna's capture to his advantage. But *we* have an advantage, too. Magic."

The ministers stir. Some uneasily, some with hope. "But without Elanna . . ." Lord Faure begins.

"We may not have Elanna, it's true. But as you're all aware"—I can't help the caustic edge to my voice—"we have been accepting refugee sorcerers for the last few months. High Priest Granpier has generously given them shelter in the temple of Aera. I'm pleased to say that two of them have already volunteered to join the fight on the border."

Devalle looks sharply at Demetra and Ciril, then back at me.

Granpier leans forward, beckoning the refugees to rise. "This is Demetra Megades, a midwife and healer, and Ciril Thorley, who can manipulate storms. They have generously offered their services."

The ministers murmur.

"We should recruit more of them." Juleane Brazeur leans toward me. "These two won't be enough against Tinan along with Paladis *and* Baedon."

"And have sorcerers slaughter us in our sleep?" Lord Marchmont retorts.

"They are here to help us!" Juleane Brazeur exclaims. "If they wanted to kill you, they'd have done it already."

An image of the murdered refugee flashes into my mind, and I wince. "We should treat the refugees with the same generosity they're showing us," I say. "No more slurs against them. Let us *welcome* them to Laon as allies." I look around the table. "A sorcerer was found murdered on the road to Laon. His feet and hands had been cut off, and nails driven through his face. This is unacceptable. If any of you know or suspect *anything*, I urge you to come forward."

They're silent this time. Some look horrified; Brazeur has put her hand to her mouth.

And Devalle's gaze flickers to Philippe. Just for the barest moment. Hardly enough even to be noticed, or to be suspicious.

Philippe simply stares straight back at me. Innocent, seemingly.

"Well," I say narrowly, "I trust news will come forward in due time." I press my hands together. "In the meantime, I will offer a public address this morning."

Devalle raises an eyebrow. "A public address, my lady?"

"The people must know that El's been taken." I hold up my hand at the predictable protests. "It is a risk, certainly. But if we don't tell them, we run the risk of being perceived as . . ." I swallow the words *callous as the Eyrlais.* ". . . as nothing but a dictatorship. I'm sure none of you want that."

"I think that is wise," Juleane Brazeur says. "The people deserve to know the truth, and they will respect you all the more for it."

A chorus of agreement runs around the table.

Lord Devalle leans forward. "There is something else that might comfort the people in these distressing times. A symbol of stability. Hope, if you would."

I eye him. He's watching me with a little smile. It's Lord Marchmont who says, "What would that be?"

"A royal marriage." Devalle smiles fully now. "Our new glorious queen could wed a nobleman. It would . . . distract . . . from the news of Elanna's capture. A royal wedding would tell the people that you are thinking of Eren's future, not just her present war. They will see that you believe yourself to be queen for a long time to come. That you commit to them."

My heart thuds in my ears. The others are murmuring assent. Of course, it sounds very good. Sensible. Inspired, even.

But why does Devalle want me to marry *now*? Now, when a wedding might seem callous in the wake of El's capture? Not to mention there is the life growing within me, which might not exactly thrill a prospective husband.

Devalle's eyes meet mine, then flick to Philippe. Back to me. A deliberate, demanding stare.

"Of course we must think of Eren's future," I say over the churning in my ears. So they do want me to marry Philippe, as I've suspected. "A wedding at this moment, however, might be seen as frivolous at best. I will first address the people and then, Lord Nicolas, we can speak more."

He smiles and, too late, I realize I responded exactly as he expected.

"The happiness of the people should come first, should it not?" But Devalle isn't addressing me. He's turned to Philippe.

Philippe gives a stiff nod. His gaze fixes on a point beyond my left shoulder—on nothing.

He doesn't seem exactly thrilled about the prospect, but on the other hand, I don't know what Philippe really wants, much less

Devalle. I don't even know if either of them is truly on my side. So I simply stand and pretend I don't hear. "Let's adjourn to the balcony for the speech."

THE WALK OUT to the balcony overlooking the courtyard seems longer than it ever has before. I'm beginning to wonder if I'm making the worst mistake of my short career as queen. What if the Butcher was right and telling the people the truth will only lead to fear and unrest?

Yet if I don't tell them, they will never trust me again. *I* would never trust me again, if I were them.

The chill air hits my face as I step onto the ornate balcony, and I'm glad I wore the warm wool shawl over my remade gown. And once I look down on the crowd gathered in the palace courtyard, I'm glad I let the palace maids fuss over my hair. I've never been afraid, exactly, making a pronouncement before. Usually there's a kind of thrill with it, the excitement that people have entrusted me with the power to aid them, to guide their futures.

But now cold fear bites the back of my neck. Normally before a crowd I feel bright and burning, on fire with the desire to stoke their love of me, but I'm rigid and afraid now. I draw in a breath and envision the muscles of my throat softening, the way I've done before performances. I pretend I'm focusing on a song I've rehearsed so many times, it's part of my breath and bone.

But this song terrifies me.

The ministers spill out onto the balcony, along with Victoire and Rhia, a ring of bodies making a half circle around me. The pressure around my temples tightens. I risk a backward glance at Teofila, but once again she doesn't really seem to see me. I catch the gaze of Lord Devalle instead. He raises his eyebrows and mouths, *Go ahead, Your Majesty.*

He must see my dilated pupils. He must know I'm afraid.

I turn blindly to the right. One of the other ministers is yawning.

Hugh looks pensively out over the crowd, and Rhia is rubbing her forehead and looking a bit wan.

Only Philippe returns my gaze. He gives me a small nod.

Somehow I release the tension in my neck enough to nod back at him. I step forward, resting my hands on the balustrade, glad no one in the crowd can see them shaking. But they'll know something's wrong. You can always tell when a singer is beset with stage fright; it compresses their voice and reduces the vibrance of their presence.

I look down into the faces assembled below. They're packed in—courtiers bundled in fine wool and fur, bourgeoisie in sturdy hats and coats, the poor mingling at the edges of the crowd. It feels as if all of Laon has come out to see me. My skin feels too thin. I can sense each one of them, the heat of their bodies, their flickering impatience, their curiosity. It's a flood of attention, and I think I might drown beneath it.

But Ruadan raised me to have steel in my spine when I need it.

I gather my voice, tight as it is. "People of Laon! Citizens of Eren and Caeris! I, Sophy Dunbarron, your queen, have returned from the border. I come before you with news. It is my pleasure to tell you that, thanks to the magic of the *Caveadear,* the king of Tinan's forces have withdrawn. And the emperor of Paladis has not dispatched his fleet." At least, I pray, not yet. "Our kingdom is safe from those who would conquer her!"

I can feel Lord Devalle smiling cynically behind my back, and some of the others mutter at my choice of words. I focus on the crowd, ignoring them as best I can. Applause scatters through the people below. I summon a smile and hold up a hand for silence.

Before I can speak, a voice below shouts, "You're not our queen! Go back to Caeris!"

What?

Other people are exclaiming. A handful of palace guards wade into the crowd, but even from above it's clear whoever shouted that damning cry has made himself scarce.

I force myself to pretend that nothing happened. "My people!" I shout, and some of the milling in the crowd ceases, though the guards seem to be arguing with several women toward the back. I plow forward. "As you know, Eren and Caeris have become a haven for sorcery! Our good High Priest Granpier has sheltered so many, and thanks to him, we have two new allies who have come forward to—"

"Witch-lover!" someone else bellows from the crowd, closer to the front.

A guard shouts. The people are milling around now. Cries of, "It wasn't me!" float up to my balcony.

Maybe I should just give up. Hardly anyone is listening now.

But that's exactly what the hecklers want.

"Listen!" I holler, but it just fades over the shouts below.

"Silence!" It's Philippe at my shoulder, bellowing over the crowd. "Your queen is speaking!"

The guards catch his cry. "Silence! Silence!"

The crowd settles down—a little, anyway. My heart's thumping in my ears, but I pass Philippe a nod of gratitude. He doesn't seem to notice. He's folded his arms, watching the crowd with an intent expression.

"We have two new sorcerers to guide the kingdom forward," I proclaim, as loudly as I can. "Master Ciril and Mistress Demetra." The two step forward, and the people below still, many of them staring wide-eyed up at the foreign sorcerers. "We are grateful for their help, especially in the face of the terrible news I must share." I swallow. My throat's tightening up again, so I focus on the sound of the words, trying to push aside the meaning of them. "It is my great sorrow to inform you that the *Caveadear* has been captured by witch hunters."

Exclamations erupt below. The guards shout for silence but only add to the general din.

"You lost her!"

"Witch-lover!"

"The Paladisans!"

"The Tinani!"

"War—"

I clench my jaw and wait it out.

Eventually, by some miracle, they seem to realize I'm still standing here, and they quiet a little.

"Yes, Elanna has been captured," I say, "but it does not mean the end of our freedom. It does not mean defeat. I have these sorcerers at my side. I have you. I pledge myself to defending this kingdom, now and forever."

A thin cheer goes up at that, but I don't miss the terror on other faces. It's so intense it pulses in my own skin. Elanna is the savior of this land, and so many have worshipped her—and depended on her. What will they do without her?

"We will communicate more in the coming days," I say. "Thank you, and may the gods' love shine down on our lands."

LORD DEVALLE STOPS me in the marble hallway as we leave the balcony. The other ministers flock away ahead of us. "Majesty, may I suggest you increase your personal guard? Those shouts were . . . unsettling."

His solicitous tone rings genuine, yet the insinuation makes me stiffen. "I would hate for my people to think I don't trust them."

"Your people would probably prefer you to stay alive," he says drily.

I open my mouth to argue, but he does have a point. "True."

"Allow me to suggest you train up some of the palace guards. Of course, Queen Loyce took her Nehish guards with her when she left—and they are, you must know, the best in any realm—but there are some at the palace who trained with them. I am sure I can discover their names for you."

I look at him. He smiles back.

"I'll interview them," I say briefly. It's not a commitment to employ them.

He claps his hands. "Splendid! I'll have those names found for you, and the men sent for. This afternoon, shall we say? You will want them in place as soon as possible."

"Thank you."

He smiles again, bows, and turns. Philippe has come up behind him. Devalle pats him on the shoulder. "You did well out there, my friend. Your presence calmed the people."

I feel my eyes narrow.

"I merely helped Her Majesty," Philippe says diffidently.

"It is very good you did." Devalle glances from him to me. "Do you not agree, my lady? Our Philippe is bold, and cuts a fine figure on the royal balcony."

A flush stains Philippe's cheeks. He moves away, forcing Lord Devalle to drop his hand.

"I am glad for Philippe," I say, "but then I am glad all of you were there."

Devalle's smile turns to a grin. "Of course, we will need to have the source of that unrest investigated. I will see it done." Before I can protest, he strides away.

"I'm afraid he's rather transparent," Philippe says to me.

I shake my head. "You should take it as a compliment, I suppose. But will you go after him and see that he doesn't offend anyone with this investigation? In fact . . ." I hesitate. I do need to have the hecklers looked into, but a few shouts doesn't mean there's an organized opposition. I'm far more worried about Lord Devalle seizing innocent people in order to make an example of them, the way Antoine or Loyce Eyrlai might have.

Besides which, does Devalle really have my best interests at heart? I suppose there's a chance he'll present me with the truth, but I am simply not sure.

"See that he doesn't make an investigation at all," I tell Philippe. "Tell him it's the people's prerogative to voice their displeasure."

He looks at me, then simply shakes his head. "As you say, Your Majesty." With a perfunctory bow, he strides away after Devalle, leaving me alone in the hall, except for a few guardswomen. I lean against a side table with a sigh. There's a flutter in my stomach, insubstantial as a moth, and I cover it with my hands. A second tremulous feeling follows the first. "We made it through," I whisper.

"You shouldn't trust either of them."

I turn, startled. Victoire steps from the shelter of a neighboring doorway; she must have been listening in on my conversation with Devalle and Philippe. Her cheeks are stained bright red, and there's a rebellious glint in her eyes.

"Do you know them?" I ask carefully. I like Victoire. She's quick to laugh and practically fearless as a spy and agitator, and in some ways, she's easier company than Elanna. But just now, I'm reminded that I don't actually know her that well.

At least she doesn't seem to have heard my whisper to the baby.

"My father did. He was finance minister to King Antoine— before the corruption caught up with him. That's why no one will trust me to take public office."

"Surely you've proven yourself by now," I say, thinking about what little I know of her family. Victoire is the sort of person whose trust, once lost, is lost forever. After we took Laon, Rhia told me that Victoire paid her father to go into exile in the country, so that he would no longer be a source of shame to her.

She scowls down the hall after the men. "Lord Devalle has lost a great deal of money, and he's keen to let everyone know it. I doubt he has anyone else's best interests in mind. And Philippe Manceau's mother was a great friend of his—and a devoted follower of the old regime."

"I'm not sure what to make of Philippe," I admit. "I don't think he misses his mother much, though."

"That may be. I don't know him well," Victoire says. "But the others will pressure him into doing what they want. You don't think they supported his bid to be minister just because they liked him, do you?"

I sigh; I should have known. "How did they support him?"

"Bribes, I suspect. Nobody much cared who he was until two months ago."

"But he . . ." I try to remember Philippe's campaign. The ministers were all elected at once a few months ago, in a flurry of short, brutal campaigns and elections. I was back and forth from Laon to Barrody to the border at the time, and I don't remember what promises Philippe made the people. Since he's the minister of public works, it probably had to do with clean drinking water, and possibly a theater. Still, for some reason I feel the urge to defend him. I say, "Maybe he made the people promises they wanted to hear."

"That might have helped, too. But watch Devalle. He's going to box you into a corner and have you agreeing to wed Manceau before you know it, and *that* would be a terrible way to find out what he really wants."

I touch my stomach lightly and force myself not to think of Alistar in Tinan.

"But then there are many terrible ways to find out the truth about things," Victoire is saying.

I drag my attention back to her. The thunderous look on her face tells me everything I need to know. "I'm sorry I didn't tell you about Elanna. I had a lot on my mind—"

"It doesn't matter," Victoire snaps, though anyone could see that it does, very much. "What concerns me is that you let her go. I demand that you send me to Ida after her."

This seems so abysmally foolish that I can't help myself. I say, "What on earth could you do to save her?"

Victoire's flush deepens. "I speak fluent Idaean. Well, nearly fluent. You know I can be charming when I need to be, and I'm as clever as anybody else. Appoint me your ambassador. I'll find Jahan and we'll save her together."

I study Victoire. She *is* charming, when she puts her mind to it, and pretty as well, with her dark eyes and glossy black hair and bowed lips. But pretty and charming enough to sway the emperor of Paladis?

"I can't let you risk yourself like that."

"I'm *willing* to risk it!" she says passionately, tossing her hair.

"Elanna is my dearest friend, and I won't let her rot in some cell or"—real tears brighten her eyes—"or face the executioner's ax."

"Elanna would never forgive me if I let you end up on the scaffold beside her," I say, even though it seems cruel to deny her. But it's crueler still to let her throw her life away.

"It would be worth it!"

"No," I say firmly. "Elanna needs you here. *I* need you here. I need you to help the people see their leadership is stable."

Victoire's nostrils flare, but she says, "I'll do it. Though I wonder," she adds as she strides away, "if you won't let me go because you're too afraid of losing your own power here in Laon."

"You know that isn't true," I protest. "I'd give anything to save her."

"Then maybe you should."

"I'm not going to risk you, Victoire. Eren can't afford to lose anyone else, and neither can I."

But she doesn't reply, just strides away. I watch her go, letting out a long sigh. I am doing what I have to do. This kingdom is more important than any one person. Ruadan always taught me to put the good of the whole before the good of the individual, and so I will—even if my adoptive father might question how much I'm putting the people first with my personal choices. But he isn't here to disapprove or dispense advice. I have to forge ahead as best I can, alone.

CHAPTER NINE

"Jahan." I breathe his name, afraid to let the guards standing outside the door hear me, or the servants who brought tea and cherry cakes to the desk. A small mirror occupies the wall between the bookshelves lined with stern, leather-bound titles. This was Antoine Eyrlai's study—though I, Charlot tells me, am the first person to actually use it in thirty years.

I try again. I reach out from within myself, trying to imagine my voice arrowing across the Middle Sea, into Ida, into his ear. "Jahan." For the barest moment, I catch the flicker of awareness. I taste the heat of the Idaean sun, sense the weight of Jahan's presence turning toward me.

Then it's gone, and I wonder if I simply imagined it. I press my fist against the wall in frustration. Of course, I reflect somewhat bitterly, I am not a sorceress. I don't know why I expect such things of myself.

In the end, I turn back to the ponderous, masculine desk and take up a piece of paper. I close my eyes. I don't know what words I can possibly use to persuade the emperor of Paladis to release Elanna and abandon his determination to go to war against us. I already know Alakaseus Saranon won't listen to an upstart girl from Caeris.

But I have to try. I can't let El go without a fight.

I open my eyes and see I've gripped the pen too tightly. Ink stains my fingers.

I write. Hours pass. When Charlot knocks on the door, I look up from a sea of crumpled papers, feeling a pulse of embarrassment at the frustrated tears welling in my eyes.

Charlot bows, professionally turning a blind eye to both my emotion and the wreck on the hideous desk. "Your Majesty, Lord Devalle has some guards to introduce to you."

I mentally curse. I had clean forgotten about Devalle's offer. Guilt worms up through my throat. El's facing death or worse, and I'm worried about employing new guards—as if anyone would want to kidnap me. With a sour pang, I wonder if the kingdom would be so unsettled if it were me, not El, who was captured.

But it's pointless—and petty—to think such things. I rise with a sigh and follow Charlot out into the hall, though Devalle is possibly the last person I want to deal with right now.

Rhia's waiting in front of a gilded painting of two cavorting nymphs, dressed in full mountain woman regalia, with close-cut trousers beneath a short split skirt and a colorful half-cloak disguising her broken arm. She casts me a severe look, and I hold down a groan. Naturally, I've managed to offend her, too.

But before she can scold me, Devalle himself approaches. "Thank you for taking the time, Your Majesty." He claims my arm in a proprietary manner and simply hangs on when I try to pull away. "This way. They're waiting in the Yellow Salon. A dozen new men—that should help with your daily rotations."

"You're very considerate." I finally yank my arm out of his grasp, scrambling to control the situation. "Please show them to me."

He merely looks amused.

Twelve palace guards are waiting for us in the Yellow Salon, facing the front in crisp ranks, their epaulets aquiver and the gold braid bright on their cut-back blue coats. I take up my place before them. Rhia stands off to the side, glaring.

Devalle casts her an exasperated look. "Lady Rhia, can we help you?"

She ignores him and addresses me. "Are my mountain women not good enough for you anymore, Sophy?"

All the gods. I want to massage my forehead—the splitting headache still hasn't gone away—but I force my hands to remain lowered. "These men would be a supplement to what we already have, not a replacement. You know I value your mountain women." The palace guards look largely stoic, except for a few of them, who watch with interest.

"With the *Caveadear* captured, we cannot afford to expose Her Majesty to the same risk," Devalle says pleasantly. "It seems to me you were present, Lady Rhia, when Elanna was taken. Were you not?"

Rhia's eyes widen. She takes a step forward, one hand going to the dagger at her hip.

"The Tinani planned El's capture carefully," I say, moving between the two of them and sending Rhia a warning look. "They had intelligence about our camp that allowed them to act as they did." I swing to face the guards. "But I can trust all of you to be loyal, can I not?"

Most of the guards clap their hands to their hearts. The ones who don't quickly follow suit.

"You wound me," Lord Devalle remarks. "I picked these men myself."

That's what worries me, I think, but I merely smile at him. "I meant that as a joke, of course. Gentlemen, will you come forward and tell me your names? I like to know who's serving me."

Rhia harrumphs but drops onto a velvet chaise, watching the guards narrowly.

One of the men steps forward and removes his decorative helmet. He's middle-aged, square-jawed, with close-cropped hair and shrewd eyes. "Marice Grenou, Your Majesty. I've been training these fellows in the Nehish style for more than a year now, with the idea of saving the crown the expense of hiring foreigners to guard the monarch."

So I'm inheriting guards first commissioned by Antoine Eyrlai. It's not the most reassuring thought.

"A good idea, and a pragmatic one, too," I compliment him. "You must have chosen everyone quite carefully."

"It has been a very select process, my lady, and open to only those I trust implicitly. Let me introduce you to the men. This is Alain, from Laon . . ."

Grenou moves down the rank of men, who salute crisply as he introduces them. Some sport neatly groomed mustaches in the Nehish style, but the rest are clean-shaven. All of them are young and fresh. I wonder if any of them took to the streets when we claimed Laon, or if they were among those who lingered at the palace, waiting to see what Loyce would do.

Grenou drones on, embroidering the details of their training practices. My feet are starting to go numb, and the splitting headache refuses to go away, especially at the discussion of how quickly they can reload their muskets. I try hard not to scowl, but at last I have to interrupt him.

"I think this will work out very well," I say, "and of course you gentlemen will receive a pay increase, though at the moment you'll understand it can only be a token. When the war is over, you'll be handsomely rewarded."

I catch one or two looks of disappointment before any emotion is hastily schooled from their faces.

I turn to Grenou. "The mountain women will remain my personal guards, but I will gladly employ your men in the palace corridors, and during all public events."

"I'm honored, Your Majesty," he says, "but these men are fit to serve you in all circumstances."

There's a muffled noise from Rhia. I carefully don't look at her.

"I have every confidence that they are, yet for now my mountain women will remain my personal guard." My mouth twists. "I'm sure Rhia will be grateful for your help guarding me beyond my private chambers, however."

Rhia says flatly, "My mountain women are more than capable of guarding you at all times."

Almost at the same moment, Grenou says, "Will I be answering to Rhia Knoll, then?" His disdain is barely suppressed.

Rhia gives him a look even less cordial. "Do you have a probl—"

"You answer to me," I interrupt sharply. "Both of you do. When we are in public, I will expect you both to work together. If we find ourselves in a crisis, Grenou, you'll have to take orders from her." I look at him. "I trust you'll find that acceptable."

"Yes, my lady. But . . ."

I suppress the urge to roll my eyes. Rhia is practically vibrating with rage.

"A mountain woman?" Grenou is saying. "I may not be able to understand her. The accent, you see."

At least one of his guards hides a grin. Rhia tenses but doesn't lunge forward with an insult, as I half expected her to.

I snap. "Captain Grenou, do you want this post or not? If you do, I imagine you'll find a way to understand Captain Rhia perfectly well. If not, the door is right there."

He stares at me. Obviously he didn't expect me to push back—or, perhaps, to even respond to his insult. Now all his guards are determinedly staring at the wall behind me, their faces blank.

"Pardon me, Your Majesty," he says at last. "I spoke poorly. I am sure I can understand the Caerisian."

"Her name is Captain Rhia Knoll, not *the Caerisian*." I'm painfully aware of my own accent, grown thicker with anger, burring through my words. I am the Caerisian, too, after all. "You will address her as such."

He bows, glances at Rhia. "Captain Knoll."

"Captain Grenou," she replies, with only the faintest curl of her lip. "You and I will meet in the morning to discuss the rotation of your men. I will also attend their morning exercises, to assess their competence." She pauses. "I do hope you understood that."

His jaw sets. "Perfectly."

I roll my eyes. If I have to deal with the wounded pride of not only Rhia but this man, too, perhaps I would be better off without *any* guards. With a sigh, I say to Devalle, "Thank you for the introduction."

He bows with a faint, amused smile. "My lady."

I nod at him and stride out of the room, my temper hardening the impact of my heels on the parquet.

Rhia storms after me. "Damned courtiers," she says in Caerisian. "That Devalle seems keen to turn you into an Ereni queen."

I snort. "Feeling better today?"

"Trying to undermine my mountain women," she grumbles. "I'll undermine *him*!"

"Which one?"

"Both of them."

We've arrived at my rooms, and without waiting for an invitation she follows me right in and stands there watching while I pour myself a cup of water. I close my eyes. This hideous headache won't go away, and my feet feel heavy and swollen. I want a nap, not to deal with Rhia Knoll's wounded pride.

"You're turning Ereni," she says all of a sudden. "You understand their games, and their manners."

I open my eyes. Her chin's up, and her eyes are dangerous. It's hard to tell sometimes if Rhia is goading me for the sake of it, or venting a real grievance. This time it seems real enough.

"There's no other reason why you'd agree to Devalle's plan," she goes on. "Why try to placate him? You're the queen! Tell him to take his 'Nehish-trained' guards and stick them up his—"

"*Rhia.*"

She glares. "It's not as if he's genuinely concerned for your safety!"

"He wants to do me a favor," I say, "so I'll owe him. I could say no, but I'm curious as to what he wants. There's also the fact that El's been captured and we obviously have spies reporting to Tinan, if not Paladis and Baedon, too—"

"Probably among those insufferable guards!"

"I doubt Lord Devalle is that much of a fool." If the guards are spying and reporting to anyone, it'll be him. I refrain from pointing this out. "I could use the extra protection, truthfully. Maybe it will even lead to some cooperation between Caerisians and Ereni."

"You heard what that Grenou called me. *The Caerisian.* He probably calls you the same."

"Well, he would at least be accurate." I sigh. "Rhia, I'm the queen of Eren *and* Caeris. It's one country—"

"And it feels like it, as long as you stay out of this damned court!"

"Then maybe you should stay out of it!" I shout back.

She stares at me.

I'm breathing hard. I don't think I've ever shouted at Rhia Knoll before; I'd have thought it was suicide. Right now, I find I don't care. "I brought you back here with me because I want your help. I *need* your help. You're more than the captain of my guard, you're my friend, and I trust you. I need you. But all you want to do is pick fights and criticize me and the people here, and tell me what a *disappointment* I am. Well, I'm sorry I'm not Elanna, I'm sorry I don't have the power of the land, I'm sorry I don't unite the two cursed countries within my person, but I'm doing my best and I wish you would respect it!"

I stop, panting. My head throbs in time with my pulse, a high, bright, raging chord.

"No one wants you to be Elanna, Sophy," Rhia says quietly.

I look at her. She's sober—not angry, as I half expected her to be. The fight seems to have gone out of her. "No?" I say. "Because it seems like this kingdom would be a lot better off if I were the one who got captured, and she were here in my place."

Tears burn beneath my eyelids. Rhia's face slides in and out of focus. I'm trying so hard not to cry, but a single furious tear slips out anyway.

"That's not true," she says.

I'm shaking my head. "Please go. I need to be alone."

She hesitates, but I say, "*Go.* Please." And she goes.

I let myself cry for exactly ten minutes, because I don't have any more time to spare. I might have told Rhia how I feel, but it doesn't make things any better. Instead I merely feel hollow and foolish. I shouldn't have entrusted my fears to Rhia Knoll; I shouldn't entrust them to anyone. A queen, Ruadan once said, should be both more and less human than any of her subjects, a figurehead upon which the people can rest *their* fears.

Yet who am I supposed to turn to, when fear is eating *me*?

I am more alone than I have ever been in my life. Alistar is in Tinan, and Teofila has hardly left her rooms since the news of El's capture. I miss Ruadan like a hole in my chest. Usually the memory of his voice, his insights, comforts me. But right now I can't even remember what he sounded like.

I pull myself together and wipe my eyes. The last thing I need is the servants whispering about the queen's indulgence in excess emotion; my detractors would have far too much fun with that one.

Fiona taps on the door. "Lady Sophy? Charlot is here. You asked him for a tour of the east wing?"

"Thank you," I manage. I gather myself. If I feel this lonely, at least I can help someone else.

CHAPTER TEN

"And here is the bathing chamber," Demetra says. She nods back toward the other refugees, whose voices hum from the great hall. "Marcos mended the pipes, so the hypocaust is working again now. Some of the others have been scrubbing the tiles. They're rather beautiful—look."

I smile, leaning down to study the tiles. When Charlot brought me here a few days ago, the bathing house was grimed and dusty, like the rest of the east wing, and the tiles looked brown and ill. Now their original paintings stand out: white backgrounds with elaborate blue-and-yellow flowers.

"It's lovely," I say. "I'm glad you're making yourselves at home here."

"The children adore it. They say they always wanted to live in a palace."

"So did I," I say, surprised to think of it. Though now that I do live in a palace, it's not exactly the stuff of my girlish dreams. For one thing, I never imagined having to deal with a hundred people all wanting a hundred different things from me, and all in varying states of dissatisfaction.

We climb the stairs back up to the main floor, where the newly cleaned great hall sits full of light. Gone are the piles of furniture and the stink of mouse nests; the refugees have transformed the space, which the Eyrlais mostly used for storage, into one both comfortable and bright. The east wing is the original palace, from before the Paladisan invasion, but Paladisan culture and style obviously took root here long before: Fluted columns adorn the arched windows, and the fireplace is carved with ornate leaf-work. It's entirely different from the style of Barrody Castle—another reminder of how different Eren and Caeris became over the centuries, even if our people were once one, a thousand years ago.

Children scamper past us, shrieking with laughter as they play a game of catch-me. I sigh. "It feels like home."

Demetra's lips tighten, and I realize I've said the wrong thing, even if I meant it well. The refugees are far from their true homes; it's unlikely they'll ever see them again.

"Though I suppose this is not nearly as pleasant as Ida," I add hastily, then wince at my own tactlessness. "That's where you're from, isn't it? I'm sorry to remind you of what you've lost. It's thoughtless of me."

She winces but says, "Truthfully, I long to talk of it. I miss it—" She makes a fist and presses it to the hollow between her stomach and breasts. "—right here. Not the city itself, but my friends. My family."

"Family?" I glance at her.

"I miss my husband." She swallows. "And my friend Tullea. She's the one who smuggled us—and so many others—out of Ida. I hear from her by a system of notes we've devised, but not often."

"A note system?" I ask, curious. "How does it work?"

"We transfer scraps of paper across great distance, with the power of our minds. Tullea invented it. It takes great effort and precision, so we are sparing in our communiqués. But we still write, when we can." She holds out a tiny piece of paper, hardly large enough to write on. "You see? I just received one before you arrived. I haven't even had the chance to read it yet."

"I wish there were an easier way," I begin. "Not only to communicate, but to—"

A noise interrupts me. It's a soft grunt—my name, spoken by

someone. I turn. Rhia has come into the great hall. She's pale. There's something raw and trembling about her, and my heart lurches. All the gods, what now?

"Soph," she says.

She sticks out her hand. She's gripping a note between her thumb and forefinger.

"Oh," Demetra whispers. She's staring down at the contents of her own note, the one she received from Tullea.

I take the note from Rhia. It's creased, soft, as if from being in someone's coat. I turn it over. Crumbs fall off the red wax seal.

"You opened this," I say, but my voice comes out flat, not teasing as I meant to.

Rhia hardly blinks. "The messenger had already done it." She clears her throat. "It's from the Butcher."

A wash of cold sweeps up my arms. I think of Alistar, deep in Tinani territory. Of the king of Tinan's troops. Though I wrote King Alfred a letter, along with the ones I sent to the queen of Baedon and the emperor of Paladis, I haven't yet received a reply.

Perhaps he deemed one unnecessary.

I break open the letter just as Demetra looks up from her note, her fingers at her lips. "Your Majesty—"

But I already know.

Word from Ida. Elanna dead. Executed by emperor. Tinani troops on the move. Emperor to dispatch black ships. Will return to Laon tomorrow so we can plan.—G.M.

I'm flushing hot and cold, and my heart is pounding so rapidly I think I might faint. El *dead*? It can't truly have happened. Not El, with her curling hair and her courage and her stubbornness. Not the *Caveadear,* whose power is immense enough to move mountains.

Or at least, it was.

"No," I hear myself saying. "Jahan's there. Jahan wouldn't let this happen."

Demetra is shaking her note. "Tullea says they believe it's true.

She says Jahan has joined the underground, fighting in Elanna's name. He escaped arrest." She looks at us. "They're planning to destroy the fleet that's meant to sail to Eren, but Tullea doesn't know if they truly have the power."

It's too much. I can't comprehend it all. "Jahan wouldn't escape without Elanna. He wouldn't leave her to die." I stare at Rhia, willing her to agree with me.

But she doesn't. She just closes her eyes.

"Teofila," I whisper, with a gasp. "All the gods, Teofila."

I have to tell her, but how on earth can I give her this news? How can I tell her that her daughter, her true daughter, is not only captive but dead? How can I break her heart that completely?

It has to come from me, though. Not anyone else.

Numbly, I begin to walk. Rhia trails me, a silent shadow. Back into the main palace; up the stairs. There's movement in the door of my chambers. Fiona comes out. She's clutching her apron in both hands. Her face is white.

She already knows.

"Is it true, Sophy?" she demands. "Is the *Caveadear* dead?"

The footmen in the hall go very still. The mountain women on duty both slowly straighten. All their eyes fall on me. Suddenly, I can't breathe. I can't be the one who bears this terrible news, the one who has failed not only Elanna herself, not only Teofila, but the entire kingdom. My heart is ricocheting wildly. I think if I try to speak, I'll scream.

Yet I have to. It has to be me. They deserve to hear this from my lips.

"We—" My voice breaks; I try again, wetting my lips. They are all watching, not only those in the immediate vicinity but those down the hall. The very rooms seem to be listening. I gather myself, though I want to shrink into nothing. To disappear. "We have only just received a preliminary report."

Fiona looks at me. She waits. They are all waiting.

"It appears," I choke out, "that the *Caveadear* has been executed as a witch by the emperor of Paladis."

Into the absolute silence, sound rushes in. Whispers rush from room to room; down the hall; from the mountain women to the footmen to the city. An overwhelming cacophony of sound. The hallway blurs. I sway. Rhia seizes my arm; Fiona, the other.

"Sophy," Rhia barks, "are you all right?"

In my womb, the baby gives a sudden, single kick. *This isn't about me,* I remind myself, though my head is still swimming. I can't collapse; I can't make a scene. This is about El. It's about the very kingdom.

And Teofila.

I turn to go to her rooms and stop. Everything falls to white.

Because she's there in the doorway, staring at me. Clutching the frame with whitened fingers. Her lips move, but no sound emerges.

She heard me. She heard me tell Fiona, the palace, the world, before I told her.

I stumble forward, but she's already pushing herself back from the doorway. Back into her chamber, her eyes hollow and wild. The door slams.

Footsteps rush up behind me. Hugh. He scarcely spares me a glance. "I'll see to her." Then he pushes past me, rapping his knuckles softly on Teofila's door. He lets himself in.

I stand there, numb. Everything is swimming again, going white and flashing back to color. Teofila doesn't want comfort from me. She'll accept it from Hugh, but not me. I can't comfort the woman who has been a mother to me, now that she lost her true daughter.

I don't think I can bear this.

Before I can crumple, there are voices behind me.

"Is this true?" a woman demands. I turn slowly. Juleane Brazeur is leading a delegation of ministers—Devalle, Philippe, High Priest Granpier, and more, along with Victoire Madoc. *All the gods,* I think, *not the ministers as well.* Juleane is saying, "Has the *Caveadear* been executed like a common criminal?"

I've never seen her so angry. Ordinarily Juleane Brazeur is solid, practically phlegmatic. I glance at Rhia. "How do they know so quickly?" I whisper. I want to say I meant to tell them later, but the truth is I hadn't even thought of them yet at all.

Rhia looks even more shaken, if possible. "The messenger— I sent him down to the kitchens. He must have told every . . ." She stops mid-word, her lips open. Staring at me in horror.

Everyone. Everyone in the palace—including the ministers' various informants—and soon everyone in the city. All of Laon will know Elanna is dead, if they don't already.

I draw in a trembling breath. If I didn't feel I'd failed all of Eren and Caeris before, I feel it now, keen and bitter. The *Caveadear* was captured on my watch, and not one of the useless measures I've employed was enough to save her. I couldn't even manage to contact Jahan.

But in Rhia's gaze is a question—a truth—even more frightening. If Elanna is dead, what becomes of us?

We have no time to discuss anything further. The ministers have surrounded us. Even Philippe looks angry.

"You should have summoned a council meeting," Juleane Brazeur says with quiet, furious reproach. "Instead we all heard the truth by gossip."

"I am told a fleet is due to set sail as well," Lord Devalle says. "Is this true, Queen Sophy?"

I press my hands to my cheeks. I can't even think straight, and suddenly, I feel all those years of Ruadan's training click in. I straighten. To Brazeur, I say, "There was no offense intended. I only just received the news myself. Apparently Jahan is planning an attack on the fleet—"

"Jahan Korakides? The crown prince of Paladis's best friend?" Devalle lifts a single, skeptical eyebrow.

I can actually feel the blood pulsing in my ears. "Jahan is a friend to Eren and Caeris. He helped defeat the Eyrlais. He—"

"You named him ambassador, did you not?" Devalle says sweetly.

Heat burns into my face. Even now, he's searching out ways to discredit me—using, most mortifyingly, the truth.

"I heard Jahan Korakides is a sorcerer," Philippe says unexpectedly. "I heard he'd been arrested along with Lady Elanna."

Devalle's mouth thins. He turns his head and looks at Philippe—a long, challenging stare. Philippe's jaw ticks, but he looks away.

"Foul rumor," Devalle begins.

"Actually, it's true," I say. "Jahan is a sorcerer. And he—"

Juleane Brazeur interrupts. "I am not interested in Jahan Korakides's identity or whereabouts." Her voice lashes at me, and I shrink backward instinctively. "What concerns me is the incompetence of this regime. First the *Caveadear* is captured—and now she is executed. The Tinani retreat—and now they advance. The emperor of Paladis appears to hesitate—and now he sends a *fleet*. Our nation is in danger and our ministry has failed to take action to save the situation."

I want to disappear, but I force myself to face her. "Even if Elanna were here, we would still be at war. You are all part of this cabinet." I struggle to stay reasonable. "We have known for months it's only a matter of time before the emperor sent a fleet."

"If Elanna were here, we would stand a chance of defeating them," she says coldly. She folds her arms, glancing at High Priest Granpier, who simply shakes his head. To me, she says, "I have supported this regime from the beginning. I stood by your side when you proposed a government that did not equally represent Ereni with Caerisians, because I believed in time we would develop new laws that would allow everyone to be treated fairly. I have advocated for sorcery to be accepted and used. But time and again, this regime has stumbled. And now it appears it is sinking."

"We can still fight, Mistress Brazeur," I say, ignoring the stinging in my eyes. "We can fight more fiercely than the Paladisans, Tinani, and Baedoni combined, for we have the most to lose."

Her gaze tells me I am very young, and terribly foolish. "There will be riots in the streets when this news gets out. The price of grain is already rising without the *Caveadear* to make wheat miraculously sprout from the earth. Soon people will not be able to afford to buy food. They will starve. They are already afraid, hard as we try to bolster their spirits." Finally, as if she's afraid I might not understand, she says, "We risk losing everything we fought to gain."

I refuse to look away from her, even though tears are filling my eyes, even though I'm sick with shame. "I will not let that happen. I fought for the betterment of this country, and for those who gave their lives to make it so, and I will again." I swallow hard. "I *always* will."

I'm glad my mother isn't alive to see this.

I address them all. "The Butcher is returning to Laon tomorrow. I will meet him in Royal Square. I want the people of Laon to see me. To know I am still here, fighting for them."

Juleane Brazeur seems to gather herself to object, but then she simply purses her lips.

"We will prepare for all eventualities," I say, and offer a brittle smile. "Lord Devalle, please prepare me a briefing on the terms we might be able to negotiate with the emperor. When Lord Gilbert returns, he will provide a report on our defenses both by land and sea. Perhaps we can recruit more men and women to the army to bolster defenses. Mistress Brazeur, please put together a report on our financial situation. Finally," I say, "we will declare a national period of mourning for the *Caveadear*. Remember, too, that I am still awaiting an official report of her death."

The others all nod in agreement; my abrupt plan seems to have calmed them, though Victoire's cheeks are still wet with tears. She hesitates, as if to speak, but then follows the others as they begin to disperse.

I release a shaky breath. The growing silence in the hall is deafening. Everyone heard the ministers; it will be all over the palace, and the city, in no time at all. The awfulness of it stoppers my throat.

I should go to my study, write more letters, develop a better plan.

Instead I turn to Teofila's door.

*

IT'S HUGH WHO answers my knock, and I see the refusal in his expression even before I voice my desire to see Teofila.

"She needs to be alone," he says softly.

I bite the inside of my lip. Alone with *him,* he means.

But then Teofila calls from inside the room, "Let her in!"

I start forward, and Hugh stops me with a raised hand. "She's frantic," he whispers warningly. "She doesn't believe El is dead."

"But the reports . . ." I press my fingers to my throat. It's true I told the ministers we needed official confirmation, yet we still have to operate with the assumption it's true. "We heard it from both the Butcher and Demetra."

He just shakes his head and stands back so I can enter.

The sitting room is a cluttered disaster. Since Teofila has hardly spoken to me since that night at the Spring Caves, I've sent her trays of food and jugs of coffee and cocoa, and even dispatched one of the footmen to the university in search of obscure musical scores. The dishes sit in a welter on one of the tables; her maid has done nothing with them, presumably at Teofila's insistence.

Teofila herself is crouched over a dish on the floor. It shines, apparently filled with water. Beside her, a candelabra flickers and burns. She's whispering, "El. El."

It takes me a moment to realize what she's doing. I kneel beside her. "Let me ask one of the refugees to look for her by magic—"

"I should be able to see my own daughter's body." Despite what Hugh said, her voice is calm. Stern. She looks up at me and my heart cracks, for it's obvious to me she's turning her grief into denial.

"You aren't a sorceress," I say, as gently as I can.

"I should be," she says, still quite reasonably. "I gave birth to one. The ability is often inherited. I've been reading some books Granya Knoll sent down from Dalriada about it."

I glance at the plush blue divan, where Hugh has sat down with a sigh. It is, indeed, covered in books. Meanwhile the spinet doesn't appear to have been opened in days. The scores I sent over sit on the bench, still wrapped in paper and a red ribbon, apparently untouched.

"I've been having strange dreams since I started the work," Teofila says. "Almost like waking. I swore I stood in the hold of a ship where she was captive. It was dark, and I heard sea shanties and the creak of ropes and wood, and a girl's frightened, ragged breathing."

I look at Hugh, unable to suppress a lurching sense of horror. I never knew Teofila wanted to work magic, or believed she could, until a few nights ago at the Spring Caves. She's been keeping this secret from me, though I thought I knew her better than anyone.

"Teofila . . ." I try again. "I'm so sorry for what's happened to El. I can't even put it in words."

"You don't need to," she says, still quite sanely. "She isn't dead."

I stare again at Hugh, and again he shakes his head. There must be something we can do, some way to coax her out of this madness. But I can't think of any words.

"You can stop looking at each other like that," Teofila adds with a shade of irritation, and I give a guilty start. "I'm not mad. I'm El's mother. Don't you think I would know if my own daughter were dead?"

This is grief, I tell myself. I remember how impossible my mother's death felt to me. How I hoped for nearly a year that they'd gotten the reports wrong and she would one day appear at Cerid Aven with her bold smile and her traveling shoes and say, *Well, Sophy, are you ready to be brave?*

"I never thanked you for the music, Sophy," Teofila says all of a sudden, with a polite but distant sort of smile. "Thank you. As you can tell, I haven't had a chance to play it just yet, but I will. You're very thoughtful, you know."

I blink at her. I feel about ten years old. *Children* are thoughtful. Queens are . . .

I kiss her cheek, pretending I don't feel the pressure of tears behind my eyes, and that the baby, who I've always imagined as her grandchild, didn't just jab me in the gut. Pretending her conviction that El's alive isn't scaring me to pieces—though it has, I suppose, distracted her from discovering the truth about the child. I don't think she's looked at me close enough to notice my expression, much less my pregnancy. I say, "I'll send a seamstress over to fit you with a mourning gown. You can wear it to the procession to-morrow."

But she's only staring into the water again, unhearing.

I stand up. I'm trembling, and tears threaten my eyes. Hugh rises from the couch, puts his arm around my back. "It's all right," he murmurs. "I'll look after her."

Tears are blinding me. For years, it was I who looked after Teo-fila, and she me. We have always taken care of each other, and now it seems as if I can do nothing for her—and that, even if I could, she wouldn't want me to.

There's nothing to say. So I simply nod and go out.

Queens are alone.

I GO TO my study, the place where I can be most alone, and bolt the door. Throw myself at the mirror between the bookshelves.

"Jahan!" I scream at it. *"Jahan!"*

The mirror shows only my own reddened cheeks, my raw gaping mouth, my desperate, glittering eyes.

"Answer me, Jahan!" I pound on the plaster. "Answer, damn you."

But of course there is nothing. Only my aching fists, the horrible catch in my throat, the hollowness in my gut.

I drop to my knees and cry—huge, heaving sobs. No one interrupts me, not even Charlot, or Rhia. Eventually, the tears seep to a stop and I'm left with the sodden mess of my face, and a faint flutter in my stomach, like the echo of a note struck on the piano, followed by another so faint it seems imaginary. It ceases almost immediately, and for a moment I'm overwhelmed by my own foolishness. I should see a midwife. I should've seen one long ago, and done what I needed to have done. The Ereni already distrust me—after today, probably more than ever. They'll positively despise me when the truth comes to light, as it will have to, eventually.

The sensation eases. I place my hands on my stomach, though the baby is silent now. This poor child is being fed on my fear and frustration. It's no way to grow. What kind of mother am I going to be?

I'll be good to this child, I vow to myself, the way my mother was good to me. And I will never, ever leave her.

CHAPTER ELEVEN

Fiona insists that I prepare carefully for the procession that will greet the Butcher at Laon's gates. It's important for us to appear strong without Elanna. I feel sick in the gut as I put on the black gown she had the modiste alter to my new style. So far no one has copied, or even particularly remarked upon, my gowns, though the maids seem to have realized I've gained weight. I heard one ask another, "Do you think she'll get fat like Queen Loyce?"

Now the maids arrange my hair, teasing it into a soft aureole into which they nestle the royal diadem.

"You look beautiful, my lady," one of them says, arranging a curl to fall artfully over one shoulder.

I stare at my reflection in the mirror. My eyes look drawn, pinched, and my heart is thudding dully. This is the first time the people will see me in public since the news of El's execution. The diadem winks at me, garish. I don't care much for the thing. It came from the Eyrlais, and when I wear it, I feel not so much like a queen as like I've stolen someone else's property. Of course, the royal diadem of Caeris vanished a long time ago, melted down probably by the conquering Eyrlais. I'm not exactly in a position to commission a new one.

I take it off, startling the maids. "I'll wear a hat."

Rhia's waiting for me in the hall, wearing a trim knee-length black coat edged in gold braid, her tall leather boots polished and shining. She looks exactly like my childhood picture of a pirate queen, and I notice the other women in the royal guard have found costumes almost the same. It will be as if I'm going into the city accompanied by a flock of fierce crows. Rhia's eyes track to the small black hat I'm wearing, and she gives a short nod of approval. I'm glad I took the diadem off.

"Ready?" she says.

I swallow. "As much as I will be."

Down in the foyer, a crowd has gathered, all of them dressed in black, as if a mourning party of crows has taken over the palace. They spill all the way out into the inner courtyard, where an open carriage drawn by four glossy horses awaits me. I sigh. The carriage is an Eyrlai relic, its gilt trimmed now with black ribbons, still too gaudy for my taste.

Demetra catches my eye. She's standing on the edge of the crowd, looking self-conscious. We asked her to be here, along with Ciril, so the people would know we still have powerful sorcerers at our side.

"Ride with me in the carriage," I say, taking her arm. The crowd parts around us, smooth as butter. Demetra looks sidelong at the courtiers and footmen we pass, her chin lifted guardedly. But though I tense, no one stares. They seem tired instead; worried, resigned.

We settle into the coach, Demetra adjusting the worn cuffs of her coat. I start guiltily. I should have given her something finer to wear, I realize, too late.

"Will we go out to the front now?" she asks, as an awkward silence seems ready to develop between us. "Ciril is eager to prove himself, and I want to help as much as I can."

"We appreciate your help. The Butcher—that is"—I correct myself when she casts me a look of alarm—"Gilbert Moriens, the minister of war, is the man we're going to welcome. He and I will decide where you can be of the most use, and then we'll send you out."

She nods, still looking troubled. "Why is he called *the Butcher*?"

"For the reasons you're probably thinking," I say, only somewhat sourly. "He . . ." He betrayed our first rebellion, all because Teofila had spurned him, and became the king of Eren's machine of war. He gave the order that killed my mother. He killed hundreds of others, maybe not by his hand but by his orders. Yet the army seems loyal to him, and when it came down to it, he helped us win our war because El took the chance to convince him—so I have been forced to be cordial to him ever since. No one has ever asked me how much it must grate. At last, I simply say, "He is a very useful ally."

The carriage bounces slightly. I look over with a start—Philippe Manceau is climbing in. I don't recall inviting him.

"The ministers felt it would be best if one of us were represented," he says, apparently reading my mind—or expression. He nods politely at Demetra. "I was volunteered."

"Of course you were," I say. I can just imagine who did it. Devalle and friends are clearly pursuing the image of Philippe as king—whether Philippe or I like it or not.

Captain Grenou leans over the side of the carriage. "Ready, Your Majesty?"

I check behind us. Everyone has assembled, but Teofila, of course, isn't there. "Yes." I turn to face the front, swallowing down my worry.

He barks an order. The carriage lurches forward. We rattle out into the city. The sky is blue and clear, and a crowd has gathered in the Royal Square. Like the rest of us, they wear black.

Bracing myself, I lift a hand to them. *It's just like any other performance,* I tell myself. Yet this is the first time I've gone out into the city knowing El isn't coming back. A tremor is running through my hands.

The crowd doesn't cheer, and the ranks of black clothing hardly shift. A girl watches me solemnly from her father's shoulders. Even the children are grieving Elanna's death. The whole kingdom is. I taste the bitterness of guilt mingling with grief.

Philippe clears his throat. "The mood is . . ."

"Tense," I say.

He looks apologetic.

The carriage stops. The crowd eddies around us and falls silent again. I force a smile at Demetra and Philippe, though I'm twisting my hands together in my lap. I've planned a speech, which I'll stand up to give once the Butcher arrives. But now, as we sit waiting, the words sound hollow in my mind. False reassurances about how we'll manage without El. A sick certainty churns in my gut. These people didn't fight for *me*. Perhaps they fought, in part, for our Caerisian ideals, but Elanna was the one who stirred their imaginations. She was a legend come to life. Beside her, the rest of us are . . . simply human. And we're not enough.

Rhia draws her horse up beside the carriage. She rides easily despite her broken arm, but her shoulders are tense. "Where is he?"

It's not like the Butcher of Novarre to be late for an appointment. It worries me, though at the same time I'm relieved I don't yet have to deal with his presence. I open my mouth to reply—but now there's movement in the street. A troop of horsemen is pressing slowly through the crowd, toward us.

It's time. I push myself to my feet—rising so quickly makes me light-headed, thanks to being with child—and shade my eyes. The riders have entered the square now. There's the Butcher, as crisp as if he's just emerged from a drawing room.

And behind him, a familiar head of spiked hair. Alistar! Despite everything, my heart soars. He's back from Tinan—alive, safe. I press my hand to my stomach.

Murmurs rustle through the crowd. "The Butcher," someone says. The back of my neck itches. I glance around. Deep in the crowd behind me, several men and women are staring me down with narrowed eyes. They're commoners, well dressed. Shopkeepers, perhaps. I turn away quickly—realizing, too late, that I should have held their gazes, or even smiled back at them. The hair lifts on the back of my neck.

The Butcher is drawing closer now—close enough to smoothly dismount his horse, the epaulets on his shoulders quivering, and make his way toward me. But my gaze catches on Alistar's wiry figure, clad in a dark coat. He's seen me now. His eyes are tired, creased with grief, but the faintest smile tugs at his mouth.

Another murmur runs through the crowd. This time I *feel* it in my body, a ripple like a wave in an otherwise still lake. The Butcher puts his hand on the carriage door. I lean toward him—

"The *Caveadear*!" someone shouts.

"The steward of the land!"

"The *Caveadear* is dead!"

"The *Caveadear*!"

"The *Caveadear*!"

The square rings with her name. My head comes up. They're mourning her, I think at first. This is how the Ereni express their grief. Tears sting my own eyes.

Yet there's another tone beneath the sorrow and the ache. A deep, glittering note. It's like the sound I heard from Teofila in the Spring Caves, only this is hard, almost faceted. Like a jewel—or a weapon.

Something comes flying out of the crowd, slamming against the carriage door. We all jump. My heart surges. I lunge forward: A rotten apple lies on the cobblestones.

More things fly out of the crowd now—lettuce, a cabbage. "She gave us food!" someone screams. The guards are shouting now. A horse bucks. Philippe is on his feet, staring at someone in the crowd. Rhia screams an order, lost in the din. The whole carriage rocks as the crowd moves, shoving the guards too close.

"Get down, Your Majesty!" Lord Gilbert barks.

I stay standing. "She was my friend, too!" I shout at the crowd, a pale approximation of the speech I meant to make. My whole body is thrumming. "We all mourn her—"

Something flies into my shoulder. I'm knocked back, banging my legs on the carriage seat, a scream caught in my mouth. I scramble upright. Another damned apple.

I struggle to get back up—to try to reason with them, to try to simply make my voice heard—but Philippe throws himself on top of me, holding me down. Protecting me. I don't need his damned protection. I struggle, trying to push him off, but he doesn't get the hint.

"Go!" he shouts at the carriage driver. *"Go!"*

The Butcher's thrown himself into the carriage. His knee connects with my leg. I struggle upright. The coach is heaving forward, rocking back. The roar of the crowd is like a physical thing, an animal that could swallow us whole. Philippe shoves me down flat on the seat, and this time I stay there.

The carriage jolts forward in a sudden burst of speed. Something hard strikes the side. Rhia screams, a feral, wordless shout, but I don't dare lift my head. The crowd's rage—their grief—pummels me. I'm gasping ragged breaths. The carriage thunders on. Overhead the blue sky stares down at me, serene.

The cobblestones change to flagstones. I pull myself up on my elbows; Philippe has finally moved off. We've made it back through the palace gates, but the roar of the crowd is pursuing us. I glance back. People pour through the gates, behind the soldiers, an angry black river.

We'll never get the gates closed—not that I have ever wanted to keep the people out. Not before this.

The walls of the palace lurch up around us. The carriage slams to a stop—the horses whinny—and Philippe grabs my arm.

"Hurry," the Butcher orders.

I'm already on my feet, throwing myself out the carriage door, running for the palace's colonnade. I'll run through, to the upper balcony. They'll all be able to see me from there. Perhaps I can gather enough breath to make myself heard. Perhaps they'll stop, and listen.

My mountain women surround me, Rhia and the Butcher both snapping orders. I pause, panting, in the marble foyer. I've lost my hat. My hair is falling down. Behind us, on the landing outside the colonnade, the palace guard is closing into a solid formation. But the thunder of the crowd still bellows overhead.

Demetra tumbles past the guards, her eyes enormous. Terrified.

I straighten, and the marble seems to tilt. That's not right. I shake my head, but it only tilts more. I'm breathing so fast I can hardly speak; my whole body is vibrating. "I need to—address them—"

"No!" Rhia and the Butcher exclaim simultaneously.

"You need to be kept safe," the Butcher says. "I'll take care of this."

I shake my head, and heat strobes through my temples. The floor wobbles. I remind myself, as I did yesterday, that this is not about me. I need to be strong for my people. I whisper, "So you'll kill them all?"

Philippe's head jerks toward me.

The Butcher's lips thin, and also fade in and out of focus. I try to concentrate, but my pulse is beating too fast, a staccato all over my body. "There will be no bloodshed, Your Majesty." Even his words seem to blur. He's gesturing to Rhia.

She grabs my arm. I throw her off. Stumble. "I need to . . ." I have to grasp for the words. "Speak to them! I am . . . the mother of the people—"

"You are a foolish girl!" the Butcher exclaims.

I swing to face him, and black spots bloom in my eyes. "I am— I am—"

Heat rushes over me.

I'm not aware of falling. The next thing I know, I'm being carried up the staircase, held in a pair of warm arms. "Alistar?" I mumble.

"No," Philippe says shortly.

Then the heat breathes over me again. I blink. He's setting me down on my monstrosity of a bed, and Demetra is leaning over me from the other side, a frown between her brows. I realize that I *fainted*—fainted in front of the Butcher of Novarre and Rhia Knoll and so many others—

And Demetra is holding my wrist, feeling my pulse. She's going to examine me.

She'll find out.

"No!" I yank my arm away, but she expertly grabs me back. "I don't want an examination!"

"You just fainted," Philippe snaps. "You need to be looked over."

Demetra's eyes have narrowed. Does she suspect? "Lie back."

I grind my teeth together. The world is still pulsing warmly, but I don't lie down.

"Lie back. You had a terrible fright, that's all." The cynical twist of her mouth belies the truth of this statement. "The servants can bring something cool to drink—"

"Sophy?"

It's Teofila. My heart pounds again, so fast I think I'll pass out a second time. She rushes in from the other room, pushing Philippe aside. Glances worriedly at Demetra. "What happened?"

"It was an apple," I mumble, "that's all." I feel exhausted. Heat sweeps over me again, and this time I lie back on my pillows. My pulse hums through my entire body.

Teofila is looking at Philippe now. "Someone in the crowd must have planned a riot," he's saying. "It turned to chaos. The Butcher and Rhia Knoll are locking down the palace."

I close my eyes. The roar of the crowd is still humming inside my skin, a counterpoint to the hot flush of my own body. They're still out there.

"I should get up," I whisper.

Three people push me back down.

"Philippe," Teofila says, "get us a report, would you?" She looks at Demetra. "You must have family you're worried about in the east wing."

I blink foggily at Teofila. She's commanding. In control. Utterly sane. How on earth does she even know about the refugees in the east wing? She's seemed utterly oblivious to everything, even though she came here to translate for them.

Demetra glances at me. "I can't leave her . . ."

"You can," Teofila asserts. "Tell me what to do, and I'll look after her. I've done so these last thirteen years. I'm not about to stop now."

DEMETRA ORDERED ME to rest, but though I'm propped up on down bolsters and swaddled in blankets, lying here is hardly restful. People keep rushing in and out—first Philippe, then Rhia, who assures me that none of the rioters have actually broken into the palace or tussled with the guards. "They're still shouting out there," she says with a small frown, as if it's only striking her now how strange it is to be the ones shouted at, not those doing the shouting.

Teofila passes me a cup of tisane without comment.

There's a thump at the door, and the Butcher enters. He looks, for once, out of breath, flustered. He scarcely even glances at Teofila, or at Philippe or Rhia, who's glowering at him. "They're starting to break up, Your Majesty. We're handing out bread."

I blink. *Bread?*

He nods. "They're claiming the *Caveadear* fed them, and we won't."

I chew on my lower lip. "Was anyone hurt?"

"Not seriously, so far as we saw. The guards are shaken."

Teofila glances at him. "I'd say we all are."

He acknowledges that with a twist of his lips.

"Where's Alistar?" I ask. I can't believe he hasn't come to find me yet.

"Lord Connell is securing the palace entrances," the Butcher says with a dark look. "Your Majesty, we need to talk." He pauses. "Privately."

"Privately?" I can't conceal the alarm pitching my voice too high. No matter what Elanna says about him, no matter that I need his help, I'm not glad to see the Butcher, and I certainly don't want to talk to him alone.

His glance cuts toward Philippe—and Philippe's mouth sets in recognition.

Teofila intervenes. "Lord Philippe, help me see that the palace staff has remained calm, since Sophy can't speak with them herself."

Philippe gives the Butcher a hard look, but he nods. "Call if you need anything, Lady Sophy."

I manage a smile. They go, and a lump hardens in my throat.

The Butcher still doesn't speak. With a sigh, I look at Rhia. Her shoulders are taut. She says to the Butcher, "At least tell me if my father is well."

He puts one arm behind his back like a punctilious secretary. "The warden of the mountains is still on the front, maintaining our defenses."

"I see." Rhia nods, but I know her well enough to recognize the disappointment tightening her lips. "Is he well?"

"Hale as a mountain wolf, and still talking of prophecies foretold," the Butcher says with genteel disapproval.

Rhia closes her eyes. "Thank you." She shoots me a warning look—a warning to call should I need her—and retreats.

The Butcher shakes his head. "Mountain folk."

"They've helped keep our defenses together on the border," I point out.

"Indeed. One can't fault them for their ferocity, except when they devolve into squabbles over honor." He lifts his eyes to the ceiling. "Is the girl certain to succeed Knoll?"

"If you mean Rhia, she's a year my elder, and I would hardly consider her a girl. And no. The mountain lords maintain lively elections. Rhia would have to make a strong case." Which I imagine she would—if she wanted to put her mind to it. I've never been sure, though, if it's what she really wants. I can't quite comprehend the reluctance, personally. She's too clever to remain the captain of my queen's guard forever.

The Butcher pulls up a stool and sinks onto it, rubbing his hand over his chin. For the first time, he looks almost human to me—tired, sore. Worried. He looks at me. "The mountain lords make up perhaps an eighth of the overall population, do they not? Yet under the tripartite rule, one of them will always be a third of the kingdom's government."

This is so far from what I expected him to say that I simply stare. "I suppose, Lord Gilbert."

"The government of Caeris," he explains patiently, "is divided among the *Caveadear,* the monarch, and the warden of the mountains. A reasonable enough balance in Caeris, where two-thirds of the population live in the lowlands, thus represented by the monarch and *Caveadear,* and the remaining third in the mountains. But this does not take into account the government of *Eren*—which in addition to being larger and indeed wealthier than Caeris, has no representation at all."

"It has . . ." I stop. It *had* Elanna. And now she's gone. But that's still no reason for the Butcher to criticize our government—as if he had any genuine interest in its formation. Carefully, I say, "Does this have something to do with the riot? Now that El's gone . . ."

I almost choke on the words. I won't say what I'm questioning, not to the Butcher of Novarre—what this means for not only the kingdom's future, but my own.

But I know the answer well enough, though I shrink from admitting it.

"Oh, that." He flaps his hand toward the distant city. "That was a true riot. They're upset Elanna's been executed." He pauses, and a shadow passes over his face. I wonder if even he feels some measure of grief, but then I remind myself that this is the man who burned an entire village in Caeris to the ground. The Butcher might have liked Elanna, as much as he can like anyone, but he won't let that cloud his thinking.

"No, Your Majesty," he says at last, "the riot in itself does not concern me."

I utter a strangled sound. A *riot* doesn't concern him?

"What worries me," he says, "is how some people might take advantage of emotions running so high."

"And that's why you asked me about tripartite rule?" It seems so irrelevant, I can't withhold my own sarcasm.

Without a word, he digs in the pocket of his military jacket and produces a crumpled piece of paper. He hands it to me. I smooth it out and flinch. It's a pamphlet—with my face on the front, garish in a woodblock print. I'm wearing the Eyrlai diadem, and my face is fat and bovine.

Beneath this flattering portrait is written, THE BASTARD QUEEN.

"Are you all right?" the Butcher asks.

I'm breathing too fast through my nose. I feel flushed all over, again. With an effort, I gather myself; the Butcher's concern is the last thing I care to receive. "Yes."

"Perhaps you shouldn't read the text . . ."

But it's too late; my eyes have already dragged down to the elaborate script below. *Tripartite rule is the rule of greed! Caeris has conquered Eren. Sophy Dunbarron is a sow who has placed herself on the throne. Does this seem equitable to you?*

"Who did this?" I say quietly, at last. The pamphlet is unmarked.

The Butcher doesn't answer immediately. Instead he says, "It is understandable that the Ereni feel they are not represented in the government of their kingdom. They are ruled by Caerisians. They want a voice."

"They *have* a voice." My vehemence takes even me aback. "We defeated the Eyrlais on the promise that everyone would have a voice. That's why we set up the local assemblies, the councils, the elections. That's why I hold public audiences. They know they only have to speak to me."

"Would you change the tripartite rule if they asked?"

I say nothing. I want to scream so badly I don't trust my own voice. My own people are protesting against me, issuing mockeries of me, mere months after I took the throne.

Part of me wants to scream at him, at them. Tell them they're wrong, that they don't understand.

The other part wants to disappear, quietly, without fuss. Back to Caeris, perhaps even to another country. Somewhere I won't be recognized; where I could live without the reminder of my own failure.

A small voice in my head whispers, *Ruadan never said it would be like this*. Months ago, *we* were the protestors.

"The people wanted us," I say finally. "We had popular support in Eren."

"You still do. But the people are afraid. The *Caveadear*'s dead, and even if the Tinani have withdrawn, your subjects aren't fools. They know Tinan is still a threat, and Baedon, and most of all Paladis."

It's exactly what he warned me would happen, and having it rubbed in my face isn't exactly heartwarming. I clench my hands together. If he thinks he could have done better, let him try.

"The price of bread is going up," he says. "We have no trade, no access to so many common goods. People are growing desperate."

"And they blame me," I say quietly. "Even though I've sworn to keep them safe."

"Well." He studies me and nods to himself, almost satisfied. As if he's pleased he's succeeded in scaring the wits out of me. "Here is what I think has happened. I fully expected fear might turn some people against us, that people would be profoundly distraught over Elanna's death, but I did not expect them to use the argument about tripartite rule. The protests about sorcery, yes, and the lack of food and goods and feeling unsafe. But not that, not yet."

I eye him. I have the feeling that, even though he's illustrating how desperate our situation is, he's obscurely taking pleasure in being right. It makes my nostrils flare.

"Someone is working to undermine us," I say flatly.

He nods like a teacher, pleased I've followed his line of thought, and I grind my teeth. I was taught by Ruadan Valtai; I don't need the Butcher of Novarre's approbation. "You're aware, I suspect, that some of your own ministers care very little for you and Caeris."

"It would be hard to miss."

"Indeed. There's more to it, though, which I didn't expect. Someone is out in the country, rallying people against you. Someone who wants the very foundation of your government to be suspect. There will be more protests—more riots."

My mouth goes dry. "The way we did—printing pamphlets, staging protests."

"Exactly." His lips quirk. "Ironic, isn't it? I suspect this is the individual who arranged for the murder of that sorcerer in Ichou."

"Why are you so convinced there's only one person behind it? It sounds like a . . . a movement."

Which depresses me so profoundly, my mind feels numb.

"Duke Ruadan started a movement in the same way, with a little money and influence."

"I see." Wretchedly, I do, only too well. "So do you have any idea who it is?"

"Yes, Your Majesty. It's a man many of us know—those who spent time in the Eyrlai court, that is. A man most Ereni know by name, whose wealth was even greater than the king's." He looks at me. "You may know his name, too. Aristide Rambaud, the Duke of Essez."

I draw in a shaking breath. So it's him—this mysterious duke whom everyone but me seems to know. An ally of the king of Tinan, a man with almost as many lands to his name as the former royal family had.

"He has already been heard to say you must be cast off your throne," the Butcher says, watching me. "I have at least two informants on him at all times. He's made speeches in town squares calling for you to be deposed. He has named sorcery as vile, anathema—an evil cancer that must be cut out of Eren."

I flinch.

"Soon there will be more protests, and the people of Eren will be calling for the same things. Sorcerers are already considered wicked by some. Rambaud is taking care to exploit that."

"Then we must counter him," I begin.

The Butcher interrupts me. "Majesty, we need to strike fast and strike hard. We need to make changes and we need to remove these pamphlets." He pauses. "We need to put Rambaud down."

"Put him down?" I stare at him, repulsed. "You mean assassinate him?"

"It might be difficult," he concedes. "Though I'm sure I can deduce his location."

My mind is reeling. The Butcher doesn't only want to "put Rambaud down"—he wants to destroy the pamphlets. Though I'd love to never see this caricature again, that's *censorship*. It's exactly what the Eyrlais did to us. Not surprising, I suppose, since he worked for the Eyrlai king and queen.

"I won't do that," I say at last. "I won't behave like Antoine Eyrlai."

He lifts a skeptical brow. "Then how do you propose to keep Rambaud from turning the people against you?"

My mind is spinning, spinning. "It's simple," I say with a confidence I don't feel. "I will make the Ereni love me."

"How?"

"I'll show them that I love *them*." I pause. *How*, indeed? The people are hungry, but I can't make wheat sprout from the fields, like Elanna. I have already granted them access to the royal granaries. And no matter how helpful, these are still only gestures. Somehow I must prove to them that I value my Ereni subjects as much as my Caerisians. Somehow I must make myself like Elanna: not only Caerisian, but Ereni as well.

The answer is obvious, but I can't say it. I see Alistar in the crowd, looking at me with that small, familiar smile. I see Lord Devalle looking so significantly at Philippe Manceau. I feel the flutter of the baby in my belly.

The Butcher is waiting for me to speak.

I refuse to let him think I'm soft. That I put my own desires before the good of the kingdom.

I say, "I will marry an Ereni lord."

CHAPTER TWELVE

The Butcher leaves, and Teofila takes his place. I'm shaken. I told myself I wouldn't give my hand away like a trophy, and here I am, declaring I'll marry an Ereni lord at the first sign of trouble. There must be another way to prove my devotion to the Ereni, to tell them I'm determined to become the ruler they want and deserve. But at the moment, I don't see anything else that would be as swift or effective.

I must be staring into space, because finally Teofila says, "What's wrong, dear?"

I just shake my head.

She gives me a knowing look but doesn't press. Instead she fusses over me, the way I've tried to fuss over her, insisting that I put up my feet when I try to rise, bringing me tea and warm chocolate, a platter of roast beef sandwiches. I do my best but the roast beef, which I ordinarily love, smells terrible.

"Is there something you'd rather have?" Teofila asks, concerned. For the first time in days—or weeks—she seems to really study me.

I squirm. Yet my stomach is rumbling and there's only one thing in the world, it seems, that sounds good. "Cream custard," I admit.

She looks at me, lifting an eyebrow, and I feel momentarily naked, obvious, beneath her gaze. But then she smiles and goes to the door. My shoulders ease a fraction. A dish arrives soon after, almost the size of my head—custard with a compote of stewed plums. I try to offer Teofila some of it and end up eating the entire thing.

Full now, I become aware of the silence between us. Of Teofila's keen gaze, and the dome of my stomach, swaddled by blankets. But is it invisible if you look closely enough? Teofila knows me better than anyone. Maybe she doesn't need a rounded stomach to tell her what a mother's instinct already knows.

She hasn't spoken of anything else important, either. Not of the riot, nor of what the Butcher and I talked about. Certainly not of El's death. I'm afraid to bring it up. For my entire girlhood, Elanna was a captive. Teofila almost never talked about it—the same way I never talked about my mother. Some losses, I suppose, are too profound to be spoken of—even between women who are like mother and daughter—and I never found a way to ask her. Besides, at that time, Elanna was safe as far as we knew; Antoine Eyrlai had brought her up like his own daughter. He might have held a pistol to her head, but he never would have killed her.

I search for words, but none come. The silence between us holds a soft, low note—a sound that seems to emanate once again from Teofila. A deep, aching sound that isn't precisely heard. I feel it, rather, in my skin, a foreign awareness that overlays my own senses. I shiver all over.

"You seem to be feeling better," Teofila remarks. "Fewer stomach upsets."

So she knows, or suspects. My heart kicks, then begins to pound so hard I can barely feel my fingertips. All the same I force my voice even—as falsely casual as Teofila's own. "I'm much better."

"Mmm." She leans forward and takes the tray from me, setting it on a side table. "I thought you were having trouble with your monthly courses, perhaps."

I feel myself go very still. The spoon clatters in my empty dish.

Teofila's dark-brown eyes are level. "I think you have something to tell me."

There's no point in trying to hide it further; it was only a matter of time before she saw straight through me. I made this choice, and it's time to face the consequences. Slowly, I sit up, as straight as I can against the pillows. She perches on the bed, facing me. I force myself to meet her eyes.

"Sophy," she says on a sigh. "What are you doing? People are going to notice. They already *are* noticing—"

"They think I'm getting fat," I say. "Fat and lazy, while you and Elanna carry all the weight of the world on your shoulders."

Her eyebrow lifts at that. "I haven't heard anyone call you *fat*. But the maids must know, or guess—the moment you decided to start a new fashion."

Miserably, I confess, "I didn't think my gowns would fit. And I'd have needed help to get some of them on . . ."

"No doubt the maids have noticed you're dressing yourself." She shakes her head. "It's a good thing you've been on the road, or they would have already figured out that you haven't bled in— what—four months? Five?"

"Close to five." I lift my chin. "I know people will discover the truth soon, and I won't be able to conceal it any longer—though I suppose that's what you're going to tell me to do. But I won't do it. I won't go quietly away into the country when my time comes. I can't. This child is . . ." I cut off the words viciously, though they rattle on in my head. Teofila hasn't been speaking to me. Ruadan's dead. Elanna's gone. Alistar is on the front. The child is all I have.

"I would never have told you to do that!" Teofila whispers angrily. "I wouldn't tell you to lie to the people."

I meet her eyes. "Wouldn't you?"

Her gaze shifts away, and I can read the truth there clearly enough. Teofila is kind and openhearted, but she's no fool. Not like I am. She'd have dealt with this, in one way or another, long ago, if I had confided in her.

She takes my hand. "Sophy," she says, "I have already lost one daughter this week. I am not going to lose another."

"It's not going to kill me," I retort, even though my heart lifts at being called her daughter.

"Maybe not. But you know what this is going to do to your

reputation. The ministers—the Ereni—even the Caerisians . . . Having a dalliance is one thing, but the *queen* having a child out of wedlock? And in the precarious position we're in?"

"I . . ." Cold tears overflow my eyes. She's right. There is no way I can justify what I'm doing, except that I want it. I want this child so badly I'm willing to risk anything for it.

And I *have* thought this part through. I'm not a complete fool. I wipe my eyes and say as firmly as I can, "I know it may look mad from the outside. But I want this, and I'm certain that the people will want it, too."

Teofila stares at me. "Darling, your enemies are going to tell the people that you're a whore."

I flush again, with anger this time. "Let them say that! A child is the symbol of the future. It's hope for our new nation. It tells the people I intend to be their queen for some time to come, and, and—"

I falter to a stop. I can't stand the pity in Teofila's eyes.

"It's understandable that you would want a child of your own," she says. "A family of your own, since you lost all your blood relatives. I know I felt the same way when I came to Caeris, though my family still lived—but they were so very far away, and hard to reach when they traveled."

I nod. Teofila's family hail from Baedon but are court musicians, traveling to one royal capital and then another to perform their music. She used to travel with them; it's how she met Ruadan in Ida.

"It was such a relief to have Elanna," she's saying. "I felt as if I had an ally. Someone I could love unreservedly, and who would love me."

"That's not why I want a child," I bluster. "I want it to symbolize unity, and peace, and hope . . ."

Teofila just looks at me. "A baby isn't a symbol, as you know perfectly well. It's a person. You haven't convinced yourself you need to have a child because of what it *symbolizes*."

I put my hand over my mouth. Tears are leaking out of my eyes.

She understands me too well, and she's not sparing any truth. I want to crawl beneath the armchair and disappear.

"Have you seen a midwife?" she demands.

"Of course not! I couldn't risk anyone knowing. You're the first person who does."

Her eyebrows draw down. "You have to see a midwife! Not only for the child's sake, but for yours. A healthy mother helps make a healthy child. You know this! Let me send for someone."

"No," I say quickly. "I can't risk someone coming to this room. People will notice, and talk. They'll ask questions."

She folds her lips, then tilts her head as another thought comes to her. "Is it Alistar's?"

I can't meet her eyes.

"Have you told him?" she persists.

"I . . . He . . ."

"Sophy!" she exclaims, and I startle. She's really angry now. Her eyes are bright. "You're putting him at as much risk as yourself. He needs to know, and soon!"

"It's not as if we're married," I say, flaring in response to her anger. "No one needs to know who the father is."

"The entire country knows you're having an affair with Alistar Connell! It won't be hard to sort out, and however much you might wish otherwise, he's going to be dragged into it." She stops, drumming her fingers. "You could get married."

"The ministers would be thrilled to hear you say that," I say darkly. "They seem to think I'm nothing more than a brood mare, best saddled with a husband to settle me down. Ruadan would never have stood for it."

"Ruadan would have had you engaged to be married by now, if Finn had lived."

I stare at her. "That is not true."

"What did you imagine your future would be? He raised you to cement a political alliance through marriage."

"He raised me to be the backup heir!"

"Yes, but he never thought Finn would die. Or that Euan Dromahair wouldn't actually come to Caeris himself. Ruadan never expected you to claim the throne, Sophy."

"So I was second choice to him, as well as to everyone else!" I burst out. "You don't have to tell me. I already know. I've always known that I come second and last. It doesn't mean that's what I want to be."

She looks at me—up at me, since I'm now on my feet. I don't know when I got up, but I'm standing now, anger pulsing through me, hot and red.

"Second?" Teofila asks.

"Second to Finn," I say impatiently. "Second to Elanna. I am everyone's second choice."

She stands, too. "Not mine."

"What are you talking about? Of course I am. Elanna comes first for you. She's your daughter, your real daughter. And I . . ."

Teofila grabs my arms. "Stop it. This is beneath you. I don't choose between my daughters."

I'm crying again, stupid, helpless tears. Without another word, Teofila folds me against her with one strong arm, cupping my head against her shoulder so that I can weep. And I do—though I'm taller than she is, though it cricks my neck painfully, though I feel that instead of weeping I should be apologizing for what I said.

"I'm sorry," I say, "I'm sorry I lost her again. I'm sorry I'm not the queen everyone wants me to be."

"Shh. Enough." Teofila sets me back, and I snuffle down the rest of my tears. She brings out her handkerchief and wipes my face, just the way she did when I was a little girl. I feel completely stupid. I can't look at her, though she sits down right beside me on the bed, her hand squeezing my kneecap.

"Sophy," she says, "have you thought of marrying Alistar?"

Marriage, again. As if in response to my sudden tension, there's a flutter in my womb. I touch my fingertips to where I felt the movement. Hesitantly, Teofila brings her hand beside mine. There's another faint flitter. "Did you feel it?" I ask Teofila. She nods her head, leaning closer. We both sit there, though the baby doesn't move again, foolish smiles growing nevertheless on our faces.

In a whisper, I say at last, "I promised the Butcher I would marry an Ereni lord."

Teofila looks up at that, sharply. "Why would he demand such a thing of you?"

"He didn't. He wanted me to use force to subdue them. I argued that showing my Ereni subjects I valued them would be more effective in the long run. So I . . ." I swallow hard. "The only solution I could think of was marriage."

She looks thoughtful. "It might help, at that. But, darling, is this what you want? Do you want to marry an Ereni lord, for a political alliance?"

I look away, thinking of Philippe Manceau, with his observant eyes and his entirely enigmatic loyalties. "It doesn't matter what I want. The good of the kingdom must come first."

"There are other ways to win over the Ereni, without giving yourself to a man you don't love."

"But I have to do *something*."

She shakes her head. "You mustn't give yourself away if you are unwilling. Your desires matter." She gives me a significant look. "You are allowed to tell Gilbert no."

I can't imagine summoning the Butcher to an audience and then telling him I've changed my mind. He would ask why, and I would have to say, *Because I'm not in love with an Ereni man*. I can just see the expression on his face. It makes me wish the bedclothes would smother me—or maybe him. He has no right to castigate me.

"You're the one who has to live with the man," Teofila says, more urgently. "Sophy, if you marry anyone, do it for love. Life will bring you such hardships, sometimes, that at least you will be able to tell yourself you wed a man because you truly loved him once."

I stare at her, but she's looking at her own hand, still cupped against my stomach. The note that pulses off her now holds both tenderness and an unspeakable grief. Of course, she is thinking of Elanna, and Ruadan. She lived with fear for so many years, and now after she finally got her daughter back, she's lost her in the most final way imaginable.

I put my hand over hers. We sit there for some time longer, speaking softly of what the remainder of my pregnancy will bring, talking of what Teofila remembers from bearing Elanna, discussing cribs and nappies and rattles and lullabies. Dreaming, together, of what the future may bring.

SOME TIME LATER, there's a knock at the door. Teofila goes to answer it. I've risen from bed and put on a dressing gown. I heard the deep burr of a male voice, and before I even have a chance to react, he strides in.

Alistar.

"I'll leave you." Teofila steps out with a last, quick glance at me.

But I scarcely hear her, because Alistar is crossing the room. He hasn't even bathed yet; his clothes are muddy and torn, his face tired. Yet his eyes light when he sees me.

"There's my lady," he says. "My Sophy."

I hold out my hands. "My hound."

Then I'm in his arms, feeling the heat of him. It's so natural, so comfortable, so *safe,* I can scarcely remember my initial trepidation.

He strokes the hair away from my forehead and leans down to kiss me. "They said you fainted when I was assisting the guards. Are you all right? Sophy, I'm so sorry, I was in Tinan so long, I couldn't make it back until now—"

"I'm fine," I say, and I feel myself smiling—a familiar wicked smile, as if El isn't dead and none of today happened and things are as they always have been. "I was simply overcome. The way I always am in your presence."

A grin sparks in his eyes. "Overcome by . . . my brooding good looks? Or perhaps my valor in battle?"

"By your goodness," I say, and my throat catches. I laugh and quickly add, "And by your roguish charm, of course."

"I am overcome by you," he murmurs. "By your beauty, your intelligence, your . . . regal . . . presence . . ."

He leans closer, pressing his lips to my throat, to the soft tender skin at the top of my breasts. He'll notice, certainly, that they're swollen.

But then he lifts his face and begins to feather light kisses over my cheeks, my forehead. I close my eyes, wrapping my hands around his neck. This is the truth about Alistar, what most people don't guess about him, because in the outside world he's so fierce and boisterous, but always, when it's just the two of us, he's so tender. Too tender, sometimes, as if he's afraid of hurting me.

He leans his forehead against mine. I pull him closer, drinking in the smell of him, even overlaid with the scent of sweat and horse. We're almost of a height, and unlike most men, he doesn't seem troubled being with a woman a scant inch shorter than he is. Not even that first night, four years ago, when we slipped out of the ball at Cerid Aven and he kissed me in the cool air beneath the oaks. We'd met before, of course; Dearbann isn't far from Cerid Aven, and Ruadan was always throwing parties, since he couldn't leave his grounds. I'd kissed other boys, mostly in the spirit of ex- perimentation. They'd been all right, but with Alistar it was . . . delicious. And safe. Awkward, because neither of us quite knew what we were doing, despite our experiments with others. And he was such a gentleman—far more of a gentleman, in my opinion, than he needed to be. When we finished kissing, he'd made an awkward bow and said, "Well, I'll be seeing you around, Miss Sophy."

I suppose he has seen me around, and then some.

Now his hands drift down to my waist and slip beneath my dressing gown, burning through the thin fabric of my chemise. My skin feels translucent. He leans his lips back down to mine. "Might I request an audience with Your Majesty?" he murmurs. "I haven't greeted the queen of Eren and Caeris properly."

"I'll have to check with my palace steward," I say breathlessly. "See if I can fit you in. A queen's schedule is quite packed, you know."

Alistar is making a persuasive argument along my jaw and down my neck. His hands slide lower, caressing the curve of my hips, moving between us to my stomach—

I jolt to my senses. Gently, I capture his hands, pressing them together between us. He's kissing the notch of my collarbone.

"Alistar," I say.

He bends lower, his breath hot against my skin. It takes all my power not to melt against him. But if I let him undress me, he'll know; he's no fool. And he doesn't deserve to find out that way.

I clear my throat. *"Alistar."*

He lifts his mouth from my body with a sigh. "Milady?"

I feel myself wince; he calls me *milady* when he's particularly teasing, or particularly exasperated. This time, it's clearly the latter; he's breathing quickly. And even though I've rehearsed this speech dozens—no, hundreds—of times in the dark hours before sleep, now that it comes down to it, I don't know how to say it. I don't know how to excuse my own cowardice in keeping this secret from him for so long. For making the choice to keep this child without ever consulting him.

For telling the Butcher I would marry someone else.

Best just to get it over with. "Do you remember the day of the dying year? Well, the night of it . . ."

He chuckles low in his throat. "I certainly do."

"Well . . ." My hands are sweating where they grip his, and he's still leaning into me, warmly, invitingly. I fumble onward. "That night, I—I didn't take precautions." What had I been thinking? It was as if I wanted this child so badly I'd convinced myself that I didn't have to be careful, though I had been a hundred times before.

He straightens abruptly, and I risk a glance at his face. His mouth is slack.

"Are you saying . . ." He glances around, a frantic movement, to be certain we're alone. We are, yet he lowers his voice all the same. "You're *with child*?"

I give a small nod.

"That's—! Soph—!" He seizes me in his arms, planting kisses all over my face, and I smile in spite of myself. But then, just as quickly, he sets me back, dropping his hands. "But that was months ago."

I wince. "Almost five. Yes. Look, I'm sorry. I—I didn't know what to do. It's not like I expected it to quicken. Or Finn to die. Or that we would actually win against the Eyrlais and I would become *queen*—"

He's retreating from me, though he hasn't moved back. He seems to grow taller. "How long have you known?"

I'm too ashamed to admit I figured it out six weeks in. "I should have told you. I've been trying to figure out what to do." Tears swell in my eyes. "I don't know how much longer I can hide it."

"You shouldn't hide it!" he bursts out. "A child conceived on the day of the dying year is a lucky child."

"A child who can see spirits."

He nods. "Blessed."

"Or uncanny. Can you imagine the Ereni thinking it's lucky? Much less blessed?"

"We should get married," he says decisively. "Then you wouldn't have to hide it. That is . . . if you want me."

Tears blur my eyes. I'm choking on the words I spoke to the Butcher. Because of course I want Alistar. I've wanted him for years—and I've had him, since Ruadan said that a dalliance was acceptable and even healthy for a young person. "And better Alistar Connell," I once heard him say to Teofila, "than some young buck without a good family." I've let him into my heart and my confidence, I've held him closer than anyone else.

And now I can't have him.

"I . . ." The words stick in my throat. I owe him the truth, yet I can't make myself speak it. "You know the ministers won't allow it."

"You're the queen. *You* tell the ministers what you're going to do."

"You know that's not how this works!" I snap. "You know what a precarious position I'm in—we're all in! With El dead—and the people rioting, and—and—" I have to hunt for breath. "You know the Tinani haven't just withdrawn for no reason. They're waiting for something, and the emperor of Paladis is just gathering his breath before he sends a fleet—"

"Those are all reasons *to* marry," he argues. "To present a united front. To show we won't be bullied by anyone."

The tears are falling down my cheeks now. I catch in a sob. "I can't, Alistar. I can't."

His mouth closes. He doesn't move to comfort me, and it makes me cry harder. We've never fought before—disagreed, of course, because we're both strong-minded people. But I've never wounded Alistar so much that he won't even put his hand out to me.

"You could have gotten rid of the child before this," he says flatly. "So I'm thinking it's me you don't want. You're willing to risk ridicule for birthing a bastard, but you're not willing to have a Connell of Lanlachlan as your husband."

My ears are ringing. I hear myself say, "I always told you this was a dalliance. I told you it couldn't be anything more."

"No, Sophy," he says. "You didn't."

He steps away, but pauses and turns back to face me. "For the record, I would gladly marry you. Not because I want to be king—that's the last thing in the world I want—but because I—I *care* for you." His voice cracks, as if the word shatters him. "And I would love to care for our child."

Tears choke my eyes, my throat. Somehow, I manage to say, "I told the Butcher I would marry an Ereni lord. Just now, before I came here. They don't trust me, Alistar. I have to make them trust me. I have to make them love me."

"*I* love you," he says so softly it's almost swallowed by the space between us.

I gulp down my tears. "I . . ."

But when I lift my head, it's to see him walking out of the room. The door slams behind him.

ALISTAR TOLD ME he loved me. He told me he wanted to raise our child together, and I told him I'm marrying an Ereni lord. I want to peel off my skin in shame. I must be the most horrible, coldhearted person ever to have lived. How can I be a mother to this child, when I treat the father the way I have? It's a good thing my mother isn't alive to see me now. She'd be so ashamed.

I come to myself in a haze of tears. I don't want to vanish. I *can't*. I might be able to live with the scorn of the people, with the disapproval of the Butcher, the disappointment of Hugh and Teofila, even my own self-loathing, but there is one person I can't disappoint. My mother. She gave her life so that I could someday become the queen of Eren and Caeris. It's what she would have wanted, and I can't back down now. Even if what I've done wouldn't make her proud, she would understand why I did it. At least, I think so.

I look around. Some kindly maid—Fiona, I suppose—has left a pot of tea by my elbow. I'm crouched in the big wingback chair in front of the fire, with three crumpled handkerchiefs littering the carpet at my feet. Hours have passed since Alistar left. It must be the middle of the night. Darkness presses against the window-panes, and I feel tears threaten again.

Maybe I should find Teofila—although I don't know how on earth I'll ever admit to the shameful way I've treated Alistar. Maybe it's Alistar himself I should go after. But I can't change course now. Shame has swallowed me whole.

I rise and change into my plainest dress. My movements are stiff. But there is a child growing within me, and for her I must swallow down the thickness of my grief.

I can't marry Alistar, and I don't want to marry Philippe. El is dead. The kingdom is in turmoil. And I haven't even done the simplest, most important thing for my child.

If my mother were alive, she'd tell me to take courage. *Are you ready to be brave?*

I wrap a kerchief around my hair, like a maid, and bundle a thick, warm shawl around my shoulders, tying it across my breasts and stomach and behind my back. I'm suddenly weary down into the marrow of my bones. A single note hums through my head, through my body—a high, intense vibration. This time, it seems to come from me—an emanation of my own anxiety.

I go to the door. By some luck, Rhia herself is on duty, and Grenou's guards are scarce. "Just the two of us," I tell her, my voice hoarse.

She looks at me as if to question where we're going and why I'm dressed so plainly, but nods. She must be tired, or she'd argue. I walk ahead of her through the halls. Darkness has fallen, and the palace smells of food and wood fires.

We descend the stairs and enter the east wing. It smells of paint and the bright tang of fresh air, and in the great hall refugees are playing games with dice on the heavy, old-fashioned tables, while children doze in the corners. It's not quite as late as I thought.

A man comes over to us. "Demetra?" I ask him.

He treats me to a skeptical look, but grows wary at the sight of Rhia. Turning to the children, he speaks briskly in a tongue I don't know. Three children rise from among the others and come over, rubbing their eyes. The oldest is perhaps eight; she cradles her little sister in her arms. "Come," she says in Ereni. They herd us out and upstairs, to a small chamber at the end of a long hallway. It must have been a study once, for Demetra is seated at an ancient, scarred desk, her back to us. The desk's surface is covered in fresh herbs.

Demetra is slow to look around from them, even with the children pulling at her elbows. When she turns, she looks at me a second time before hurrying to her feet. "Your Majesty?"

"Please wait outside," I tell Rhia.

"Go." Demetra shoos the children after my guard captain, despite their protests. The door closes behind them.

I'm alone with Demetra in the old stone room, the weight of my secret between us. I draw in a breath.

"I need your help," I say, simply. "But I must swear you to secrecy. I have a condition, you see, that no one must know about."

Demetra's eyes are red and tired. Her gaze flickers down to my stomach. "I see."

My face grows hot. "You guessed?"

She actually laughs. "There's only one reason why a woman would come find *me* in the middle of the night. So tell me, Your Majesty, how far along are you?"

"Almost five months," I admit.

"And have you seen a midwife?"

I shake my head. It does seem foolish, in retrospect.

"No one at all?" she exclaims, then shakes her head. "I suppose you had no one you trusted. And who will I tell?"

I manage a smile. "Something like that."

She clicks her tongue. "Let me examine you, then. Lie down."

I obey. A warmth is building under my ribs—the comfort, the relief, I realize, of finally trusting Teofila and Demetra with the truth. Demetra gently squeezes my hand before touching my stomach. She presses her hands firmly on all sides, puts her ear against my abdomen to listen, and then, apparently satisfied, sits back. A single note radiates out from her, deep and golden and potent. It shivers through me until my body hums like a plucked string—and the child growing in my womb somehow begins to hum, too. A note like mine, but ever so slightly different, a faintly higher pitch. So subtle I almost can't hear it.

I gasp a little, but Demetra takes no notice. My whole body seems to have transformed—humming, alive, in a way I have never felt before.

Demetra leans back over me. "You have a healthy child, as far as I can tell. Though no thanks to the strain its mother is under! You must be more careful to rest, and to eat well. Make sure you get enough sleep."

I sit up, with her help, and she looks at me knowingly. "You already love this child."

I cup my hands over my stomach. "More than anything."

"But it is difficult for a queen to have a child without a king." She smirks a little. "Even in Eren."

"Especially in Eren," I say darkly.

"Will you marry, then?"

I lift a shoulder. "Apparently I must."

She looks at me. "Once you're a mother, you'll realize no one can make you do what you don't want to do. Especially when it's about your child."

I smile a little at that. "Maybe I will still find another way." I pause. "The note you sang—is that your magic?"

"Note?" she says, confused.

"The music you made while you were examining me." I gesture, but she just stares blankly. I hum the sound myself. It vibrates through the dim room, echoing through my body once again, a comforting warmth.

"I did not make that sound," she says firmly.

"But I heard it," I insist. I can't be going mad on top of everything else. "It sounded like magic."

She frowns, but her gaze sharpens as she studies me. "Perhaps it is yours, my lady. Your magic."

I'm staring at her, and at the same time, the floor seems to be dropping away. "But I don't have magic. Elanna's the one with magic. She's the *Caveadear.*"

"Perhaps it's only awakening in you now," she says. Her head tilts. "A musician friend of mine used to say that everyone has a note they hum at. Perhaps your magic is hearing others'."

"No." I stand up. "I was very upset. I must have imagined it. Thank you for your time, Demetra. And for your secrecy."

She seems bemused. "Of course, my lady. But if you—"

"I don't think my ministers could survive a sorcerer ruling the country." I smile at her, though I'm thinking how rapidly I could be deposed. "Please don't give it a second thought. Good night, Demetra."

But as I leave—warmer now, and oddly comforted—I find myself thinking of the women in those villages outside Laon. Women who had no magic before, at least to most eyes. Women whose magic is awakening, who never dreamed themselves sorcerers. I sent Juleane Brazeur to find them days ago now, and she never reported back to me on her activity there. I will have to ask her again, even though she's angry with me. I wonder if they are the only ones whose magic has begun to awaken. If, perhaps, there are more of us than we can even guess, now that Elanna has woken the land. If the very fabric of the Ereni and Caerisian people is changing in our altered land.

I wonder.

THAT NIGHT AS I lie in bed, I prop myself up on pillows and put my hands on my stomach, feeling for the child silent within me. I hum first, using the melody I pick up, instinctively, from the baby. A spreading yellow song, tentative as a tree beginning to blossom in spring. Quietly, I begin to sing.

My body softens. I sense the breadth of my blood and bone, the weight of my lungs, the pattern of my heartbeat. And within my body, tucked into the gentle darkness of my womb, I sense the outline of the baby. The curl of its tucked-up legs, the bubble forming at its lips. Its delicate fingers.

No, not it. I breathe in, sensing more deeply. The child's song unfolds within me, blossoming with possibility. *Her.*

A giddy smile bursts over my face, throwing me from the reverie. Can my intuition truly be correct—it's a girl?

Every scrap of knowledge inside me whispers, *Yes.*

I hug my arms over my stomach, still smiling, even as worry gathers beneath my breastbone. Who am I, to bring a girlchild into this world? How can I even help her grow? How can I protect her?

All I know is that I will do my best. Every day I will struggle forward.

And if this is magic . . . I hum again, and the note hangs in the air, rippling, its color a delicate green. I have never seen sound before, but it seems *something* in me is changing, even if it isn't magic, because I see it now, in my mind's eye. I lift my hands and see that color clings to them—a faint, vaporous indigo blue. I look down at my body. The color covers me like a mist, from my feet to my shoulders. Only my stomach is different—there, the blue is touched by a soft, glowing yellow-gold. It seems the child has a color of her own.

I don't know if this is sorcery. Surely if it were, I would have discovered it before now. I would have spent my life repressing it, like Elanna, or carefully tending the secret of it, like Jahan. It would not be blossoming out of me now, from nowhere, at the age of twenty-one.

And yet . . .

The land has woken. Even now, deep under the palace, I can sense a powerful hum, the kind that sinks deeply into my bones. I'm almost certain it comes from the Hill of the Imperishable and the stones atop it—or perhaps all the way from the Spring Caves.

I close my eyes. Colors shift behind my lids. White. Blue. Palest gold. The colors have a pulse, a rhythm, and the rhythm contains a song.

I part my lips and let it ripple out, so softly. A lullaby for me and the baby. A song to cradle us both until tomorrow.

CHAPTER THIRTEEN

"Sophy!"

I lift my head from the pillow. Fiona's flinging back the curtains. I slept deeply, and I'm muzzy from dreams. "Did I oversleep?" I mumble.

"You need to get up. Now. The guards . . ." Her voice shakes, and I sit up at the warning sound of it, wincing as cold air invades my bed. "There's been an incident with the sorcerers."

"An incident?" I repeat.

"You need to go, quickly. Someone . . ." She bites her lip. "I think someone might be dead."

Dead? I push myself out of the bed, reaching for the robe she hands me, shoving my feet into slippers. Now she's said it, I *hear* something, a black cacophony like music on the edge of my hearing. I hurry into the sitting room and out the door, my hair falling loose and heavy down my back.

Rhia meets me in the corridor, her face sharp with worry. "There you are! Come on."

She charges down the hall, and I hurry to catch up, my robe flapping behind me. "What's happened?"

"One of the sorcerers tried to leave the east wing around three o'clock this morning. He wanted to enter the palace. The guards were alarmed. They thought he was going to attack someone." She rolls her eyes, but hisses a breath through her teeth as she jostles her broken arm.

We're practically running now, down the back stairs to the east wing. At the bottom landing, I jerk to a stop. The hallway ahead of me, which was perfectly intact last night, appears to have split in two. A massive black scar shears the length of the eastern wall, and stones have crashed inward, leaving a pile of rubble on the floor.

In the rubble lies the charred remains of a corpse. My stomach lurches in revulsion, but I force myself to look long enough to identify the decorative helmet that's fallen from what's left of his head.

Beyond the corpse and the wreckage, the palace guards make a seething knot before the east wing doors. A harsh silver pulse emanates from them—one of the most violent sounds I have felt. They're . . . kicking something on the floor. Beating it with the blunt sides of their sabers.

No—*someone.*

"Stop!" I shout. *"Stop!"*

Rhia has a better battle cry. *"Stand down in the queen's name!"*

On the other side of the mess of men, I see Captain Grenou flanking the door. He hasn't been beating the person up—he's been watching. Cold crawls down the back of my neck.

He's registered our arrival. "Enough!" he bellows at his guards.

But to my horror, only two of them seem to hear. The rest, at least a dozen men, continue to pummel the figure on the floor.

"Stop this now!" I shout. My hands are shaking, but I point a finger at Grenou and he finally steps forward, wrenching one man off the victim. Rhia lunges forward to wrestle more of them back, one-armed, and more of my mountain women appear, pulling the men from the body. I grind my teeth, waiting. Grenou's gaze keeps flickering to me.

"Let us at him!" one of the men shouts.

Rhia actually shakes him. "Your queen is here!"

The men sober at that. They step back at last, making an uncomfortable semicircle around the body lying on the floor. Its back is to me, and it wears black. I can't tell if it's a man or a woman, alive or dead.

I snap my fingers to the mountain women still flanking me. "Send for Demetra. Hurry!"

One runs off, and I turn back to the men.

"What," I say quietly, "is the meaning of this?"

"He killed Thierry!" one of the guards cries out. The others have stopped moving, but the violent rage still quivers off them.

"Silence." Grenou steps forward, still breathing hard from the effort of subduing his men. He gives a short bow. "Your Majesty, the men reported that Ciril Thorley attempted to leave the east wing early this morning. They refused to let him out."

I fold my arms. "On what grounds?"

"He's an evil bastard!" one of the guards exclaims. "He wouldn't go back in. He killed Thierry, Your Majesty!"

I point at the curled figure on the floor. "Is that the sorcerer?"

The men look at each other, and cold crawls up my spine again. Captain Grenou waits, apparently impassive.

"No, Your Majesty," one of them says at last. "Ciril Thorley escaped."

"Then," I say carefully, "who is this?"

"He's another one of those bastards, who tried to get out of there. Came to see if his friend had killed us all."

Bile rises in the back of my throat. I force it down and walk forward. The guards all go to attention. I pause in front of the body and make myself look into the face of each man. Some flinch. Several stare back. Most drop their gazes.

I end with Captain Grenou. He returns my stare, challenging.

"You have a great deal of explaining to do," I say. Suppressing my nausea, I kneel beside the body. The man's face—what I can see of it, anyway—is a mess of blood. His nose is broken, at the very least, but there's so much blood they must have done a good deal more damage than that.

I touch his shoulder. There's a twitch—a humming beneath my fingers. Even without fumbling for a pulse on the man's neck, I know he's not dead. Life, feeble and graying, whispers through him.

Demetra had better get here soon.

I climb back onto my feet. "You're lucky this man is still alive," I say to all of the guards. "We don't live in a kingdom where we beat a man to death because of what his friend has done."

This time, most of them have the grace to look ashamed. A few just look sullen.

"I assume that is Thierry." I gesture to the charred body behind me. "What happened to him?"

Grenou nods to one of his men, who draws in a breath. "The bas . . . the sorcerer struck him down with—with lightning! Your Majesty." Even his attempted bravado can't hide the note of fear souring his voice.

Cold washes through me, again, but I need to show the men I'm not afraid. And I cannot let this spread any further.

"We will gather Thierry's remains," I say as calmly as I can, "and see to his funeral. I am certainly sorry for his loss. That being said, you are all revoked from duty until I have a complete understanding of what has happened here. Rhia, see to it that new guards are put in place, and inform the refugees that I expect an explanation from them, as well. Captain Grenou, you and your men will meet me in the Yellow Salon at once. I will be there as soon as Demetra arrives."

DEMETRA BURSTS FROM the east wing on the heels of the departing guards. Her face is drawn with panic. "Marcos!" she cries out, pushing past us in a bright rush of panic. "Let me see him." She crouches to examine the fellow on the ground, pressing her fingertips to his pulse.

"Will he survive?" I ask quietly.

Her nostrils flare. "They struck his head, didn't they?"

"Yes. I think they did." My lips tighten.

"All he did was go to the door and ask what had happened! We all heard the explosion—we saw Ciril come back—and then we heard shouting." Her face contorts with pure anger. "He wanted to *help*."

We both look down at Marcos, crumpled on his side, blood crusted below his nose.

Quietly, I say, "I am sorry, Demetra, and I'm going to put this right. Tell us what you need."

"I want to transfer him to a bed. I need to examine him properly."

I nod. To the mountain women, I say, "Help Demetra in whatever way she needs."

They immediately surround her, helping her lift the other refugee onto a stretcher. He groans softly, and I feel a stab of hope.

"Make sure Thierry's body is taken away," I add. "I expect he's due a state funeral, though that depends on the testimony I receive."

I stride off, Rhia on my heels. "I'm not leaving you," she informs me, fiercely, when I glance at her.

I manage a small smile. Though I'm angry enough to defy Grenou on my own, I'm still grateful she's come. I need to appear strong.

As ordered, the guards are waiting for me in the Yellow Salon, in neat if sullen ranks. They salute crisply as I arrive. Grenou bows. I march to the front of the chamber, crossing my arms over my dressing gown.

"Explain," I say shortly.

Grenou nods at the guards. "Alain?"

A tall, thin young man steps forward with a bow, sweeping off his helmet to show straight, sand-colored hair. His eyes meet mine—level, serious. The faint humming sound of him is as solid and level as his gaze. "Thierry, Sebastien, and I were on the night duty, Your Majesty. That Ciril Thorley came to the door around three o'clock and tried to leave the palace. We refused him . . ."

"Why?"

"Thierry thought it was suspicious that he wanted to leave at that hour of the night. He was the ranking officer, and he thought Ciril seemed too dangerous to be let out into the city at night."

I drum my fingers on the arm of my chair. "Did you ask him what he wanted in the city?"

Alain hesitates. "He wouldn't tell us, Your Majesty. He grew belligerent."

"And did you grow belligerent in return?"

His silence is answer enough.

I utter a sharp sigh. "How did Thierry die?"

"We—well, he wouldn't go back in. Thierry told him he had to or he'd pay for it. He still wouldn't go back, so we seized him. And he . . ." Alain's voice breaks. "He gave a great shout and a bolt of lightning burst through the hallway. It flew—it went straight into Thierry! Burned him. And fire—fire erupted in the walls! We let go of the sorcerer for a moment and he got away."

"Where did he go?" I ask neutrally.

"Bolted back into the east wing."

Well, I can certainly imagine he'd get as far away from my guards as possible. "We'll find him. So the fire?"

"It took hours to put out." He shakes his head. "We had to summon half the company! Then one of the other damned refugees puts his head through the door and demands to know what's happened to his friend. He accused us of murdering him! When he's the one who killed Thierry! And then *he* demanded to be let out and find you, Your Majesty."

"So you gave him a lesson?" I say.

Alain flushes. He doesn't answer, but his gaze cuts toward Grenou.

"He took Thierry's life!" one of the other guards cries in protest.

"Ciril did," I say to the company at large. "Do you have any evidence that the second man helped him?"

The guards look chastened, or at least some of them do. Alain says in a small voice, "No, Your Majesty. We did not."

I look at Captain Grenou, who stares bullishly back at me. The guards might have been angry and upset and frightened, but I can't imagine them attacking the second refugee without encourage-ment. "When did you arrive at the scene, Captain?"

"Around four o'clock, to help put out the fire."

"And what did you do when the door opened a second time, and the second refugee came out to find what had happened to Ciril?"

He stiffens. "I ordered him seized as a co-conspirator."

"Did you also order him beaten to death?"

His gaze moves past me. "Certainly not, Your Majesty. He did not die."

"Yet," I note. "Let me ask this again. Did you order the men to beat him, or did you stand by while they did it?"

He says nothing.

"Captain Grenou!" I'm aware, like the soft hum of music build-ing, of the guards' anger, their confusion, pulsing from Grenou to me. If I push Grenou too hard, I risk turning all of them against me. Yet I'm not about to let them think this behavior is acceptable—and I know I saw guilt on their faces. These men did not attack the sorcerer out of malice. Grenou did. "You will answer."

"I would like to speak with you privately," he says.

My hackles rise. "First you will tell me the truth in front of your men!"

Grenou clenches his jaw.

But Alain steps forward again, squaring his shoulders. Anger beats off him now in heavy, drumlike waves. "The captain encour-aged us, Your Majesty." When Grenou whips toward him, he gives the captain a defiant stare.

"Is this true?" I ask the assembled guards.

No one else answers. But most of them glance at Grenou, though they seem too afraid to confirm Alain's story.

"Very well," I say. "Captain, you will remain here. The rest of you are dismissed, for the time being. I will be asking the refugees for their version of events. And we will give Thierry a state funeral."

The guards file out. I am alone with Captain Grenou, and Rhia at my side.

"The men were angry, madam," he bursts out. "They demanded to punish the refugee."

I lift an eyebrow. "And you were unable to restrain them?"

"I . . ." His face has reddened. Now he points at me. "Those refugees are a blight on our society! We don't know what's become of Ciril Thorley! If he had attacked you, you would not be interrogating me this way!"

"Attacked *me*?" I echo. "Ciril was nowhere near my chambers. Captain Grenou, I think you forget that I employ Ciril Thorley. I also employ you. Remember that. You are dismissed until I have a satisfactory version of these events. Alain will function as captain in your stead."

He doesn't move. If anything, he seems stunned. "Alain? But he's only—"

"Yes," I say firmly, "Alain. He seems to have a more level head than you do."

He just stares.

"That will be all," I say.

Now he jabs a shaking finger at me. "You should be careful, Your Majesty!"

"Is that a threat?"

"Careful," he collects himself, somewhat, "of the refugees, I mean. You don't know the danger in your own palace."

I stare at him. I am tired of this man and his arrogance. So I simply say, my voice short, "You are dismissed, Captain Grenou."

His lips pouch, and he glares at Rhia. But he goes. I release a breath, trying to loosen the tightness in my shoulders.

Rhia scowls after Grenou. "Too bad you can't dismiss the smarmy ass entirely," she mutters.

I sigh. "Yes, we would hate to distress Lord Devalle." It gives him more power than he ought to have, curse him.

At least I no longer have to force Grenou to cooperate. Now it's time to try to hunt down a renegade sorcerer.

*

CIRIL THORLEY HAS apparently vanished. The refugees report that he came back into the east wing and left through another exit. No one knows where he's gone, or why.

"We can't let the word out," Alistar says. He's arrived, tired and unwilling to look at me, but still worried. "After the riot yesterday—there would be chaos in the city streets."

There's a rap at the door; Rhia comes in. We've retreated to my study to talk. "We didn't find anything in Ciril's room."

I curse softly. We're going to have to hunt him down somehow, or there will be another riot. If he hadn't decided to storm off to the gods know where, I might be able to contain this situation fairly easily. But without him here to reprimand, it will appear I'm punishing Captain Grenou and not the refugee who murdered a palace guard.

I look at them both, thinking of how much Ciril unnerved me. "We need to find him, and fast."

"You have some way to capture a sorcerer?"

"No," I admit. That scares me more than anything.

I've never been frightened of a sorcerer before, I realize. They've always been on our side—we've always been fighting for them. But I don't know what Ciril wants, or what he's capable of. He's willing to fight against his own people—but then, in some ways, we all have done the same.

And it infuriates me that he's making the rest of the refugees look bad by extension.

There's a rattle in the corridor. I get to my feet just as Lord Devalle marches in, the Butcher and Philippe close behind.

"What's this?" Devalle is demanding. "A royal guard is dead, and you've demoted Captain Grenou? What are you thinking?"

"Gentlemen." I nod at them, even though I want to order them out at the same time. "I'm still trying to get to the bottom of what happened."

"One of these sorcerers murdered an Ereni guard," Lord Devalle says flatly. "That is what happened."

"And our Ereni murdered a sorcerer on Rambaud's lands," I

snap. "Has there been justice for that death? No. I have requested that anyone who knows what may have happened come forward." I look from Devalle to Philippe. "No one has."

Philippe grimaces, but Lord Devalle waves this away. "That was a case of local justice. Who knows—maybe that sorcerer tried to murder them, just as this one has!"

"If he could have killed one of them, I doubt he'd have allowed himself to be killed *by* them," I say darkly.

Devalle runs right over this. "Your Majesty, we need to make clear that nothing like this will ever happen again. You need to make an example of this sorcerer. Let justice be done." He pauses. "You need to put Grenou back in his captaincy."

"Grenou's demotion is temporary," I retort, "but it is the punishment he deserves. He allowed and encouraged his men to beat another man almost to death! An innocent!"

Devalle barely controls his contempt. "Most likely he feared that man would attack them the way Ciril did."

"Demetra said that Marcos opened the door to find out if they needed help." I shake my head. "I will *not* tolerate such behavior in my own household, much less in the rest of my kingdom. I witnessed what happened. My guards were beating that man because they could. Because *Grenou* told them to. It was nauseating."

Devalle opens his mouth. "Your Caerisians would do the same thing if—"

"It was *unacceptable*," I interrupt. "If I witnessed a Caerisian behaving in this manner, it would also be unacceptable. I will not permit such behavior from anyone in my palace or in my country. Do I make myself clear?"

"You do, my lady," he says, a glint in his eyes, "but Captain Grenou has many friends. They might find his demotion equally *unacceptable*."

We stare each other down. Somewhere, I hear a clock ticking.

"You may need Captain Grenou," Devalle says at last. "Especially if you cannot find that sorcerer quickly. Once the people hear what has happened, there will be protests in the streets. Fear is already running high. Your refugees . . ."

He's threatening me—and I can only suppose it must be through a connection he has with Rambaud. I can't afford another riot, and I certainly can't risk people harming the refugees in any way.

Ruling, Ruadan always said, is about compromise. I wish he hadn't been quite so prescient.

"Captain Grenou will return to duty as usual at five o'clock this evening," I say coldly. "It will give him a few hours to think over what he could have done better."

Lord Devalle bows. "A wise choice, Your Majesty."

With a last glance at Philippe, he leaves.

Philippe doesn't acknowledge the departure, though the tension in his shoulders eases a fraction. He's watching me, a line between his brows. "They didn't harm you during the altercation, did they?"

"No, not at all." It dawns on me that I'm still wearing my dressing gown, and my hair is falling over my shoulders in a fury of snarls. At least the dressing gown is heavy, unbelted, its thick quilted fabric loose enough to cover my growing figure. I cross my arms over my breasts. "Thank you for your concern, but I am perfectly fine."

The Butcher steps forward, speaking for the first time. "And Ciril? You have put him under guard, I assume?"

I glance at Philippe. He's still frowning. I suppose this is another opportunity to test his trustworthiness, though I would rather tell the Butcher in confidence.

"He's gone," I say baldly.

The Butcher actually pales, and Philippe stares at me. "Gone?"

"He seems to have stormed back through the east wing and left. No one knows where." I look at the Butcher. "I intended to ask you if you had given him any instructions about locations, or planned to meet with him again."

"No." I've never seen the Butcher look shaken before, but he does now. "I did not. As far as I know, there's no possible reason for him to be out in the city."

I study Lord Gilbert for a moment. Ciril's disappearance has frightened the man who spent most of his life pretending he felt less than nothing. I wonder whether it is Ciril himself—or whether, when it comes down to it, magic makes even the Butcher of Novarre uneasy.

The Butcher clears his throat. "You have a plan for finding him, I assume?"

I'm glad he credits me with enough intelligence to already be working on this. "Rhia found nothing in his room. We'll have to track him."

He nods thoughtfully. "If Lady Rhia could bring me something with his scent on it, we could use dogs. We had best hurry, though. Time is already running out."

"I'll send for some of his clothes," Rhia says.

"We'll find him," Alistar promises me, though he still hasn't actually looked me in the face, and I flinch a little at his curt tone. He's already following Rhia out.

I'm alone with the Butcher and Philippe. Quietly, the Butcher says, "I don't wish to trouble Your Majesty further, but I've received reports this morning from my informants in Roquelle and Marsan. After the riot yesterday here in Laon, protests flared up in both towns. No one was harmed, but . . ." He glances at Philippe. "People were heard shouting catchphrases. Demanding the queen be unseated from her throne. Denouncing sorcery as a great wickedness. Catchphrases," he says, "coined by Aristide Rambaud."

There's a cold twinge between my shoulder blades. The Butcher warned me about this just yesterday, but I didn't expect the protests to spread so quickly. But like him, I wait for Philippe to speak.

"That is a great shame," Philippe says at last. The sound of him is taut and blue, pulsing so rapidly I feel it as a discomfort against my own skin. "The people should know Queen Sophy only has their best interests at heart."

"Mmm," the Butcher says.

I intervene before this can turn into an interrogation. "What can be done, Lord Gilbert?"

"Nothing at the moment," he replies, "except finding Ciril, before his disappearance adds fuel to the flames."

I nod, though the idea of continuing protests against me makes my skin crawl.

The Butcher's eyes flicker from me to Philippe. "I'll leave you," he says, significantly, "to fetch the dogs and their masters."

He strides off, and I swallow down a burning embarrassment. I don't have time to discuss marriage with Philippe, not now. And not after what happened with Alistar yesterday.

"I know Captain Grenou may not be entirely agreeable," Philippe says abruptly. "But you're wise not to antagonize Devalle—or the captain—further."

I look at Philippe. Worry still pinches his brow, though the hum of his tension has eased now that the Butcher is gone. It's obvious he knows something I don't, yet I also have the sense that he's told me as much as he's willing to—or as much as he safely can.

There is, however, another matter he might be able to help me with. "I need to know about Aristide Rambaud," I say. "If he's inciting people to the streets, calling for me to be deposed, I have to take a stand against him. But it's like fighting a shadow. I've never met him. I don't know how to feint back."

Philippe's gaze darts away, and I lean closer, gripping his arm. "I need your help, Philippe. You can't play me for a fool—I know you know him." I pause. "And I wager you also know where to find him."

His mouth tucks down. For a long moment, he simply stands, thinking. The sound of him is eluding me now, beneath my own urgency. I don't release him. His forearm is warm under my fingers, slighter than Alistar's. At last he says, "I'll see what I can do."

TEOFILA FINDS ME soon after, as I'm walking back into the palace from the courtyard. "Any word on Ciril?"

I shake my head. Alistar departed with Rhia, some of his Hounds, and a number of actual dogs. I'm growing increasingly agitated, wondering what's come of them; I feel almost naked without them here. If Ciril was willing to kill a guard . . . It galls me that I must simply sit here waiting and wondering and worrying.

We arrive at my chambers and Fiona emerges. She curtsies, which she ordinarily never does. I stand up straight. "Pardon me, Your Majesty," she says, "but two young women are requesting an audience with yourself."

I exchange a mystified glance with Teofila; we both go into the sitting room. "Please send them in."

Fiona steps aside, and two young women enter the sitting room. I recognize them as, respectively, a chambermaid and the char-woman who lights the fires in my rooms every morning. The char-woman is twisting her fingers nervously in her skirt, her eyes a little too large; I can't imagine why, since I have never been anything but polite to her. I even know the name of her pet cat, and a full list of its digestive ailments.

The chambermaid, however, curtsies and meets my eyes with determination.

"Hello, Estelle," I greet her. "Dorothée."

The charwoman, Dorothée, bobs, as if she's startled to be called by name.

"What can I do for you?" I ask. Fiona is watching the two like a hawk.

"There's been talk belowstairs, Your Majesty," Estelle says, with a defiant edge to her voice. "We came to ask if it's really true, if the sorcerer who killed Thierry is on the run."

My heartbeat swoops into my ears. I should have expected this; of course the servants are talking.

"We will find him," I say with as much confidence as I can. "You and the palace staff are quite safe."

Estelle bobs a curtsy, and Dorothée belatedly follows suit. "Thank you, milady, but my parents live outside the city. Many of us have family in Laon and out in the country. Should we send word to them to watch out?"

I stare. All the gods, this news is going to spread like wildfire, if it hasn't already. If these maids are frightened enough to seek an audience, the entire palace must be in a lather.

"Rhia Knoll and Alistar Connell are pursuing Ciril Thorley even now, and they *will* find him," I say firmly. "Your families have no cause to fear. He has no reason to harm anyone."

Of course, he had no reason to kill a palace guard, either, but he did. And, as I suspected, my reassurance does not have much impact on the fear tightening the girls' faces.

"Please, Your Majesty," Dorothée begins, rather breathlessly, "what about the other sorcerers? Will you send them out of the palace now?"

I feel myself rooting into place. I should have known this is what they'd want, and fear.

"The other sorcerers pose no threat to any of us," I tell them, more sternly than I meant to; Dorothée winces. "They are only seeking refuge for themselves and their families, just as any of us would if our lives were threatened. Ciril acted alone. No one else would risk their current safety by harming any of us. You must understand that."

But judging by the looks on their faces, I'm not sure that they do.

"We—the whole palace staff—we would all feel better if they weren't here," Estelle says boldly. "We don't want to cast them out of Eren, Your Majesty. We're not heartless. We've all seen the little children and how scared they must be. But do they have to live in the palace? Can't we send them into the country, so the rest of us can sleep at night?"

I look between the two of them, Dorothée trembling with nerves and Estelle gazing defiantly into my face. They're protecting themselves, their friends, their families, and unlike Grenou, there's no hate in their eyes. Only fear. They don't understand the sorcerers, and now Ciril has given them no reason at all to trust them. Despite my frustration, I can understand why they're afraid.

"Perhaps it would comfort you to meet the refugees," I say. "Talk to them. I can arrange for you all to work together. You'll discover they're people just like the rest of us."

The girls exchange a glance. Then Dorothée's chin firms. "If you don't send them away, lady, then we're resigning. All of us."

My mouth drops open. They're threatening me? "*All* of you? The entire palace staff?"

Dorothée nods, and Estelle says, "Except me. I'm not afraid of magic or foreigners. That's why they sent me up here."

I close my mouth. If I let my staff go, I'm doing right by the refugees. But then their fear will spread through Laon—out into all of Eren. I can't afford to let my people think I'm choosing the refugees over them, or that their lives are in danger. I can't let them think I don't value their fears or their personal safety.

"I'll see what I can do," I say at last, though it feels like capitulation.

"Thank you, my lady!" Dorothée exclaims, obviously relieved.

Estelle curtsies with a bright little look. She knows they succeeded in unsettling me. With a swish of her skirts, she follows Dorothée out.

I press my hands to my cheeks. I can't stop thinking of Demetra. Her children. The people who crossed to Eren overland from Tinan, who left behind almost everything but their lives. I pledged to help them, and there *must* be a way. If public sentiment is running this high, perhaps they're safer out of the city, anyway. It would be far worse if something happened to them . . .

In time, I can heal this. Perhaps those who stay can help.

"Fiona," I say roughly, "send for the Butcher. I need him to accompany me to the east wing."

CHAPTER FOURTEEN

My gut rebels at what I'm about to do, but nevertheless I walk the long hallways back to the east wing. The Butcher, at my request, follows me. I can't make myself even look at him. Nor can I shake the feeling that I am about to trap the refugees in a situation all of us will regret. And I'm not sure it will be enough to comfort the palace staff, or the people of Laon.

But I don't see what other choice I have.

I find Demetra sitting by Marcos, packing his bruises with poultices of herbs. He's sleeping, breathing fluttering breaths.

"He'll live," Demetra says in answer to my unspoken question, a flutter of angry green sound hanging on her words. "No thanks to your brutes of guards."

I hesitantly sink onto a stool beside the bed. She gives me a look but doesn't order me off. Quietly, I say, "Where do you think Ciril has gone? Lord Gilbert has said he didn't give either of you instructions."

Demetra frowns and glances at the Butcher, who lingers beside the door like a particularly malevolent spaniel. "No," she says shortly.

I smother a frustrated sigh. I don't blame Demetra for being angry, but it simply makes all this harder. "You said you were awake when Ciril tried to leave. Some of you witnessed what happened with the guards."

She nods. "The lightning strike woke most of us, as I said. I thought we were being attacked. It shook the entire building. I ordered the children to stay in the room and came running out, along with a handful of others. We all saw the fire raging in the hall and were going to offer help, but then Ciril stormed back through. And the soldiers started screaming at us. We bolted the doors to keep them and the fire out."

"You must have waited a long time," I remark, "before Marcos went to see what had happened."

"As I told you, we heard them shouting. Fighting the fire." She sits back from the patient and looks at me. "Finally it quieted, but we didn't know what had happened. We were afraid for our lives. Marcos said we should try to speak with you. But when he went out . . ."

"To see if they needed help," I prompt.

"Yes. He made us close the doors behind him. We could hear them out there, shouting insults at him. Telling him to go back where he'd come from. Screaming all the horrible things they would do to his family, and the rest of us."

I reach forward and grip her hand. She looks for a moment as if she'll push me away, but then her fingers squeeze mine tightly. "I'm sorry," I manage, "I'm so terribly sorry you had to witness that."

"I thought they were going to kill him," she says flatly. "We all did."

I grimace. "Please tell the other refugees that I am doing my best to guarantee your safety. And I'm terribly sorry for my people's appalling treatment of Marcos. It's . . . barbaric." I fumble for the right words, but they don't seem like enough. I don't know how the refugees will ever trust any Ereni again.

Demetra seems to share my thoughts. She just presses her lips together.

"And . . ." I hesitate. "Ciril didn't have any friends among you? Anyone who might know where he's gone?"

"He kept very much to himself. Only the children like him, because he tells them stories." She corrects herself: "*Told* them."

I sigh. The Butcher looks at me, obviously waiting. I swallow. It's time.

"Demetra," I begin, and she looks up sharply, reading my tone. "There have been complaints from the palace staff already. I am— I'm concerned for your safety, and that of the other refugees, if you remain here."

She stares at me. Her breathing has quickened, but she takes a long moment before she says, "What do you mean?"

She isn't going to make this easy on me, but then I can't blame her. I lean forward, bracing my elbows on my knees. I've decided to be forthright—especially since she is one of only three people who know my secret. "I'm afraid I don't have the power to protect you. We've already suffered through one riot here in Laon. More have been happening in the countryside. Once word of Ciril's actions gets out—not to mention the fact that he's disappeared— there's one obvious target. You."

"I see," Demetra says. Her tone is cold, and I see in her eyes the weight of my secret. The power she could wield against me, if she chose. The revenge she could take.

"I will do everything I can to help you." My voice cracks a little. "Though I can only do so if I am free to act."

Her eyes widen slightly as she takes in my meaning. She hesitates, thinking, and the pulse speeds up in my throat. Behind me, the Butcher is surely wondering why Demetra is deliberating, but he keeps silent.

At last, she gives a tiny shake of her head, and I realize she's angry—both with herself and with me. "I took an oath," she whispers. "Much though I sometimes regret it. Some matters are confidential."

I breathe out, unable to hide my rush of relief. Quickly, aware of the Butcher's gaze on my back, I say, "If you are still willing to fight for us, on the front or even here in Laon, I think I can keep you here. And if anyone else is willing to use their sorcery to aid us . . ."

Demetra makes a soft, derisive noise.

I grimace. "I didn't think so. If you, or anyone else, *is* willing to stay, however, perhaps you can do more than help us fight. Perhaps you will be able to help us change how sorcery is perceived in Eren."

Her shoulders hitch up; she isn't interested in glory. "What happens to the rest of us? Are we being sent from your country, then?"

"No, not at all!" I exclaim. I force myself to meet her gaze, though guilt is constricting my chest. This woman has shown unspeakable courage and determination—as well as kindness—and look at what I am doing in return. I want to tell her I have no choice. That I don't know what else to do. There seems no better way to protect both her people and mine.

Yet the Butcher is watching. And though I tell myself I don't care what he thinks, I don't want to shoulder his derision at my womanish sentiment. So I simply say, "They will be sent to safety in the north, in Barrody. They will be far safer there than here in the capital."

Her jaw tightens, the angry green hum vibrating from her once more, and I think of her children. They're so young. I can't force her to abandon them. My stomach is knotting now, but there's a certain approval in the Butcher's gaze. I want to turn on him. He knows I'm forcing Demetra's hand, and it's wrong. He has daughters of his own, but does he feel any sympathy? I don't think so.

"I see." Her glance at the Butcher tells me that she does, perhaps better than I'd wish. She speaks to me. "Of course I want my children, and my friends, to be safe. But we were supposed to be safe here. We were supposed to be protected by Eren. Will Caeris be any different?"

I meet her eyes. "The people of Caeris have always been better friends to sorcerers than the Ereni. But . . ." I swallow. "These are difficult times. We will do everything we can to protect them."

She looks away, blinking fast. "If I remain here," she begins, "if I—I *help* you . . ."

"Our people will take care of your children."

"So will my friends among the other refugees." Her lips press together, but she seems to come to a decision. "Very well."

"Thank you." Some of the tension eases in my neck. "Let us know if anyone else will remain. We'll have the others sent to Barrody immediately, by our fastest coaches, with a guard to keep them safe."

Demetra gives the Butcher a glinting, dangerous look but says, "I understand."

As we turn to go, she calls out, "You might consider how to use your own magic, Your Majesty. Perhaps you're not as helpless as you believe yourself."

I can feel the Butcher's gaze burning the back of my neck. I leave without answering.

Of course, he follows me. "Magic, Your Majesty?" he says, with a touch of irony. "Might you be able to save us with a miracle, like the *Caveadear*? Strange that we have not heard of your abilities before."

"It's nothing," I say flatly. "Just a fancy of Demetra's. She sees sorcery everywhere."

But even as we walk back to the main palace, I sense the music everywhere, the shifting, brilliant colors of it unspooling from every room. Pulsing with life, a rhythm I could manipulate, if only I knew how.

JULEANE BRAZEUR FINDS me in the east wing courtyard, where I've gone to oversee the refugees packing up into coaches. I flinch instinctively at the sight of my minister's close-cropped hair and grim mouth, though I try to hide it. We haven't spoken since she condemned me following the news of Elanna's death.

"You sent for me, Your Majesty?" she says, solid and forbidding in her short, fitted navy-blue coat and crisp skirt.

The air lies brittle between us. I can almost taste her continued disapproval. "In light of the growing unrest," I begin, unable to hide the tartness in my tone, "I wondered if you had looked into the task I set for you. The women in the villages outside Laon who began developing magic—"

"I remember," she says brusquely. "I went out to Tristere and Fontaine myself and spoke to the women and their families. They refused to leave their homes. Nothing could be done."

I look at her. She stares back at me, unrelenting. "A sorcerer murdered a man this morning," I say. "Word is already spreading. Those women are going to be in great danger."

"What would you have done with them? Would you send them to Barrody with the refugees?" A dark edge of contempt underlies her tone. "Not everyone can simply be delivered to Caeris for safe-keeping."

"But they need to be kept safe!" I flare. "If it means sending them to Caeris, then yes, I would do that."

"Doing so would break up their families."

I grasp for the shards of my temper. "Their families are already broken. Their *lives* are at risk—"

She holds up her hand. "Very well. I will send someone to speak with them. But if they refuse to leave their homes, what would you have me do? Forcibly evict them?"

"Of course not," I say beneath the judgment in her eyes, though every instinct in my heart is saying *yes*. "They should at least be given the choice, though."

"I'll see to it." She pauses. "Was there anything else?"

I don't know what she's waiting for—an apology, an admission of my failure to keep Elanna alive, to protect the refugees? I wish I could apologize to her. But I am clinging to control with all my might, and my mind is too exhausted to find a way to forge a truce between us. So I simply say, "No, thank you."

She goes, taking the dark-yellow hum of her disdain with her, and I remain where I am somewhat longer, watching the refugees carry their few belongings from the east wing. Some of the children exclaim with excitement—"We're going to live in *another* castle?"—but the others stare at the coaches with tired, wary eyes.

They've had too many homes in the last months, and I know so well how what can seem like a great adventure at first grows too long, too tiresome, always running, always being pursued. I vow to myself that this is the last time these children will be forced to move. If they do so again, it will be by choice.

Demetra comes to join me, and together we wave the refugees off, unspeaking. No one else has volunteered to stay and fight except her—and I have the feeling she's only remaining here on principle.

Despite the refugees' swift departure, by evening two kitchen staff and one footman have resigned, citing the missing Ciril as a threat they cannot endure. The maids are whispering that a boy from the city went up on the Hill of the Imperishable and the magic in the stones possessed him, turning his eyes silver and making him hear whispers that aren't there. So far I haven't seen evidence of the boy himself, and I'm unsure whether to believe the whispers.

But I do believe the other news, brought by the Butcher, that there have been riots across the south of Eren today, mimicking the one in the square yesterday. It puts my teeth on edge, yet what on earth am I supposed to do about it? If this Rambaud character is using El's death to foment unrest, it's not as if I can bring her back from the dead to put everyone at ease.

I pace the front balcony. Rhia, Alistar, and the others haven't returned. There's no telling where Ciril has gone.

"Your Majesty." Charlot has appeared behind me, polite and almost soundless. I startle. He hands me a note. "This just arrived for you. The mayor of Montclair invites you to make an appearance in her town square. Her people are well disposed toward you, and she believes it may help mitigate the recent protests."

I rather wish Charlot would stop reading my mail. I take the note. It says essentially what he recapitulated, although more enthusiastically. *The people of Montclair would love the opportunity to honor the queen! We would like to host a ceremony granting her the keys to the town.*

"Montclair . . ." I say.

"It's just north of Laon, on the eastern side of the Sasralie," Charlot says deferentially. He's still quite convinced that my Ereni geography must be abysmal, since I'm from Caeris. I'm not sure he even believes I know my cardinal directions. "Two hours out of the city, at most."

I nod slowly. "It's a hill town, isn't it?" Philippe, Rhia, and I passed it on our way to Laon. Philippe said something about Rambaud being associated with someone there—was it the mayor herself? How very curious, then, that she has suddenly decided she wants to meet me, and in Montclair. I'm only a few miles away; she could have come to the palace anytime. I start to say, "Tell her—"

Sophy.

I stop dead. It's a whisper in my head. Someone else's voice, speaking into my mind.

Sophy.

"I'm sorry, Charlot," I babble, thrusting the note into my pocket. "I'll consider this—we'll send a reply to the mayor later. I must go—I've just remembered . . ."

Sophy.

Charlot is staring—politely, of course. I grimace a smile at him, then fling myself through the doorway, moving through the halls almost at a run. My mountain women pant after me. "Your Majesty—"

"It's fine." I almost go into my chambers, but then veer straight. My study is probably the safest place, with only one entrance. I throw open the door myself.

Sophy.

I swing back to the guards—Kenna and Moyra. "Keep anyone else out of here for at least a few minutes."

Sophy.

I slam the door shut and fetch up before the mirror beside the bookshelves. The reflection is not mine. I gasp, even though I'd hoped. A man is squinting into the mirror. The rough beginnings of a beard cover his jaw, and his dark hair has grown even more unruly. The collar of his shirt hangs open; he looks as though he's been in a fight.

"Jahan?" I say, my eyes stinging.

His gaze flickers away from me, into the purple twilight surrounding him. He's outside on a high, dusky hill. "You bastard!" I cry out, pounding a fist against the wall. "I called and called for you. What's happened? Where *are* you? Where—"

Just a minute, he interrupts, with the flash of a smile. *There's someone who needs to talk to you more.*

The reflection in the mirror jogs, capturing only a blur of light, and my heartbeat thuds into my ears. I'm choking on hope.

Then the image settles, and I actually scream aloud. It's her. Elanna, with her tumbled chestnut-brown curls and her freckles and that rueful twist to her mouth.

Alive.

"El," I'm saying, "El, I thought—"

She breaks in. Tears are silvering her eyes. *Is Rhia—is she—?*

She must think Rhia is dead—that she died on the Ard. "She broke her arm," I assure El. "She was madder than a hornet. We practically had to tie her down to keep her from going after you. She called me a tyrant!"

Sure enough, that makes El grin, even though her tears still seem ready to fall. I'm crying myself, sharp cold tears that taste almost sweet in my mouth. *She* would *say that,* El says.

"What happened?" I demand. "The emperor sent me this horrible, threatening letter—and then they were giving out that you were dead . . ."

Yet she is very much alive, with color in her cheeks. All the gods, I can't wait to tell Teofila.

I was rescued. El's gaze flickers toward Jahan, presumably. *Not everything is as it seems here. But tell me first what's going on at home. Have the Tinani . . . ?*

I shake my head. "They quieted down for a while, after you flooded them out on the border." I hesitate. I don't want to burden her with further guilt—there is already something haunted in her gaze—but she needs to know the truth. "But people got word that you were dead, El. There have been protests all across Eren. There's this horrible man—Aristide Rambaud, the Duke of Essez—who says that sorcery is evil and vile, and that I must be pushed off the throne. He's allied with the Tinani. It's . . . it's ugly."

Then I need to come home, El says immediately. But before the tension in my chest can unclench, she begins to cry. *Except—oh, all the gods, Sophy—they took my sorcery from me. The witch hunters—they stole it.*

My ears are ringing, even though I only hear her words in my head. My horror must be written all over my face. To have El alive, but stripped of her magic—it's beyond what I can comprehend.

At last, I find words. "It's enough for me—for all of us—to know that you're alive. You're still our *Caveadear.* This is still your home." Yet without sorcery, how can she even help us? She must be desperate to return home, and afraid at the same time. I don't know how she'd even get out of Ida, and if her magic has been somehow destroyed, there's no point in her risking her life. Firmly, I put aside the fears I want to tell her about—the Tinani, and the refugees, and the protests—and I say, "If you and Jahan can work against the emperor from the inside, I can hold out here a little longer."

Elanna throws a glance at Jahan. It's stark with worry.

His voice comes through the mirror, though I can't see his face. *We'll do what we can here. And then I promise I'll send El back to you.*

I breathe out. I need to tell Teofila at once. "Thank you, Jahan."

Jahan destroyed the emperor's fleet, El says. *The one he was planning to send to Eren. There's hope, Sophy.*

I feel my eyes widen. "He did? Did the emperor—"

A sudden rap at the study door interrupts me. "Your Majesty?" It's Philippe's voice.

"I have to go now," I whisper to the mirror quickly. "I'm sorry.

Summon me again, please, as soon as you can. It's so wonderful to see you both. I—I'd begun to think I might not again."

I'll be back as soon as I can, El says fiercely. *I promise.*

"My lady?" It's Kenna on the other side of the door.

I start to move from the mirror, though not before I hear Jahan add, *Take care, Sophy. Give Alistar our regards!*

Guilt starts through me. "Yes, yes," I say quickly, grimacing a smile at El, and turn away from the mirror.

I'VE HARDLY FINISHED speaking when Philippe swings through the door. The guardswomen follow him, and he gives them an irritated look. "We need to talk privately."

I feel my eyebrows rising; Philippe is more sharp-edged than I've ever seen him. Interesting. I gesture the guards to leave. They go, both still eyeing Philippe warily.

He's pacing stiff-legged around the study. "You said you want to know more about him," he says abruptly, and when I just blink, he adds, "Rambaud. He's back in Laon. There's an event. If you want to know what he's really like, you should just come and see him."

I'm staring. Philippe is impassioned—angry—as I've never seen him before. It's interesting, but also a little alarming. And if Rambaud is back in Laon . . . that's not a good sign for me, I suspect.

"Surely if I attend an event, I'll be recognized," I point out.

"No." His lips press together. "We wear masks. And . . ." His gaze flickers over me. "You'll be with me. They'll assume . . ."

"What will they assume?" I feel a stab of amusement, mixed with annoyance. "That I'm your paramour?"

His guilty look tells me the answer.

I fold my arms. "You're full of surprises, Philippe Manceau."

Now he looks confused, probably because I didn't take offense, nor entirely accept his offer. With a little shake of his head, he holds out two objects—a green velvet cloak, and a mask. It's black, simple, with two openings for eyes. The least intriguing mask I have seen.

I take it, studying Philippe. I told the Butcher I would marry an Ereni lord. I suppose if I'm going to, I should test his mettle. It could be a trap, of course. Yet surely Philippe doesn't think I'm quite this much of a fool.

"Why?" I ask all the same. "Why take me there?"

"Because otherwise you're fighting shadows, as you said yourself. You should see what you're up against." He pauses. "And I saw him in the crowd at yesterday's riot."

I startle.

"It seems only fair that you have the same opportunity to observe him," Philippe says.

"And your mother?" I ask.

"Still in Tinan." His mouth twists. "For the time being, anyway."

This is, I suspect, a small mercy. "How will we get there?"

He gestures at the bookshelves. "There's a passage hidden behind one of these."

I survey the innocent ranks of books with a mental curse. I should have known there's another entrance to this room! Laon's palace has more hidden passages than a rabbit's warren.

"If you're willing to go without your guards," he adds.

"Mmm."

"We'll walk down the streets together." He coughs into his fist. "Everyone will think we're a courting couple."

I lift an eyebrow, and he winces slightly. "Not to presume, Your Majesty."

"Well . . ." I know it's a terrible risk, but I have to admit to curiosity. I want to see this Rambaud person. I'm interested in spending some time alone with Philippe, as well—especially if I have to marry him.

Perhaps most of all, though, I want to know who else is at Rambaud's party. Even if they're wearing masks, I should be able to identify some voices. It should be a great insight into my own court.

I take up the cloak Philippe gave me. It's a worn, dark-green velvet—his own, presumably. It smells surprisingly nice—the way, I realize, he must smell, a comfortable odor of bergamot and leather. For some reason it makes me terribly sad. I busy myself wrapping my hair under the scarf I've been wearing, and put the mask in my pocket.

The mirror reflects my image back at me—the black, fine scarf dulling the brightness of my hair, the too-large velvet cloak swamping my frame. The wide hood settles, heavy, on my shoulders. "I look absurd," I mutter. But I suppose at least I don't appear pregnant.

Philippe smiles faintly. "You look like a rebel."

"I *am* a rebel," I point out. "I'm the rebel queen."

He raises an eyebrow. "No, I think you're just the queen now."

I stare at him for a moment, then find myself laughing. "What do I normally look like, then? Regal, I suppose?"

"No, you look . . . nice."

Nice?

"Friendly?" he suggests, seeing my mouth open in indignation. "Kind. Approachable. You're far less intimidating to most than the *Caveadear,* for instance."

I huff a sigh. It figures that Elanna looked the part of a damned rebel even though she grew up in this massive gilded palace, and I, who spent my childhood at the insurrectionist's knee, look *nice.* Perhaps if I stomped about in a greatcoat and trousers, people would take me more seriously.

"Lady Elanna is rather terrifying," he adds. "Even to those who knew her before."

"Yes," I agree, too eagerly, and have to swallow down a giddy smile. I need this evening to unfold *before* I tell Philippe Manceau the truth about Elanna. As gravely as I can, I add, "Or she was."

His face shutters. "I'm sorry. Let's look for that door. There's supposed to be a lever on this wall."

He walks along the bookshelf to my right, tugging volumes out, seemingly at random. I watch him, growing skeptical—and starting to worry that my guards will notice our absence. "How long will we be gone?"

He shrugs. "An hour or more, I would expect."

The guards aren't going to like that, and perhaps it's unwise of me to be doing this. But now I know El's alive, and I feel like being a little bit reckless. Philippe could be offering me the perfect opportunity to study those who are working against me.

Or perhaps leading me into a trap, though I don't entirely believe it of him.

Either way, if I go with him, I can see these people at work. I'll know who's against me, and what they're planning. I'll know whether I stand a chance of keeping my crown.

I open the door a fraction. The guards look around with a flap of their brilliant cloaks, light-haired Kenna swallowing down a heavy cough. "Are you well?" I ask, worried.

"Yes, my lady." She straightens with a brisk smile, though her eyes are a bit red.

I decide not to press the issue. "Lord Philippe and I have some work to do," I tell them. "Please see that we're undisturbed."

They both nod, and I close the door. On second thought, I bolt it.

Philippe is still pulling at books, rather unsuccessfully. I pace over to him, drawing the hood of the cloak low over my head. It's difficult to see around it, but if I can't see out, hopefully no one will see my face. "How do you know about these passages?"

"Rumors, mostly. King Antoine used to be quite paranoid of spies—and assassins—and there were always stories about the passages he'd place guards on." His mouth crooks. "They used to joke that an assailant could always get into the palace through the king's study, since he never once used it."

I utter a hollow laugh. Naturally, no one has ever told me about such rumors—not even the oh-so-helpful Lord Devalle and his guards, who know perfectly well how much time I've been spending here lately. Philippe glances at me, but just then he must have grabbed the right books. There's a faint clicking noise. We both lean closer. He tugs at the books, and with a low groan a section of bookcase shifts slowly forward.

Cool air breathes out from the opening. I pick up a candle from the desk and lead us into a narrow passageway, pausing on the threshold to examine the floor. It's dusty, unmarked. Either no one knows how to access this passage, or they haven't deemed me worthy of spying on, at least not in my study. I feel strangely disappointed.

I slip into the passage, with Philippe following. It's straight and narrow, and it quickly becomes apparent that the study is merely the last in a series of secret doors. We pass three on the left and four on the right, some cobwebbed, some not. Here, footsteps have clearly disturbed the dust. My skin tightens. What if we meet someone? I whisper to Philippe, "Do you know where we are?"

He hesitates, then admits, "I think we're passing the state bedchambers. Yours. The ki—the *Caveadear*'s."

A chilly hand seems to run up my spine. So Philippe still instinctively refers to Elanna's chambers as *the king's;* they were once Antoine Eyrlai's. And mine, which I claimed from Loyce, are also accessed by this secret corridor. I shiver.

I have no idea where the secret door is in my bedchamber. Perhaps I had better find out.

The thought spooks me, and I hurry. At the end of the passage, a cramped staircase winds down. I follow its spiral, stiffening every time a noise echoes through the walls. But we meet no one, and the stair ends at a narrow door. I open it cautiously and find myself facing a small hedge. On the other side is the promenade that runs the length of the palace grounds, and a gate leading into the city. I blow out the candle and tuck it into safety under the hedge—and freeze. It appears to be a popular hiding spot. A lantern also huddles beneath the greenery. Someone must have left it for future use, and not long ago, either. The glass is shiny and unblemished.

"I wonder if Lady Elanna used this passage," Philippe is saying, "when she escaped from Loyce's guards."

"Perhaps." I rise, shaken. Clearly someone has used this lantern much more recently than that. He's gazing around thoughtfully; he doesn't seem to have noticed the lantern. I take his arm, and he starts in surprise. I smile at him, as much to distract myself from the thought of unknown persons wandering the secret passage as anything else. We might as well play the part of the courting couple.

We emerge through the gate onto the grand avenue. "Did you know Elanna?" I ask, curious. "Before?"

"Not well. She . . ." He pauses as if searching for a diplomatic word. It strikes me, for the first time, that even though El grew up here, not everyone might have liked her. "She kept to herself. Very interested in her botanical studies. Of course, Loyce treated her cruelly, and the king doted on her . . ."

"And you?" I ask. We cross the street, and the fresh spring wind blows, catching the edge of my hood. I grip it quickly to keep it in place, though no one appears to give me a second glance. It's strange to emerge into the city unrecognized. Coaches and pedestrians throng past, oblivious to the two of us, the press of traffic blocking the long rows of white houses from view.

"Me, what?"

"Were you close to the king, or Loyce?"

He's quiet for a moment, his head bowed. "Not as close as my mother wished me to be," he says at last. "Come this way."

We turn down an alley that darts between the gleaming white row houses, and in the mix of Ereni voices I find myself missing Caeris more than ever. I miss the mossy oaks at Cerid Aven, and the quiet. This is not my city. Why did I ever think these people would accept me easily? If it had happened the other way, I'd feel the same way they do. Yet I still feel guilt, as if thinking this makes me disloyal to Ruadan.

The alley leads us to another street, and another tall alley. We're between the grand houses of the nobility now, and Philippe seems to be counting the back gates. At last, he stops at one with a fence ornamented with wrought-iron birds, and lets us through. I smell winter roses; the gate is cunningly placed to hide the house from view, except for the high slant of its gray roof. Philippe draws me to a stop beneath a small tree—a pear, I think—its branches tipped with red buds.

He gestures at my face. "Your mask."

I pull it out, tying it neatly under the deep hood. My heart is thumping. I look at Philippe, with his fine, precise features, his neatly groomed hair. So respectable. Not like Alistar at all. Something flips in my stomach. At first I think it's the baby, but then I realize it's me.

Then Philippe covers his face with his own mask, and the moment passes.

The gate creaks behind us—there's a whisper of conversation—and he takes my hand. Quickly, we tramp along the garden path. A butler is waiting at the back door, wearing a mask, too.

"The true king," Philippe murmurs, and the man lets us in.

The true king? I feel my gaze narrow.

Philippe hooks his arm through mine. "Relax," he murmurs in my ear. "You look like any other wealthy girl pretending an interest in rebellion."

"As long as I don't open my mouth," I mutter.

He holds me closer. I suppose I'll have to get used to it, if I marry him.

The house is as wealthy as I expected, with high coffered ceilings and expensive carpets and paintings by Paladisan masters. The murmur of voices draws us toward a pair of double doors, flanked by two footmen. Their uniforms are carefully neutral. They let us through.

People crowd the room beyond—a ballroom, to judge by the size. There are women in wide silk gowns with rouged lips, and men in jeweled coats. They all wear masks.

A man's voice rises over the crowd, and suspicion tightens my chest. I turn to Philippe. "Whose house is this?"

His eyes are unreadable behind his mask. "It belongs to Lord Devalle."

And what, I wonder, have I ever done to Devalle? Of course—

I curse under my breath—his damned merchant ships. So much for his claim that he wanted to help us reinstitute trading; it seems he's decided to bypass me for a better patron.

Two women pass us, their silk skirts swishing. "A little bird told me the Bastard isn't much longer for her throne—unless the people are willing to have a queen who can't keep her skirts down."

The other gasps. "She's with child?"

"So the mice in the walls say. And by that filthy Dog person, too."

Someone must have been listening through the walls—when I talked to either Teofila or Alistar. Or both. There's a ringing in my ears. I will—

Philippe nudges my arm. He's snagged two glasses of punch. I grab mine and take a hasty swallow. He gives no indication that he heard the ladies gossiping, though he's not deaf and they made no effort to be quiet. Perhaps, I think darkly, it's old news. Maybe the entire kingdom knows.

But—*the Bastard*? Is that all I am to them? I suppose it is. My defining feature is that my mother didn't marry my father. And that, according to some of the more pointed slurs I've heard, I stole the throne from him. Even some Caerisians think so.

Philippe nudges me again. "There," he murmurs, nodding his chin.

I look. Over by the windows, identifiable despite his mask, is Lord Devalle, sleek in a gray silk suit. Standing beside him is another man, his face bare. He wears his dark hair long, gathered back in an old-fashioned queue, though he's not old—forty, perhaps, at most. He dresses simply in a black coat and trousers, but there's an expensive sheen to the fabric. His eyes are a pale blue, the skin around them creased, as if he has spent a lifetime being mildly amused.

The women who passed us earlier flurry over to the two men. "Your Grace!" one of them coos.

So this is him—Aristide Rambaud, the Duke of Essez. The man who wants to remove me from my throne. He's so comfortable—so assured of his own safety—that he doesn't even trouble to hide his face. His cheekbones are high and aristocratic, and he smiles as the two women curtsy. I feel for the sound of him. It's bright and fine as cut glass.

I edge closer, pressing between the clusters of chatting nobles. The ranks of windows have deep bays and heavy curtains; it's easy enough to drift into one, sipping my punch and staring out at the lawn. Listening. Philippe arrives at my elbow, huffing an exasperated breath. He starts to speak but I nudge him silent.

". . . your time in Tinan?" one of the women is asking. "Did you see the former queen?"

"Alas, yes." Rambaud's voice is deep, and bright with irony. The women are already laughing, and so is Devalle. "King Alfred has assigned her a home in the country—as a hint, you know—but since her husband is his cousin, he can't forcibly remove her from court. She lives a shadowy approximation of her former style."

"No doubt Alfred refuses to pay for her whims," one of the women says.

"Have you spoken to her?" the other asks, still giggling.

"I have been given a cold shoulder each time we inhabit the same room." Drily, he says, "I gather she blames me for not coming to her rescue when the Caerisians claimed Laon."

In spite of myself, I wince. I never pitied Loyce Eyrlai before, but now I realize how much it must sting, not only to be removed from one's throne, but to discover that one has no supporters. Even those who want to get rid of me don't want Loyce back.

"I confess to missing Queen Loyce, on occasion," Lord Devalle is saying. "Though she had markedly less intelligence, she was more malleable than the Bastard."

Philippe makes a soft noise, but I ignore him. I want to hear this.

"Yes, Rambaud," one of the women says, and though she's teasing, there's an edge to her voice, "you might have kept the Caerisians out of Laon. They're a cursed inconvenience, bumbling about court, inciting all our neighboring lands to war!"

"We've had to ration the food on our estate," the other woman remarks. "You wouldn't believe how much the peasants complain we're starving them, and talk on and on of their rights! Why, they've even threatened to vote us out of politics. Yet a noble-woman's duty is to be mother to the people on her lands."

I suppress a snort. I wonder if it's ever occurred to her that the people don't want to be mothered—not by her, anyway. Of course, I have been known to call myself the mother of the people as well. Perhaps we're both deluding ourselves as to what the people really want. It's a gloomy thought.

"You shan't have to endure much longer," Rambaud says sooth-ingly. "King Alfred and I are in agreement, and the true king will be here soon enough."

The true king? He can't mean *our* true king. Can he? I stare over my shoulder. My movement catches Rambaud's eye; he looks at me with that faint amusement.

I toast him with my punch glass. Why would Aristide Rambaud have anything to do with Euan Dromahair? Unless he's simply using the same catchphrase as a mockery of all things Caerisian.

"I do look forward to that," the high-voiced woman remarks, "but do you have a plan to remove the Caerisians? I fear you don't understand, since you've been gone so long. They cling like bar-nacles. *Barnacles.* And the people support them!"

"Naturally, we have a plan for all these matters." Rambaud is still watching me, one eyebrow lifted. "You'll find the people real-ize they love the Caerisians less than they think."

"I am relieved to hear it," the woman replies frostily; there's a warning in her voice.

Interesting. Clearly, despite Rambaud's protestations, no one ac-tually trusts him to keep his promises.

He's still got an eye on me, so I turn to Philippe. My punch glass is empty, and I'm feeling a bit light-headed. "Oh, *darling,*" I coo in my best, perhaps slightly exaggerated, Ereni accent. I swing against him, and instinctively his arm comes around my back. I lean into his warmth and bat my eyelashes at him. "More punch, please?"

"You're getting soused," he mutters. "We should go."

I look at him. With a sigh, he takes the glass.

When he's gone, it's easier to turn to face the room, pretending to wait for his return. I listen, hoping for more discussion of this *true king,* but Rambaud's conversation has turned toward family matters.

"Is Hermine still in Tinan?" one of the women is asking. "How does she fare?"

"My dear wife is enduring her exile as best she can," Rambaud says, still with such an ironic slant I can't decide whether he means it or not, or whether he even likes his wife. "Veronique Manceau is keeping her company. I receive communiqués almost daily praying for their swift return to Laon."

Philippe's mother. I tug in a breath; it's a good thing he's still at the punch bowl, distracted by another lord.

"And the children?" the woman presses. "How is darling Claudette? I still cherish the memory of her dancing for us last summer!"

Rambaud hesitates. "Claudette has been unwell, alas. I've kept her in Eren, but in the country."

"Oh, the poor child!"

Both women are exclaiming, and so is Lord Devalle. Rambaud smiles reflexively, but his gaze has wandered across the room. I've probably gleaned as much as I can from this conversation. Philippe is still at the punch bowl, both his hands occupied with glasses, stuck there while the other lord gestures at him. I smirk. I start to edge forward to rescue him—

"I don't think we've met, madam."

I startle. Rambaud is at my elbow, having seemingly abandoned his other companions. One of the women glances after us, a frown puckering the skin above her mask.

I curtsy, trying to think fast. Philippe was right—my mind is fuzzy with punch, and I know I can't fake an Ereni accent well enough to fool Aristide Rambaud. So I say, as winsomely as I can, "I grew up in Caeris, alas. We have not met."

"A Caerisian, indeed?" He looks rather pleased. "You are most

welcome here. I take it you didn't arrive with your fellow dissent-
ers."

He gestures across the room to a knot of men and women on the
other side of the fireplace. A stone seems to sink in my stomach.
One of them is speaking loudly, her Caerisian accent cutting
through the din of Ereni accents.

Even my own people?

"I didn't think I had any fellow countrypeople here," I say,
rather stupidly.

"I imagine you've come for the same reason," Rambaud says,
but there's a question in his voice.

"The—ah—" I think quickly. "I can only imagine they're angry
that Queen Sophy stole the throne from her father. Like I am. They
want a ruler who doesn't throw us into war with the entire world."

Rambaud's shoulders ease. "It is a complaint I've heard, and in
future days it will only grow louder. The true king—"

"Your Grace." There's a movement behind me, and then Philippe
pushes into our circle, shoving a punch glass at me. He seems
slightly out of breath. I glare at him; I could smack him for interrupting just when Rambaud was going to tell me about the *true
king*. He ignores me. "Such a wonderful gathering you've organized."

Rambaud brightens. "If it isn't Philippe Manceau! You came
after all."

"How could I miss it?" Philippe is starting to sound more hostile than friendly. I take the punch glass and nudge him in the ribs,
but he doesn't seem to take much notice. "All of my dear colleagues in one room, scheming against the queen."

I wince.

Rambaud's eyebrow has hitched up. "How fortunate that we
still enjoy your company, given such sentiments. But then I hear
almost daily from your mother."

"And I as well," Philippe says darkly.

"She is eager to be quit of Tinan."

"Actually, I think she's in her element." Philippe nods brusquely. "If you'll excuse us, I meant to introduce my friend to—"

"My fellow Caerisians," I supply, having taken a drink of punch. Philippe looks at me, and I sense he's suppressing a groan. "Yes."

"It's been a pleasure," Rambaud says to me.

I just nod; Philippe is already maneuvering us away—past the Caerisians, to the door. I struggle against his grip. "We just got here!" I whisper at him. I need to see which Caerisians are in that group.

"You're getting drunk," he says flatly. "We came; you met him. We're leaving."

"I am *not*—"

But we're already out in the corridor, and as I stumble over the carpet, I realize maybe I am. Not drunk, perhaps, but still the small amount of alcohol is making my head spin.

Philippe takes my arm, and I let him. We move back through the elaborate house, passing Devalle's wife without greeting her. By the time we reach the garden, my tipsiness is draining into a cold horror. Then we're outside, passing through the darkened city, back to the palace, climbing through the cold secret corridor to my study.

When we finally emerge into the dim chamber, I'm vibrating with anger. There's so much to be angry over, but one thing sticks in my gut. I throw off my hat and whirl on Philippe.

"Who?" I demand. "Who are they replacing me with? *Him?*"

He doesn't immediately answer. His gaze lowers.

"Tell me, Philippe," I say, "who is *the true king*? Is it Euan Dromahair? Is it *you*? I presume that's what they all want: your mother, Devalle, Rambaud . . ."

"No—" He gives a quick shake of his head. "That was before."

"Before what?"

He looks at me. "Before I told them no."

I look at him and then, despite all of it, I laugh. "So we're both replaceable."

He grimaces. "It would seem so."

There's a bitterness to him; he's not comfortable among those people, doesn't like them, even though he grew up with them. Slowly, I say, "But you were their first choice."

He won't look at me.

"It's all right, Philippe." I draw in a breath. "Perhaps there's a way we can beat them at their own game. If we were to marry, for instance."

His gaze jerks up to mine. There's no horror in it, as I half feared, but no hope, either. He looks genuinely shocked. Slowly, he says, "How exactly would that be besting them at their own game?"

I hesitate, then decide to tell him. "I've just received news that the *Caveadear* is alive."

Philippe stares.

"But she can't get out of Ida," I continue. "We're in a difficult place, even though she lives, and even though the emperor's fleet has been destroyed."

"Destroyed?" He looks even more astonished.

I nod, without admitting to how I've come by this knowledge. "I need to take people's minds off their fear. I need to give them something to look forward to."

Philippe's eyebrows have hitched up. "I see."

I utter a self-conscious noise that can't quite be called a laugh. "I didn't think I was such a terrible prospect as all that."

I wait, but he just rubs the flat of his palm over his forehead. The whole sound of him has muted.

"It seems I've miscalculated," I say, my face hot. "Please forget what I said."

He looks at me and sighs. "You're not in love with me."

"Is that a requirement for a royal marriage? I haven't been given to think so."

"I'm a romantic," he says flatly. "I don't believe anyone should marry where there isn't at least affection between the two. Desire. Not political expediency. Not a wedding to distract the people from their own fear, to try to prove you're one of our people, as if I can somehow give you the credibility you haven't earned."

I feel myself freezing into place.

"And then there is the matter of . . ." He draws in a breath. "Alistar Connell."

"What about Alistar?" I say coldly.

"You've been dallying with him since before you took the throne!" he exclaims. "You're with child by him if the gossips can be believed! The entire kingdom will soon know of it. What do you plan to do—keep him on the side, or remove him? Removing him would damage your relations with Caerisians; they'd think you've gone Ereni. But no husband would want you keeping him."

I pull away from him; I can feel my nostrils flaring with anger. "That is enough."

"You want me to marry you," he shoots back. "You treasure honesty, so I'm giving you my honest opinion. Or at least, you *think* you want me to marry you." He looks at me. "Perhaps the truth is that you don't want to marry at all."

"I do what I must for the good of my kingdom," I retort.

"Then marry someone who doesn't care what your motives are, or what you do behind his back."

His hands are on his hips. He's glaring, and so am I.

"I would never live with Alistar while I was married to someone else," I say furiously.

"Why not? Other people in your situation do it. Loyce did it."

"I am *not* Loyce Eyrlai!"

His mouth tightens. "No, you're not. You're the one who threw her off her throne. You shouldn't be trying to live the way she did, feel like you need to make the same moves she made. You claimed this kingdom. You can write your own rules."

I look at him. "And here I thought there was a chance you'd say yes."

"You don't want to be sold off like a prize cow," he says, "and neither do I."

Without another word, he strides away, slamming the study door behind him. I stay where I am for a moment, leaning against the bookshelf. Absurdly, ironically, I miss Alistar more than I ever have. I want his steady arms around me, and the smell of him, and his breath against my cheek when he tells me he will hold me forever.

But he isn't here, because I've pushed him away, too. I feel entirely alone.

I open the door with a sigh. I've been gone more than two hours, and the guards will be worried by now. But when I emerge into the hall, neither of them even react. I turn to stare at them.

"I'm sorry, Your Majesty." Kenna is swaying and her face is gray, her voice ragged.

"You're ill!" I exclaim. "You shouldn't be on duty."

She shakes her head. "No one else can work, my lady."

I stare from her to the other guard, Moyra. Her skin is pale and sweating, and her eyes have a glassy look. She barely acknowledges my gaze. All the gods, I hope I don't get ill as well—though I haven't noticed anyone else taking sick.

"You're both ill," I say, stating the obvious. "Did you eat anything suspicious? Why isn't someone filling in for you?"

"Because everyone is ill, Majesty," Kenna says wretchedly. "All the queen's guards. Isley came down with it yesterday morning, vomiting and feverish, and now we've all got it."

"*All* of you?" I certainly don't want to expose myself to them, in that case. Although if they've all got it . . . "Are you certain you didn't eat something? Do I need to have someone test your food?"

They exchange a confused glance, and Kenna says, "We all ate the same thing."

"I was feeling all right this morning," Moyra mumbles. "I swore I was fighting it off."

"You should both be in bed!" I say. Perhaps it's simply influenza. "You could be getting the rest of the palace sick with whatever you've got."

"But then you would have no guards, Your Majesty."

I mentally curse. It's long past five o'clock, and I'm sure Grenou has returned to duty, as I promised Lord Devalle he would. "No, I do. I have Captain Grenou and his palace guards."

Kenna draws herself up. "They can't guard your private chambers."

"They'll have to," I say, though it galls me to rely on Grenou for anything. Over Kenna's protest, I say, "It's only one night, or two at the most."

"But my lady—"

I gesture for them to be silent, and call for a footman. "Send for Captain Grenou!"

He bows and hurries off, and I let the women follow me back to my chambers.

"As soon as he arrives, you must go to your own rooms and rest!" I tell them both sternly. "I'll have the kitchen send you up extra soup and tisane. You should have told me at once!"

"You have so much on your mind, my lady," Kenna says, almost apologetically. "You said we shouldn't disturb you."

Perhaps, if I'd had any common sense, I would never have gone with Philippe in the first place. I look at her. "Maybe, but the first thing I should know is whether or not my guards are at their best. You must take care of yourselves. You're not putting only yourselves at risk by not doing so."

The words have their intended effect. Moyra gasps, and Kenna presses her hand to her heart. "We would never expose you to greater risk!"

"Yet that is exactly what you have done today," I say severely. "And if Rhia were here, she would agree. She would also see you stay in your beds until you are fully recovered." I pause outside my rooms. "Now, as soon as Grenou arrives with his men, you are to go. Understood?"

They both nod, thoroughly chastised.

"Rhia should be back in the morning," I add. "She'll see to everything."

I go into my chamber—it's empty even of maids—and drop onto

the bed. My eyes throb with exhaustion. It's been such a strange day. I should rise and go to Teofila's rooms, tell her that Elanna is alive. But it's late, and she's probably asleep by now. It will wait until morning.

There's a scratch at the door. I heave myself up. It's Captain Grenou, crisp in his uniform, the sound of him humming with a low buzz that seems a lot like satisfaction.

"I've stationed two guards at each door," he says self-importantly, "but please permit me to remain inside your chambers tonight."

A thread of unease runs up my spine. Surely Grenou doesn't have anything to do with my royal guards' illness—does he?

"You shall hardly know I'm here," he promises. "It's the safest arrangement."

Of course, I let the mountain women stand guard within my rooms at night—but there is a vast difference between them and Captain Grenou. I study Grenou's face, trying to detect anything to substantiate the distrust I feel, but he simply projects a professional concern. Even the sound of him is brisk and businesslike. I tell myself I'm simply reading into the situation because I dislike him, nothing more.

"You may station yourself in the sitting room," I decide at last. The passage between the sitting room and my bedchamber is deep, with a small bathing chamber and a linen closet opening off either side. It will offer some privacy.

The captain lifts an eyebrow. "But you do not sleep in the sitting room, madam."

"I will leave the door open. If someone attacks me in the middle of the night," I say drily, "you will hear me scream."

He bows and retreats toward the wall.

CHAPTER FIFTEEN

I fall asleep singing to the baby, and wake curled on my side, with the certainty that something woke me. I was dreaming that I was at Cerid Aven, in my comfortable bed surrounded by floral curtains. I heard music—the twining, breathy melody of a flute—and I rose and walked out of the house, determined to find the player. Only when I emerged outside, a woman was moving away from me, over the soft moss beneath the oaks, the light catching in her golden hair, the deep blue of her gown. I called after her, but she seemed not to hear. She kept on, releasing notes on the flute.

Then, behind me, someone cried my name. I turned and saw a girl on the house's back steps. A slight child, perhaps eight years old, with my own reddish-gold hair and Alistar's black eyes.

She uttered my name again, but this time it did not emerge in words. It came out as a glowing sound—a deep and brilliant purple note that shivered through every part of me. The sound most like my own self.

Now something creaks again in the room, and I startle out of the remnants of the dream. It must be almost dawn, for the fire has burned low, but the charwoman has not yet come on her rounds. I lie, listening. A soft cough echoes from the sitting room. It must have been the guards I heard. Maybe they changed watch.

The weight of the child is pressing against my bladder, but I snuggle deeper into the blankets. Already the girl's face from my dream is slipping away from me. I try to remember whether her chin was oval like mine, or sharp like Alistar's. For a moment, as I lie there drowsily, I pretend he's here, too, holding me and the child against him.

A bitter smell sifts into the room. I lean up on my elbows. Sneeze.

There's an echoing sound. A creak.

Smoke. The smell is smoke.

Yet the fire hasn't been lit, and the charwoman hasn't come—

I shove myself upright, just in time to see a flame ripple in the semi-darkness. My eyes are dazzled, blinded by the light. I can't see him but I sense someone there in the dark. I catch the ragged sound of him, the staccato patter of sound mirroring his heartbeat.

"Who's there?" I whisper.

There's a breathless pause. The person is hesitating. In the dim light, the sound of him is amplified, his panic echoing toward me. My heartbeat surges into my ears. Instinctively, I reach out, not with my hands but with my inner senses, trying to grab onto the shape of him, trying to—

A soft gasp in the darkness. A pulse of blue flares from him. There's a creak, and his shape slides out of my grip.

The smell of smoke is growing thicker. Deeper. Something cracks. Snaps.

There's the faintest *click*. A door closing. The secret door?

I lunge onto my knees just as flames sweep my bed curtains in a sudden *whoosh*. I cry out. The flames pour up, over the foot of the bed—too late, I see the viscous trail of oil snaking across the coverlet. That man came all the way in here. He stood over me and traced oil across my bed—across me.

I'm standing on the bed now, rocking unsteadily on the down mattress. I reach for the man with my mind, but the sound of him has vanished, and my mind is sparking with panic. "Help!" I shout. "Help!"

Nothing. Where the hell is Grenou? They better not have gotten him, or I'll have to feel sorry for the bastard.

Unless, of course, this was all his doing.

I seize a pillow, holding it in front of me like a shield. My bed is completely engulfed. Smoke thickens the air. I inhale and begin, helplessly, to cough. I need to move before it smothers me.

"*Guards!*" I scream through my choked throat. Instinctively, I scrabble for Grenou with my mind, trying to feel for the sound of his presence. But there's nothing. He's not there.

None of the guards are there.

I grab a second pillow. The flames are racing around the back of the bed now, smoldering up into the canopy. *Are you ready to be brave?*

I charge forward, stumbling on the mattress, and throw myself over the line of fire. There's a burst of heat. The flames snatch at my nightgown, my hair. Something's burning my legs. Someone is screaming.

Then my feet hit the floor, and I crash onto my knees. My elbows. I'm coughing into the pillow.

My back is on fire.

I fling myself over, my shoulder blades hitting the carpet hard. There's a last, throbbing burn before the fire goes out.

At least, the fire on me. I pull myself upright, scuttling backward toward the table in front of the silent fireplace. Sheets of orange fire blaze around my bed, and the canopy collapses. Sparks fly out onto the carpet.

I slam the charred pillow over them. Somehow I'm on my feet. The palace sits around me, completely silent. There's only me and this roaring fire.

I sprint into the sitting room. As I sensed earlier, it's empty; Grenou's gone. Before I can open the door into the corridor, a crash sounds from the bedchamber. A woman shrieks.

I run back in. The charwoman, Dorothée, has entered through the servants' door and dropped a load of firewood all over the floor. She's screaming, and the fire is blazing. "Queen Sophy! Help!"

Then she sees me, and startles wildly. "Your Majesty—all the gods—"

"Get help!" I say, before I start choking on the smoke again.

She hesitates, then races back down the servants' stair. The fire is eating hungrily into the floorboards below the bed now. I reach for the heavy carpet, trying to drag it backward.

There's a shout behind me. "My lady!"

I drop the carpet and instead seize a poker from the fireplace. I turn, the flames heating my back, as Captain Grenou pounds through the brief hallway behind me.

I raise the poker, and he comes up short. He's not panting hard. I didn't sense him in my room, but he can't have run far. Perhaps he was simply in the hallway.

Or perhaps he was the one who entered my room and drizzled oil over me.

I advance on him, the poker raised. He holds his ground, staring from me to the blazing wreckage of my bed. "Your Majesty—the fire—"

A shout erupts behind me; the servants have plunged up through the other door. There's a hiss as a bucket of water is thrown at the flames, but it does nothing whatsoever to dim the heat at my back. Whatever Grenou may or may not have done, we need to put this fire out.

"Go," I tell Grenou through my clenched teeth. "Get help."

He just stares at me. At the poker.

"Get help!" I scream at him.

He bolts away.

I swing back to my burning bedchamber, heaving in a breath as sudden fatigue hits me. The fire is spreading, and the smoke has thickened so I can no longer see the servants. There's a repeated hiss as they throw more water at the flames. Their shouts are smothered by the roaring fire. Gathering myself, I run back out to the sitting room and heave up the carpet from beneath the divan and armchair.

The door bursts open as I'm wrestling the carpet back toward the bedchamber. "Sophy! What's going on? Are you all right?"

It's Philippe—what is he doing here at this hour? I decide it doesn't matter. "Help me!"

He grabs the other side of the wide carpet, and together we haul it into the bedchamber. With a heave, we throw it onto the flames. The fire gives an angry gasp, but dies back somewhat. Smoke stings my eyes. On the other side of the room, more vaporous hisses rise. The servants seem to be making progress with their bucket brigade.

"Your Majesty!"

I turn. The guards are pouring in now, hauling a wooden contraption among them—a fire engine. It's almost too wide to fit through the doors. Grenou is nowhere to be seen; Alain is the one who barks orders, and points Philippe and me toward the sitting room.

We squeeze past the fire engine. The guards are operating the pumps on either side, and a sudden spray of water bursts from the contraption's long nozzle. The fire hisses wildly.

Philippe takes my arm. "Sophy, your hair—"

I don't even hear him. Grenou is coming into the sitting room, frowning terribly. He stops when he sees us.

Suspicion runs cold fingers down my chest. "Philippe," I say quietly, "did you send for the guards?"

"Yes," he says, but there's a flicker in his gaze. "I smelled smoke."

Grenou is staring at us.

I pick the poker up from where I dropped it earlier, ignoring the tightness of my breath. The weight feels good in my hand.

"Sophy," Philippe begins.

"Stay back," I bark at him. I'm advancing on Grenou.

The chief of my guards begins to babble. "Your Majesty, it must have been that sorcerer. Ciril. How else could it have happened so quickly? We didn't even hear you struggling . . ."

"You're a terrible actor, Grenou," I say flatly.

"My lady?"

His tone is startled. Innocent. But just for a moment, his hand went to the pistol at his hip.

"You weren't in my rooms. No guard was stationed at the servants' door."

He blinks. "You did not tell me to put one there, Your Majesty."

"Indeed," I say sardonically. "I thought that's what you might say."

His gaze flickers to Philippe, who is staring him down. "It was the sorcerer, madam," Grenou says, but he's still watching Philippe. "That Ciril. He must have played with our minds—"

"A man who can summon lightning entered my chamber and set fire to the place with a torch and oil?"

He swallows.

The poker is weighing down my arm, but I keep it trained on him. "You could run," I say. "Join Rambaud. Of course he probably wanted you stationed here, and you failed him, didn't you?"

He wets his lips. "I told you those refugees would lead to nothing but trouble."

Softly, I say, "You're being a fool, Grenou. Admit to what you did, and I might see you pardoned. Keep lying, and I'll be forced to treat you as an enemy, and a traitor."

There's a shout behind us. Two guards come running. "It's out!"

I lower the poker. Grenou doesn't move; Philippe goes to stand beside him, putting his hand firmly on the guardsman's shoulder. In the next moment, there's a creak of wheels, and the fire engine trundles back into the sitting room, pushed by the flushed, triumphant guards. Grenou seems to take no notice of his men; his gaze has fixed on the wall behind me.

"Well done!" I congratulate the guards.

Some servants have followed them, Fiona at their head. "Sophy!" she exclaims. "Are you—" She takes in my nightgown and my hair, which must be a singed wreck, and the red licks of burns up my legs. She swings to the other servants. "Send for a doctor!"

"I'm fine," I insist, putting my hand to my stomach. My lungs feel wrung out. "Thank you all for what you did."

But no one listens to me. Fiona is ordering the other servants about, and the guards are wheeling the fire engine from the chambers. Alain marches up to me. "How did they get in, my lady?"

At least he doesn't assume poor, stupid Ciril tried to kill me with a lightning strike. I send Grenou a sour glance. "Through the door to the secret passage, I expect." I look at him. "Alain, did Captain Grenou appoint anyone to guard my bedchamber last night?"

"Captain Grenou?" He frowns, utterly confused. "But Isley is the deputy of your queen's guard, while Captain Rhia is . . ."

He trails off, staring around the room as he realizes there are no mountain women here.

"That's what I thought," I say grimly. I gesture with my chin at Grenou. "Take your men and arrest this man. Make sure you disarm him, as well."

Alain stares from his captain to me. Fiona and the servants, realizing a new drama is unfolding, have withdrawn to the corners of the room. The remaining guards are watching, wide-eyed.

"You heard the queen," Philippe says gruffly.

Alain snaps to attention. "Your Majesty!" He marches forward and takes up position beside Grenou, wrestling the pistol from the captain's side. Three more men step over to flank them.

"Lock him up in a spare room." I add drily, "And make sure you guard *all* of the exits."

Alain salutes, his expression now perfectly neutral. Grenou doesn't look at me; the sound of him burns, heavy and flat with rage. The guards close formation and march him away.

Fiona takes my arm. "The doctor's here, Your Majesty."

I pull away. "I don't need a doctor . . ." But now that Grenou is gone, I'm aware of the burns stinging my legs, and the smoke still caught in my lungs. I glance down, trying to see my legs, and glance again. I'm wearing only a white nightgown, trimmed with fine lace. The gathered fabric hides my stomach.

A man bustles forward through the servants. It's a doctor, a mild, middle-aged man carrying a leather bag. He gestures to a plushly upholstered chaise. "Please, Your Majesty. Sit."

I turn to Fiona, gripping her arm. "Not him. I need Demetra."

"You've been in a fire! You need more than the foreign midwife."

"It's only a slight burn." My heartbeat thunders in my ears. "Send for Demetra."

"Sophy," Fiona says firmly, "you—"

"No!" I shout at her. The doctor will take one look at me and know. He'll know that I—I—I stumble. Everything stings and aches. Heat's building in my head, tingling out along my limbs. I can't breathe. I—I—

"Sophy." It's Fiona, gripping me tight.

I blink. Slowly, the room stops spinning. I gather my breath. "I'm fine. Just bring me a robe."

Fiona gives me a skeptical look, but sends the order.

I'm still light-headed, so I let the doctor guide me over to a chaise. Philippe comes to join us, frowning. The doctor is a kind man, with spectacles and a fatherly look. "My lady, you must lie back. You've been injured, and you've had a terrible scare. Please, let me examine you."

Tears threaten my eyes. I want Demetra. I want to have chosen differently. Has the fire harmed the baby? Surely it can wait.

"Sophy!"

There's a scuffle at the door, and then Teofila runs through the crowd of guards and servants, Hugh on her heels. She throws herself on her knees beside the chaise. The doctor, with a dubious look, shifts over to examine my legs.

"What happened?" Teofila clutches my hand. "Who did it?"

"I don't know. Grenou tried to blame Ciril, but it was obviously a setup." I look at Hugh, then back at Teofila. "Rambaud is behind it, I'm sure."

Teofila's eyes darken. "I'll kill him."

"Not if I do first." I touch my stomach, and her gaze follows mine. She looks from me to the doctor.

"Hugh," she says, "go fetch Demetra Megades from the east wing."

The doctor sits back on his heels. "Ladies, I assure you that I am perfectly competent if you'll just let me do my job."

More voices echo out in my sitting room. I push myself up. The ministers have arrived, a collision of sound and color, and I won't be found sitting here like an invalid. "Thank you," I tell the doctor firmly, "but we will examine any wounds I have later."

Fiona hands me a robe; most of my clothes were in the dressing room, and left safe. It's a fine, slippery silk. Without thinking, I stand and pull it on, tying the belt at my waist.

But the fabric is as rebellious as water. The sash slides up underneath my breasts, silhouetting my stomach. I snatch for the sash again, but it's too late. The doctor's staring at me. Surprise and shock pulse from him, bright and tangible as a fist. His mouth opens. "Your Ma—"

"No questions," I snap, and he stares at me again. All the gods, this is the last thing I need. I don't have time to silence this man. I don't know whether he *will* be silent, even if I demand it.

I untie the sash, for all the good it does. Philippe is looking at me, too; I suppose he saw. The hang of the robe disguises my outline, but it's no use; the secret's out now. Teofila has drawn in a breath.

Panic grabs at my throat, but there's no time to think of what I should say, or to bargain with anyone for their silence. No time for anything. The ministers have surrounded me, a cacophony of questions and buzzing, bright white fear. Even the Butcher looks concerned. Victoire has arrived as well, her hair and eyes wild.

"Who did this?" Juleane Brazeur is demanding.

"It must have been that refugee," Lord Devalle says with a gasp. "Fire! Like the lightning strike that killed poor—poor Thierry . . ."

I look at him. Just look. But he sees me, and the words die in his mouth. The other ministers fall silent, too, watching me. Juleane Brazeur's eyes have drifted down to the sash dangling from my waist.

"I woke this morning to someone in my chamber," I say, loud enough for the servants and guards to hear as well. "They had doused my bed with oil and set fire to it with a torch. I glimpsed them for only a moment before they disappeared into the hidden passage behind my rooms. I assume," I add drily, "you all know what passage I'm referring to?"

None of them speak.

"Curiously," I go on, "Captain Grenou did not appoint anyone to guard my chamber last night—except, presumably, himself. He did not answer my shouts for help. He did not appear at all, in fact, until Dorothée discovered me and sent for more servants to aid us. Even more curiously"—I look at Lord Devalle—"Grenou also blamed Ciril."

Devalle can't hide a wince.

"I've had him arrested," I say conversationally, and the minister swallows.

"Your Majesty," Juleane Brazeur interrupts. She's pointing at my stomach. "Are you—"

"I have not finished speaking," I rap out, and she falls silent, out of surprise as much as anything else. I draw in a breath and look at all of them, watching me with varying degrees of concern. My hands have begun to tremble, but I know in my bones it is time to tell them. It's time to speak the truth. Ruadan would want me to.

"As you can see, I've survived," I say. "Not only I, but the hope for what lies ahead. The life I'm carrying, the symbol of our kingdom's future. The child I am bearing has survived, too."

THERE IS A moment of absolute silence. The echo of my words seems to hum in the air. The ministers don't seem stunned, exactly. The sound of them is too calm for that. They are staring from one another to me, as if they can't believe I actually told the truth. I wonder sourly how long they've known. Even Teofila looks surprised.

So does Philippe. I can't look at him. He will hate me for this, I suppose, even if by his own admission the gossips have already guessed.

Lord Devalle starts to back toward the door.

"Guards!" I bark. "Arrest the minister of finance."

The guards hesitate. Devalle laughs, but a little too high-pitched, a little too uneasy. "Your Majesty surely doesn't mean to suggest I had anything to do with this unfortunate incident this morning . . ."

I look at him. Mere hours ago, I would have felt obligated to placate this man—to play his game. But if he is willing to participate in an attempt on my life, then I am done being nice.

The bastard should have known better than to threaten my child.

"Perhaps you didn't hear me before," I say. I'm still trembling, but this time my anger feels good. It warms me down to my bare, aching toes. "When I was *screaming for help,* Captain Grenou did nothing. Like him, you have suggested the perpetrator was Ciril Thorley. It's hard to fathom why Ciril would fake his own sorcery with a torch."

Devalle opens his mouth.

"We are done with this discussion," I say. "And I'm done with you. Guards!"

This time, they obey, surrounding the minister of finance. For once he has the sense not to protest.

I look around at the other ministers. Most of them have shrunk back from me. The Butcher looks neutral, and I bite down the urge to curse. He probably knew even before he heard me speaking oh-so-subtly to Demetra. Hugh is watching me steadily, and Teofila stands firmly by my side. Victoire has folded her arms, but she gives me a minute nod.

"Your Majesty . . ." It's Juleane Brazeur. "Forgive me, but are you truly with child?"

"I am carrying a symbol of hope for our kingdom." I lay a hand on my stomach so they can all see its roundness. "Let this be a message to Tinan and Paladis and Baedon, and whoever else thinks they can destroy us. We are not going anywhere!"

None of them react quite as I'd hoped. Hugh starts to say something, then glances at the others and falls silent. Philippe is frowning at me. I stare back.

Juleane Brazeur sighs. "The father, I suppose, is well known to us."

My shoulders tense. Quietly, I say, "The identity of the father is immaterial."

Teofila looks at me, and I keep my gaze focused on the ministers. The words echo in my ears, blunt as a betrayal. As if Alistar doesn't matter. I feel as if I don't recognize myself. Yet I plow on, determined to appear strong.

"I won't marry to hide the fact that I am bearing a child," I say with conviction I don't quite feel, even though the words are true. "I am proud to soon be a mother."

There's a silence.

"My lady," Juleane Brazeur begins, "with respect, we are in a difficult position, with the black ships due to arrive, and the *Caveadear* dead—"

"Elanna is not dead." I nod at their universal shock. "I saw her with my own eyes yesterday afternoon, along with Jahan Korakides. They spoke to me all the way from Ida. The *Caveadear* has not yet found a way home, but she is alive and well. And," I add, "the emperor's fleet no longer poses a threat. Jahan destroyed it."

There is an astonished silence. Then Teofila turns to me. She whispers, "Is this true?"

I turn to her, grasping her hands, feeling a smile burst over my face. Finally, it seems I've done something right. "Yes. She's alive, and well, and once we tell the people, things will improve."

"But this won't change anything," Philippe says quietly, "and you know it."

He's watching me with a heavy gaze—a sharp reminder of our conversation last night.

He glances at the other ministers. "The people believe Elanna is dead. They won't change their minds because you shared some sorcerous form of communication, Sophy. No one will believe you—particularly not with magic involved. And the same goes for the fleet. Telling them that Jahan Korakides single-handedly took it down? It sounds impossible."

"But he *did*," I say tightly, "and Elanna *is* alive. I told you so—and I would never lie." He might have mentioned some of these doubts last night.

"Perhaps not, but there are people who will accuse you of doing so." His jaw is tight, as is the sound of him, and I stiffen. Something has changed. He seems to be angry with me—or perhaps angry at the world. Maybe I shouldn't have proposed to him; maybe it insulted him.

My mouth has gone dry, and he's still speaking. "Your Majesty, I'm only saying what Aristide Rambaud and his followers will say. This is perfect fodder for them. They will use this to destroy your reputation. They will portray you as fickle, weak, uncertain, a *liar*, and . . ." He hesitates. "A loose woman."

To my horror, tears prick my eyes. But I can't cry, not in front of all the others. I can't let Philippe see how much he's hurt me. So I say, though the words taste bitter in my mouth, "You mean they will call me a whore."

He looks away.

I swallow back my tears, and feel them turning to rage. Rage that Philippe thinks he has the right to shame me. Rage that the ministers believe they and the kingdom at large have the right to both know and determine what happens to my body. I look around at them all—the ministers, Victoire, Hugh, the Butcher. Teofila.

"This is my body," I say. "If I choose to have a child, it is my choice. Whether this baby will become the future ruler of Eren and Caeris is a choice that belongs to the people—but bearing the child is *my* decision. If Aristide Rambaud and his friends' outmoded morality makes them accuse me of being dissolute, then let them accuse me."

Philippe bites his lip but says nothing more. Juleane Brazeur seems about to speak, yet hesitates.

"You're worried about what people will say." The truth is, I am, too. But the trembling inside me has as much to do with fury as fear. "Tell them this: that I am alive—and not only that, I am bearing a child who could be our future monarch. Tell them Rambaud attempted to murder a pregnant woman. Tell them Elanna lives, and the Paladisan fleet has been destroyed." I raise my eyebrows. "Tell them we should be celebrating."

They hesitate, but I say, "Go!"

They begin to file out, talking among themselves. I catch the Butcher's eye. He nods, lingering beside the fireplace.

I call after Juleane, "Did you send someone back to those villages to look after the women?"

She glances back at me, surprised. "Yes, of course."

"Good." I nod, though I don't know that this latest news will do much to persuade the women to take my offer of help. "You can go."

Hugh comes over to clasp my hands. He looks searchingly into my face. I have never really heard the sound of Hugh before, but it is as quiet and contained as I might have expected; the notes that make him up have a fluency like poetry. Quietly, he says, "Congratulations on your good news, Sophy dear." He hesitates. "But is this quite the way you want it spread? I can send for Alistar, bring him off the hunt for Ciril. You can—"

"No!" I'm vibrating with anger again. Did Hugh not listen to a word I said? "I'm not going to get married to conceal the fact that I'm carrying a child. The people deserve the truth, and the truth is that this is my body, and I chose to conceive a child so that our people could have hope for the future."

His glance slides toward Teofila, and I realize my pregnancy isn't exactly news to him. "If that is what happened . . ."

I feel my eyes narrow. He probably knows perfectly well that the baby was conceived well before Finn died—before I even thought I might become queen. All the same, I insist, "I am always putting the good of the kingdom first. *Always*. Just as Ruadan taught me."

"Of course." He pats my hand, and I smart at his tone. I won't be patronized, not even by Hugh—especially not by Hugh, who has known me most of my life and should have the decency to respect me. Especially when I'm afraid he might be right—not only about how the people will react, but about Alistar.

He steps away, and I finally allow myself to drop once more

onto the chaise. I'm still trembling. I shouldn't have gotten angry; I'm not usually so quick to temper. But they threatened my child. Ruadan used to say, *If you are going to lose your temper, take control of how and where you do it. Let it drive policy. A good statesperson lets their rage be for something bigger than themselves.*

It doesn't feel as if I've succeeded in that. I feel more as if I've made a mess—particularly of my personal life. I should never have said that about Alistar.

There's a movement in front of me. Philippe crouches down. I jerk back instinctively.

He doesn't seem to notice. "Sophy, I'm afraid it might not be wise to arrest Devalle."

"*Wise?*" My temper surges back into my ears. "He wanted me dead, Philippe! He knew about their assassination plan—he probably helped devise it! Yes, I think it's wise to put Devalle in prison. I value my life."

"I know, I know. But with things so volatile . . ." He lowers his voice. "You saw Rambaud last night—and Devalle. They'll see this as an attack. And . . . they'll strike back."

"It *is* an attack. I'm tired of placating people like Devalle. I'm sick of these games." I look at Philippe. He seems sincere, yet his eyes aren't quite meeting mine. He knows something, or suspects it. And suddenly I find myself wondering how Philippe Manceau ended up at my door this morning, before the guards even arrived. Before anyone else knew what had happened. Last night, Rambaud said Philippe's mother had been writing to him—and Philippe didn't disagree. I remember how Philippe looked at Grenou, and how Grenou stared back. How Philippe told me, just yesterday, that it was wise not to punish Grenou.

Slowly, I say, "How did you come to be in the hallway this morning?"

I hear the note pulse from him, high and bright. A sound like panic. The sudden awareness startles me; my own body is humming in response.

"I . . ." His gaze darts past me. "It was a hunch."

"A hunch," I repeat. I think back to last night, to Rambaud saying that *the true king* is coming. For a time, clearly, Devalle and the others wanted Philippe to marry me—an easy way for them to exert influence. But perhaps, in recent days, they decided they didn't need to bother with me at all.

Philippe said that he told them no. And maybe he truly doesn't want to be king. He certainly made it abundantly clear that he doesn't want to marry me. It doesn't seem to be power he's interested in.

But he's mixed up in this plot somehow. If he won't come clean, then I'm left with no choice.

I stand up, ignoring the ache in my legs, and snap my fingers. The guards are learning; two of them trot over. I gesture at Philippe. "Arrest the Count of Lylan."

"Sophy!" Philippe exclaims. "What—"

But the guards have already grabbed him by the arms, yanking him up. He struggles.

"I'm trying to help you," Philippe says. "You have to believe me, Sophy, please—"

"I don't have to do anything," I say coldly. "Unless you are prepared to tell me the truth about your involvement in this plot, I do not want to hear from you again."

He's staring, his mouth fallen open.

"And," I add, "you have no right to call me *Sophy*. Guards, take him away."

"SOPHY!"

The shout carries all the way from the hallway. I look up in time to see flying dark hair and a billowing coat before Rhia shoulders past the guards and practically flings herself on me. She smells of road dust and sweat. The doctor, who's bandaging my burned legs, gives her an exasperated look.

"What happened?" she's demanding. "Someone said that cur

Grenou attacked you—or maybe it was Lord Devalle. Are you hurt?"

"Nothing serious." I wince as the doctor tightens the bandage, and reach out with my free hand to squeeze Rhia's wrist. "Any news on Ciril?"

But Rhia is looking around the room, her face thunderous. "Where are my mountain women?"

"They took ill . . ." As I say it, I realize what a fool I've been.

"Took ill?" Rhia's glowing with rage. "*Took ill?* Someone took *you* for a fool, Sophy Dunbarron! Where are they?"

With a hasty apology to the doctor, I get up, stuffing my feet into slippers, and hurry after her. Rhia's raging through the sitting room, sending everyone spinning out of her way. I race after her into the hallway. My heart thumps dully. I don't want to imagine what might have happened to my queen's guard. What a fool I was—what a damned fool—

Ahead of me, Rhia takes the stairs to the third floor two at a time. I follow suit. I'm panting raggedly by the time we reach the top, and she swings back to face me.

"Be careful, Sophy!" she bellows. "You don't want to lose that damned babe after all this."

I'm gaping at her. "You knew?"

"Anyone with eyes and a brain would know!" She tosses her head, but comes over to touch my shoulder with real concern. "I've spent months at your side, Sophy Dunbarron. When all the rest of us were complaining of getting our monthlies at the same time, you were puking every morning."

"Oh." Heat suffuses my face. In a small voice, I say, "You *all* knew?"

She raises an eyebrow. "My women can keep their mouths shut. I supposed you had a reason to keep it a secret, though . . ." Her lips quirk. "You might have trusted me."

"I should have." Looking back, I don't know why I didn't seek out at least one ally. "Though I know what you would've said."

"Do you, now?" Rhia looks amused and a little offended. "And just what would I have said?"

"You'd have called me the biggest fool you ever met."

"Now, that's where you don't know me as well as you think, Sophy Dunbarron." She shakes her finger at me. "In the mountains—if you'd troubled to consider our customs—you'd have known it's acceptable for a mother to bear a child out of wedlock, if she sees fit. Just like the queens of old."

She swings off, and I start after her. "Which queens of old? Rionach and Tierne were both married . . ."

She flaps a hand. "The ones before them. The ones in Wildegarde's time."

"You mean *Aline*?" I want to laugh. "She got pregnant by a man who took the shape of a black bear by day! And then he got murdered by that rival shaman."

"Well, so it wasn't too pragmatic to marry him, now, was it? She raised the child alone, as I recall."

I've never thought of the story that way. Aline, the queen of Caeris, fell in love with a sorcerer who'd been cursed to live as a bear by day, and a man by night. I suppose in Aline's opinion she got the better end of the deal; he must have been quite a man. "It's a legend," I point out.

"Her daughter Morvenna is your direct ancestor." She raps on the nearest door. "Isley!"

There's an awful, extended silence. Then the door opens and Isley leans out. Her face is wan, and she's clutching her gut. "Captain? I'm so sorry, we've all got the influenza . . ."

"Food poisoning," Rhia says. "That's what you've got."

Isley's gaze moves from her to me, and her lips part in comprehension. "All the gods!"

"Incompetent assassins, incompetent poisoners," Rhia grumbles. "Let me in. I want to examine your dishes from last night."

I start to follow her but catch myself. The women are terribly ill, and the last thing they need is to feel they have to perform for the queen. "I'll visit later," I tell Rhia. "Let them know how sorry I am."

"We're all sorry!" she exclaims, shutting the door behind her.

I turn to go—and discover the Butcher climbing to the top step behind me. He pauses to catch his breath; the steep stairs make even him pant. "You wished to see me privately, Your Majesty?"

It's not exactly what I said—and I never *wish* to see the Butcher privately—but I find myself nodding slowly. Perhaps he's the one I should turn to about this matter, though I wish it were anyone else.

"Walk with me." I start down the corridor, and he follows. We're passing servants' rooms—I'm taking the chance that they're unoccupied during the day, and no one is lurking, eager to over-hear us. The thwarted assassination attempt should give Rambaud and his followers a stumbling block, if nothing else.

The Butcher falls into stride next to me. I still feel stiff and strange walking alone next to him, as if every stride is a betrayal of my mother's memory.

"Those were several startling arrests," he remarks, and I shake myself back to the present. "Grenou, Lord Devalle, Philippe Manceau."

"I suppose you think I should have exercised more caution."

"Not at all. I've suspected for some time that Rambaud planned to put Philippe on the throne, if he could."

I glance at him. "Yet Philippe doesn't seem to want the throne. And"—despite Philippe's refusal to tell me the truth—"I don't think he much cares for Rambaud. It's hard to see how Rambaud would control him."

"Oh, Manceau is the perfect pawn. A rebellious youth, a few mistakes . . ." The Butcher shrugs. "I have no doubt Aristide Rambaud has all the leverage he needs over that boy."

"Leverage?" I repeat. No one has ever told me anything about Philippe's youth—Victoire didn't seem to know—and now it's too damned late. "You might have mentioned this before."

He shrugs. "I don't know the details. He quarreled with his mother more than once—hardly a surprise there, given my experi-ence of the woman—and it ended quite badly just before we deposed Loyce. Apparently he stole quite a large sum of money from her, and she threatened to disinherit him."

"Why would he steal money?" I ask, bewildered by this sudden influx of knowledge.

"That, I haven't been able to discover. But it's been enough to keep him to heel."

"You should have told me this before." I can't keep the stinging anger from my tone. "If I'd known, I could have talked to Philippe. We might have offered him protection!"

"Protection, against Rambaud? Against Philippe's own mother?" The Butcher has the gall to look amused. "Philippe Manceau is no fool. Our position remains too precarious to offer him true protection, and he knows it. His mother won't hesitate to remind him. Countess Veronique is not above that sort of manipulation."

Our position might be less precarious if we informed each other about matters like this, I think darkly. Perhaps there's still a way to talk to Philippe—at least, once we establish who's in control. I say, turning the conversation, "I'm still surprised they stooped to murder."

"I can only surmise that they heard Jahan Korakides destroyed the imperial fleet, and became desperate." He pauses. "Though if Aristide Rambaud wanted you dead, I suspect you would be."

I glance at him. His chin is lowered, sunk in thought. "What do you suspect?" I ask warily. "I could have died."

"You could have, but you didn't. I imagine they weren't trying to make an attempt on your life so much as to sow discontent—and distrust of the refugees. They wanted it to look like Ciril's handiwork, after all."

I feel my mouth tighten. They also want me to look like a fool for trusting foreigners, especially a Tinani man. "I'd trust Ciril over my own people," I say, rather bitterly.

"Mmm. It's good you're taking decisive action."

My lips twist. The idea I've had will require more gumption than just a few arrests—and it demands I trust this man, of all people. "I imagine everyone else is as surprised as you are," I say, unable to swallow down my resentment completely. "It means there might be an opportunity for a further surprise, and I need your backing."

We've slowed in the corridor, and he faces me. His eyes are too neutral for me to read, and the sound of him is as muted as his expression. It's maddening to find him so opaque. I want to shock him. Coolly, he says, "What sort of opportunity?"

"The mayor of Montclair sent me an invitation to come to her town yesterday. To speak to her people." I lift an eyebrow. "I've been told Montclair is an independent town, but the mayor is on excellent terms with Aristide Rambaud. It's a perfect opportunity."

"You think to go to Montclair?" he says, incredulous. I've managed to shock him after all, but the dismay in his tone makes it a lot less satisfying than I imagined.

"As I said, it's an opportunity." I fold my arms. "Rambaud and this mayor must be trying to trap me"—though it's a bit galling to admit they think I'm that much of a fool—"but you must see this is our chance to trap *them*. I've arrested Rambaud's highest-placed supporters. No doubt he still has spies, but they can't be as close to me. This is our chance to lure *him* out. If we capture Rambaud, on top of all the others, the opposition ends."

He looks pensive. "It might give us leverage with King Alfred of Tinan, as well, given that he and Rambaud are friends."

"Yes. It may help prevent war."

But the Butcher is still frowning. "Montclair will be difficult to infiltrate. When I was last there . . ." He shakes his head a little. "It may be possible, with suitable planning. First we must ascertain that Rambaud himself will be there; I'll ask my informants."

I nod. "And if he is? Will you help?"

He's considering it; there's a hum of anticipation about him. "Rambaud isn't a vain man, but he can be smug. If he thinks he's won, there's a good chance he'll appear himself to lord it over you."

"That's the impression I have as well," I say, thinking back to the man who so smoothly controlled last night's party. Rambaud won't be able to resist showing me up—especially after our brief acquaintance. He'll be insufferable.

"Then we should try," the Butcher decides, and I control my instinctive flush of victory. "We'll need to keep the element of surprise, but tomorrow is the earliest we could manage. I would need to bring soldiers in, secretly, from the eastern side of town. I suppose the mayor would take you to the square, thinking they will secure the gate and bridge . . . We would have to secure the bridge, then, as well."

"I can bring a force with me," I point out. "After all, I was almost assassinated this morning. I think I can justify guards."

"No," he says quickly, "that will make them suspicious. You'll need to go in with only a few supporters."

I stare at him. "*That* won't make them suspicious? They'll think I'm a fool!"

He doesn't disagree, and I clench my teeth together. Perhaps this is how I appear to the Ereni—a gullible, overly trusting girl. Well, if that's the case, I suppose I'll have to play it to my advantage.

"If you have too many guards, Rambaud will be wary," the Butcher says. "If we truly want to lure him out, you must appear vulnerable."

"You want me to be a decoy. A sitting duck."

"Sometimes that requires more bravery than the soldiers who will surround the square."

Bravery. My eyes sting. It almost feels as if the Butcher is using Ma's words against me, though he can't possibly have known them. *Are you ready to be brave?*

Today, I am.

"I'll do it," I say briskly, "as long as I have Rhia Knoll at my side."

"Of course." He nods. "I'll reach out to my informants. We'll need a map of the town, and then we can make a plan."

"Let's meet again in an hour. Perhaps there's a map in the archives—"

He shakes his head. "That won't be necessary. I've been there before."

CHAPTER SIXTEEN

The next morning dawns brilliant and clear, though the Butcher had hoped for rain and fog. We move out through the streets of Laon, my open carriage—no longer draped in black for mourning, but shining a brilliant gold—flanked by only five guards, the hilts of their sabers flashing on their shoulders. Rhia rides to my right, bolt-upright despite the sling on her arm, her brightly woven cloak flapping behind her. I feel naked with so few, but the Butcher insisted I must appear an easy target, and the other mountain women are still too ill to accompany us. Teofila and Hugh wave to me from the steps of the palace. Publicly, I've left them in charge of the city for the day; privately, I gave them instructions on what to do should I not return. Rambaud would enjoy holding me ransom, but at least if worse comes to worst, we have three of his people to bargain with.

It's impossible to feel at ease, though at least I don't have to endure the Butcher's company. He went with his most trusted men to Montclair in the dead of night; he knows of a little-used exit on the southeastern wall, through which his informants have been smuggling information since yesterday afternoon. Rambaud, it seems, is waiting for us; according to our intelligence, he's spent several days in Montclair. The mayor responded to my acceptance of her invitation with apparent delight.

So here I am with a scribbled map of Montclair in my cuff, and a burning determination in my stomach. I tug down the sleeves of my long scarlet riding coat, and adjust my little black hat, trimmed with a gold tassel. Even in the carriage, I'll stand out for a mile— which is supposedly a good thing.

Doors and windows open as we pass, the people of Laon emerging to stare at our small, gleaming party. Children call to me. I wave at them, forcing a smile. At least my people can see that I am alive and well—even while so wickedly bearing an illicit child.

We cross a bridge over the river Sasralie and emerge into the countryside. The day is even more brilliant here, a blush of warm southern air stirring the red buds on the trees. Eren's fertile green hills roll out from the city walls, while to the west the Hill of the Imperishable slopes up above the gray roofs, a heathered monolith. Farmers emerge from their fields to lean against the stone walls and watch us pass. A few cheer—"Long live the queen!"— though some are silent.

No one riots or throws produce at my head, and it feels entirely surreal. My forced smile makes my cheeks ache.

We skirt a small hamlet, where commoners are emerging from humble thatched houses to watch us pass. Some join the tail end of the party, having heard that the queen will be speaking in Montclair. They shout after me, calling for the blessing of a favor, or at least a glance from me. It's a strange counterpoint to the riot of two days ago, and my muscles tense even as I wave to them.

The road curves, climbing a hill above the Sasralie, and the sharp peaks of town roofs punctuate the horizon. As we draw closer, walls of severe gray stone differentiate themselves from the town's silhouette. I draw in a breath—the walls are thick, ancient. No wonder Rambaud has cultivated a friendship with the mayor, and is trying to ambush me here.

The horses snort at the hill's steep grade. Riding beside the carriage, Rhia points. "Looks like a welcome party has arrived."

I squint. I can just make out a blur of figures crowding the ramparts, and more standing in the maw of the town's gates, watching us come. A trickle of sweat runs down the neck of my riding coat. It's hot under the sun.

"Flowers," she adds. "And bunting, from the looks of it."

"You can't be serious." I squint harder. The people are carrying bright objects, softening the forbidding stones. It looks as if I'm being not only welcomed, but celebrated. Tension pinches the back of my neck. It seems the mayor is taking her part in this charade seriously, too.

Rhia snorts. "It's a bit much, isn't it?"

We're approaching the gates now. All looks just as the Butcher marked it on my map. The street slopes upward on the other side, thronged with people in their finest clothes—all bright colors and wide smiles. They throw flowers at the guards and shake the cheerfully colored bunting. The guards glance at me, and I nod for them to smile back at the people, even though it feels like madness. I wonder if they're all hiding weapons under their clothes, or whether the mayor has simply played on her people's love of pageantry.

Now I'm passing under the shadow of the gates, a gasp of cold in the warm spring day. For a moment, I'm blinded, and my heart kicks with sudden panic, the certainty that I should not have come. Then sunlight flares into my eyes, and a shout rises from the people gathered on the street.

"The queen!"

"Queen Sophy!"

"Long live the queen!"

Rhia and the guards fall back, and I lift my hand. Somehow, through an effort of pure will and Ruadan's training, I smile and wave. A child tosses a bouquet of early-spring flowers at me, and I catch them clumsily, spilling meadow rue all over the carriage.

"Long live the queen!" they call again, insistently, as if expecting an answer.

"As it is willed!" I call back, although I have always found the traditional Ereni words uncomfortable. Who wills the queen to rule? Not the gods, certainly; I don't have that kind of arrogance, to believe I have been placed on the throne by divine right. No, I rule thanks to the will of the people. These people.

And the people who control their lives, whether they know it or not.

The street climbs past tightly packed old houses, up and up, toward a wide stone bridge. I force myself to breathe. This bridge is our control point; our opponents, if they suspect our trap, will most likely anticipate we'll attempt to control the gate behind me, and the street. But with his southeastern entrance, the Butcher doesn't need to control this side of town. He plans to surround the square and blockade the bridge from the other side with the very carriage I'm riding in.

I just have to assume he and his men got into place.

The coachman urges the horses across the bridge. I lean up, fisting my sweating hands in my skirts. Rocks shear down on either side to a river boiling white below, a tributary of the Sasralie, which shimmers in the distance, visible now from the height of the bridge, twining through the farm fields on the other side of the town.

On the far side of the bridge, at last, spreads the wide-open town square, surrounded by a small pillared temple and several solemn, aged buildings that must be used for town governance. Only two narrow streets lead off it, and a small dark alley darting past the temple.

A deputation occupies the temple steps: a woman in a long, old-fashioned black mayoral robe, and a party of perhaps ten others, all finely dressed. Behind me, the guards stop in the middle of the square, on the Butcher's instructions; from their vantage point, they can signal to our hidden soldiers. My carriage sways over to the temple steps.

I glance up at the building, thinking I caught movement, but I see only the triangular-shaped frieze in the Paladisan style, gray with age. Below it are three low, square windows like black eyes. A humming tension rises from the very stones, and I know I didn't imagine the movement above. The Butcher suspected they would use the temple. At least his predictions have been accurate so far.

"Your Majesty," the mayor calls from the steps. "Welcome to Montclair."

The carriage halts, and I stand. Rhia has already dismounted, leaving her horse with a groom. I glance back. None of the festively dressed people have crossed the bridge. Rather, they seem busy on the other side, hauling heavy objects through the crowd. A blockade, presumably. My palms itch with sweat, even though it's exactly as the Butcher and I anticipated.

Around me, in the black windows surrounding the square, I feel the press of eyes watching my back. Some must be Rambaud's, but the rest, I am sure, are ours.

I climb from the coach as slowly as I can. I don't have to fake the deliberation in my movements; my legs still ache from yesterday's burns. Rhia falls in at my shoulder. The coach is guided away. I stay where I am, looking up the steps at the mayor. The Butcher told me to remain out in the open as long as I could.

The mayor frowns at me. Her silvered hair is teased into a small tower on her head, and jewels wink beneath the high collar of her black robe. Even the sound of her is frosty. She doesn't bother with an obeisance.

"Mayor Faustine, I presume," I say coolly. "Thank you for this generous welcome."

"You honor us with your presence, Your Majesty." Her gaze flickers to my stomach. "I trust the journey wasn't too much for you, in your delicate condition."

"Not at all." I feel an edge to my already forced smile. Where the hell is Rambaud? "I feel better than I ever have in my life."

"How marvelous," she remarks. "Will you not come into the temple?"

I make a show of glancing over my shoulder, in as foolish a country-bumpkin manner as I can manage. "Should I not address the townspeople? They seem to have been waylaid."

The cool glint in her eyes lifts the hair on the back of my neck. "We meet in the temple first, Your Majesty."

"But I must speak to the people," I insist, as innocently as I can. "It's what they expect!"

The mayor casts an exasperated glance toward the others flanking her.

"Perhaps you can introduce me to your colleagues," I press.

Rhia shoots me a look. I give her a minute shrug; I need to play this along as far as I can. Around us, the humming tension has grown even more taut, plucking at the hairs on my neck like a high-pitched string. The entire square is trembling with it.

There's movement again in the temple windows above, and this time I sense the bright vibrating scarlet of the men who hide there.

The mayor sighs. "Your Majesty . . ."

There's a rustle in the colonnade behind her. "Were you waiting for me?"

Aristide Rambaud saunters out onto the temple steps, his hands in his pockets, the cut-glass sound of him more brilliant than ever. He smiles right down into my eyes.

I stare back at him. "Yes," I say, "as a matter of fact, I was."

He just laughs and snaps his fingers.

Something scrapes in the temple above us. I glance upward, to the three black windows directly overhead. Finally, the movement above has resolved.

Long metallic objects protrude from the windows. Three—six—nine—

They fire, and I whip around in time to see my five guards collapse, thrown from their horses. Rhia shouts, throwing herself in front of me despite her broken arm.

More shouts echo behind me, but before I can turn, the people flanking Rambaud and the mayor are running down the steps, toward us. A volley of shots erupts across the square. I risk a glance backward. Our coachman has blockaded this side of the bridge, but he's being shot at. The snouts of muskets press through the broken glass windows of the buildings behind us, trained on Rambaud and his people. The Butcher's soldiers are in place.

A shot bursts out, spraying into the cobblestones near my feet. I'm not sure who fired. Our would-be assailants seem uncertain, too. For a moment, everyone pauses.

Into the silence, there's a shout. "Duke Aristide! You are surrounded. Surrender now!"

It's the Butcher. He's stepped from the building behind us, shouting with the stridence of a man used to making himself heard on battlefields. I can see our men in the windows above him, their faces fierce.

Rambaud stares from the Butcher to me, to the carriage blockading the bridge. Then his gaze drifts a little farther down, toward the wall just beyond the carriage.

The wall, over which a man is climbing.

Rambaud smiles. "My friend is, as they say, a crack shot."

"Lord Gilbert!" I cry.

But the man has already swung himself over the wall. He's ten yards from the Butcher, no more. He raises a pistol, setting it on his arm, sighting down the length of it. He's pulled a second one, smoking, from the front of his coat. I'm pointing, frantic. The Butcher turns toward the assassin.

The man shoots. Once. Twice.

At such close range, he doesn't miss. The Butcher catches the shots full in the chest.

His mouth opens. He's staring, shocked. Blood bleeds through the pale fabric of his coat.

Someone slams into me—Rhia. I stumble.

"Seize them!" Rambaud shouts.

Rhia shoves me again, but I'm staring. Stricken. Up at the broken windows.

Our men are falling. A blow to the head; a dagger plunged to a throat. One drops to his knees, throwing up his hands in surrender.

Rambaud knew. His people have swarmed into the building behind the Butcher's soldiers, claiming their lives.

Rhia drags me, one-armed, across the square, but there's nowhere to run. Blood slicks the cobblestones, a deep crimson. The five fallen guards lie before us. Two are still alive, struggling to move their wounded limbs.

Something is rising in me. A deep, humming bellow. My rage is bigger than this square, bigger than our attackers. Bigger than this damned town.

A hand grasps me from behind. I'm wrenched backward. Rhia lets me go, fumbling one-handed for her dagger. I spin around, bringing my fist with me. It connects into my assailant's face. The man stumbles backward, clutching his nose.

But others are coming after him, held at bay only by the sweep of Rhia's dagger. Her teeth are bared, a fierce, furious battle grin. Somewhere, Rambaud and the mayor are watching, and across the square the Butcher's lifeblood is seeping out. Rambaud's people pour from the temple and from the buildings, into the square to surround us.

And I'm trembling with fury—not only that, but with the sound of all these people. The scarlet hum of their blood and their fear thrums into my own body.

I'm shouting. Roaring. I reach out with my mind, and I *pull*.

A gasp, like an indrawn breath. Bright, thrumming panic spirals into my mind.

I let go. Open my eyes.

The square lies silent. Around us people have collapsed to the ground. Our attackers slump over the feet of the fallen guards. The men who emerged from the building have collapsed, too. Even Rambaud and the mayor. All of them, except Rhia, and me.

She's staring at me, her good hand still outstretched, blood bright on her dagger. A vicious hum whines through my ears.

"Sophy?" Rhia whispers.

I can't speak. I didn't kill them all, did I?

No—over on the temple steps, Rambaud is moving. Pulling himself shakily to his knees. He leans down and touches his fingertips to the mayor's throat. Her head moves ever so slightly.

Rhia's gone, if possible, even more still. "We need to go. Now."

I start toward my fallen guards. "Two of them are still alive—"

"No, Sophy." She grabs for me, drops her dagger, swears. Across the square, the mayor lifts her head. "We need to run."

Still, I hesitate. Perhaps even the Butcher is still alive. We have time—

Rambaud looks up, and his eyes meet mine.

I stare back at him, unflinching.

Rhia grabs my arm; she's got her dagger put away now. I let her pull me along, refusing to drop Rambaud's gaze. "Sophy!" she hisses.

I pull my gaze from Rambaud's, and we run.

CHAPTER SEVENTEEN

"They're still looking for us," Rhia says.

I squint at the sun, lowering over the western road that makes a ribbon along the Sasralie. When we left Montclair, we ran for the southeastern exit, marked on the Butcher's map. But in the unfamiliar streets, we lost time determining the route and almost missed the narrow gate itself, tucked deep into the wall. By then, distant shouts—and a few shots—told us the people in the square had come to. We threw ourselves through the gate, out onto an unfamiliar path beneath a plunging waterfall. It brought us out into a dense, ancient forest, and by then more shouts echoed, closer to us. They guessed, of course, how we planned to get out of the town. So when the path descended to the road, we kept to the forest, hiding as best we could. Now from our vantage point on a rocky overlook, Rhia spots riders moving north along the Sasralie.

"We don't know they're from Montclair," I point out. The riders appear to me as nothing more than fuzzy spots on the horizon.

"They're armed. Not wearing royal colors."

I chew at my lower lip. The rolling hills block our view of Laon, though it can't be more than five miles distant. The riders will certainly arrive in the city before we do—if that's where they're going. If they're searching the countryside for us . . .

"We have to wait until nightfall," I say at last. We can't risk getting caught—even if they are heading for Laon. Whatever I did in the square didn't keep them out for long enough, and soon it'll be dark. Teofila and the others will know something's gone wrong, since we failed to return. I just have to trust that Teofila and Hugh have taken whatever measures they must to protect our people.

Rhia flops into the lee of the outcropping, and I lower myself more gingerly onto a mossy spot. It's slightly damp, but cushions my aching body better than the bare rock. I'm glad I wore sensible boots; my gown is torn and muddied. I rub my hands over my face.

"We should've taken water from that falls," Rhia says. She digs in her coat pocket and produces a flask, which she tosses to me.

I unscrew the lid and can't suppress a smile when I sniff the contents. "You can always tell a true Caerisian by whether or not they carry whiskey."

"The smell reminds me of home."

It does me, too. Peat bogs and long lakes and the scent of oak woods. I blink back the sudden pressure of tears, and swallow a mouthful of the liquid, letting it rest on the back of my tongue before it slides, burning, down my throat. I never thought I would miss Cerid Aven so much. And Rhia's mountains are even farther away. Did either of us understand that this was what it would be like, when we said we wanted to rule Eren and Caeris?

I hand the flask back to her. The whiskey gives me the courage to say what I haven't yet. "I don't know what happened."

"That you're a sorceress?" She presses her lips together.

"Maybe I am. But I don't know what I did. It just . . . happened." And in retrospect, it sends shivers of both excitement and terror through me.

Rhia crosses her good arm over her chest, and scowls. I tense for the verbal assault, but instead she just blows air out of her mouth. "Why is *everyone* a sorceress except me?"

I'm so startled I laugh. "That's not true."

"Elanna is, and now apparently you are, too! I'm the one who grew up in the mountains," she grouses. "*I* memorized all Aunt Granya's magic books when I was a child. But do I have sorcery to knock half a town unconscious? No."

"You know how to use the shifts in the land, though," I point out, fighting down the urge to smile. "You could use one of those to get us back more quickly."

She looks dour. "I haven't felt any nearby. We'll have to keep going until we find one. If the Ereni had just mapped them properly, instead of insisting they didn't exist for years and years, it wouldn't be such a problem."

"We'll find some." I hesitate. There's another thing we haven't discussed. "The Butcher went down."

Rhia's fingers tighten on the flask. "There won't be any bringing him back."

"No," I say very softly. I stare up at the sky overhead, turning a tremulous pink. "I don't know how we'll be able to hold Eren without him." Though I can't say I actually miss him—but it seems ill luck to speak against the dead, even the Butcher.

With an angry grunt, Rhia tosses back a swallow of her whiskey. "I never wanted to be in this damned kingdom. We should have freed Caeris and left Eren to rule itself."

"They wanted us," I protest.

"Some of them did. Or thought they did." She kicks at a pebble. "We should have kept to our home. The kingdoms have been separate for too long to ever be one again."

I say nothing. Have we really been such fools? Everything seemed so possible when Elanna woke the land. Now I don't know anymore.

The sun drifts lower; neither of us speaks. Cold gathers, thick and damp, over my skirts, pressing against my face. I shiver, cupping my hands over my stomach, hoping our flight today has not harmed the baby.

There's a rustle as Rhia clambers to her feet. It's not full dark yet, but a deep-blue twilight. "Come on," she says. "If we wait any longer, we'll break our ankles going down this hill in the dark."

I stumble after her through the black shadows of the trees, downhill. Where the ground levels, it's now full night, and a farmhouse looms like a pale ghost in the darkness. Within, a dog barks. We keep to the stone wall, until we find a stile that guides us onto a muddy, rutted lane. As we walk, more farmhouses come into view like ships marooned in the darkness, their windows dimly lit. Smoke from wood fires itches my nose and makes me long for warmth and my own soft bed. It's been a long time since I ran at night like this, a fugitive in my own kingdom.

Neither of us dares to talk, though I sense Rhia glancing at me from time to time, as if she's chewing over some thought. Eventually a half-moon rises, barely enough light for us to see by.

The lane trips down to the main road. We pause in the ditch, listening hard. Nothing, not even a rustling squirrel.

We walk, clinging to the edge of the road. Only once does a vehicle pass us—a post-chaise, lanterns swinging, leaving bright spots on my night vision. We watch from the shelter of the ditch, the earth's dampness seeping through my thin clothing.

After the post-chaise passes, we top a low rise and come into sight of Laon. The city gates sit dark and forbidding—closed. Teofila must have blockaded the entrances; I hope she acted in time.

Rhia hisses a sigh through her teeth. "We'll have to skirt around. Come in by the Hill of the Imperishable. At least there's a fold in the land over there."

I nod. Laon isn't completely defensible; though the gates can be closed on the royal road running north and south, the old city walls don't enclose the Hill and the aristocratic neighborhood, nor the university and factory district on the other side of the city. Even the palace is quite vulnerable. If Rambaud's people march on us, we could easily be overrun. Not a particularly reassuring thought.

We cut across more farm fields, slipping in cow pats and rousing guard dogs. At last Rhia grabs my arm—we've reached the Hill of the Imperishable, where the fold hums through the land, difficult to sense and impossible to use unless you walk carefully along the path it creates. Rhia knows how to, and the space before us melts into a familiar city street. I stumble a little; the shifts are always something of a shock. But we're in Laon now, and the palace lies just down this street.

Rhia breaks into a brisk walk, and I follow suit despite my protesting feet. At Royal Square, we both slow. Rhia motions me to stay back. We sink into the shadow of a townhouse and peer into the darkened square. It's empty. Silent. On swift, quiet feet, Rhia darts across to the fountain that occupies the center of the square. I curse softly and follow her, dropping low to let the fountain block my presence. From here, I can just make out the bulk of the palace gates, their wrought-iron bars thin in the night. The gates have been closed. The silhouettes of guards occupy the gatehouses, their plumed helmets distinctive even in the dark.

Rhia starts toward them—but I seize her arm, pulling her back. The sound of the guards presses softly through the night, the dull gray of boredom. For a breathless moment Rhia and I hover in the shadow of the fountain, listening. Waiting.

It comes again: a soft wooden tapping from the buildings behind us.

I turn, scanning the porticoes of the massive townhouses. A whisper threads over the cobblestones to me, a wordless hum that sounds like my name.

"Come on," I whisper to Rhia. She's gone still; maybe she feels it, too. We back away together from the fountain, as quietly as we can.

There's a clatter from the gate. I glance back. A man's standing behind the wrought-iron bars. The bayonet in his arms gleams in the faint moonlight. Does he see us? He doesn't call out; the sound of him is blue and quiet. Then from behind us, I hear the faintest whisper, floating just beneath ordinary hearing.

The square is empty. The city is silent.

A sorcerer is aiding us. Rhia doesn't seem to hear. I grab her arm, pulling her along with me across the vast square. Even with the whisper threading just below my ordinary awareness, my shoulders tense in anticipation of a shot.

We turn down a wide avenue, and the whisper that is not quite a name intensifies. The wooden tapping comes again. Silver flickers in the mouth of an alley ahead of us. I slow, and tug Rhia's dagger out of its sheath on her belt. She makes a muffled noise of protest.

Cautiously, we both creep forward. The grooves on the dagger's hilt dig into my palm. I listen for the sound of the person in the alley—their tension so sharp I can almost taste it. As we move closer, the person speaks. A woman's voice, young and a little breathless. "Your Majesty?"

Rhia's fingers tighten on my arm, and I clench the dagger more tightly. "Who is it?" I hiss.

A shadowed figure detaches from the alley, putting back the hood of a cloak. Not that it does much good: Her face is little more than a silver sphere in the moonlight. She sees the dagger and blanches.

"It's Felicité, from the temple of Aera," she whispers, and I startle with recognition. It's the novice who seemed so alarmed by the refugees. "High Priest Granpier sent me. Come quickly. They have guards at the palace gates."

"Do we go?" Rhia murmurs to me.

"Who has guards at the gates?" I ask Felicité, still pointing the dagger at her.

"Duke Rambaud. They took the palace late this afternoon." Her voice quivers. "Please, we must go!"

Her fear is convincing, and I can't believe Granpier would betray us. Nevertheless, I keep the dagger in my hand as I hurry after her, Rhia at my heels, down the narrow alley, darting across the main streets. The city lies silent—unnaturally so. All the houses sit dark. "Rambaud's followers aren't celebrating their victory," I whisper to Rhia. It makes me oddly relieved that the streets aren't packed with people reveling in my downfall.

"Shh!" Felicité hisses.

Ahead, the smooth dome of the temple gleams in the moonlight, and the sweet smell of an herb garden seeps through the night air. Felicité is bringing us in through the back. Rhia elbows me, but I just shake my head, refusing to give the dagger back.

We dart across the open space where the back of the temple faces the river, and Felicité fumbles with the latch on the back gate. It swings open and we pile into the garden and the soft shapes of its shrubs. Felicité closes the gate carefully behind us.

I turn to her. "Are you a sorceress?"

"No! I . . ." She bridles a bit but deflates. "Well, when I use my beads and concentrate, sometimes people can hear me, even though I've said nothing. Only since the *Caveadear* woke the land . . ."

She holds up her fist: Prayer beads are wrapped around it. That accounts for the wooden tapping we heard. Perhaps she knocked them against a wall to get our attention.

"Come." She guides us toward the temple door, skirting the raised beds of the garden. "They're waiting for you."

"They?" I echo, all my nerves going taut. "Who's waiting?"

"Lady Teofila, and the others," Felicité says impatiently. "Come!"

I hesitate, but the girl is already pushing open the door. I step cautiously closer, Rhia on my heels. A gust of warm air brushes my face, and light flares through the open doorway. For a moment, I'm blinded.

"Sophy! Rhia! Come inside!"

It's Teofila. Even blinded, I obey instinctively, throwing myself into the warmth. In the next moment, she crushes me against her, and I have to scramble to keep the dagger from sticking her. Rhia snatches it out of my hand, then shuts the temple door. "I thought—" Teofila gasps, "I thought—"

I let my face fall into the hollow of her shoulder. My legs have gone weak with relief. I sag against Teofila. Just for a moment, I pretend I'm safe. That everything will be all right.

Then she releases me, and I see Hugh's waiting at her shoulder, his face more haggard than I have ever seen it. He embraces me swiftly. I force myself not to clutch at him. We're in the temple kitchen, and High Priest Granpier is watching us from a table where food has been set out. Demetra sits next to him, looking at us with empty eyes.

Granpier rises. For once, there's no twinkle about him; his countenance is grave. "Your Majesty."

Hoarsely, I say, "What happened?"

Teofila grips my hand. "Rambaud's people took the palace, as

Felicité must have told you. We hardly had any warning." A muscle moves in her jaw. "Philippe Manceau saved my life. And Hugh's."

"What?"

Teofila shakes her head. "He got free. We think Captain Grenou ordered his release, believing him loyal to Rambaud. Grenou himself was already out by then. He must have convinced someone in the palace guard to let him out as soon as you were a safe distance from Laon. He took command of the guard. Hugh and I were in the music room. The door burst open and Philippe rushed in, saying we had to run now, that our lives depended on it. He said we had to come here, to the temple, that High Priest Granpier would take us in."

My hands are clamped to my mouth. "What about Fiona? The servants? The mountain women?"

"I don't know." Teofila's hands close into fists. "We had no time to stop or even ask questions. We got out through the hidden passage; Philippe knew where it was. We just ran."

Feeling dizzy, I look at Rhia. She's just staring at the floor, wordless.

I say, "And Philippe?"

"He stayed at the palace."

I press my fists into my temples. So Philippe Manceau saved Teofila's and Hugh's lives, though he could have had them killed or continued to keep them imprisoned. Perhaps he *has* been trying to help us, but forced to cleave to Rambaud's side. Yet why was he in the palace when Rambaud's people set my bed on fire? Had he come trying to save me? Well, he was too late for that.

And Grenou escaped. He turned the palace guards against me.

"Were you followed?" Rhia asks. Her face is pale.

Teofila and Hugh glance at High Priest Granpier, who shakes his head. "As far as we know, no. No one has guessed that they came here. Lord Philippe must have covered their escape. Perhaps he told Rambaud they went after you, into the country."

I turn to Demetra. "How did you come to be here?"

She shudders. "I must have known it in my bones. I came down earlier to offer prayers to Aera. Then the news hit the streets . . ."

"That's lucky," I manage, and she simply nods. I think of her children, hopefully safe with the other refugees in Barrody. At least we got them to a place of refuge before this all imploded.

"The gods were looking out for us all today," High Priest Granpier says.

"And . . ." I press a hand to my chest. My heart is beating so fast. "Did anyone return from Montclair?"

Granpier looks at me with a kind of infinite sadness. "No, Your Majesty. Not that we know of. A party arrived from that town this evening—Rambaud himself with a number of his followers. They're claiming you're dead."

"But you knew I was alive. You sent Felicité."

Teofila's grip tightens on my hand. "A mother always knows."

I swallow hard. "The Butcher . . ."

"Dead in Montclair," Hugh says, "and the few men who survived surrendered and swore themselves to Rambaud. Or so they say."

"I saw him fall," I whisper, and beside me Teofila shudders. I hug her. So he really is dead, and I'll never have to face the man responsible for my mother's death again. But still my legs are shaking. "Most of the men must be dead, or grievously wounded—" I draw in a trembling breath; these aren't the only lives on my conscience. "We need to find out what's happened to everyone at the palace, too."

"We'll look into it as soon as we can," High Priest Granpier says from behind us; I turn to him. He gives me a firm nod, though his eyes are worried. "It's the one advantage to being a charitable organization. The temple can help local people make inquiries to see if their family members survived. I imagine any who live are being pressured to swear allegiance to Rambaud and the true king."

"The *true king*," I say bitterly. "I suppose they freed Philippe so he can lead them?"

Granpier shakes his head. "Philippe Manceau hasn't claimed the throne. As far as I can tell, no one yet has."

"Then who?" I say. *"Devalle?"*

No one even laughs, and none of us speaks the name of the man we all must suspect. Teofila is frowning at her hands. "Juleane Brazeur and I stocked the Spring Caves with food and supplies. Perhaps we should go there."

I'm entirely surprised. "When did you do that?"

"After we heard El was dead."

"Well, you must remain here tonight," Granpier says firmly. "It's far too dangerous to be roaming the streets now. In the morning, we will know more."

I rub my hands over my face. Morning seems like a long time to wait.

THE DAWN BRINGS no news, only a thickening tension that thrums throughout the temple. "We need to get you out of the city," High Priest Granpier says over a thin breakfast of rationed bread and preserves, and watered-down tea. He looks as though he hardly slept any more than I did; deep pouches underscore his eyes. "Rambaud didn't intend to lose you when he claimed Montclair. He'll have people searching for you. It isn't safe to stay here."

Leave the city—run away with my tail between my legs? The idea leaves me sick.

"I need to go north," Demetra says. Her eyes are red-rimmed with weariness. "I need to be with my children, and the others who fled here with us."

We can't let her travel across country, alone, up to Barrody. I bite my lip.

"Perhaps," she adds hollowly, "we should leave entirely. Find a ship to carry us across the Great Ocean to the Occident. They are rumored to be kinder to sorcerers there."

"Demetra, no!" I exclaim. I reach across the table and squeeze her hand. "We will fight this together. I pledged to help you make a home here, and that's still my promise—if, of course, you're willing to stay."

She looks slowly around the room, and I hear the bright tremor of her skepticism and her fear. "But I need to go north to my children. I need to see their faces. Make sure they're safe."

I suppose my guarantees haven't been worth enough in the past. "Please allow us to try to help you. We can take you to Caeris." I close my eyes. "We can *all* go to Caeris. As far as we know, Rambaud has only claimed Laon. We'll be safe in Barrody, and from there we can discover what Rambaud means to do, and what the people truly want."

High Priest Granpier visibly relaxes. "That would be an excellent solution, Lady Sophy."

Of course it would. I curse myself silently. If I remain here, even out in the Spring Caves, it not only puts us in danger but endangers Granpier and his novices, too, and anyone else who might help us.

"I would like to meet with the old resistance first," I say. "Tell them our plans."

He nods. "I'll contact Victoire Madoc. Hopefully she is still walking free."

I suppose I shouldn't be surprised that Victoire is likely still in the city—and that she's his contact.

"We could use the river," Felicité offers. She's been sitting at the end of the long table, watching me and Demetra shyly. "When you escape, that is. The fishermen tie up their barges below the temple steps. If we . . . appropriated . . . one of them, we might be able to fit all of you. We could float downstream, out of the city, and then cross the country north to Caeris."

High Priest Granpier looks at her kindly. "And the barge afterward? How would we return it to the fishermen, so that we don't deprive them of their livelihood?"

Felicité casts a glance around the table, but we all wait for her to answer. "We temple novices could bring it back. The barge would be light enough to pole back upstream, once it's empty."

"A neat solution." Granpier nods.

"And," she adds, sinking self-consciously toward the table, "with my magic, I could—"

A shout interrupts her. One of the other novices bursts into the kitchen. "Father Granpier! Rambaud's people—they've got one of the refugees—they—"

They have a refugee? We're all on our feet in a moment, Demetra's hand pressed to her lips, while the boy stutters an explanation. "They're bringing him through the street—they said he tried to kill Rambaud—"

My heart thumps, and Rhia catches my eye. Her nostrils are flared. She's guessed the same as I have.

Somehow, they have captured Ciril. And he tried to kill Rambaud—but why? *How?*

Demetra has already bolted out. I hurry after her through the temple corridors, Rhia on our heels. Felicité comes running behind—"Here!"—and throws three blue robes at us. We wrestle into the long, plain wool robes, and the round hats that accompany them—a safer disguise than the usual fillets. My robe is inches too short and squeezes me tightly under the armpits, but I'll just hope no one looks at me too closely.

From the front steps of the temple, a crowd is roaring. A bell clings, and my hackles rise. A witch hunter?

People fill the open square in front of the temple, crowding the street. The steps afford us a view, and I can make out a procession moving slowly down the street—a collection of horses and carriages and soldiers. If the sorcerer's there, he's lost in the crowd.

"Come on," Rhia says. I follow her down the steps, dodging the spectators who have gathered, Demetra on my heels. People talk among themselves, leaning up on tiptoe for a glimpse of the procession.

Then I hear it—toward the front of the crowd. Several men are running along ahead of the procession, calling out, "End sorcery! End sorcery!" Some shopkeepers in the crowd obediently take up the shouts, while most others just stare. They're not here in protest, I realize—or at least most of them aren't. They seem bewildered and tired, and more than a little frightened. They've come out not to scream Rambaud's bywords, but to find out what's happened to their city, to see who's claimed it this time.

It makes me unspeakably weary.

Close to the street, Rhia slows and grabs my arm. She has to rear up on tiptoe, but I'm tall enough to see why she stopped moving. So is Demetra. Both her hands are pressed to her mouth now. Between the ranks of guards, a man is stumbling forward. Iron shackles bind his hands and ankles, and his face is grimed with dirt beyond his ragged beard. He can't walk so much as shuffle, and keeps falling to his knees and struggling to rise again. The two men leading him just drag on his chains. Several people in the crowd jeer. Ciril stumbles back onto his feet, only to fall again a few steps later.

It's hard to imagine this man attempted to kill Rambaud—and I can't imagine he even knows who Rambaud is—yet this is the person who brought down the lightning that murdered a palace guard. I don't know what he wants, or even what he's really capable of, yet my heart is shattering to see him like this. Rhia's gripping my arm—or perhaps I'm gripping hers. The bell peals out again, and Ciril grunts as if he's been stabbed. But no witch hunter appears in a blue coat. I finally spot the owner of the bell: Rambaud himself, seated on a horse, following Ciril.

"We have to do something," Rhia whispers. "They're going to kill him."

Demetra stares at us, but I just shake my head. Maybe they're going to kill him, but they're going to send him mad first, the way witch hunters famously do in Ida. More than that—they're going to make an example of him.

They'll do the same to Demetra if they catch her. And—it hits me with a painful impact—me. The sound of the bells clangs like teeth into my head, and I shudder. But the sound doesn't stop; it ripples on and on, now fading, now growing stronger, growing taut. No wonder they invented this torment to undo sorcerers. It makes me want to bolt—not just for the temple, but for Barrody. I want to get as far away from here as I can. Yet we can't simply leave Ciril and the others. Can we?

The crowd's pressing around us, blocking our retreat. So though the throbbing in my head propels me to leave, I'm forced to stay. To watch, and pretend I feel nothing. To squint through my watering eyes. And so I see them.

The carriages, first: gilded and worked with filigree designs. Flanking them, men in fine coats on horseback. Women occupy the carriages—women in silk gowns, their hair elaborately dressed. They look out over the crowd with cold, satisfied faces, though a few seem frightened. Maybe they think we'll rise up and overthrow them.

"It's the nobles come back from the country," someone says to my right—a café owner, to judge by her stained apron and odor of coffee. "Don't you recognize them from the gossip papers? Soon Countess Veronique Manceau will be back from Tinan, along with Duchess Hermine Rambaud."

"What about Loyce Eyrlai?" the woman's companion asks with disgust. "Will we have to see her again as well?"

The first woman laughs. "She won't be back. She never wanted to be queen."

"Well, if she comes back to Eren, *I'm* moving to bloody Tinan."

Behind us, several people shift and break away. The carriages have passed by, and there are mutters of, "Damned nobles back from a country holiday. You'd think the Caerisians could have held the throne longer."

"My money was always on the Rambauds."

"Mine, too, but my *hope* was on Sophy Dunbarron. She meant well, anyway."

"Nonsense. If she had her way, we'd be at war with the entire world. I value my head, thanks."

My teeth clench, and the bells echo in my head. Rhia hangs on to my arm. It takes all my strength not to bolt—or face them and declare that if they didn't like what I did, they could have told me so to my face.

Though in a way, I suppose they did. No one is exactly protesting Rambaud's coup.

It's Demetra who breaks away first, her mouth grim. We cross slowly back through the square, and I touch her arm. "I'm so terribly sorry. You don't know if he really would have attacked Rambaud, do you?"

She's shaking her head. "Whatever happened to him in his native country—Tinan—was so horrible he wouldn't speak of it, not even to those of us who also had horrible stories. I suspect . . ." She swallows hard. "I suspect his children died, and he vowed vengeance on whoever killed them. He wasn't a gentle man or even a kind one, but he's one of us. Just to see him go like that . . ."

"We might still be able to free him," Rhia begins.

Demetra cuts her a glance. "If it's a choice between Ciril and my children, and all the others . . ." She draws in a breath. "I have to choose my children."

I squeeze her arm. My heart feels so impossibly heavy. "Perhaps once we're gone, High Priest Granpier can argue for mercy. Granpier knows Rambaud. The duke might listen to him." Or more likely, Rambaud will arrest Granpier, too, as a sympathizer. It's what the old king of Eren would have done.

"It would be good simply to know he'll try," Demetra says. "At least Ciril will know he wasn't forgotten."

I look over at Rhia, but she doesn't say anything. I suppose there is nothing more to say, though I want to protest, demand that there be a better answer. But there isn't. None of us speaks as we climb the temple steps.

High Priest Granpier is waiting for us at the door. There's an actual smile pulling at the corners of his lips.

"They're dragging a man through the streets," I begin angrily.

He interrupts me. "You need to go in and see who's just arrived. Rhia and Demetra can fill me in on the details."

Rhia and I exchange a glance. Then I hurry through the doors, past the statue of Aera, and back down the hall to the kitchen. The door stands open. A man is seated at the long table, clutching a bowl of porridge in both hands.

I stop short. "Alistar!"

He turns. His hair is matted and dirty, his clothing rent. A long red scratch angles across his cheek. "Sophy!" He rises, shunting his chair backward, then checks himself. Glances at my stomach.

Heat burns into my cheeks. His gaze moves back to meet mine. He doesn't need to say anything; I know what I've done. I told the world I was with child. And by telling them the way I did, I told them the father didn't matter.

"You're alive," he says at last, then adds, "But then you've got Knoll there with you. I should've known."

"Where have you been?" Rhia demands, having followed me despite Granpier's injunction to remain with him. I can't seem to form words myself.

"Tracking Ciril." He nods toward the street and procession we just witnessed—and toward Demetra, who's come in with Granpier, her arms folded. "I have to admit I haven't done a very good job of it. I would have given up days ago, except I was outside Laon, in a village Rambaud was passing through, and I saw Ciril. He was in the crowd of Rambaud's followers. Watching Rambaud, the way a hawk watches a snake. He didn't even realize I was watching him."

"But why would he have pursued Rambaud?" I ask. "How would he even know who Rambaud *is*?"

"I can only tell you what I saw," Alistar says.

"Did you talk to him?" Rhia asks. "Ask him what he was doing?"

"I ran after him, but he disappeared in the crowd. But it gave me a hunch." He pauses. "I decided to follow Rambaud instead of Ciril—which is, if possible, even harder." He glances at me. "I didn't get to Montclair until it was too late."

"We were all too late," I say softly.

Alistar nods. "Ciril was there, too. He attacked Rambaud last night."

So Ciril really did attempt to kill Rambaud. I shake my head. "You were there?" All the gods, we might have been together, had I known. "But I still don't understand why Ciril would have gone after Rambaud."

Demetra draws in a breath. "The Butcher mentioned Rambaud to both of us. I remember now. He was talking of Eren's defenses, and he said that the greatest threat wasn't from outside, but from within. From Aristide Rambaud, who had just returned to Eren."

Coldness walks up my spine. "You think he did it on Lord Gilbert's orders?"

"No. We hadn't been given any order. It was simply part of the conversation; I didn't think anything of it until now."

"Rambaud's been in Tinan," Rhia points out. "Perhaps Ciril met him there."

"Ciril is from Darchon, the capital," I say, remembering, but then I shake my head. They may both have been in the same country, perhaps even in the same city, but it's hard to imagine Ciril's rough path crossing with Rambaud's cold and deliberate one.

"Perhaps Ciril simply understood the politics better than I did," Demetra says, "because he lived here. Maybe he understood the threat when the Butcher mentioned it, and decided to take matters into his own hands. Ciril was rude to the rest of us, but he was kind to the children. Perhaps he did it for them, because he had lost his own family. Maybe he thought it would keep them safe."

Wordlessly, High Priest Granpier takes her hand. Demetra's head is bowed, her lips tight.

I say nothing. Even if Ciril knew Rambaud's name, it doesn't seem enough to prompt a single-handed manhunt—especially without telling any of us what he was doing. There has to be something more at work here. But the only way of discovering it will be to speak with Ciril himself—which is currently not an option. I bite my lip, thinking of the shackles that bound him, and the obvious pain he was suffering.

"Well," Alistar says at last, "they're calling it an assassination attempt. They're blaming all of us—especially you, Sophy."

"Naturally," I say with some bitterness. As if Rambaud needs further ammunition against us. I almost wish Ciril hadn't even tried—though I can't pretend I'd have been sorry had he succeeded.

"There's another thing." Alistar hesitates. "I—I didn't try to stop Ciril. I saw him come into the town square, and instead of going after him, or any of them, I hid. I've never . . . *hidden* before. But I hid, and I watched. Ciril summoned lightning, just the way he did when he killed Thierry. It should have killed Rambaud. But . . . It didn't. It . . . *erupted*. Sprayed away into nothing. It was as if Rambaud was protected by an invisible shield. Ciril tried again, and the same thing happened. By that time the other men had surrounded him. They beat him down and tied him up. And Rambaud . . . he acted as if nothing had happened."

My skin is prickling. "You think Rambaud's a sorcerer?"

"Maybe. No." Alistar shakes his head. "I don't believe it was him, or he couldn't handle the witch hunter bell he's got. I don't know who it is . . . or what. But, Sophy—he's thrown you out, and he's denouncing magic, all while *he's using sorcery himself*. I just need to find out how—or who's doing it."

I nod slowly. Somehow this doesn't surprise me as much as it should. Then I catch Alistar's last words. "You mean you're going to spy on him again?"

"I'll help here first, but I have to figure out who it is. If we know, we can take them down. We can defeat Rambaud."

I press my hands over my eyes.

"Isn't that what you want?" Alistar says. He looks around at all of us, alarmed. "Don't you want to smash the bastard back into the hole he crawled out of?"

"I have no throne," I say quietly. "I have no palace, no guard, no army. The people are exhausted by this tussling over the crown. Who is going to support us? Who wants us back in power?"

He just looks at me, dogged. Trusting. "We can fight them, Soph. Elanna will be back soon. We'll have more power than Rambaud can even imagine."

I shake my head. There's no point in claiming power if no one wants us to have it, but Alistar doesn't seem to hear me say that.

So I simply square my shoulders. "There may not be much we can do now," I say to the room at large, "but we can go to the meeting of the Laon underground. Then we'll go north. We'll leave Eren. In Caeris, we can make sure the refugees are safe, and we can meet with our people and make a plan. And then . . ." I stop. And then the gods alone know how I will help my kingdom. Especially if Rambaud's *true king* really is Euan Dromahair, whom Ruadan once touted as the savior of all Caeris—the man whom Caerisians have spent decades waiting to claim his throne.

The thought isn't particularly comforting.

CHAPTER EIGHTEEN

Night falls. Victoire arrives at the temple, dressed entirely in black, her silence speaking volumes of her despair and worry. I try to speak to her, but she doesn't seem to even hear.

We slip from the house, taking the back alleys down to the warehouses that bulk up along the river. The city curls around us like a creature sleeping with one eye open. We take narrow steps down between two buildings and emerge onto the riverfront. The Sasralie rushes nearby, softly gleaming. I feel it like a whisper in my own body. The nighttime dreams of all the people around us, thick with hope and love and fear, press close, a twining symphony of color and sound. I touch my stomach.

We approach the warehouses; a narrow door leads us into a cavernous, hushed space. Victoire pauses to light a candle, which she places into a lantern. Then we edge past barrels and crates stamped with an Ereni merchant company's logo—THE EREN TRADING CO.—and deep into the underbelly of the warehouse. It's cool, the floor slightly damp on account of the river's nearness; all the barrels and crates sit on wooden pallets to keep dry. Finally we approach a long, rolling door.

I touch Victoire's arm. "Why this place?"

"The Ereni rebels used to meet in this spot," she says, her voice distant. "I spoke here myself once during the rebellion."

The Ereni underground. I know their leaders, of course, for

these are the people who made our victory in Eren possible. But until now, they never gave me any of their secrets; none of them told me that there might be a way to find the secret lines of resistance, still alive in the time after my victory. Of course, I didn't dream it would be necessary.

Victoire rolls the door back, and light pours over our feet. Several people rise from their seats on the wooden crates and barrels. I'm startled by the sight of Juleane Brazeur and her friend Lord Faure. She acknowledges me with a cool dip of her chin. "Sophy."

I hide a wince. Clearly we've dispensed with the honorifics. If I needed a more potent reminder that I'm no longer the queen of Eren and Caeris, this curt greeting is it. I don't know whether she's angry with me or the situation itself.

Victoire looks around the circle. "Are we all here?"

Brazeur nods. "Josie couldn't make it tonight. This is all of us."

"Why are we meeting?" one of the men asks. He's a stocky fellow, wearing a plain black jacket.

I start to speak, but High Priest Granpier puts a hand on my forearm and shakes his head. I fall silent. Clearly this isn't my meeting. Most of them haven't even acknowledged that I'm here. I swallow hard.

"There is some rather upsetting news," Juleane Brazeur says drily. "Our old friends are back in power."

"Yes," the man in the black jacket says with some impatience, "but they're bringing in the king they fought for." He flaps his hand at Rhia and me.

Brazeur and Victoire exchange a glance. Coldness unfurls down my spine. "What do you mean?" Juleane says, glancing at me.

"Euan Dromahair," Black Jacket says. "They're bringing him in from Ida, along with some 'very powerful' supporters." He snorts.

It's nothing more than what I suspected, but still a hollow chill spreads through my blood. So Euan Dromahair really is the *true king*. He chose Rambaud over us.

Juleane Brazeur faces me. "You must have known."

"I guessed," I say unsteadily, though I'm thinking that I should have pressed Philippe harder the moment I heard that password at Rambaud's party. "But you can understand why I might not have wanted to believe it."

"Mmm." Her mouth quirks. "It's a cold game, politics over one's own kin."

"Maybe he's angry," Victoire says, her black brows knotted. "Since you didn't summon him here and cede the crown to him yourself."

"Maybe." As if I would have given it up to a man I'd never even met.

Victoire is giving me a cynical look. "Maybe he thinks you stole the throne out from under him."

I fight the urge to glare at her. I should have taken action the moment I suspected the truth, though I don't know how I could have prevented my father from coming. Now we're left to scramble against Rambaud's plan, which in all likelihood will be a masterstroke.

High Priest Granpier squeezes my shoulder as if I'm a child. I want to disappear.

"So," Juleane Brazeur says at last, "we have a foreign king about to be installed on the throne, and he's allied with Rambaud. The Butcher is dead, so we've lost control of the army. This isn't good news."

Black Jacket folds his arms. "It may not be, but they've barely been in power for a day and a half. What use is it to fight against a regime that hasn't even had a chance to do anything?"

I stare at him. I feel as though I've been kicked. "They killed the Butcher."

No one seems to even hear me.

"We know what life will be like under Rambaud," Juleane Brazeur says briskly. "Things will go back to exactly the way they used to be. We'll lose everything we fought for."

"Maybe not. He's bringing in the so-called king of Caeris."

"Who is an unknown factor. He's lived in Ida all his life. Does he even speak Ereni?"

Black Jacket looks skeptical. "So what do you propose we do?"

"I think we need to prepare for all eventualities." Juleane Brazeur hesitates, glancing at me. "And we probably need to get Sophy and her followers out of Laon."

"I don't want to run," I protest, even though I promised the same earlier.

Black Jacket rides right over me. "Why not have her contact Euan Dromahair? He's her father, after all."

They all look at me—and I can't say it's an improvement on being unnoticed. Quietly, I say, "I have contacted him. I wrote him five letters after I took the crown. He never answered one of them."

"Maybe he'd show mercy if you grovel," Victoire says.

I meet her eyes. "Yesterday Rambaud and his friends tried to kill me and my entire retinue," I say flatly. "It doesn't exactly inspire confidence."

Rhia intervenes. "We have a refugee we need to smuggle out of the city. Demetra."

"And the others are in Barrody—hopefully safe for now," I add. I wonder what's become of Fiona, the mountain women, the palace staff. "Have any of you heard what happened to the other Caerisians at the palace? The Ereni staff?"

"The staff are safe," Lord Faure volunteers. "The takeover happened so quickly they were all too stunned to fight back. But there's no word on the Caerisians."

I close my eyes. Grenou and Devalle won't treat the mountain women kindly, nor my Caerisian maid. Yet I can't put anyone else at risk trying to smuggle word out. Maybe once I reach Caeris, I can write and ransom them. If they're still alive.

Black Jacket is talking again. "I still think the best policy is to wait and see. People are tired of all this upheaval, and obviously the Caerisian regime didn't do much good."

I wonder how insulted I should be by this.

"Rambaud hasn't done anything to us," he goes on. "In fact, he's been campaigning for a more just and equitable system of governance. We might give him a chance."

Juleane Brazeur is shaking her head. "A wolf doesn't change to a dog. Rambaud knows exactly what he's doing—much the way Duke Ruadan did. We need to be careful. Take precautions. We need to put the communications system back in place."

Black Jacket huffs. "Juleane, your faith in humanity is really rather disappointing . . ."

"I'll make things easier for you," I tell him. "We'll go to Caeris and regroup. I'll take power in Barrody." The Caerisians will always be loyal to me, after all. At least, I think so.

"Maybe," Black Jacket begins, but just then there's a thud from outside the storage room. We all go very still. Silent. A fist raps on the door. Rhia puts her hand to her dagger.

The door rolls open. A man rushes in, throwing off his hat. "You need to get out of here! Soldiers are coming!"

I stare at Philippe Manceau. My mouth seems to have fallen open.

He spares the briefest glance for me. He's obviously come from the palace—he's well dressed in a gleaming brocade coat and matching trousers, impeccably groomed. "They're five minutes behind me, if that. We need to go."

"How did you find us?" Juleane demands.

"I have spies," Philippe says bluntly. "On Granpier in particular. Now, *hurry*—"

"You have spies on Granpier?" I'm utterly taken aback.

He gives a bitter smile. "They're my mother's, if you must know. We need to go!"

"How do we know Rambaud didn't send you?" Black Jacket asks in a spectacular about-face. "And how would *he* know where we are?"

"He has spies, too!" Philippe practically shouts. "Everyone has spies, and if you don't, you're a fool! There are guards coming to *arrest you*. He wants to destroy any resistance."

"That's absurd. He's hardly been at the palace—"

I take charge. "We're going. Victoire, out. Rhia, you check ahead. How many exits are there? Will they follow you, Philippe?"

He nods. "I expect so. I wasn't subtle enough. Didn't have time."

"Then we go out another way." I point at the man. *"Move."*

We all run out into the warehouse—but we're too late. I *feel* them in my skin, drawing closer. "Douse the lights!" I order.

We plunge into darkness. Somewhere ahead, over the black shadows of the crates, a light flickers and blooms. Boots crunch over the graveled floor.

"This way," Juleane breathes in my ear. We ease to the right along a path through the crates. I'm aware of my too-shallow breath, the weight of my body.

The lights flicker closer. We move so silently, then stop all at once. Between the crates, I catch the barest glimpse of a man's face in the lantern-light. Grenou. He's motioning them toward the sliding doors.

"We're going to have to run," Juleane whispers.

I nod. "As soon as they go in."

There's a squeal as the door is rolled back.

We bolt, racing in a ragged line through the crates, careless of noise. My breath is hot in my mouth. There's a precarious moment as we run for the warehouse doors.

Then a voice shouts behind us. "Halt!"

We don't halt. We're sprinting now, catching ourselves against the hard corners of the crates. Lights flicker madly behind us. "They're out there—"

A doorway. It looms suddenly in front of me. I burst out into the night. Several figures are racing away down the waterfront, just visible against the glinting river. Someone grabs my elbow. "This way." It's Victoire.

I run with her between buildings, Rhia, Philippe, and Granpier on our heels. Behind us, the guards shout again. "Stairs!" Victoire hisses, and I lift my foot just in time. We rush up them. My thighs burn. Behind us, the guards seem to have scattered, unsure whom to pursue. I hear Grenou's caustic bark.

Then we reach the street. I have the barest moment to gasp in a breath before Victoire is running again, and the rest of us charge after her.

Philippe grabs my arm. "Sophy—the temple—"

"They're there, too?" I gasp the words between breaths.

"Yes—he knew—suspects—you're there—"

Curse it all! We ease around the café blocking the entrance to the temple square, and slow. Sure enough, a parcel of guards have gathered on the front steps.

High Priest Granpier makes an abrupt about-face. "This way!" he whispers.

We plunge after him down an alley and emerge in the open space behind the temple, facing the river. Beads clack. I breathe out. "Félicité." Over the balustrade, I glimpse a boat shifting on the water.

Granpier is panting hard; he points Rhia and me toward the steps leading down to the river. "Go. I'll stay. Head them off." He takes off to the temple's back gate before I can protest.

Victoire turns to go as well. "I'll stay here. Send you messages by the usual routes. Go to Barrody and build your support."

"I will." Impulsively, I hug her.

She hugs me back, briefly. "Go!"

I glance around for Philippe and see him starting to turn away. "Philippe—"

"Yes?" He looks back at me, his gaze impenetrable in the shadows.

Quietly, I say, "It seems I ought to have trusted you."

"It's all right." His teeth flash in the darkness: a sudden, self-deprecating grin. "I wouldn't have trusted me, either."

"Rambaud," I begin, "your mother—the Butcher told me—"

"Did he say I stole my mother's money?" Philippe's voice is flat in the dimness. I'm aware of Victoire lingering by the nearest building, listening in that intent way of hers. "That she threatened to disinherit me? Because I was *irresponsible*?"

"Well, he didn't say that."

"But it was implied." Philippe lets out a huff of air and glances over his shoulder. For the moment, we are still alone, watched only by Victoire and Rhia. Swiftly, he whispers, "I told you about the printing press, didn't I? How I had to burn it down? It wasn't the only thing I was made to do. I saw what we do to the people beneath us, Sophy. I *participated* in it. The threats. The extortion."

He pauses to draw in a breath. Victoire has drawn nearer again, her arms folded. I can't make out her face, but I know enough of her story to recognize that Philippe's is not so far from it.

"So yes," Philippe says, "I stole my mother's money. I was going to send it to the north, to Duke Ruadan. I read all those pamphlets before I burned them, and I knew if he meant even half the things he said, his regime would be better than the Eyrlais'. I shouldn't have done it. I should have taken everything I had and simply run all the way to Caeris. But maybe my mother would have found me there anyway, and found some way to force me back to her."

"You should have told me," I begin.

"I tried! But Devalle and the others were watching me." He hesitates. "My mother threatened to disinherit me, it's true, and she has every day since if I don't obey her orders. But worse than that could happen, now that Rambaud's in power—and Euan Dromahair. They could make an example of me, you see."

I do. I nod wordlessly.

Roughly, from behind him, Victoire says, "You took too much of a risk coming here."

"My people ordered that fire set," Philippe says fiercely, "the one that could have killed Sophy. They massacred your people at Montclair. I can't stand idly by anymore. I have access to my mother's spies—I have access to Rambaud. I can use that to help you."

I reach out and grip his hand. "Then if you're willing, send messages through Victoire. I'll leave you to arrange a system."

"Yes," he says, "you need to go."

I nod, and then on second thought, I hug him quickly, the way I did before. I whisper in his ear, "Be careful."

"Sophy . . ." Rhia nudges me along the street, and I go, leaving

Philippe and Victoire behind. When I glance back, they have both already melted away into the shadows.

I follow Rhia down the shallow steps to the fishing docks. The barge lingers by the shore. Alistar is waiting in the boat, peering up toward us through the dark. He reaches up to help us into it, his hands warm on mine for the briefest moment. I settle down beside the bundled, silent figures of Teofila and Hugh, across from Demetra, whose head is bowed. No one speaks a word. I glance back at the shore and the domed roof of the temple, where Granpier has gone to meet with the guards.

Then the temple novices ply the poles, and the barge slides around the river bend, downstream. Alistar glances back at me but says nothing. The city murmurs around us, a gathering tremor that hums into my very bones. So many people and colors and sounds my head throbs, and my heart aches with the knowledge that I'm abandoning them. I hum a few soft notes, but of course nothing happens. I can do nothing but go.

We slip slowly down the dark river, leaving Laon behind.

WE EACH TAKE a turn poling the barge downstream. In the silence, with only the soft splash of the poles and the quieter sounds of the people around me, I feel oddly bereft. It doesn't help that Alistar still doesn't quite look at me, though he's sitting directly in front of me in the barge.

On the outskirts of the city, we drive the craft into the shallow reeds on the riverside and clamber out. Alistar grips my elbow fleetingly as I climb from the boat, and I feel again the distance between us. I plant my aching feet on the shore; my body curls on itself, tight and cramped and unutterably weary from our flight. Around us the night lies deep and quiet. A few frogs chorus. Nothing is left of Laon, not even a faint glow in the sky.

I shiver and hug my coat tighter. Perhaps I was never meant to be an Ereni queen.

But I am determined to keep Caeris, at least, safe.

"Goodbye," I call quietly to Felicité, who is already poling the barge back into the river. If she replies, her voice is lost in the hush of the water around the pole.

"The road's over here," Alistar says, his voice deep in the night air. We shuffle through the soft riverbank. The royal road going northwest is quite close, the route muddy from melting snow and spring rain. In the depths of the dark night, we should be safe using it, as long as we keep an ear out for anyone approaching by chance. As we tramp onto the road, I absorb the fact that we'll have to walk all the way to Barrody, unless Rhia can find a place to shift the land. The journey takes the better part of five days by coach. I don't even want to think about how long it will take on foot.

I fall back to walk beside Rhia. "Any chance of shifting the land?"

"We'll come to a spot eventually." Her voice is rough. Tired. "And once we do, I'll do my best to move us all through, though there are a few more of us than I usually take. But I'll manage— that's what a Knoll does."

I can't see her expression in the darkness, but I can imagine her scowl well enough. She's definitely annoyed. "Your father can retreat up into Caeris," I say at last, finally realizing what must be troubling her. "He may even be over the border now. We'll send word to him as soon as we reach Barrody."

"Hmm." Rhia stumps along beside me, unspeaking. At last, when I'm beginning to wonder what I said wrong this time, she says, "We don't know what sort of military presence Rambaud has. If he—they—have people in the army willing to overthrow its leaders."

I hesitate. She's right to worry, of course. Ingram Knoll is leading a group mostly made up of Caerisians, but there are some Ereni among them, and if they turn on them . . . But we have to get to Barrody first. We can't simply bumble around the country looking for Ingram Knoll; we don't even know his location.

"I'm sorry, Rhia," I say finally.

She makes a brusque movement in the darkness, wiping at her cheeks. "I know."

We don't speak much after that. The road winds through a small town, which we avoid by tramping through a series of muddy farm fields. After we stop to rest, I find myself beside Alistar. My heart leaps as it never has before, not even the first time we kissed, or that night when we sneaked off into my bedchamber to make love for the first time. I was a girl then; I'm a woman now, and I've made a woman's mistakes. I wouldn't blame Alistar if he doesn't want anything to do with me.

"You're all right?" he says gruffly. "And the—the child?"

I touch my stomach self-consciously. "We're both fine."

The silence stretches between us.

"It must sting," he says at last, gruffly, after we've walked through more darkness, and I've splashed through a puddle. I hardly even notice; my feet are already soaked. "I know how much the crown meant to you."

An undeniable bitterness underlies his words. I flinch. "I'm sorry, Alistar."

He doesn't respond. Just waits. I stare out ahead of us. The others are walking behind us on the road, talking quietly; only one lantern lights the way. Yet here at the head of our little party, looking into the darkness before us, we feel entirely alone.

So there's no one to rescue me. I have to fumble through the words myself.

"I'm sorry," I say again, "that I put the crown before you. I knew how desperate the situation was. I was trying to hang on with everything I had. But that doesn't excuse the things I said to you."

He's quiet for a long moment—so long I start to wonder whether he'll respond at all. "No," he says at last, "it doesn't."

I wince. "I deserve that. But I'm glad we're here now."

"You are?" He glances at me in the dark, surprised.

"It means you're speaking to me again."

He grunts. It might be a laugh—a surprised one. "Aren't you still planning to marry that Philippe?"

I think of Philippe, the way he looks at me. He's a good man. A helpful one. But he's not mine. "No."

Alistar glances at me again, swiftly. I feel his surprise—and then, as I might have expected, his smirk even in the dark. "He's not man enough for my Soph, is he?"

I roll my eyes. "This isn't a contest . . ."

"He has that perfect hair." Alistar's warming to his theme—clearly he's given quite a bit of thought to this particular matter. "And that noble expression, like a stallion bred for show. You know, all glossy. And—"

"That's enough!" I'm actually starting to laugh, and I refuse to give Alistar the satisfaction. "Do you want me to change my mind?"

"Have you made up your mind for me, then?" he says, challengingly.

The words are sharp in the darkness, and we're both silent for a moment. But I refuse to lose the tentative ease between us. I reach for his hand and, after a hesitation, he lets me hold it. I stroke my fingers along the back of his, the way I always have. Softly, I say, "I want you, Alistar Connell. Some days it seems like I always have. But I can't give myself to anyone, not now. You know that."

"I do, I suppose." Lightly, he covers my hands in his, stilling them. "But I helped create that child you're growing, and I want a part in its life. Don't forget that, Sophy Dunbarron."

My throat tightens. "I won't."

Behind us, Rhia calls out, "This is the place. I can shift us from here; I feel it."

And I do too, I realize. It's a soft, deeper hum within the land, as if the threads that make up the fabric of the earth are looser here, ever so slightly.

Alistar tucks his fingers through mine, and I clasp his hand against my chest. Just that small gesture; nothing more. But it's more than enough. We turn back, together, to cross the land to Barrody.

CHAPTER NINETEEN

We shift through the night, across Eren. We pass from the muddy road to an empty meadow, dew gleaming under the moonlight. Then we emerge into a place so deep in the forest I can hardly see my hands before me. "What sort of magic is this?" Demetra mutters warily to me.

"Rhia can feel the thin spots in the land, where there's an old stone, or a sacred spring. They link to others of the same kind."

"Oh," she says with sudden understanding. "That must be how you took Laon so quickly!"

"That, and armies of walking trees." I sigh, and in the safety of the dark I find myself confessing, "I wish my magic were more useful."

There's a silence. Then Demetra says, "It seems to me you don't truly know what your magic does. It might be useful for many things."

"Feelings, mainly," I say wearily.

I can hear her faint amusement. "But you hear things. You sense sound. Sound is powerful—one of the most powerful tools in the world. When I had my midwifery practice in Ida, I would engage a harpist to play for mothers before and after birth. They had no magic, those musicians, at least not in the way we think of magic. Yet you should have seen how their music soothed those women. A touch of the strings could relax them, could help them sleep and raise their spirits. I even had one assist with labor." She pauses. "If that is what an *ordinary* use of sound may do, just think what you might be capable of? You might touch the very fabric of our beings."

I force a laugh; the baby is shifting. "I think you overestimate any possible skill I could have."

"No. The foundation of sorcery is sound. A summons, for instance. If you speak the name of another sorcerer with enough command, no matter where they are in the world, they will hear you." She gives me a significant look. "Powerful sorcerers can even force someone to come to them, just by speaking their name."

"That sounds a bit . . . manipulative."

She shrugs. "Sorcery isn't good or bad in itself. It depends on who's using it, and for what purpose, like anything." She makes a twinkling sound, not quite audible. "You might even find yourself more powerful than your steward of the land."

I manage a laugh again, though my breath catches. To have even a sliver of El's power . . . "I can't imagine such a thing."

"It's hard to, since you don't know all that you are capable of."

Ahead, Rhia is guiding us toward the next shift. The magic hums through the dewy morning air, trembling like a living thing in my very blood. I say to Demetra, "How do I even begin to figure out what I'm capable of? It's not as if there's anyone who knows enough to teach me . . ."

"The same way anyone else does," she says. "By using one's mind, and making an educated guess. By trying things."

Tentatively, I begin to hum—a fall of deep-blue notes like the sound I hear glimmering from Demetra. Her eyes widen, and I hum a little more. The sound seems to take shape in the air between us, an indigo vibrance with shining chips of gold, overlaying Demetra. It *is* Demetra. It's as if she's growing more solid—as if I've taken some essence of her and brought it into form.

Her eyes have eased now, falling almost closed. "What is that song? It makes me feel so strange. Dense and light all at once."

"It's the sound you make," I say.

We look at each other. I'm starting to grin, and there are tears in

Demetra's eyes. "It's as if you brought my soul into my body. Sophy, it's like nothing I've felt."

We're both grinning now, possibility humming between us. Then Rhia calls, "Here it is!" and we step forward, together, through the shift in the land.

The next shift brings us to a valley below a high waterfall. The sky overhead is turning pink with dawn, and the air is cool, scented with pine. I drink it deep into my lungs, and smile at Demetra.

"We're in Caeris."

Rhia is growing tired, and the next two shifts take longer to find. But at last we step, impossibly, from a cow pasture to a high, bare hill marked by a circle of tall upright stones. A wind is shearing down from the distant mountains to the north, ruffling the hair on the back of my neck. Below, the hill slopes steeply down to a castle, its many towers bronzed in the morning light. Beyond it spread the gray slate roofs of the town, and the silver waters of Lake Harbor, one of the long narrow Caerisian lakes that feed all the way out to the sea.

Barrody. Home.

Tension drops out of my shoulders so suddenly I feel unmoored. Song seems to pulse from the stones—the rhythm of the magic Elanna released in them.

Demetra turns to me. "This is it?"

I nod. I'm smiling; tears are itching my eyes. I have missed Caeris so much. Roughly, I say, "Come. We will give you a proper Caerisian welcome."

We start down the hill in a ragged line, clinging to the steep path. I glance at the castle. I've scarcely been here since El woke the land, since she surrounded the city with a forest filled with the specters of our ancestors. It's such a relief to be back, even under these circumstances. My throat is tight. Alistar, just ahead, looks back at me with a swift smile.

Teofila drops back to walk beside me. "Sophy . . ." She gives me a searching glance. "Rhia told me it's Euan they're bringing."

I stare down at the peaks of the castle roofs. "Yes."

She touches my wrist. "We need to talk. Did your mother ever tell you about him?"

I give a short laugh. "She barely mentioned his existence. I had to deduce from meeting other children that I must have had a father, not sprung full-born from Ma's womb."

Her hand tightens on my wrist. "Then you don't know."

I look at her sharply. "Know what?"

But we're interrupted by a shout from below. We've been spotted, and people are running out through the gardens.

"Queen Sophy!" The cry rings against the castle walls, bouncing up the hill.

"It will wait," Teofila says.

I glance at her, but she's already waving to the people below.

The castellan, Fairbern, is hurrying up the hill to us. He's a thickset, capable man of about Hugh's age, dressed in a wool herringbone coat, for it's always a bit cold in the castle. Surprise hums from him, bright and orange, and underlying it a warm buzz that sounds like gladness. "We didn't expect you!"

"No," I begin, but I falter over the explanation. In the end, I simply say, "We had to leave Laon quite suddenly."

It's Alistar who tells everyone the truth. "An Ereni lord staged a coup. We've been thrown out of Laon. You need to double the city guard, and station someone here to watch the hill, in case they have an ally who knows how to walk the folds in the land."

"Yes, sir!" Fairbern swallows his alarm and gestures to two footmen, who run back into the castle to carry out the orders.

"Send word to the watchtowers on the old border as well," Alistar adds, his hands on his hips. "We'll need to mount a defense there. And if Ingram Knoll has reached Caeris—"

"We had word he's less than a day's ride away," Fairbern reports.

"Send him a messenger telling him he's needed, as fast as he can arrive." Alistar nods, then glances at me. A slight frown creases his brow. "That is, if the queen approves these orders."

"I do," I say. I'm fighting down a surge of pride. If the Ereni ministers could see him now, they'd never doubt Alistar's fitness as my consort. "Send word to whichever ministers are currently in Barrody, as well. We'll need to convene a council as soon as possible. I want reports on our defenses, as well as our munitions supply."

Fairbern nods. "Consider it done, milady."

I smile—and there's a sudden, painful twinge in my back. I put a hand to my stomach. Clearly walking all night with a child in my belly is not the best plan. I'm abruptly aware of my swollen feet, the sweat sticking my chemise to my body, and the exhaustion dragging down my limbs.

"The council meeting can wait until afternoon," I decide. If we meet, I might simply fall asleep.

"If you don't mind my saying so, you look like you could all use food, rest, and a visit to the bathhouse," Fairbern says with professional diplomacy. His gaze slides toward Rhia, whose face is worn, and her sling spotted with mud.

I glance at Demetra. "There is another thing—Demetra needs to see her children."

At that, Fairbern actually smiles. "Three bright young things named Alexis, Matilda, and Larissa? We've housed the refugees here at the castle, you see. They've already been informed."

Indeed, a shout is rising from the castle door. "Mama!" Demetra's children race into the garden, throwing themselves at her like eager puppies. She falls to her knees in the grass and hugs them tight, kissing their faces, asking questions so fast my poor Idaean can't keep up.

I glance at Alistar. His eyes are on Demetra and her children, his face lit with a slow smile that makes my heart feel too large for its cage.

Teofila presses my shoulder with a knowing look. "Let's go in."

We tramp into the castle's stone halls. Unlike the royal building at Laon, this is a true castle, its thick stones barely tamed by carpets and antique tapestries; most of the furniture is decades old, and the glass in the windows is heavy and blurred. It smells of age and stone.

The castle staff have gathered in an informal mass to greet us, and I think how little I miss the starched aprons and tidy caps of those in Laon. These people are dressed simply but more color-fully, a jumble of red gowns and blue coats, an insistence on indi-viduality that the Ereni have had forced out of them. The sound of them is as bright and varied as the clothing they wear. "Hello, Byron," I greet one of the men. "Did your wife have the baby yet? Is she doing well?"

"The finest little bear cub you've ever seen," he says proudly, and the others start laughing. I gather Byron tells them about his babe every chance he gets.

"And Annis!" I turn to the young maidservant watching me with wide, adoring eyes. The sound of her trembles in the air, a blush of pink. "Did your mother recover from her lung infection?"

"Oh, she's so much better, milady! I can't believe you remem-bered!"

I just smile. It feels so good to be back among these people.

"Let the queen be, now," Fairbern says in mild reproof, gestur-ing for the others to scatter. "She's had a long journey."

"Is it true we've lost Eren, milady?" one of the maids asks as they begin to file away. Fairbern gives her a quelling stare, and she says quickly, "I mean, we just heard Lord Alistar talking of it out-side . . ."

"It's all right," I say with a sigh. "And yes, it seems to be true. For now."

"It must be a horrible shock," she says. "But we're all glad it means you're back in Barrody, milady. It seems too long since you've been here, and it's good to see you. That's the plain truth."

I give her an impulsive hug. "Thank you."

She looks at me. "You're the queen we chose, and we want you here. Those Ereni don't know what they've lost."

"So you don't mind being just Caeris, not Caeris and Eren?"

She pats my arm—a familiarity none of the maidservants in Laon would ever dare. "We fought for our own freedom. If they want to lose theirs, let them. We have the *Caveadear*—or we will soon, from what they say. You and she are all we need."

I'm grinning now. It's so damned good to be home.

"Now," Fairbern says firmly, "the bathhouse is waiting."

I glance around. Teofila and Hugh have already disappeared— "Together," Alistar informs me. He raises his eyebrows roguishly. "What do you think of that, now?"

"They deserve happiness," I say, though in truth, it makes my heart feel stretched and strange. I knew Teofila wasn't entirely happy with Ruadan—which is perhaps putting it too kindly—but I didn't expect her to recover from his loss so quickly. Or to take up with his right-hand man.

But Teofila started growing away from Ruadan years ago; I never once saw them truly close. And maybe, I reflect, Ruadan never really understood what it was to love someone. He certainly made me wonder. Perhaps Teofila deserves every moment with Hugh, and more.

I shake my head and follow Rhia the rest of the way to the bathhouse. The small, vaulted chambers are billowing with steam; I groan when I sink into one of the pools. I let myself float for a few minutes, alone with my aching body. The child flutters in my womb. I hum the soft tone I gather from her, a yellow as bright as marigolds. I think back to the song I hummed for Demetra. Did I really sing her soul more fully into her body?

My mind is too dull with weariness to truly contemplate it. Instead I wrap myself in a fresh chemise and robe and climb back upstairs on aching legs—followed by both Alistar *and* Rhia. Alistar lets himself straight into my bedchamber, and I'm too weary to protest at how blatant he's being. Besides, it's not as if it matters much anymore. I pause in the doorway and turn to Rhia.

"Go to bed," I tell her. "You're swaying on your feet."

She blinks and says, "Someone needs to guard you."

"No one's going to assassinate me in the next few hours." At least, I'll take the risk. "Go rest, Rhia. You've earned it."

She gives me a stubborn look—and then yawns mightily. Her jaw cracks. "Fine. But if you die, it's not my fault."

She goes.

I enter my own chamber and close the doors. There is the old, comfortable bed hung with flowered curtains. Alistar is already curled up under the blankets, half asleep, his dark hair dampening the pillows.

I kiss him, then nudge his hand gently aside when he tries to pull me to the bed. There's one more thing I need to do.

A mirror hangs on the opposite wall. I approach it, my heart-beat rising into my mouth. I taste the sticky tang of failure. But I have to tell them—at least tell them some of the truth.

"*Jahan,*" I whisper. There's nothing. I concentrate, conjuring his image in my mind's eye: a hawk-nosed, sharp-witted Paladisan with a wry smile. I whisper his name again, imagining the sound winging all the way to Ida. It doesn't seem likely to work, even though I can feel the current of magic rising within me. I try once more. No matter what Demetra says, that speaking another sorcerer's name summons his attention, I don't know if I can believe that I'm really a sorceress.

Maybe, just now, I wish I weren't. Then I wouldn't have to confess this.

It's too late. Jahan's voice bursts into my mind: *Sophy!* Then the image in the mirror is shifting. It *worked.* I vanish, and it's him, his hair mussed as if he just got out of bed, his shoulders wrapped in a blanket. And behind him, leaning over his shoulder, bleary-eyed, is El.

I clap my hands over my mouth. "Oh, thank all the gods!" I never expected it to work. It feels like a miracle, a conjuring trick. Tears prickle my eyes.

What's wrong? El demands. Her hair is a chestnut tangle. I must have summoned them from bed.

I dig my fingers through my own hair. "Do you remember I told you there had been protests all across Eren, when everyone thought you were dead? Well, now the protestors are claiming—" I wince at my own words. *Have claimed.* They *have claimed* a victory. But I can't say it; I can't confess my own abysmal failure to Elanna and Jahan, with their tired faces and weary, worried eyes. "They're claiming a victory. Their leader made an attempt on my life—but I found proof—"

We've won here, El says, and my heart stutters. *We've taken Aexione! That should be enough to dissuade them.*

I'm shaking my head, tears falling down my cheeks, despite my fragile, momentary hope. No one in Eren cares what's happening in Aexione or Ida. And I have failed so completely.

I pull in a breath. "That doesn't matter now," I say, "not to them. They say they've found a replacement ruler, that he's on his way to Eren." I pause, choke out the words. "He's coming to take my throne. To claim it's rightfully his."

Elanna makes an impatient noise. *Who could possibly do that?*

I swallow hard. "Euan Dromahair. My natural father."

There's a moment of silence as they both stare at me.

But he has no right! Elanna exclaims at last. *And he has no support—no means—*

Jahan interrupts her with a gasp. His eyes have widened. *Sophy,* he says urgently. *What do people say about his supporters?*

"That they're powerful and influential—all the usual things." I roll my eyes despite my tears, thinking of Rambaud. "Why?"

In the mirror, El has turned to Jahan, her lips parting. As if she's had the same realization he has.

Augustus and Phaedra Saranon, Jahan says. He clears his throat. *Leontius's younger siblings—they wanted his throne. I have no proof. But Sophy, I would wager they are Euan's supporters, and they're headed to your shores, with him.*

I'm staring. "The Saranons? But why would they come here?"

Probably because they have nowhere else to go, El says grimly, *and for some reason they've allied with Euan Dromahair.*

They're opportunists, Jahan says. *They see Eren's weak, and they want to take advantage.*

El looks at me. *We're coming, Sophy. We'll be back in a few days. Just hold out a bit longer, if you can.*

I draw in a breath, and nod. "I will."

Their images fade from the mirror, and I turn, shaken. Shaking. So my father is coming here with the Saranon siblings. Perhaps they are united in a hatred of magic, though I don't know why my father would fear it—he was obviously willing to support Elanna as a figurehead in our rebellion. No, there must be more to it. My head feels thick, stupid. I can't see it.

Unless maybe he never intended to ally with us at all.

Alistar is sitting up in bed. "Sophy," he says gently.

He holds out his arms, and I clamber over the bed, into them, pressing my face into his warmth. His lips brush my forehead, my hair. Then his hands slide up my robe. He lowers his lips to my neck, and heat flares in me.

"I—I need to think," I say. "I need to plan . . ."

"You need to rest." His teeth nip my ear. "Let me comfort you, Sophy Dunbarron."

His fingers find the sash of my robe. I help him slip it loose. My chemise slides over my shoulders, and he pushes it down, kissing the hollows of my collarbone. I bury my hands in his hair. My eyes have fallen shut. Warmth is humming through me, an urgent desire. Yet at the same time I want to take this slow. So slow. I want to make it last as long as possible.

My chemise is around my waist now, and Alistar leans down, putting his ear to my stomach. There's a delicate movement in my womb, like a tiny bubble bursting, brief and gone.

"I felt it!" he exclaims. "Like a butterfly."

I laugh. "I am not going to give birth to an insect."

But then Alistar rears up, and there's no humor in his eyes, only an ardent wonder. My breath catches. How could I ever have denied him the chance to be a father?

"I love it already," he says.

"Her," I correct him. I'm smiling.

"A girl," he says wonderingly.

"She hasn't even been born yet," I say, for the look on his face is softening my tired heart. "How can you love her already?" As if I don't, too.

"I just know I do." Tenderly, he kisses me. I let myself sink into him, the warmth of his body, the hum of resonance that is so uniquely his. The thread of my own song rises to meet it. He's kissing me, and my breath and body are quickening, and as our bodies come together it seems that our songs do, too, melding into a unity that carries us both to that moment of profound release.

Afterward, I hold him against me. My heart aches too gently for words. I simply kiss him, slowly, sleepily, until we both fall into dreams, his hand still cupping my stomach.

I WAKE SOME time later, disoriented. The day has mellowed into afternoon, and a heavy bar of gold light lies across the bed. Somewhere, someone is singing. It's a melody I know in my bones—a warm cradle of sound that mothers me and pulls at the aches in my heart at the same time. I sit up, careful not to jostle Alistar. He wraps his arms around a pillow, still breathing slow, sleeping breaths. The baby kicks, once, twice, and I feel a foolish smile warming my face. For a moment, I'm caught looking at him, wondering whether our child will have his nose, his dark, thick hair or my ruddy-gold.

Then the song drifts nearer, and I look up again. It must be Teofila, though it sounds a bit deeper than she usually does. I slip carefully out of bed—no need to wake Alistar—and shrug into my dressing gown. I slept only a few hours, but feel vigorous and alert. I pad out into the hallway to find Teofila.

Only it's not Teofila. It's a woman in a long blue gown, walking away from me down the hall. Her thick blond hair is caught back in a braid that sways as she moves, and her gown is the deep blue of summer dusk.

The castle sits quiet around us, strangely so, in the middle of the afternoon. But fear doesn't spike through me. There's another tone rippling behind the woman, harmonizing with the song she's singing—or perhaps, I think, confused, she *is* the song. The melody weaves through the dust motes clinging to the air behind her, so vibrant it seems tangible. I reach out my fingers, and touch a pulse of pure sound.

The woman glances over her shoulder, and I see I'm right. She isn't singing. The song is simply emanating from her.

"Come," she says softly.

I hesitate. I grew up in a land where seeing a ghost is as common as sighting a crow, yet I have never been one of those people who stumbles upon one. I've never had an ancestor step through the veil and summon me. I saw the ancestors Elanna called up, of course, when we claimed Barrody and Laon in our rebellion. But none have ever woken me from dreams. None have ever wanted nothing but me.

There's a circlet on her brow, I realize, as she stands there waiting for me to make up my mind. The gold winks in the sweet, sleepy afternoon light.

"Who are you?" I whisper.

She simply smiles. When she begins to move away, I follow her and the twining music through the silent castle corridors and down the tall, wide-hewn stairs. Ahead, a door swings open without a touch. The gardens are flooded with the same thick, golden light; it shines between the stones high on top of the ridged hill. My heart sinks. She must be taking me up there, to the stone circle. Like Elanna.

But instead we skirt the base of the hill, until we approach a tiny glen I never knew existed, tucked between the fold of this hill and the next. We seem miles from Barrody and as I step among the ancient trees, I think this is what Caeris must have looked like a thousand years ago or more. The trees cluster around, enormous, gnarled, and a carpet of moss softens my footsteps. The light drifts through, so dense it seems to catch on the branches like gold.

My guide leads us past the trees, to a tumble of rocks furred over in verdant moss. Several vertical stones have been placed at the bottom of the rocks, where a small pool of dark water glints.

The woman steps to a flat stone on one side of the spring and turns to look at me. Softly, she begins to hum.

A river of gold seems to open inside me. I blink, and the world is clearer than it has ever been. I'm stretching out into my body, sensing every pore breathing in my skin, feeling the weight of the baby in my womb, the pulse of my blood, the breeze on my face. The woman begins to sing, now, a wordless golden song that twines around and through me, and I feel the weight of my own bones, the strength of my feet pressing against the earth.

This, I understand now, is what Demetra meant when she said she felt I'd brought her soul more fully into her body.

"Sound," the ancient queen says softly, "makes up the fabric of the world. *You* are song."

Understanding travels into me, slow, curious. If I am song, then maybe what I sense is the true essence of people. When I sense others around me, when I hear their emotions humming from them—maybe I'm feeling who they really are—the fabric of their beings. Their souls. Maybe, when I knocked the men unconscious in Montclair, I actually snapped the souls *out* of their bodies for the briefest moment. The idea makes me blanch.

Around us, a deeper song has begun to weave itself between the trunks of the trees, and I look around in sudden realization. "Golden pines," I whisper. The magical trees that used to grow throughout Caeris; legend has it that their sap sings. Yet it's more than that. It's the trees themselves singing. It's me. It's her.

It's the world around us, interwoven, humming all at once.

The ancient queen nods. "You are beginning to see," she says. "Open your eyes, Sophy Dunbarron."

I look at her. There is something particular, yet elusive, in her face, as if I am dreaming at the same time I'm seeing her. She is both a breathing woman, and nothing more than a collection of shimmering, humming motes of light.

"Queen Aline," I whisper. Not the legendary Wildegarde, but the monarch she served.

I look at her—

And she's gone.

I'm curled on my side in the mossy rocks, my cheek pressed against my fist. My mouth tastes of sleep and golden light. When I sit up, something hollow clatters against the stones. I reach for it blindly.

It's a flute. A flute made of *bone*—white and fine, with six holes for my fingers. I put it to my lips and play a tentative note. It hovers mothlike over the water, speeding through the air. The flute itself is humming—not merely with the echo of the music, but with a deep, potent vibration. Magic.

Sound. If everything in the world is made of sound, then one sound can change everything. Put a man to sleep. Inspire a woman to dance. Bring comfort to an aching heart, and joy to one already happy. It can transform any emotion, any person.

I find myself whispering the words aloud—the ancient poem about Wildegarde. About Aline.

The queen spoke a word and the world heard it. When she whispered a truth, the people felt it in their hearts. When she sang, every living thing caught the rhythm of her song. She sang the heat of the sun into a sword, and the shining of the moon into a cup.

I rise from the ground, clutching the bone flute. There's no sign of her now. The light is once again ordinary; an afternoon like any other. Yet the trees and the spring whisper with the memory of her presence.

I tuck the flute into the pocket of my robe. At last, I think, I am beginning to understand what I am meant to do.

CHAPTER TWENTY

From the edge of the glen, I see a woman walking through the castle garden. She's coming along the same path I took: Demetra. I can't believe she's up already—and let her children out of her sight.

"I heard something," she says as we draw closer together. "A song." I look at her, and her lips part in understanding. "Someone came to you?"

"Yes." I glance back toward the glen, then pull the bone flute from my pocket. It pulses in my hand like a living thing. Demetra looks at it, her eyebrows rising. "Do you know if it's possible to—to put magic into an object?" I ask, stumbling around a question I don't quite know how to ask.

Demetra's lips twitch. "Like a magic sword?"

"A lot of Caerisian kings supposedly had those," I say, and we both snicker. Sobering, I say, "There was a queen of Caeris, back in the time of legends, named Aline. She had a magical cup, and a magical harp, and a magical cloak . . ."

Demetra takes the bone flute from me, running her fingers over the holes. When she looks up, she's not laughing anymore. "It feels like there's magic in it."

I swallow. "I think there is."

"It feels like . . ." She purses her lips and gestures above us to the stone circle crowning the hill. "It's like a tiny piece of the circle's great power, caught in here."

Slowly, I say, "If the circles—and springs, and places like that—if they are the sources of magic, perhaps sorcerers tried to capture that power into an object, for when they left the place."

"So they could still have a source of power!" Demetra snaps her fingers. "So they wouldn't have to draw upon their own life force."

I blink. "Is that what you had to do in Ida?"

"Yes." She gestures around us. "But here, there is magic to be had near any of these circles. I can use sorcery without draining myself, the way I did at home."

"There must be something like our circles and springs in Paladis."

"I suppose there is, but the use of it has been lost, the way yours was until the *Caveadear* woke the land. Perhaps Tullea and Jahan and your Elanna found it, in Paladis." She hands the bone flute back to me with a little shiver. "There's something powerful in that, Sophy. It feels . . . larger than it ought to."

"I'm not sure what to do with it, exactly."

She looks amused. "Well, I would think you'd play it."

I grin, and just then a shout raises over the palace. A ululating cry. "That's Ingram Knoll!" I exclaim. He's here earlier than expected—they must have traveled by way of the folds in the land.

Leaving Demetra, I hurry along the graveled path that takes me to the front of the castle. A party of mountain lords are dismounting from their horses, their brilliant cloaks flapping bright, along with a small band of Alistar's Hounds of Urseach, their hair spiked as if they're ready for battle. They all shout when they see me. "The queen! Queen Sophy!"

"Hello, everyone!" I can't seem to stop smiling; it is so good to see their faces, to hear the familiar burr of their Caerisian accents. I pass through the party, clasping hands and patting arms, barely self-conscious even though I'm only wearing a dressing robe. Finally I glimpse Ingram Knoll himself over by the palace steps, in intense discussion with Hugh.

The warden of the mountains swings around when he sees me and actually lifts me up in a bear hug, kissing me resoundingly on either cheek. "Congratulations, Sophy darling! I hear you're bearing a future Dunbarron."

A chorus of congratulations rises from the men behind me.

It's so completely opposite of how the Ereni ministers reacted—not to mention the Ereni themselves. And they call me by my name, not *Your Majesty*. Hugh is smiling, too, in a way he never let himself in Laon. Gratitude overwhelms me; I can feel a smile warming my own face.

"Thank you for coming so quickly," I say to Ingram Knoll. I glance at Hugh. "Hugh's probably told you what's happened."

Ingram Knoll's face darkens. "That he has. It's a cruel trick the Ereni played on you, and no surprise our kingdoms forged different identities these last thousand years."

Only the mountain lords would view this conflict in the context of centuries. I start to laugh, despite everything. "I don't know," I say to him, "the mountain lords have played some even cleverer tricks in the past."

His expression lightens; he winks at me. "That's a secret between us, now. Don't go letting those Ereni know."

"I shall not whisper a word south of the border," I say virtuously.

"That's another matter," Hugh interjects, in a serious voice. "Alistar was wise to bring it up this morning. The border watchtowers need to be manned once again—"

"Or woman-ed," I point out.

He flashes me a smile of acknowledgment. "We'll have to raise a force of men *and* women. I doubt we have enough forces at our disposal now to cover the entire length of the border. It's possible Rambaud isn't interested in taking Caeris, but I presume it's a particular goal of your father's."

"Euan Dromahair." Ingram Knoll's lip curls in clear disgust. "The man should have come back himself if he wanted Caeris, instead of sending that boy Finn to die for him."

"He may be willing to work with us," I say, "but I would feel better with a firm guard between him and us."

"We'll see to it," Ingram Knoll promises me. He reaches into his pocket and produces a rather crumpled note. "From Count Hilarion, in Tinan. We've been in touch. Forgive me for opening it—I wanted to be certain it wasn't information I needed to act on."

I take the note. Four lines scrawl across it, in Hilarion's elegant handwriting:

Now that the old eagle has died and the young eagle has claimed his throne, the lion questions where he has made his lair. I see him wondering whether the she-bear might be a safer ally than the magpie, for all the magpie is his friend. The young eagle is, it appears, both a friend to sorcery and the raven whom we know well, and the lion sees the changing tide. If the she-bear sought an alliance with the lion, she might receive an audience.

"He's always afraid it will be intercepted," Ingram Knoll says with a sigh. "Though in truth, I think he just enjoys his little code."

I snort a laugh. "Let me see if I understand this. The old eagle must be Alakaseus, and the young Leontius, if he's a friend to sorcery and the raven—who I suppose is Jahan. So Leontius has taken the throne, then?"

"It appears so. If Hilarion could be bothered to explain himself . . ."

"The lion must be Alfred of Tinan. So I am the she-bear and . . . is Rambaud the magpie?" I squint at the paper. "Hilarion thinks I should try to ally with Alfred, now that Leontius has come to power."

Hugh, who has been listening, leans forward now. "Alfred's no fool. If Leontius has claimed power, and he is a friend to sorcery . . ."

"The treatment of magic throughout the world may change. Alfred must see the score." I glance past him; the castellan Fairbern has emerged onto the steps and caught my eye. I nod and tuck the note into my pocket. "Ingram, Hugh, if you'll come in, we're as-

sembling the ministers to begin a meeting. The men will find re-
freshments in the kitchens as soon as they've stabled the horses. I'll
join you soon."

Hugh nods, and goes to pass the word to the men. But Ingram
Knoll draws me aside before I can go in. "How is my Rhia?" he
asks in an undertone, a frown deepening his brow.

My heart softens. Someday Alistar will scowl just this way over
our child's safety. "Her arm is still holding her back," I tell him,
"but her spirit's as strong as ever, if her tongue is anything to judge
by."

"My Rhia is a sharp one!" He chuckles, but says more soberly,
"Thank you for taking her back to Laon. I'd have worried about
her on the border. I want to keep her in one piece. She's meant for
more things than, well . . ."

"Being a royal bodyguard?" I say wryly. "I agree. But I think she
believes her only skills lie with a sword."

He sighs. "At least you see there's more to her. You'll help bring
it out of her in time, I'm certain of it." He pats my shoulder once
more.

I go in. The staff greet me, and I fall in stride with plump Annis,
who's carrying a load of linen upstairs. She refuses to let me take
any of it, though her cheeks are bright pink—but perhaps that's
more from nerves than from effort.

"Congratulations on the baby!" she exclaims. "The future king
or queen of Caeris."

"No, Annis!" I stop right there in the corridor, and she does,
too. She's flushed again; the poor thing looks mortified. I hasten to
explain. "I mean, thank you, of course. But I was elected, like the
kings and queens of old. If my child becomes the next monarch,
she or he will put forth their name and be confirmed by election,
too."

"Oh, but don't you think it's a given?" she says doubtfully. "If
you raise your child to be the next ruler . . ."

My child, whom I claimed would be the future of Eren and
Caeris. Yet Ruadan raised me to know my history, and now that

I'm home, I'm reminded that it isn't up to me. The Caerisians claimed their freedom so the best candidate could take the throne, and no matter what I dream of, the good of the people comes first. Besides, the child growing within me *isn't* a symbol, as Teofila rightly told me. She's simply my daughter. "The Dromahairs weren't always the kings and queens of Caeris; they've tried to keep it in their family, but before they claimed it, the crown switched hands if the people found an heir wanting. Or sometimes simply if a better candidate came forward. Unless you're the only claimant, as I was, it could become contentious. My child will be raised with a royal education, but she'll still have to prove herself." Annis still looks doubtful, so I try another tack. "My mother was a maid. Like you. If I can become the queen of Caeris, you, or your daughter, or your daughter's son, can too. That is what we fought for, and it is my promise to you."

"That's quite a thought," she says slowly.

I smile. "One to think about." I step away, letting her return to her work, and step down the corridor to my door.

And I slow. Two men are standing in front of it, waiting for me. One of them steps forward as I approach, beaming. "Sophy! Welcome home." It's Lord Aefric, one of my Caerisian ministers, a dignified man with graying hair and a cheerful mustard-colored coat. I've known him since I was a girl; he used to visit Ruadan at Cerid Aven. "We came to congratulate you!"

I touch my stomach. "It's wonderful everyone has been so excited—"

"Well, it is marvelous news." Lord Aefric clasps both my hands in his. "The king coming to Caeris!"

I jerk back as if I've been slapped. "The king?"

The other man, Lord Gavin, a minister I know less well, is watching me intently. He's younger than Aefric, and the sound of him is less bright. Indeed, if there's warmth in Aefric's sound, the sound and shape of Gavin are brown and blunt. "The king from across the sea, of course. The one we fought for."

"Your father," Lord Aefric says, lifting an eyebrow, "Euan Dromahair, coming to claim his throne at last."

"I—" I bite the inside of my cheek. No one else has mentioned this yet. The palace staff got their news from me, though—and the only other person I've talked to is Ingram Knoll, who shares my sentiments. Carefully, I say, "Where did you hear this? I didn't think the news had reached the north yet."

Lord Aefric and Lord Gavin both look surprised—genuinely so, to judge by the change in sound frequency from both of them. "It's been all over Barrody," Lord Gavin says. "Did you not send us the letter yourself?"

"The letter," I echo.

"Yes, telling us the good news."

Rambaud. This has to be his doing. He's so damned clever that he forged a letter from me, knowing the effect Euan's impending arrival would have on the Caerisians. Of course, they haven't yet gotten word that Rambaud and his followers seized Laon through a bloody trick—and if Rambaud had had his way, I'm sure that news would never have found its way north. I should have anticipated Rambaud would do something like this; this is why he allied with Euan, so he would have the largely unconditional support of Caeris. So he could undermine me among my own people.

Now it will be my word against the legend that Ruadan built. The promise of Euan's return, so potent our people rose up in revolt. The irony tastes sour in my mouth.

I withdraw my hands from Lord Aefric's. "How interesting that you received this news; I can assure you it did not come from me. I only discovered that my father is coming to Eren yesterday."

Now Lord Aefric looks surprised, and Lord Gavin's eyes narrow slightly. Their sounds diverge—Aefric's high and uncertain, Gavin's low and taut.

"I discovered it," I say with an edge to my voice, "after Aristide Rambaud seized Laon in a coup and killed the Butcher of Novarre."

Lord Aefric has gone utterly silent; white shock pulses from him. "All the gods."

"We're here not to celebrate, but to mount a defensive." I look between the two of them. "My father seems to have allied with Rambaud. I don't yet know what it means for our future, but I came back to Caeris so that the Caerisians would have someone they know and trust in Barrody Castle, should they choose to keep me."

There's a silence around us; I can feel the castle staff, including Annis, watching us.

Lord Gavin bows. "We'll meet you in the council chamber, then."

He turns to go, but Lord Aefric doesn't. He says, "I have long wondered if Euan Dromahair is a trustworthy ally and future monarch." The words pour out, humming with truth, as if he's been holding on to them for years. Maybe he has. "I wondered at Ruadan supporting him, when the man never set a foot in Caeris, and then again when instead of coming himself, he sent that sorry lad of his to die for him, Finn. Then we won, and still he did not return. Now"—his voice rises, incredulous—"he returns by invitation of one of our *enemies*? When his daughter is queen? His allies write a letter to trick us, thinking we Caerisians are such a stupid, credulous people we believe a forged note, a false legend, over the woman we elected queen?" He shakes his head. "I don't like it, Sophy. I don't like it at all."

I'm staring. "Well," I manage, "he is the king from across the sea. I thought the Caerisians would want to give him a chance . . ."

"A chance across a heavily guarded border," Lord Aefric says darkly, "with a few hundred cannons at our backs." He nods. "That is the recommendation I'll make before the council."

With that, he sweeps away after Lord Gavin, who has been watching us from down the hall. Our eyes meet, and Lord Gavin nods. The sound of him has grown markedly quieter. "We know who the true ruler of Caeris should be," he says, with a ring of truth.

"Damned right we do!" Lord Aefric agrees.

I retreat into my sitting room, shaken. But I'm smiling, at the same time, in a kind of wonder. Lord Aefric *believed me*. He took my side over Rambaud, without even requiring proof. It was as if I'd said what he was longing to hear. Of course there may still be people in Caeris who will say Euan is the true king—that we should let him prove himself. But here is Lord Gavin, looking at me with approval. Maybe even the deep-dyed supporters of Euan will begin to change their minds, once they see what his followers have done.

Unless, of course, Rambaud has done more than send a false letter in my name. The man certainly seems more than capable of outmaneuvering me. I suppose time will tell.

I slip through into the bedchamber. Alistar stirs under the bed-covers. "Come back," he mumbles, holding out his arms.

I lean over him and drop a kiss on his forehead, then dodge away when he tries to pull me closer. "Council time!"

"I should never have fallen in love with a queen," he groans.

I just smirk as I pull a simple blue gown and soft stays from the clothes press. A metallic gleam catches my eye. It rests on top of the nearby vanity, old and tarnished: my mother's locket. I pick it up, turning it around in my hands. The clasp is stiff, but the small lock of hair still lies within, bound with a black ribbon.

Perhaps I'll need it, though I'm not sure what for. Euan Droma-hair doesn't seem keen to have proof I'm his daughter. But I open the clasp all the same, and reach up to fasten it around my neck.

A moment later, Alistar's hands have closed over mine. "Let me do that," he murmurs in my ear.

He fastens the necklace, but lingers there, kissing the back of my neck. I lean into it for a long moment, then force myself to break away. I tap his bare chest. "You are going to make me late. I suppose you could come with me, although . . ." I raise an eyebrow, surveying him. "It would be a shame to put clothes over all that."

He grins. "So I'm to be your boyish favorite, am I? Handsome, but not too bright?"

"Actually, I choose my paramours based on their talent for tactical thinking." I tug my gown over my shoulders and give him a mock-challenging look. "As well as for their rugged good looks, of course. Hurry up!"

He moves to gather his shirt and trousers, but pauses at my dressing gown. "What's this?"

He's picked up the bone flute. Even from here, I feel its eerie hum like a current in my own body.

"I don't know exactly," I say. "I had a—a kind of waking dream, of Queen Aline. She took me to it."

"It's a gift from the ancestors, then." He hands it to me. "You should keep it with you."

I tuck it into the pocket of my gown, and the current deepens, almost like a song whose melody I can't quite catch. I need to play it, to experiment with the music as Demetra suggested. First, however, I have an opposition to organize.

RHIA'S WAITING FOR us in the corridor. Her eyes are bruised from lack of sleep, and she looks perfectly cross. "Can't the damned meeting wait?" she demands.

"Good afternoon to you, too," I say, my arm wrapped through Alistar's. "You don't have to come. Go back to bed."

"Well, I'm here now." She looks at us both balefully. "Fairbern woke me up out of a nice dream, too."

"Don't blame me," I protest. "I didn't send him."

"Maybe he has a grudge against me. That would explain it."

"Perhaps you should challenge him to a duel," Alistar says with great solemnity. "Though how would you resolve it? Fisticuffs? With your broken arm . . ."

"Poetry," I say, just as seriously. "I hear that's how they're doing duels in Ida now. *Epic* poetry. No one dies, except of boredom."

"I rather like epic poetry," Alistar says.

Rhia glowers. "Neither of you takes me seriously."

Her mood improves, however, once we reach the council chamber, where the smell of coffee wafts up the hall. Rhia bolts ahead to claim a cup, while Alistar and I follow at a more sedate pace.

Unlike my council chamber in Laon, this room is all ancient oak paneling, scarred by centuries of use, the walls hung with banners depicting the great clans and cities of Caeris.

The room already bursts with vigorous debate—all the ministers, and more people still, crowd the oblong table. One minister is arguing heatedly in favor of sending a delegation to Laon to meet with Euan; Ingram Knoll asks whom he thinks is likely to volunteer, since most people prefer to keep their heads on their bodies. Oonagh Connell, Alistar's older sister, is arguing in favor of shutting the border down entirely. "The Ereni were never part of our original rebellion, and when we split our kingdom into two capitals, it weakened us."

"But Eren and Caeris used to be one," Lord Aefric protests.

"In a time best recounted in legends," Oonagh retorts.

I take up a chair, and Ingram Knoll and Hugh both pound their fists on the table. Eventually, there is silence, of a sort. "The people of Eren supported our rebellion," I say to the table at large. "It's their rulers—not only the royal family, but the wealthy nobles—who did not. They are the ones using our rebellion to claim power for themselves. There's still a chance the Ereni people may want us again"—under a differently structured government, I reflect with a wince—"but for now, we must take care of our own."

"Is it true that the *Caveadear* is coming back?" Oonagh asks.

"Word travels fast," I say with a smile. "I spoke to her this morning, and Jahan Korakides, too." I look down the table, at their dear Caerisian faces, and I smile. "They won. They claimed Aexione—and from what Count Hilarion told us, Leontius has claimed the throne."

A cheer runs up and down the table.

"Unfortunately," I add, "we suspect that Leontius's siblings are accompanying my father here, to Eren. They tried to seize power in Paladis, and now that they've been kicked out, they seem to be seeking a new base here."

"What do a Paladisan prince and princess want with us?" Lord Aefric asks doubtfully.

"I don't know for certain," I say. "Sanctuary, perhaps? I gather Leontius would have stripped them of their power if they had remained in Ida. We'll need to be wary of them. I don't know how much influence they have over Euan."

Teofila leans forward. She looks well rested, and her eyes have brightened since I mentioned Elanna's return. "They must be quite desperate to come to Eren. In Paladis, our country is seen as little more than a backwater. They would never come here if they had another choice." She looks around at us. "Perhaps there's a way to make them all more desperate—not only Euan and the Saranon siblings, but Rambaud and his followers as well."

I nod. "I think our minds are moving on the same lines." I tug Count Hilarion's symbol-ridden note from my pocket and smooth it on the table. "It appears that once Emperor Alakaseus died, and Leontius came to power, King Alfred of Tinan began to question his alliance with Rambaud. It seems Leontius is a friend to magic, as well as to Jahan Korakides, and Alfred is aware of the shifting dynamic."

Hugh nods. "Alfred's a pragmatic man. Even though he and Rambaud are friends, he won't directly oppose the emperor of Paladis."

"Which means," I say, "that he may be open to negotiations . . . even from those he once considered enemies. Particularly if they are allied with the new emperor."

Ingram Knoll looks thoughtful. "It may help. I'll send a letter to Hilarion at once."

"Excellent. Tell him I'd prefer to meet with King Alfred myself, if possible," I say, "somewhere on the border, in neutral territory."

Oonagh drums her fingers. "Of course, there's Baedon as well."

"I imagine the queen of Baedon will fold more easily than King Alfred," I say. "She doesn't have his army, or his personal connection to Rambaud. As far as I can tell, she mostly opposed us because the emperor of Paladis declared war. Now . . ."

"I knew Queen Sylvestra when I was a girl," Teofila says unexpectedly. She pauses, then admits, "In fact, I taught her how to play the pianoforte. She wanted to learn from a girl her own age. We had great fun. I'm sure she would remember me."

I blink. "Would you *go*? To Baedon?"

"It's a long journey," Teofila says, "but not so long as some. If I leave now, from Threve, I can take a Caerisian ship and get there by sea in a matter of days. I know Sylvestra will admit me to the palace, if nothing else." She winks. "I can tell her Alfred is allying with us, too, even if it isn't *strictly* true."

The others laugh and agree that it's a wise idea. But my chest is swelling. I look at Teofila, still too thin after the long winter. She's the closest thing I have to a mother. The journey by sea to Baedon isn't arduous in itself, but what if Rambaud has the foresight to already control the Ereni fleet? What if he has her stopped? What if Queen Sylvestra *doesn't* listen?

What if I lose her, too?

Teofila turns to me, and she must see some of what I'm thinking because she reaches across the table and grasps my fingers. "This is something I can do, Sophy. Let me help you."

I close my eyes, but I say the words, because I have to. I must honor Teofila's willingness to do this, and the simple fact that she will be our most effective ambassador. "Then of course you should be the one to go."

She smiles. "I think I have a way for us to keep in touch, as well," she whispers.

"Will it be enough?" Lord Aefric is saying. "Allying with everyone around Eren—pinching Rambaud and Euan Dromahair the way they pinched us. If they have no allies, nor trade . . ."

"Perhaps they'll cooperate," Hugh finishes.

"Yet we still don't know their plans," Alistar points out. "Or what forces they may be bringing from Paladis, though it can't be many if they had to flee so abruptly. Manning the watchtowers must be our first priority."

"Without question, that is important." Lord Gavin leans forward. "But Queen Sophy should perhaps begin by speaking to the people first. Not everyone may understand why we are thinking in terms of war and enemies. Some people still believe Euan Droma-hair is our ally—the true king." He turns to me. "Arguably it is most important for you to convince them otherwise."

A chorus of agreement runs around the table, and I nod, pleased Gavin has brought this up. "Please make arrangements for me to address people as soon as possible. Then, once the letter goes out to Alfred, and Teofila departs for Baedon"—my mouth goes dry just saying it—"we must turn immediately to Caeris's defenses. I want a thorough report on every watchtower on the old border, and an inventory of the food and supplies stockpiled here in Bar-rody. We may be in for a dry spring."

"Starve in spring," Hugh says, the old Caerisian maxim, "feast in fall."

Ingram Knoll nods. "We tighten our belts now to survive the next weeks. And soon," he adds, "the *Caveadear* will be back."

"That's another thing that may help us," Oonagh says. She's starting to smile. "Not only the *Caveadear*'s power, but that of other Caerisians. Magic has been awakening in people throughout the land. There have been stories of women who could glimpse the future, and supposedly a man turned himself into a stag up in the mountains."

"Really?" Rhia says, frowning. She sounds almost envious.

"A similar thing seems to be happening in Eren," I say, "though of course they're much less happy about it. The awakening sorcer-ers are being locked up by their families, or treated as mad."

"Southerners," Ingram Knoll says with comprehensive disdain.

"But the *Caveadear* will have an idea how to help them learn their power," Oonagh says, "along with the lore the mountain lords keep. Who knows what we might be capable of?"

I feel the bone flute humming in my pocket. Who knows, in-deed?

Rhia raises her cup of steaming coffee. "To Elanna."

We all lift our drinks. "To Elanna!" we chorus.

Ingram Knoll raises his cup and nods to me. "To Sophy!"

They all chorus the words, so deep they resound in the chambers of my heart. *"To Sophy!"*

I FIND TEOFILA in her chambers some time later. She's packing two small trunks, with the help of the maid Annis. I thought Teofila might be tense or even tearful, since she won't be here when Elanna returns, but she seems almost excited. "Oh, good, Sophy, you're here!" she exclaims. "Annis has volunteered to come with me, as a traveling companion."

I stare at mild, plump Annis, who seems like the last person in the world to sign up for something so dangerous. "Have you really?"

"I was thinking about what you said earlier, milady," Annis says, with unexpected confidence. "That my daughter—well"—now she blushes—"that my daughter could become the queen. Not that I'm planning to have a baby now, or anything like that. But . . . if I do have a child, I want to give her or him all the chances they can possibly have. And that begins with me taking some chances. For myself."

"Of course," I say in a strangled tone. I wonder if this is what my mother was like, when she packed her bags for Paladis, brimming with hope, determined to overcome her fear.

"So I'm going with Lady Teofila, to see a bit of the world," Annis concludes.

Teofila smiles at her. "And I'm so glad you are. I think that's all my things packed. Go put your luggage together, and we'll move out."

"Yes, ma'am!" Annis hurries off.

Teofila closes the door behind her. "I hope she doesn't get seasick—we need to spend the whole voyage practicing her Baedoni. She doesn't speak a word of it." More soberly, she says, "I wanted someone to go with me, for reasons of safety if nothing else. Annis will enjoy it, in any case. I'll show her the Promenade, and the Gardens of the Gods—"

"This is starting to sound like a sightseeing expedition!" I say, trying to keep my tone light.

Teofila looks at me and winces a little. "I imagine we'll spend most of our time in negotiations with Queen Sylvestra. But when we're free . . ."

"You'll want to explore the city, of course." I hesitate. "You seem . . . excited."

She closes her eyes. Quietly, she says, "Yes, I am. More than I imagined I would be. Sophy . . ." She looks at me now with a kind of infinite sadness. "My family is there. My parents—my brother—his wife and children. I haven't seen them in more than fifteen years, since Ruadan's first attempt at rebellion. We've written letters, but it isn't the same. I'll get to hug them. See them. Hear their voices. Eat the food they're eating. Speak in my own language."

"That will be . . . it will be wonderful." I choke a little on the words; my throat is so tight.

"It will be strange, too. Awkward. It's been a long time." With a little sigh, she crosses the room and folds me in her arms, cradling my head against her collarbone just the way she did when I was a girl, even though I'm much too tall for it now. She whispers, "I'll come back. I promise."

My whole body stiffens at those words. "You shouldn't make those kinds of promises—"

"Well, I am. *This* is my home now. I will come back."

I pull out of her arms, shaking my head. The sadness is so old and black I think I might drown in it. "You don't understand. Sometimes we make promises and—and the choice is taken away."

She touches her fingers to my chin, and I look up at her. Quietly, she says, "Your mother did a noble thing, Sophy. She saved you, knowing what would likely happen to everyone else in that village. I've thought about that for many years. Sometimes I've thought, if she could see you, she'd understand that she'd been selfish. That she tricked you, in order to give herself hope. That she should have given you the choice, even if you were a little girl."

I swallow hard. I can't even speak.

"I've asked myself if I would have done the same thing," she goes on. "And every time, the answer is yes. Yes, I would."

I close my eyes. "But you're only going to Baedon."

"Only," she echoes, with some irony. "I know it's a risk; a journey by sea always is."

It is, and I'm both grateful and worried that she's undertaking it. I just hug her again. "You told me you had some plan for communicating with me?"

"Ah, yes." She pulls back, excited again, and fetches a small object from her trunk. It's a hand mirror, the back covered in gilt curlicues. "I've been practicing! Go to that mirror."

Obediently, I step across the room, to the mirror hanging on the wall.

"Sophy," Teofila says, and then she whispers it again, more insistently, this time only in her mind. *Sophy.* Yet it's so loud, so vibrant, I hear it, too, humming through the air between us. I feel the effort it takes her to establish the connection. But just as I turn to offer that another sorcerer could do this for us, my reflection fades. The face in the mirror is Teofila's.

"There!" she says triumphantly, but her voice catches. She grimaces at me. "It's a bit of an effort, but I can manage."

"You can indeed!" I hug her again.

"And now I just have to do it in Baedon." She grins.

There's a tap at the door, and Hugh looks in. I kiss Teofila's cheek quickly. "I'll meet you at the coach before you leave, to say goodbye," I tell her, and squeeze Hugh's elbow on the way out. They deserve some time to themselves.

In the corridor, Lord Gavin is waiting for me, along with Rhia. I smother a sigh. It's part of my role, I suppose, that I can't get any time to myself, but it does get tiresome.

"He wants a favor," Rhia tells me.

Lord Gavin just shakes his head. "In fact, I thought you might be interested in a short excursion into the city, Lady Sophy, to examine the food storage situation. It would also be an opportunity to talk to some of Barrody's citizens, as we discussed earlier, and reassure them about your plans for securing the kingdom. I've taken the liberty of arranging a carriage."

"Excellent work," I say, surprised. He's followed up quickly on his suggestion.

"I thought it might be easier than a speech." A nervous flicker pulses off him, and he gives an awkward smile. "The possibility of war makes me uneasy, and the common people must feel the same. They'll be so reassured to see you moving confidently about the city."

I look at him, hearing beneath that single nervous pulse a thready beat—a desire to please, I think. The poor man, I suspect, isn't only worried about war; he's afraid for his position. I offer him the most reassuring smile I can muster.

"I'm happy to come." I glance back at Teofila's door. "As long as we return in time . . ."

"I'll see you back here before she leaves," he promises, with a cool hum of relief.

Rhia raises an eyebrow. "He did say he had food in the carriage." She adds, "And coffee."

"You've drunk enough," I tease her. "You're still vibrating."

She shrugs, and we start down the hallway, Gavin leading the way. "I will say I'm less keen on the carriage, though," Rhia says. "Blasted things. One day I shall have an entire day where I stay in one place and never go anywhere."

"You'd get bored," I tell her.

"Not just for a day, or two." She sighs gustily. "I could *read*. And no one would bother me."

Rhia Knoll has never struck me as much of a literary type. "What would you read?" I ask, curious.

"The old histories and legends were always my favorites as a girl. Especially the ones about Queen Aline."

"I'm surprised. She wasn't very bloodthirsty."

"I don't like books all about battles. What?" she says when I start laughing. "Military tactics bore me to tears. Adventure stories are much better. One of my favorite books is all maps—maps of every country in the world." She adds, "Of course, our library is ancient, so the maps are all from two hundred years ago."

I laugh in earnest now. Having Rhia along does make things better.

Lord Gavin's carriage is a large, well-sprung affair, and it smells of fresh bread and coffee. I pause, nevertheless, at the door. We've emerged into a side courtyard, empty except for the carriage driver, Gavin, Rhia, and myself. The driver doesn't look at us, but I glimpse his hands tight on the reins. Tension hums off him.

I swing back to face Gavin, only to find him staring me down. Not nervous now, or attempting to smile—instead a red, angry pulse strains from his body.

I reach for Rhia's arm, though she, too, has slowed. The courtyard lies quiet around us. Too quiet; the walls too high, their windows too empty. No ministers here, no servants. If this is a journey to a public audience, the public certainly hasn't been notified.

"I'm sorry," I say to Gavin with false brightness, aware of the hard beat of my heart. "I forgot something inside! How stupid of me."

I start to back away—but suddenly Gavin is there, behind me. He throws me forward. My knees bark against the carriage step. I stagger, instinctively trying to protect the baby. Rhia shouts, but it's cut off in a grunt. I glance back. The coachman has fallen on her, knocking her to the ground. I scrabble for something, anything, I can use as a weapon, but Gavin's behind me. He grabs me by the waist, shoving me hard into the carriage. My flailing hands smack a coffeepot on the seat, and burning-hot liquid sluices over my skin. I grab the pot anyway, trying to winch myself around so I can strike Gavin across the face. But he's bearing down on my legs—on my stomach. I flinch back, and he manages to wrestle the pot out of my hands. I kick at him, but he grips my hair, forcing my head back. He jams the spout of the coffeepot into my mouth. Hot liquid burns my teeth, my tongue. I try to turn my face, but Gavin holds me tight. More bitter liquid floods my mouth. I'm choking. I have to swallow, and swallow again.

The pressure eases. Gavin releases me. I try to kick at him, but my limbs don't seem to obey me. I try to pick my head up, but it's too much effort. Black spots bloom in the corners of my vision. "What . . ." I slur.

Gavin's talking brusquely to the coachman, but my ears seem to have gone stupid, too. Next I know, he's reaching back in, wrestling me into a semi-sitting position against the seats. Then he and the coachman fling Rhia onto the seat behind me. Maybe they forced the poison-laced coffee down her throat, too; she's not moving. I note with bleary satisfaction that the coachman has a bloodied nose. Even with a broken arm, Rhia Knoll's a force to contend with.

Then Gavin climbs in over us, taking a seat on the free bench. The door slams. I still can't seem to gather myself. Lassitude tugs at my limbs, though I know I need to move, to stop him, to free us somehow. But my neck feels thin as a dandelion stalk. Maybe I should have seen this coming, but I was so happy to be home, so grateful to be accepted, that I wasn't even looking for it.

I blink up at Gavin, and he looks back, his gaze slightly narrowed. Impatient.

"Poison." I force the word out of my mouth. "You. Poisoned. Us."

"It's laudanum." Lord Gavin checks his pocket watch. "Opium. You won't die. Now be quiet and go to sleep."

I try to struggle upright, but it seems as if a great weight is shoving me back against the floor. The carriage has begun to roll forward; the high gray walls give way to gray sky. I seem to be floating in a cloud of numbness.

Finally I manage a last word. "Why?"

"You shouldn't have stolen the throne from your father," he replies. "We ought to have known from the beginning a girl like you wouldn't have the strength to manage the crown, or to reward her supporters as they should have been."

I try to answer, but his face is rippling and the carriage is tilting, and the next thing I know, the world is black.

CHAPTER TWENTY-ONE

I wake, disoriented, with a foul taste in my mouth. My hands are numb. The carriage has stopped, and the light is dim. The seat across from me is filled with Rhia's slumbering form. Her hands are bound awkwardly in front of her, twisted up with the sling on her healing arm.

I look down. My wrists are bound, too, with a length of rope. No wonder they're numb. I've no idea how much time has passed. I try to sit up, and my head pounds.

The door opens. Lord Gavin. He looks at me. "We've stopped to change the horses," he says conversationally.

I find my voice. It's hoarse. *"Why?"*

"You usurped your father's throne. We are returning you to him, so he can mete out justice." He holds up a water flask. "Drink?"

I shake my head, but he grabs my hair again and forces the flask to my lips. I choke and splutter but the water still pours in, and I'm forced to swallow.

He grunts with satisfaction and lets go of my hair.

I jerk my head toward his. My forehead collides with his mouth.

"Gods damn!" he exclaims, jerking back.

I try to lunge up, but my limbs are like molasses. Naturally, the water must have been spiked with more laudanum. I can't move fast enough, and Gavin shoves me back down.

"When I have power again," I growl at him, "you're the first person I'm going to execute."

He just glares at me, putting hand to bloody lip. Red anger pulses from him.

"Did I hurt you?" I coo. *"Good."*

Of course, I'm probably too damned softhearted to even threaten him with torture, were I in power. Though if all this damned laudanum harms my baby in any way, the man is going to pay. Let him stew on it, anyway.

There's another voice outside the carriage. "All right there?"

Lord Gavin sniffs. "Bitch gave me a split lip."

Footsteps scuff outside. Then a man peers in at me—an all-too-familiar square-jawed face.

"Grenou," I snarl.

He gives a mocking bow. *"Majesty.* You've slept the night away. It's morning, and you're well into Eren now."

I want to struggle against my bonds—but the last thing I really want is more laudanum forced down my throat. I stay still. "Where are you taking us?"

"To Laon, milady." He purses his lips. "So your father can decide what to do with you."

I LOSE TRACK of the time again; when I sit up next, we're rolling past the gray buildings of Laon, into the circle before the palace. It's late afternoon, though I don't know if it's even the same day. Regardless, we've arrived more quickly than should be possible; perhaps Gavin knows how to travel through the shifts in the land, or the coachman does. It's awfully inconvenient having Caerisians in the opposition, I think muzzily, just before the door opens, revealing several palace guards. They bundle us out of the carriage. My mouth still tastes foul, and my mind is slow and sticky. Still, I look at the guards and greet them by name: "Alain. Sebastien." Neither of them can look at me. Rhia's guards, noticeably, have fewer qualms. Her good arm is wrenched behind her back, and the daggers are stripped from her hips.

"Search her," Grenou barks. "The bitch probably has a saber hidden under her skirts."

Rhia stares him down, her eyes wide, nostrils flared with contempt. "Better to be a bitch than a traitorous cur. How would you have lived with yourself, if the fire had killed the queen? How do you live with yourself now, since you—"

He strikes her across the cheek. Her head snaps back sickeningly, and anger punches through me.

Rhia's head comes back up, and he hits her again.

"Enough!" I cry out. "She's done nothing to hurt you, Grenou, only wounded your damn pride."

He swings toward me, his eyes black with rage. "She'll kill me if she can."

Rhia's cheeks are scarlet where he slapped her, and her hair's coming loose from its braid. "All because you couldn't tolerate answering to a woman," she mutters.

"What did you say?" Grenou rounds on her.

But a footman hurries up, interrupting. "Rambaud is ready for them now."

Alain adjusts the rope on my arm; it's too tight, and I grunt.

He winces. "Sorry, my lady," he breathes, and loosens the bindings just a fraction, so the numbness leaves my hands.

I hardly have time to comprehend his kindness. He prods me toward the palace entrance. I stumble forward. Rhia stalks beside me, her jaw taut and angry. The marks on her face are going to bruise. I fight down a pulse of pure rage. I always knew Grenou was trouble—I should have done something about him when I was queen, when I had the power to remove such men. Now we're stuck with him, and this miserable situation.

We climb slowly up the grand staircase, Alain hanging on to my elbow as if I'm an old woman.

Sebastien notices this, too. "You don't need to cosset her. She isn't the queen any longer."

"She's with child!" Alain says, as if that explains everything. At least someone doesn't seem to hold it against me.

We pace down the hall, passing servants who stare at us, wide-eyed. I know their names, too, and the names of their families. Their histories. It's strange; in my deepest fears, when we were fighting Antoine and then Loyce Eyrlai, this is exactly what I imagined, being brought before them to be humiliated. Only we claimed the palace for ourselves, and now I am a prisoner in the place I was beginning to think of as home.

"The duke?" Alain asks a footman. Grenou has been left behind in the courtyard.

The footman's gaze catches on me. His mouth opens.

"Hello, Basile," I say quietly. Have they even noticed that I remember all their names? It doesn't seem to matter how hard I tried. Maybe they were always going to betray me.

Basile closes his mouth and points wordlessly to a door down the hall. The Yellow Salon. I walk forward of my own accord, and the guards quickly close around me again.

The salon is warm and quiet. Only two people occupy it: a young man with auburn hair seated at a writing desk, pen in hand, ink staining his fingers. And Rambaud himself, standing before the fireplace, his hands linked behind his back, head bent in thought.

He turns, and I tear my gaze away from Philippe, who has looked up with a quickly concealed frown. Rambaud takes us in. Slowly, he begins to smile, and the sound of him pulses warmly, reflecting his apparently genuine pleasure. "Well, it looks as if Lord Gavin made good on his claims."

"He caught them in Barrody, I'm told," Alain says. "And brought them south to Captain Grenou."

Rambaud looks at me and shakes his head. "Some friendly advice," he says to me. "Never deprive a man of the rewards he expects to reap from his service to you. Gavin's family used to be the high judges of Caeris. You knew that, didn't you?"

I say nothing. I did, but I didn't think it mattered. Not this much.

"You replace them with the wardens of the mountains, who have jurisdiction over justice." He gestures at Rhia. "So he doesn't get his tax break on his pension, and he can't buy all those things he's been dreaming of once he got better access to trade. And quick enough, he starts to wonder if Euan Dromahair wouldn't have listened to him better. If a king would be better than a queen." He snaps his fingers. "It's not far from there to him believing you stole your father's rightful throne."

"I see," I say coldly.

"If only you had spoken to him at that party at Lord Devalle's house, perhaps you would have known not to trust him."

I go very still. He's watching me with a cool amusement. So he knew who I was all along. I suppose it shouldn't surprise me. "Did I give myself away so obviously?"

"Not at all." He glances at Philippe, and I wince. Of course Rambaud knew perfectly well who Philippe was—and, I finally realize, must have ordered him to bring me there. No wonder Philippe seemed so angry about it. "But it was a fine attempt at deceit," Rambaud adds. "Almost as fine as our Philippe's own in attempting to aid you."

"I told you I gave that up," Philippe says calmly. "Mother reminded me of all I stood to lose."

Rambaud's gaze is shrewd. "Indeed. And you have been exceedingly gracious about it ever since. You haven't attempted to rescue this woman from a certain fire, for instance. Or happened to leave the palace during the raid on a certain warehouse."

I feel my jaw clench. So Philippe isn't here simply to serve as Rambaud's amanuensis—Rambaud stationed him here for this moment. At least I can finally guess what Philippe was really doing outside my rooms during the fire: He must have caught wind of the plot and come to rescue me, despite his mother's threats.

Philippe doesn't waver. "I told you, I didn't trust Grenou not to slaughter them all. I went after him thinking I could prevent bloodshed."

"And our opponents conveniently escaped," Rambaud drawls. He's watching me.

"That's hardly my fault." Philippe's voice is bland.

I simply shrug, struggling to keep my expression neutral. Somehow I doubt Philippe has managed to smuggle any messages to Victoire.

"Oh, well," Rambaud says. Disconcertingly, he smiles at me. "I'm glad you survived Montclair. Well done."

"You might have caught us," I point out.

"We decided it was unnecessary to pursue you further," he says. "Since your father is, after all, the rightful king, it somewhat diminishes your claim to the throne. I presume you heard he's coming back?"

"It was hard to miss," I say flatly.

"Oh, good. I pride myself on being able to effectively disseminate information." He looks Rhia over, then comes back to me. "Lord Gilbert was our true target. Justice has been served!"

"Praise the gods," Philippe says, still in that bland tone.

"I'm certain your mother is overjoyed to hear the news," Rambaud says.

"No doubt." Philippe pauses. "But revenge is a cold bedfellow."

"I suppose she'll take it, since the Butcher robbed her of your father. And my mother." Rambaud looks at me and clicks his tongue. "Didn't you know? Philippe's father was a spy—in the employ of my mother, a wicked degenerate working for the Paladisan emperor. Rather inconvenient for Antoine Eyrlai, since the Count of Lylan was also a member of the cabinet. One fine day our parents met outside the city to exchange some particularly sensitive news. Little did they know the king knew. They didn't expect to be thrown to their deaths." He pauses. "Not over the bridge in Montclair."

A cold shiver runs down my spine. Montclair wasn't only meant for me. It was a message sent to the Butcher—a message he dismissed, because we both believed we could spring the trap Rambaud had set. He must have guessed it wasn't coincidence that Rambaud chose Montclair—but maybe, at the same time, he didn't imagine it portended his own death.

"Antoine Eyrlai made a poor choice that day," Rambaud adds. "He might have had our parents interrogated, made to answer for their crimes. Instead he chose to kill them. A foolish choice, for they were well liked. Loved, in fact." He gives me a significant look. "And never forgotten."

My mouth feels full of butterflies, but I say, "Remind me never to murder any of your family members."

"You are, I suspect, far too gentlehearted to attempt such a thing." He pauses. "Although there was that sorcerer who tried to kill me."

"I didn't send him."

"Oh," Rambaud says, somewhat patronizingly, "I know. I was just wondering whether you would take responsibility. You're wise not to."

My chin comes up. "Did you not try to murder *me*?"

"Oh, no," Rambaud says with a smile. "If I'd wanted you dead, you would be dead. I was merely trying to ensure there was a certain degree of discord. My colleagues, however, got a bit . . . over-zealous."

"Hmm," I say, "and of course having such a blunder on your personal history would be terribly embarrassing. No wonder you don't want to take responsibility."

Rambaud laughs out loud. He says to Philippe, "I like her."

"A lot of people do," Philippe replies.

Rambaud raises an eyebrow. "With the exception of the ones I've paid not to." He laughs again at my expression. "Isn't that how you bought loyalty to your little rebellion, *Your Majesty*? Your currency was promises of power and autonomy rather than gold, but it seems to me it worked much the same way."

"We'll have to agree to disagree on that point," I say flatly. "What do you plan to do with us?"

"A good question." Rambaud tilts his head. "I wasn't expecting you to land right in my lap. What do you think, Philippe? What should we do with Sophy Dunbarron and Rhia Knoll?"

It has the tone of a trick question, but Philippe meets Rambaud's eyes with an apparently even temper. "The king will be here tomorrow or the day after. Sophy is, after all, his daughter. You might leave it to him to decide."

"A logical proposal." Rambaud chuckles. "Maybe he'll make her his heir! Wouldn't that be ironic?"

"Or," I say, "you could let me go, and treat me as queen of the sovereign nation of Caeris. We could discuss the terms of our alliance."

"Clever, little queen," Rambaud says, "but do you really think the people of Caeris will side with you against your own father? Oh, I am sure you made your plans and fortified your defenses. But once Euan Dromahair is here, the king from across the sea? How can you compete with a legend?" He claps his hands. "Guards, see these women are comfortably situated until the king's arrival."

Alain steps forward. "We can hold them in the east wing, sir."

Rambaud nods and gestures the guards to take us out. "See it done."

I'm careful not to catch Philippe's eye as we leave.

We emerge into the corridor. A man is approaching us with a swift, confident gait. He's sleek, bright-eyed. It's Devalle.

He pauses. Smiles directly at me. Then he goes in to see Rambaud.

THEY TAKE US to the east wing, through the great hall and up the winding stairs to a small study, to a room with a single bed and a desk cluttered with a drift of dried rosemary. I almost laugh, though my mouth is dry. Somehow we've been directed to Demetra's chamber. The bolt slides home, echoing in the small chamber. Rhia bangs her fist on the door, just once, in frustration.

I approach the desk, wondering. A kind of hope is caught in my chest. But the desk is bare, and I drop to my knees. On the other side of the heavy oak, wedged between it and the wall, is a sheet of paper. My heart pounds as I tug it free. It's been written on in Ereni—a simple, stark phrase. *I will try.*

I sink down on my heels. Alain might have left the note, but the handwriting looks more like Philippe's. Are they working together, I wonder, or did Philippe just happen to mention this room to Alain? It's impossible to guess now, and I can't risk asking the guards. I shake my head. However it got here, it's hard to put much stock in the author's optimism.

"What?" Rhia says. "Did Demetra leave you a secret message?"

"It's from Philippe, I think."

She takes the paper and snorts. "That's not any help."

I sigh and drop the note to the table. "I know." I hunt in my pocket for the bone flute. I don't see a reflective surface in this room—nowhere to contact Jahan and Elanna, or Teofila. But perhaps my flute can help somehow.

Yet I stop before I put it to my lips, staring at Rhia. She's paced the length of the small room to the high, narrow window. Now she leans down and pulls off her right boot. I blink. She's wiggling the heel, and finally, with a grunt, twists it to the side. She pulls out a small, rounded blade no larger than the palm of her hand.

"I'm not sure what amazes me more," I remark. "The fact that you have that blade, or the fact that it even occurred to you to put it in your boot."

Rhia sniffs, but she can't hide a little smirk. "I took precautions when I first came into your lowlands."

"Our lowlands are a bit more civilized than your mountains!"

"Oh, really? I can't recall the last time a mountain lord overthrew the warden of the mountains and took them prisoner."

I think hard for a moment. Then I point at her. "The Lords of the Western Isles, in 4123, common time. A Blair took a Browne hostage and she escaped from a tower with her wits and a penknife she had hidden in the lining of her stays."

"You know all my influences," Rhia complains, dragging a stool over to the wall and standing on it so she can work the blade around the edge of the window.

"She used the penknife as a handhold so she could climb down the side of the tower, didn't she? Jammed it between the stones?"

Rhia looks long-suffering. "A solution that could have worked if I were imprisoned alone."

"And if your guards were deaf and blind." I pause. "I doubt Rambaud is that much of a fool."

With a grunt, Rhia digs her fingernails under the edge of the window and pries it open. A gust of bright spring air pours in. I get to my feet, inhaling. It smells like hope.

Rhia leans her head out the window, and with a twist, her shoulders. But the frame catches around her arms, and she yelps at the pressure on her barely healed bone.

"Do you need me to pull you back in?" I ask, almost laughing, though I glance anxiously behind me to make sure the guards haven't heard.

"No," Rhia says with as much dignity as she can muster. She winches herself slowly back into the room and turns to glower at me, clutching at her wounded arm. "There's a roof directly below. We could get out if the window wasn't built for children!"

"I doubt they designed it so someone could crawl out of it." But my brief flare of hope is sinking away. If the window's too small for Rhia to wiggle out, there's no way I can squeeze my larger, pregnant body through.

I shake my head and lift the bone flute to my lips. I play a short, sweeping series of notes. The flute's sound is lovely, just the right amount of depth and sweetness. When I close my eyes, it's as if the music heightens my senses. I hear the strains of all the people moving within the palace, the city, the hum of the land itself. It brightens my awareness of the world until this small, dark room seems almost incandescent.

Yet nothing happens. The music is beautiful. And useless.

"Maybe you can play that and summon a white knight to rescue us," Rhia says dourly, dropping onto the pallet bed. "Except they'd better bring a potion to shrink both of us, because that's the only way we're getting out that damned window."

I lower the flute with a sigh. Jahan might be able to walk through walls, but clearly that is not what the bone flute is designed to do.

"Perhaps Euan will take pity on us," I say drily. "He is my father, after all."

She casts me a skeptical glance, and I shrug.

"It's possible, you know."

"Mmm-hmm," Rhia says, but she doesn't argue. We both know it isn't going to happen. Darkly, she says, "Those bastards better not have imprisoned my mountain women, that's all I have to say. Or they'll pay the price."

It worries me, too—the fate of not only the mountain women, but Fiona and any other Caerisian servants in the palace. "We'll find them," I promise her, though the words sound hollow even to me.

She just closes her eyes.

I step over to the window. The spring breeze teases my hair—the wind that is bringing my father to Eren. Once, that would have been a source of hope.

I put the bone flute to my lips. I play my heart into the song, a series of notes rising to a desperate height and then sinking, so softly, away. I wonder, as I play, whether Teofila left for Baedon. If Alistar and Hugh and Ingram Knoll have uncovered the truth about our disappearance. The day darkens as I play. Over the palace roofs, I see no rescuers appear. Only a distant bell rings somewhere deep in the city, a sole, empty sound.

CHAPTER TWENTY-TWO

We're brought food twice a day, and Rhia uses the window to dump out the contents of the chamber pot. Our only options seem to be to attack a guard and thus steal out of the east wing—admittedly unlikely, as we don't even know how many are on duty, or where they are stationed—or to wait for my father's mercy.

He *is* my father, I tell myself. Blood binds us together, even if my mother never spoke his name. It's possible he isn't aware of how viciously Rambaud and his followers overthrew us, and will decide he wants to work with us. Perhaps—and this, I have to admit, is the unlikeliest thing of all—he'll even decide he likes me. True, he didn't much care for Finn, nor Finn for him. But my half brother, who died too young, didn't truly want to be king or even prince, at least according to Elanna. He died before he could ever discover what he truly wanted to be. Our father never gave him another option in life.

Kind of like Ruadan did me. Once I came into his care, what choice did I have but to inherit this crown, after Finn died, whether I wanted it or not?

The difference between Finn and me is that I do want it. If that truth is a weakness, so be it. If I am honest with myself, I want this crown, and I always have.

And I won't let my father, or Rambaud, or Phaedra and Augustus Saranon, take it from me without a fight.

Perhaps there *is* something I can do. Not to stop them, but to influence how they perceive me. To persuade my father not to look at me with hatred or, worse, indifference. Maybe there's a way I can use my magic—not the bone flute, but my ability to sense emotions. Perhaps I can work it to my advantage.

When Rhia and I hear the blare of trumpets from the front of the palace, I prepare myself as best I can. I pin up my hair and shake the crumbs and dust from my clothes. My gown is stained, the hem torn. Though I don't have a mirror to check myself in, I'm afraid I don't look much like a lady, much less a queen.

Ruadan always told me it is not the clothes one wears, but the way one carries oneself, that makes one a king or a queen. It is the heart within.

So when the guards rap at the door and throw back the bolt at last, I am ready. I put back my shoulders and tell myself I have the heart of a queen. That, regardless of what I wear or how I am treated or who has claimed my throne, I am still a monarch.

And I will behave as such.

They sent eight guards to bring out two women. I let myself smile a little as I step out into the corridor. The men are palace guards.

"Hello, Alain," I say cordially, and he lowers his head. I look at each of the others in turn. "Basile. Charles. Duncan. Ambrose. Yves. Manfred. Sebastien."

The men look away from me, uncomfortable, unable to meet my eyes. They don't even try to touch either of us. Alain simply gestures me forward, Rhia at my back. The guards fall into a tight square around us and begin to walk.

"Yves," I call, "did you recover from that sprained wrist?"

There's an awkward silence. Several of the others glance surreptitiously at Yves. At last, he says, "It's much better, Your Maj—my lady."

"I'm glad to hear it. And Sebastien, is your mother better after the croup?"

Another silence, and then, "She's still coughing some," Sebastien mutters. "But she's better."

"The draught Demetra sent helped?"

"Yes," he says hesitantly, "it did."

I don't want to think about Demetra and the others in Barrody, or Teofila presumably on her way to Baedon, or Elanna and Jahan returning to this shambles of a kingdom. I'm just glad this one guard is willing to admit that sorcery made a difference for his mother's health.

We pass through the scarred wall and into the palace proper. Up the familiar staircase. My heart thumps once, twice. I suspect where our path is taking us—to the most elaborate salon the palace has to offer. A room so roundly criticized for its opulence that I hesitated even to enter during my time here. The Diamond Salon.

Clearly neither my father nor Rambaud shares my qualms.

The filigreed doors stand open, and we enter the glittering splendor of the room. I take in the twinkling chandeliers for which it's named; the tables of clear, fragile glass; the chaises of velvet and satin. Portraits of Eyrlai kings and queens populate the walls.

And standing under their eyes is Euan Dromahair.

I recognize him immediately, though I have never set eyes on even a likeness of him before. He's tall, like Finn, like me, the famous ruddy-gold hair darkened to a dull brown; like Finn, his profile is long and narrow. Courtiers surround him—Rambaud, dressed in a fine red coat sewn with gemstones, Philippe somber in his customary black, and many others. Set apart from the others are a handsome olive-skinned young man wearing a knee-length coat that seems to be woven of gold, and a thin young woman in fluttering pink satin on his arm; they must be the siblings from Paladis. Many others crowd the chamber, along with a handful of foreign guards—presumably part of the Paladisan force the Saranons brought with them. I don't know most of the Ereni nobles, except for Lord Devalle, who has the nerve to smirk when he glimpses me. I can't resist sending Lord Gavin and the three Caerisians flanking him a dark look.

Our arrival is announced, though the words pass clear, unheard, over my ears. My father is turning toward me and all thought goes out of my head. My heart beats so hard I feel each pulse like a hammer throughout my body. I'm hoping, even though I know I shouldn't.

Rambaud is talking, moving, gesturing to us, but I can only see my father. And the sound of him . . .

All the hair lifts on my arms. The sound of him is heavy and black as a fugue.

". . . Sophy Dunbarron," Rambaud is saying. "We took her prisoner in Caeris, where she'd fled pretending to be queen again. And her guardswoman, Rhia Knoll."

As if a guardswoman is all that Rhia is.

I try to reach within as Demetra taught me, for my own feeling, for warmth and kindness to emanate from me, disarming them. But my voice only comes out dry. Raw. Shaking. "Hello, Father."

Euan's gaze snaps to me. His eyes are blue, like Finn's, like mine, and as dead as ice. A pulse of emotion bursts off him, like a splatter of liquid ink, dark and viscous.

"I have been looking forward to meeting you for a long time," I continue, trying to push feelings of goodwill and welcome toward him. But I can tell it's not working. All I can feel is the sound of him, the low note that unsettles my very bones, though I can't even say why. I taste bile in the back of my throat.

The birdlike Idaean princess—Phaedra—brings a hand to her stomach. "Such a pity to see the fate that befalls women who take whatever they want," she declares in pinched Idaean, so high and quick it takes me a moment to understand. Her tone doesn't make it seem like much of a pity at all, though; more the fate I deserve.

Her brother—Augustus, it must be—is staring at my own hand on my stomach, the gesture Phaedra unconsciously echoed. His eyebrows keep rising.

"So this is her?" A woman has grasped Philippe's arm; she's watching me with a supercilious curl of her lip. She wears a wide, stiff gown, and her hair is piled up in an old-fashioned tower. The mother, no doubt, who thinks it's acceptable to threaten her son if he doesn't do what she wants him to. "You did well to avoid marrying her, darling. Look how far gone that belly of hers is. I wonder if the child will be dissolute like her."

I meet the woman's eyes. Clearly this is Philippe's mother; strange to think I slept in her bed.

"At least everything I have done, I did for the good of Eren and Caeris," I say, unable to bite down my anger. "At least I didn't clutch my gold and finery to my chest and dole out poor rations to my servants, and force them to remain indebted on my lands, and tell the people they had no power in the governance of this country, all while I lived in a veritable palace." I glance at Lord Gavin and the handful of other Caerisians in the crowd. "I gave the people the promise of a better nation, and you all fought me for it because you didn't want to give up even a fraction of your wealth." I point at Rambaud. "You bought your way back in here, and when the people turn on you, you had better not forget that you paid for your power in coin instead of merit."

My voice echoes into a stunned sort of silence and I feel my eyebrows rising. Maybe I've put the seal on any chance we had of bargaining, but at least I spoke the truth. No one has responded; I'm not sure the new arrivals even understood me. The Idaean siblings look confused, and a deep frown has appeared between my father's brows. I find myself wondering how well he understands Ereni; he's never even set foot on our land, after all.

"Well," Rambaud says eventually, in Idaean, "now you have witnessed an authentic display of Caerisian temper. No wonder they won—and lost." He gives me a mocking smile. "Your Majesty, what would you like done with your daughter?"

I hurry to speak before Euan can reply; maybe I can salvage this situation yet. "I bow to your insight, of course, but I want to tell you that I am uniquely qualified to manage the governance of Caeris. Ruadan Valtai raised me at his knee, with all the education of a queen. One might say I have spent years practicing for the position. The people of Caeris—or most of them"—I can't resist an ironic glance at Lord Gavin—"trust me. Perhaps we could forget our ill beginning. In time, you might even learn to think of me as your daughter."

"Silence."

That's all Euan Dromahair says, that one word. I stop. I was wrong. His eyes aren't dead. There's a rage in him, so old it's hardened into a fossilized thing. Now it's coming alive.

He begins to walk toward me. The guards move out of the way. I freeze, then square my shoulders and stare him in the face. He's coming closer and closer, and all I can hear is the wrong sound of him. *Wrong, wrong, wrong*—

Euan Dromahair pauses before me. He studies my face. I scrabble for the locket I've shoved into the pocket of my skirts. "Here," I say, thrusting it at him, even though the sound of him warns me not to. But I'm not going to back down. I won't let him see me be weak. "From my mother."

He takes the locket. Our fingers brush together, and I struggle not to jerk back. The mere brush of his skin brings the wrong sound of him far too close.

He gives me an odd, calculating look, then throws the locket into the fireplace. It disappears into the coals. My heart thumps, and the baby kicks. I stare at my father.

But he's no longer looking at me. He's turned to face the rest of the chamber. "For twenty years, I have been the king of Caeris," he says in a flat, hard voice. "Living in exile. Waiting. A man called Ruadan Valtai promised me the throne. Twenty years have passed, and I never got it."

"I wrote to you—" I begin.

"*Silence!*" he roars. His hand flies out and catches me across the mouth. I stagger backward, numb with shock. I didn't expect him to hit me, and the shock stings more than the physical pain.

Euan has already turned from me. "First my son Finn failed to claim the crown," he's saying, his voice a dull, angry beat. "Died a failure. Then this—" He points a shaking finger at me. "This *creature* claimed it. As if I would name a filthy Caerisian harlot as my heir."

The floor seems to sway under me. Ruadan was wrong about this man—so utterly wrong I can't even fathom it. Euan Dromahair did not want to fight for a better kingdom, for a people's freedom and rights. He wanted a crown handed to him, earned by others' blood, not effort. He wanted to sit on a throne.

"And she thinks I would back her against my friends, the Saranons," he goes on, angrily. "She asked me to fight against Alakaseus, the late emperor! The most charitable man I have ever known."

Charitable? He's talking about the man who ordered Elanna executed. The man responsible for witch hunts; the man who declared war on our country.

Augustus Saranon clears his throat. "We do mourn our poor, late father."

"Deeply," Phaedra Saranon says in a high, clear voice, as cold as cut glass.

Neither of them mentions their still-living brother, the current emperor, but his name seems to hover like a ghost in the room.

Euan has turned his back to me completely now. He's talking to Rambaud. "I have waited twenty years for my crown, and you will get it for me."

"I had a plan for Caeris," Rambaud says in careful Idaean. His gaze flickers to me. "Unfortunately, it didn't work as well as expected."

My heartbeat surges into my ears. Caeris must still be free. Ingram Knoll, Teofila, Hugh, and Alistar must have succeeded in putting at least part of our plan in place, even though Rhia and I were captured. All the same, I don't dare trust the hope pulsing in my chest.

Augustus Saranon's mouth quirks. "It seems you need a different plan."

Rambaud gestures at me. "We have the Caerisian queen. She's the ultimate bargaining piece. Whatever you—"

"What did you call her?" Euan Dromahair demands.

Rambaud's mouth closes.

"It seems he called her the queen of Caeris," Phaedra Saranon says lazily. "Though of course his Idaean is difficult to understand, being so provincial."

"I am the king of Caeris," Euan Dromahair says, his face close to Rambaud's now, his voice cold with anger. "There is no other ruler."

Rambaud's chin has lifted, but he's too consummate a politician to lose his temper. He gently deflects. "You are now the king of Eren, as well. It is a rich kingdom. Fertile. The climate is—"

"I am not interested in the climate," Euan Dromahair says coldly. "I have taken Eren, and it is mine. But I have also been promised Caeris, and I will have it. It belongs to me."

There's a stir among the Ereni nobles. Presumably they don't understand the desire for my country.

Rambaud hesitates. "I understand, of course," he says, though he clearly doesn't. I'm not sure any of us do. "But Caeris is a rough, hardscrabble sort of place. The people are notoriously difficult subjects. In truth"—he laughs a little—"you may not *want* Caeris."

A sigh explodes from Euan Dromahair. He nods at Augustus Saranon.

"We do want Caeris," the Paladisan prince explains, patiently. "It has resources that interest us. People, mainly. We plan to conscript the Caerisians into the army, so they may help us retake Ida."

There's a silence. I glance at the Ereni nobles. Most of them seem stunned. They must have thought Euan was coming here, for them, to be their king—not to help Phaedra and Augustus Saranon take the empire of Paladis, so that Eren could become a vassal state. Philippe is frowning; I catch his eyes, and he shakes his head minutely.

Phaedra Saranon is looking at me, too. I don't like the small smile touching her lips.

"Well, if you want Caeris," Rambaud says at last, "we must use Sophy Dunbarron as our bargaining chip."

"We will not bargain," Euan Dromahair says coldly. "We will begin as we mean to go on. The Caerisians—and the Ereni who supported them—must learn that no rebellion will be tolerated. The girl is a pretender, not a queen. She will be treated as such." He nods at me. "See she is executed tomorrow."

Executed. I'm swaying, but I force my legs wide. I force myself to look at him.

"I am the queen of Caeris. And I am your daughter. You have no ri—"

Euan moves fast. Too fast. The back of his hand connects with my nose. There's a sharp crack. Pain. Hot liquid trails onto my upper lip. Blood. My eyes water; I stagger, fetching up against Alain. He holds me up.

"This is not a child of mine," Euan Dromahair says coldly. "Remove it."

My vision's swimming. A hot trickle of blood is running from my nose. I try to focus on his face, but he's already turning away.

Then, as if he remembers something, he swings back. I flinch instinctively, but he only snaps his fingers. "And the other one." He nods at Rhia. "Take her into Royal Square and have her whipped in front of the people. She has a man's position, she can take a man's punishment."

"Sir—" Philippe's voice.

"I will not be questioned," Euan Dromahair says, his voice tired. As if he has been questioned so often, and is so weary of it. "I am your king. You should remember that I control your positions here."

"We understand, sir," Rambaud himself intervenes, "but the Knoll woman is so small. If she's flogged—"

"I am not interested." Euan waves a hand. "Guards!"

Alain and Sebastien seize my arms, pulling me backward. Through the haze of pain, I glimpse Rhia's face, red with rage. Everyone else in the room seems to have frozen.

"Rhia," I try to say, but my voice is thick with pain and blood. But the guards are already pulling me from the chamber. Alain puts his arm around my waist, supporting me. I shake him off, even though it's hard to see straight. I won't be carried like a sack of flour. "Rhia!"

She's being dragged in the opposite direction. I lunge for her, but Alain holds me back. "No, Your Majesty." He and Sebastien try to wrestle me forward, and I throw them off once more.

"I'll walk," I say with all the dignity I possess.

And I do. I walk the long corridors back to Demetra's chamber, where Alain whispers, "I'm sorry, my lady," before bolting the door.

I stand in the center of the small room. I'm alone. Alone to contemplate my death.

And to wonder what will become of Rhia.

CHAPTER TWENTY-THREE

The day darkens to twilight. I have stood on the stool and tried to squeeze my body through the window, toward the stain of urine on the roof below. I have snapped the bones of my broken nose back into place, gasping at the pain but staying conscious. I have pounded on the door and demanded the guards tell me what's happened to Rhia.

They have not answered, and Rhia hasn't been brought back. I bite down on my knuckle, as if it can keep me from bellowing in pure rage. I pace the small, dim room yet again. There is no budging these four walls. I'm not Jahan, who can shift the particles that make up our very existence; my magic, if it can be called that, is a small and practically useless thing. I can sense the humming song of the guards outside the door, and the baby kicking in my stomach, but that is all.

I keep seeing my father's face. The old and terrifying anger in his eyes. Keep feeling the crack of his hand on my cheek.

He's no father to me.

I pace again. My back is cramping. Aching. I have to stop and brace myself against Demetra's desk. The cramps grip my hips, my buttocks. A wave of nausea dizzies me. I crouch, pressing my forehead against my arms. The cramps knead through my lower back again. I grind my teeth together. "It's all right," I whisper to the baby, to my own aching body. "It's all right."

But my body—or the baby—must know I'm lying because another cramp racks me. Tears water my eyes. They are worse than any ache I ever had with my monthly courses, and I slowly curl my hands into fists.

More cramps ravage my back. I cry out inadvertently, clutching my belly. Another cramp doubles me over.

"No," I'm whispering aloud, "no no no—"

This can't be. I can't be having my baby here, not now. Not months early.

I lurch toward the door, hobbling in pain. I thump my fists against the wood. "Help! Alain! Sebastien! Help! I need a doctor!" I try to keep my voice level, but it's rising into panic. I scream, *"I need a doctor!"*

Silence. I press my forehead against the door, sobbing though my eyes are dry. Another cramp grips my back. I pound again. I'm going light-headed, either from my panic or from the premature birth. I can't be giving birth now. I can't lose the child.

I'm not going to die like this, and neither is my baby.

Voices murmur in the corridor. *"Alain!"* I scream, trying to push my voice through the wood. Trying to demand, with the power of sound, that they listen. "My baby—I'm losing my baby—I need a doctor!"

The voices fall into abrupt silence. Tears leak from my eyes, and a fresh wave of cramps rolls over me. They must think I'm lying. That I'm trying to trick them into letting me out. They must think this is a ploy.

Unless this is what someone planned all along. I ate the food they brought us, unthinking. What if someone has poisoned me?

But Alain said he was sorry. There's no reason for him to fake the pity in his eyes. These guards worked for me for months; I remember their names and their families. They might be angry and frustrated with the things that I have done, with the death of Thierry, but they don't hate me. I'm sure of it.

But they still don't trust me enough to open the door, or fetch a doctor.

Once again, pain contracts my back. My skin is slick with sweat; my legs are shaking. "Help!" I cry.

Nothing.

I stumble back to the bed, but it's too far to bend over, so I turn to the desk again instead. I grip it, panting through my open mouth. If this child is coming now, four months before its time, I will do everything I can to see we both survive. I have no other choice.

Though my father has ordered me executed. Unless I can come up with some plan, I'm due for death anyway.

I lean against the desk, drawing in a long, shaky breath. I'm trembling all over. I've lost everything, and everyone—my crown, my kingdom, Teofila, Alistar, Rhia, my friends, my people, my guards. And now maybe my daughter as well. I don't know what will happen when Elanna and Jahan return, if they even arrive; I don't know if I'll survive to see them.

Voices echo out in the corridor. I turn woozily toward the door, bracing myself against the desk. Is it Rhia? A doctor?

It's a woman's voice, raised.

The bolt slides back in the door. My heart is pounding with hope.

Candlelight.

A woman stands on the threshold, clenching a burning candle in one birdlike hand. The lace sleeve of her robe has fallen, exposing the length of her arm. The hauteur of her face is breaking into horror.

"What's wrong with you?" Phaedra Saranon demands.

I press my free hand to my stomach, riding out another wave of cramping. In slow, careful Idaean, I tell her, "I need a doctor."

Her gaze flickers from my hands to my rounded stomach. Her face pinches in disdain. I could overpower her. I could break out into the corridor.

Into the arms of the guards? No. That won't work.

"I need help," I tell her again.

She looks me up and down, frowning, as if I'm not measuring up to whatever she expected. The sound of her snakes into the room, though I can hardly feel it over my own pain. A complex tangle of notes that sounds, if anything, annoyed. Does she not understand that I'm with child, that I'm going into labor, that I need help? What is she even doing here?

I find myself shouting at her. "Get me a damned doctor!"

She straightens, and real anger flares in her eyes. A scarlet, humming thread rises from her. I suspect no one ever speaks to Phaedra Saranon this way. She's sneering because I spoke Ereni. "I don't know your backwater lingo."

"Then why are you here?" I cry out, in Idaean this time. A cold sweat has broken out on my forehead. The room spins a little. "What do you *want*?"

At that, she steps forward and hunkers down before me, as if we're at the fireside having a chat. Softly, she says, "Someone told me magic is awakening in people throughout these lands."

I roll my eyes, hard. "Did you—bring a witch hunter?"

"Alas, my friend Alcibiades is dead. I miss him," she adds. "We had such illuminating conversations. I learned a great deal from him, you know."

I just grunt. My back aches.

Phaedra Saranon tilts her head. "I wanted to have a look at you. The rebel queen. Do you have sorcery?"

"What makes you think I'd tell you?" I say through gritted teeth, though I can feel the outline of the bone flute in my pocket, humming. "So you can lock me up and send me mad?"

"You shouldn't judge before you understand," Phaedra tells me. "My father was the kind of fool you're describing, and so is my brother, to some extent. So is that boor you call your father—Euan Dromahair—who simply spouts whatever line he thinks will catch him a crown. But I . . . I see that sorcery is coming back into the world. Times change, and those who are wise change with them."

I stare at her. "Are *you* a sorceress?"

Phaedra bursts into bitter laughter. "Perhaps if I were, it would be me, not my brother Leontius, sitting on the imperial throne."

Another cramp racks my body, and I grind my teeth together. "I need. A. Doctor."

"It's no good talking to you," Phaedra informs me. "Especially when you're . . . like that." She grimaces, flapping her hand at my contorted body.

"A doctor," I whisper. *"Please."*

"Mmm." She seems to consider, then shrugs. "I'll think about it. Euan wants you dead, and while I'm sure I could persuade him otherwise, he's so damned tiresome. And honestly, I don't quite see how useful you can be to me."

I stare. She'll *think about it*? A slow-burning anger boils up through my throat, strangling me.

"It's a pity," Phaedra says. The sound of her has dimmed, now, as if she's no longer curious about me. She rises and steps back through the door. "Guards, close her in. I'll let you know if you're required further."

As the door swings shut, I glimpse Alain's face. His gaze jerks from my stomach to my face. I must look like a cornered she-bear, both terrified and ferocious. Then the door falls closed.

And I am alone, once again, in the dark.

GRADUALLY, MY EYES adjust. There's some light from the almost-full moon, coming through the still-open window. I crawl over to the desk and brace myself against it once more. The cramps are growing worse. I draw a breath through my open mouth. I will survive this. I *will*. I'm not going to sink into panic and fear. I won't pound on that damned door again.

If my baby comes now, I will birth it myself. We will both survive, just to spite the cursed man who sired me.

Through the pain, I start to sense sound. The sound of me, or of the child, I don't know, but it is a humming that begins somewhere in my bones and spreads through my womb, twining around the child pressing upon my birth canal.

Between the pangs of the cramps, and my own ragged panting breaths, I start to sing. Hitches of song. Hardly more than breaths.

At last my eyes close. I fumble for the bone flute in my pocket, feeling its power hum into my body. The cramps are still coming, but my breathing evens. For a strange, lucid moment, I think I feel hands on my shoulders. I think I smell my mother's scent, and then it is gone.

The door opens.

Footsteps run across the floor behind me. "Sophy!" It's a breathless whisper.

I must be hallucinating. But there are real hands on my shoulders now, warm and trembling, and a sliver of light behind me. I turn.

"V-victoire?" I whisper, and then grunt at the onslaught of another cramp.

It is her, dressed in black, with her dark curls captured under a knit cap. "Can you walk?" she asks urgently.

"I—I can try."

She takes my arm; I clutch it hard. Together, slowly, we cross the length of the room.

Out in the corridor, Alain and Sebastien are waiting. We emerge, and with a hard look Alain closes the door behind us and once again locks it.

"You're going to have to walk fast, Sophy," Victoire says to me. "Once we get out of the east wing, we're going to have to hurry."

I look blankly around the corridor. We seem to be entirely alone. "Where—?"

"You're the only prisoner, for now." She nods at Alain and Sebastien. "These two have been 'demoted' to looking after you without rest or food, because they didn't carry you bodily from the Diamond Salon."

Alain looks at his feet. "We couldn't leave you to d—in there alone, Your Majesty. So we sent for Mistress Madoc."

Despite everything, despite the cramps moving through my aching body, I feel a swell of gratitude. And hope. I look from Alain to Sebastien. They've both drawn back toward the wall. They know what will happen to them, in return for their mercy.

"Neither of you can stay here like this," I say. "You need to come with us, or—"

"We can't do that," Sebastien interrupts, then looks ashamed. "I'm sorry, my lady, but I need the pay. My mother depends on it."

I glance at Victoire. She nods, reading my expression. "Then I assume you gentlemen don't object to a short sleep?"

They both swallow, but neither objects. Victoire tugs a small brown vial from her pocket—"Laudanum," she says, apologetically. The men each take a sip, then settle themselves on the ground, sprawling themselves out as if they succumbed to a struggle. Both of them have already fallen unconscious before Victoire and I slip away.

"They'll be awake soon enough, and no worse for wear," she whispers, then touches my arm. "Can you walk?"

Another cramp digs through my back, but I reach into my pocket, gripping the bone flute. The humming pulse of it floods through my body, a numbing counterpoint to the cramps. If I focus on it, I can move.

"Let's go," I whisper.

WE CIRCLE DOWN through the east wing. The cramps are growing worse again; I bite my fist and grip the bone flute tighter. The corridors lie echoing, deserted. "Where are all the guards?" I whisper.

"I paid them off," Victoire replies. "My family's wealth has to be good for something."

We emerge through a back exit from what was once the kitchen, into an overgrown garden. Ahead, past a thick hedgerow, city homes bulk up out of the dark. Victoire winds past the ancient garden stakes to an old gate whose hinges squeak mightily when she opens it. On the other side lies a promenade, full of night. We dart across to another gate in the hedgerow. This one has also been abandoned by its guards. We emerge into the street. A fine rain has begun to fall, wetting my head, sliding beads of moisture into my mouth.

Now, on the wide avenue, with clouds scudding over the moon, Victoire hesitates. "You go on. I'll give you directions—"

"No." My legs are trembling, a hard, racking pain, but I shove the discomfort deep down, into another part of my mind. "We stick together."

Victoire's head turns toward me, but in the dark I can't make out her expression. She says, "Then hurry."

We hurry. She leads us down the wide avenue—back toward the palace and Royal Square. My heart begins to pound, this time entirely unrelated to the cramps gripping my back. I have a feeling of what's awaiting us.

The square is wide and dark, eerily silent except for the scuff of our own footsteps. We both stop, listening hard through the thickening rain. A bulky shape has been newly placed beside the still fountain. Something square and pale sits at the top, visible even through the rain.

Victoire gives a low, soft owl's hoot. A pause. Then a cautious hoot comes out of the rain.

"Stay here," Victoire orders and dashes across the square, toward the bulky shape that can only be a scaffold, with Rhia bound bonelessly atop it. I glance toward the palace gates. The rain is lancing down in great sheets now, and the gates are lost in a muddle of water and darkness, along with any guards who might be overseeing them.

A spasm wrenches my back. I grind my teeth together, refusing to cry out.

Through the rain and my own squinted eyes, I can dimly make out fleeting movement on the scaffold. Then it's gone so fast I wonder if I imagined it. Water drips down my ankles. It makes puddles in the cobblestones. There is nothing but darkness and the sound of falling rain.

Their shadows emerge so subtly they seem to be part of the night: Victoire, followed by a man. My heart leaps so hard my whole body shudders. "Alistar!" I whisper as loudly as I dare.

"Soph," he hisses back. He's carrying Rhia's limp body wrapped in a length of cloth.

"Is she—" I begin.

"Yes, she's alive."

"Demetra's back at the house." Victoire snaps her fingers. *"Go!"*

We go, stumbling through the dark, slick streets. I splash through puddles. Water splashes up my skirts, down into my boots. I'm shivering and cramping and yet my eyes are clear and I've somehow never felt stronger in my life. Alistar is at my back. Free. Rhia and I both are free; and alive.

Victoire leads our pack, diving away from the royal avenue down side streets, stitching us farther and farther from the palace. The buildings gather more tightly around us; we pass shop fronts shuttered for the night, and swinging signs whose words are lost to the rain. As we cross a main thoroughfare, a large, pale stone shape rises out of the shadows to our right: the bridge. We're right up against the river, north of the temple, in the district of shopkeepers and warehouses and merchants. The houses have turned from pale-gray limestone to dark brick, their definition lost in the darkness.

Victoire turns into an arched opening. I stagger after her, Alistar on my heels. We're in a garden courtyard, with houses looking down on all sides. She leads us directly across to a home with a small portico, barely large enough to fit us all. But we don't have to wait: the door opens immediately.

We fall into the dry warmth. A grunt escapes me. The door hushes shut behind us, and we are left in more complete darkness than we had on the street. All I can hear is everyone else's ragged breathing.

There's a soft hiss, and light blooms. I blink, momentarily blinded.

"You found them," a familiar voice says. I stare at a woman with short-cropped hair, wearing a dressing robe.

"Funny how a bit of coin will do the trick," Victoire says. "That Euan's a fool if he thinks our palace guards have the slightest loyalty to him." More grimly, she adds, "Where's Demetra?"

"She's coming," another woman says. There's a creak, and another stream of candlelight: Teofila is coming down the stairs toward us, her hair loose and wild around her shoulders. She cries out when she sees me. "Sophy!"

She runs to me, and I hug her hard, breathing in the bright humming sound of her relief. "But you're supposed to be in Baedon," I whisper. Tears are running down my cheeks.

"No, darling. We found out you'd been taken before I left. I couldn't go when you'd been captured. Alistar and I followed you south. Even Demetra insisted on coming."

"We're together now." I stare over her head at Juleane Brazeur, despite the cramps and my own panting breaths. Slowly, my mind dull from pain, I'm putting it all together. "This is your house."

"Indeed, I make a practice of only smuggling fugitives into my own home." But then Juleane relents; the sound of her softens. "You're safe here; we're the only ones in the house. I sent my housemaid to safety in the country days ago, and have been meaning to depart myself. But Mistress Madoc—and your refugee midwife Demetra—made a strong case for rescuing you." A nod. "And Lady Rhia."

I turn to Alistar; her body seems so small in his arms. Another cramp seizes my back.

"I'm here." Demetra hurries down the hall, brisk and professional. "Tell me what's happening."

"Cramps—it hurts so badly—"

"Not surprising to go into false labor, given what you've been through." She tugs me forward. "Come; we have a room prepared." To our companions she says, "Bring Rhia."

I slow. "Take care of Rhia first."

"I have no desire to lose either of you. I will do my job," she says firmly. "Come."

I let out a hissing breath. My legs are shaking again. I hobble forward, kept upright mostly by Demetra's support. Somehow we arrive at a small, neat room outfitted with two pallet beds and a warm fire. I groan at the pleasure of its warmth, then immediately begin to sweat, overheating.

Demetra helps me out of my sodden robe while the others settle Rhia onto the first bed. She stirs a little as she's set down, with a little cry.

"It's all right." Teofila crouches beside her, holding Rhia's hand. "We've got you. You're safe."

Rhia Knoll opens her eyes and bursts into tears. Teofila leans over her, hugging Rhia against her, whispering reassurances. Alistar and Juleane back out of the room, leaving the five of us alone. Victoire helps Demetra wrestle my wet clothes off, bundling me into a fresh chemise that smells of lavender.

"Breathe," she instructs me, and crouches before me, pressing her hands to my stomach. Her head tilts, as if she's listening to the baby's movement. I hear a sound myself, teasing the edges of my hearing. There's a quiver in my stomach, and a tingling runs up my spine.

Demetra nods. "We still have time."

She turns away to a table where she's set out several jars of dried herbs. She uncorks one, letting a faint horse-like smell into the room, and spills a measure of light-colored, chopped, dried roots into a mortar. With practiced swiftness, she crushes them with the pestle. "This will slow the contractions. It will help your body to heal, and carry the baby. You've gone into premature labor; I've seen it in other women. It can be stopped."

"I've been singing," I say hoarsely. "To the child. To my body."

Demetra glances at me. "Perhaps that helped you through. How long have you been having cramps?"

"Since . . ." I try to remember. "Sundown?"

Her eyebrows lift, though she quickly schools her expression into professional neutrality. "That's quite some time. Your magic must have helped you mitigate the pain and maintain the pregnancy."

I nod. "I sang . . ."

But I'm swaying with exhaustion now, and Demetra gestures me to be silent while she works. It's a relief simply to be quiet, watching her. She mashes the roots into a fine powder, then empties it into a small pan that's been heating on the hearth, stirring it briskly. She hands it to me. The smell of honey and horse almost overwhelms me. I choke it down fast, though it scalds my tongue; I hardly taste the honey-and-herb mixture.

Demetra nods, satisfied. "I'll make you another dose in a few hours. Lie down, if you can, on your side. And . . . it might help to keep singing."

I look at the other pallet. "But Rhia . . ."

"We will take care of Rhia," Demetra says firmly. "You need to take care of yourself, and your child."

My back still aches, but I sense that if I don't obey, Demetra will force me to lie down. So I settle on the bed, tucking a pillow between my legs. The pallet is softened with a feather mattress and I feel as if I've stumbled upon a cloud; or perhaps this is what paradise is like. Exhaustion reaches up out of my bones. Teofila comes over, frowning a little. I hardly feel the weight of the blankets as Demetra tucks them over me.

But I force my eyes to stay open a little longer, while Demetra and Victoire turn Rhia onto her stomach. Long enough to see the angry, red, weeping wheals on her narrow back. Long enough to see Rhia swallow the draught of the medicine Demetra makes up for her, and for her to fall asleep while Demetra leans over her, touching her fingertips to the whip marks. Near sleep, I think I *hear* the sound of Demetra's magic, cool and comforting, soothing the ache of Rhia's wounds, though she can't close them over entirely. She and Victoire begin the painstaking process of cleaning and bandaging Rhia's back.

Teofila stays beside me, a firm, warm presence. "Don't leave," I whisper.

She squeezes my hand. "I won't. I won't leave you, Sophy."

There's a noise at the door, and Alistar comes in. He crouches on the other side of my bed, so close his breath stirs my hair. I turn and try to speak, but he just smooths my forehead. "Hush."

They are both here, and I'm safe. I hum a little, to the baby, and sleep claims me.

*

"SOPHY."

I open my eyes. The little room is dark, the fire banked. I've been asleep in the same position so long my arm and hip are stiff. There's a twinge in my stomach. My back still aches, but the cramps have faded.

"Sophy?" The whisper comes again, from the other pallet.

I lift my head. "Rhia?"

"You're there." Her voice is high and breathy with relief.

"Yes." I reach out. The beds are just close enough for my fingers to reach her blankets. She fumbles her hand to mine and hangs on tight.

"I'm here, Rhia," I whisper. "We're safe. We're safe."

A wordless animal noise comes from her. She squeezes my hand once more, then lets go, burying her face more deeply in the pillow.

I tuck my hand back against my heart. Perhaps we are not completely safe but just for now, here in the dark, warm and dry, I will us both to believe it.

CHAPTER TWENTY-FOUR

I wake again too early, before dawn, startling out of a dream that my father struck me so hard I fell to the floor and a girl with fair hair came running to rescue me—and he struck her, too. I lie rigid, listening for the reassuring sound of Rhia's breathing. My mouth is dry, and the child flutters once in my womb. It's my mother I'm seeing in my mind's eye, my shining mother with her brilliant hair and her winsome smile. My mother, who fought for the man who threw me down and ordered me executed. She lay with him, this man whose anger is so old and frightening I feel it even now in my marrow.

Or did she?

I sit up in bed, one hand plucking at my throat, feeling for a locket that isn't there. My body is still trembling with the exhaustion of a few hours ago. I remember standing in a kitchen like this one, north in Caeris, beside Ma in a circle of Caerisian rebels. Someone spoke of the true king, and Ma turned on him.

We're fighting for our own freedom, she said fiercely. *For our right to speak our language and keep our own customs. We're not fighting for any king, no matter his pedigree.*

I remember my own sting of shock, that she would speak against Euan Dromahair. The others must have felt it as well, because one said, *Didn't care for the king when you met him, eh, Mag?* And I startled again, with a child's naïveté, because though I knew Ma had met the king, it had never occurred to me that she might have anything but the deepest respect for him.

She never spoke of him. Never told me stories about him; never gave me the slightest glimpse of the man who had fathered me. I was left to imagine their union had left no particular feeling; my mother's complete disinterest in my father's existence meant that I both was curious about him and dismissed his importance. At least, until I learned he was Euan Dromahair—but by then it was too late to pull the stories out of her. She was already gone.

What did Finn call him? A cold, nasty bastard.

I clamber out of bed and wrap a blanket around my shoulders. A hollow ache lingers in my stomach—the cramps, though improved, are still not gone. I wonder whether I'll have to endure this the rest of the pregnancy. Quietly, so as not to wake Rhia, I pad out into the kitchen.

Teofila is standing there, the teapot in her hand, as if she heard me rise—as if, somehow, she knew.

"Are you—" she asks.

"I'm better." I lower myself onto a stool, hugging the blanket tight around my sore lower back. I can't quite look at her, even when she silently fills a cup with tea and pushes it over to me. The steam gently touches my face.

Teofila says nothing at first. She settles herself at the table, her shoulders hunched. For the first time, she looks old.

"Ma never talked about him." The rim of the cup blurs. It's hard, even now, to speak of Ma; to remember the force of her, her love so large it seemed as if it could lift me, as if it could save me. "I never knew if they were—in love—or . . ."

"Your mother loved a lot of people," Teofila says. "Euan was not one of them."

I blink at her. She looks levelly back at me.

"Mag Dunbarron was more than a beauty," she says. "Men were attracted to her—everyone was attracted to her—because she had that . . . *brilliance* about her."

"She was a force of nature."

Teofila nods. "Do you know why she went to Ida with Ruadan?"

"Because she was serving in his household, I thought."

"Well, she was." Teofila laughs shortly. "In more ways than one. They were having a dalliance, Sophy, your mother and Ruadan. He was in love with her, and he found her completely impossible at the same time. They argued constantly. It was the source of all sorts of gossip, the lord and his fiery housemaid. Then he came to my concert, and met me." Teofila's mouth softens. "I'd been warned about him, but even so, I couldn't resist."

"You knew he was having an affair with my mother?" My voice is high. Shocked.

"He broke it off for me. He was a romantic, Ruadan was, and he gave his all to everything." Teofila gives me a wry glance. "I wasn't jealous, if that's what you're wondering. She let me know on no uncertain terms that she was glad to be rid of him, and that I was making a mistake letting such a callous bastard into my life."

Despite myself, I utter a laugh. Somehow, in all the years of living at Cerid Aven, it had never occurred to me that this was how Ruadan knew Ma—in all the ways a man knows a woman.

"So she went and found herself a prince instead," I say hollowly.

"No, Sophy." Teofila's mouth tightens, and so does my heart. She leans heavily forward on her elbows. "Your mother loved other men, and women, too. But not Euan Dromahair. She did not love him at all."

Cold bursts all over me. There's a flitter in my stomach, and I feel a strange sound in the room—the ghost of a presence. Like my mother, watching us. All the hairs rise on the back of my neck.

"Did he . . ." I begin. The words stick in my throat. I can't say them. Don't know how to say them.

"He caught her in the back stairwell," Teofila says flatly. "It happens, especially to maids. It shouldn't, but it does, and no one ever does enough to stop it. Euan was one of those young men who's silent. Not reserved, but resentful. Angry. He took what he wanted from whoever he could get it from, and your mother was no exception, despite her ferocity. Perhaps *because* she was so fierce. He wanted to subdue her. He tried. And she came to Ruadan, saying we should cut Euan's balls off, that he was a vile cruel man. She showed us her bruises. She said Euan might forget her, but she would never forget him."

"What did you do?" I ask with all the horror I feel.

"Do?" Teofila spits the word. "*Do?* What does anyone ever *do* to men like that? Your mother was a maid. He was a prince. Everyone looked the other way."

"But Ruadan . . ." I feel sick.

"Mag urged him to drop his support of Euan. Find someone else to put on the throne. Your mother wasn't the only woman Euan abused. He was notoriously cruel to all his servants, men and women alike." Teofila's hand closes into a fist. "Ruadan wouldn't do it."

I can't speak. I taste bile at the back of my throat. Even after he struck me, even after he ordered my death, this is not what I expected, yet somehow, in the marrow of my bones, it rings ancient and true and real. It feels as if I have known the tang of this grief forever.

And Ruadan, who knew the truth about Euan, led a rebellion on the back of this monster. He drummed up stories about the king across the water; he created a dream of a better future for everyone in Caeris, when he knew what the "true king" was really like. My mind can't stop circling around this small, heartbreaking fact. *He knew.* He knew, and he still used Euan. He used Finn, and Teofila, and my mother.

He used me. He used me not only for this, but in other ways. He forced me into a mold that no human being could possibly fit, that of a woman who sacrificed everything for her people, who put the greater good above all else. He taught me to be a rebel and, at the same time, a dutiful daughter who denied her own feelings when they became inconvenient.

Ruadan was the only father I had known, and I would always love him for that, and for the many kindnesses he showed me. But in some ways he took advantage of us all. I had just never allowed myself to see it so clearly before.

A cold fist seems to have closed around my heart. My hands are spread wide on the table. It's hard to breathe. Still I feel as if the not-quite-sound lingers in the room behind me, an undeniable yet intangible presence. If it is my mother, if she is watching, I hope she knows I'm sorry. I hope she knows how bitterly my heart has cracked.

Teofila clears her throat. "Your mother still had her revenge."

"What do you mean?" I say raggedly. "She fought for his damned rebellion and died nameless in the conflagration at Marose. She's dead because of my—my—" I can't say the word. "—Euan. Finn is dead because of him. Ruadan, too. Even the Butcher of Novarre, whom I never imagined I would mourn. All because of that man."

"It's true. But she had her revenge, nevertheless." Teofila looks at me, her eyes both infinitely tender and infinitely sad. "She had you."

"Me," I say bitterly. The queen without a crown. Kicked off my throne by my own people.

"Mag made sure she had a lock of reddish-gold hair to prove you were Euan's. She made sure Ruadan knew it, too."

I look up at her. "And he? Euan. Did he know?"

Teofila presses her lips together. Quietly, she says, "She sent him a letter telling him of your birth. She suggested he acknowledge you."

I feel myself freezing into place. Somewhere, a clock is ticking, too loud. He knew. All that time, when we were running for our lives, when my mother died in Marose, he knew. He could have sent for us; he could have brought us to Ida, and saved us.

He knew, and he didn't care.

"He never wrote her back," I say. "Did he? It didn't matter to him. He didn't care that he had another child. Finn was all he needed." And look how Euan treated him.

But my mother endured what happened to her, and she remained strong. Perhaps she fought harder than ever because of it—because of me. Mag Dunbarron, who could set alight a room. My brilliant, bright-burning mother, who kept me alive even on the brink of her own ending.

I wonder whether I would do the same for my own daughter, and I know without question that I would. I know that brilliant, raging love already.

Teofila reaches over and enfolds my hands in hers. I look at her, the woman who has been a mother to me, and I know she feels it, too. For me, for Elanna, for her grandchild as yet unborn.

Together, we will face anything my father attempts. For we are stronger than he can ever be.

A SHOUT ON the street startles me. There's a sharp sound like breaking glass.

"What's going on?" I rise, wrapping the blanket tighter still, and move to the window, ignoring the twinge in my back. Teofila follows me. People are streaming down the street, waving banners and loaves of bread. They're exuberant. *Cheering.*

And moving in the direction of the palace. My gut clenches. The last time the people cheered this vigorously for me was when we claimed Laon months ago. I haven't done anything to make them this happy since. Now they're cheering like this for my father—with his dead, angry eyes and his cold hatred of us all.

Alistar emerges on the heels of the noise. He's pulling a cap low over his eyes. "I'm going out there."

"Someone might recognize you," I begin.

He shakes his head. "I'll be careful." Swinging over to me, he boldly drops a kiss on my lips before marching out the door.

I hesitate, feeling the lingering cramps kneading through my gut and back. But if he's going out there, I should, too. I was once the queen of this kingdom. I have a duty to see what's going on—even with my body aching.

Before I can act, Juleane Brazeur comes into the room; she's pulling on a coat. Victoire's with her. They both seem rather tired. "We need to see what all the racket is about," Juleane says, somewhat irritably.

"I'm coming, too." The words burst from me.

"You'll be recognized," Victoire says impatiently. "And you were so ill last night—"

"I'll take the risk. And I'm better now." Though I can't help grimacing with discomfort. I hope going into the city won't bring on fresh cramps, but I suppose if it does, I can sing to my body until I get back here. That's one advantage of being raised by Ruadan: I have learned to put my own needs last when I have to. This time is no different. "I won't be recognized if I put on a maid's costume and cover my hair. Juleane, you said you sent your housemaid to the country, didn't you? She must have left some of her clothes here." Besides, Alistar's out there, and I refuse to let him risk all the danger alone.

"She may have . . ." Juleane hesitates, glancing at Teofila, as if hoping she'll dissuade me.

But Teofila says, "I'll remain here with Rhia and Demetra. I'm more readily recognizable in a crowd of Ereni."

Juleane purses her lips but nods. "We stay at the back of the crowd, and we do *not* draw attention to ourselves."

"I think you'll find I'm very good at making myself unnoticed," I say.

She snorts, but simply guides me upstairs to the maid's empty room. The woman did leave some items: a lace-edged cap, and a simple dress of dark yellow embroidered with white flowers. They're fine clothes—probably she judged them too fine for the country. I dress quickly, struggling to close the front of the gown over my stomach. On the way out, I pause to glance at myself in a mirror. I feel a pang. My stomach rounds comfortably beneath my skirts, obvious. This is how I would have dressed every day as my mother's daughter, if she had lived. My face looks simple, wholesome, framed by the white lace. I shiver.

"Sophy!" Victoire calls, and I follow her and Juleane out the door, wincing a little as I step onto the cobblestones. Each step seems to send a fresh pinch of pain traveling up my legs and back.

I pat my stomach. "Stay strong," I whisper to the baby.

Perhaps it's my imagination—or my own sheer stubbornness—but the ache seems to recede somewhat. I push myself to hurry after Victoire and Juleane. The main pulse of the crowd has already gone past, and we join up with a few stragglers who seem as bemused as we are.

"Why were they waving bread?" Victoire asks a woman wearing a pair of spectacles.

She shakes her head. "They think Euan is going to give them bread and open the ports again for trade. That's why they're celebrating."

"And is he?" Juleane wonders.

The bespectacled woman shrugs. "So they say. He's expected to announce it."

I say nothing. Clearly the people of Laon do not yet know my father.

The walk up to Royal Square doesn't seem as long as it did last night, but my heart has begun to pound and my palms to sweat. Perhaps I shouldn't have come. Every shout is making me jump.

Victoire takes my arm. "I told that woman you're new, fresh from the country," she whispers. "Don't worry—no one will recognize you. You look like a damned milkmaid."

I force a smile, but I no longer share her confidence, and after last night our brisk pace is stealing my breath far more than it should. I find myself hugging Victoire's arm tightly as we enter Royal Square, its spacious cobblestones packed with people chanting "Euan!" and "The true king!" and "Bread and coin!" Someone is singing, and someone else is shouldering through the crowd trying to sell suspicious-looking skewers of meat. My stomach rebels at the sight.

I force myself to ignore my discomfort. Over the hats and heads,

I can just make out the palace gates standing open, and the plumed helmets of the guards within. I hope Alain and Sebastien survived their deceit last night; at least I don't see their bodies hanging from gibbets. As I watch, the guards shift ponderously forward and a gold carriage moves slowly into the opening. Victoire, who's several inches shorter than I, tugs at my arm. "Who's there?"

"My—Euan, I think," I say, squinting. One man must be wearing a gold diadem; the sunlight glints off it. "And Rambaud, from the looks of it."

Around us, the crowd is going mad, jostling forward, shouting about bread and trade and jobs—all the things that I, apparently, failed to give them. And they think my reprobate father is going to do a better job? Anger floods hot into my head. How dare Euan Dromahair take advantage of the Ereni people like this?

A trumpet blasts, and the crowd settles somewhat. Everyone's leaning forward, even me, to hear what Euan Dromahair is going to say.

But when he speaks, his voice is low. Even from here it sounds bored, though I can't pick out the words, only the tone of them.

"What?" people are demanding. "What did he say?"

"Something about the army?"

"The army? But we want trade! The war is over!"

Cold runs down my back. Victoire is gripping my elbow. My father is talking again.

Someone shouts, *"No!"* over the crowd.

"What did he say?" Juleane demands of the people in front of us. "He said—"

Deeper into the square, more voices take up a new shout. "Bread and coin! No war!"

War?

The man ahead of us looks over his shoulder, his face pale. "He says we're to sign up. All able-bodied men under thirty are to join the army. We're to retake Paladis."

Just like Euan said they would. I feel my lips twist. He certainly hasn't wasted any time.

"But Leontius Saranon is emperor of Paladis now," Juleane says. "Euan will never defeat him!"

Shouts are rocking through the square—a dozen voices, a hundred, more.

"No more war! No more war! Bread and coin!"

"Euan Dromahair is willing to execute his own daughter," Victoire says abruptly to those around us. "Is there any limit to what else he might do?"

The man stares. "You mean Queen Sophy?" He has to shout to be heard.

The bespectacled woman is nodding. "He had that Caerisian bodyguard flogged here in the square."

The crowd is roaring, a living thing, and I am suddenly glad not to be in that carriage between the gates. "We welcomed you!" someone is bellowing at Euan. "And this is how you repay us?"

"Bread and coin! No more war!"

The gilded carriage retreats through the gates, and the crowd surges forward, following it. Sudden knowing pricks me. I grab Victoire's arm. "I have a—"

The first shot bursts out, interrupting me. Then another. And another. People are screaming, running. The sporadic shots turn into a volley. People are stampeding now—a wave of humanity bursting toward us.

"Run!" I shout, and then I'm sprinting back down the street as hapless as any fish caught in the current. Aches course up my legs, and cramps are knitting my back, but I push onward. Behind us, the shooting stops and resumes again, an incessant volley. Tears mingle with sweat on my cheeks. People are screaming names, mothers crying out—to no answer. Doors and windows are flung open, people leaning out to demand what's going on. None of us respond.

Then we're at Juleane's house, bursting to the door. Teofila answers. "Were those shots—?"

"Where's Alistar?" I demand.

She points, and I whirl to see him sprinting into the courtyard. He pushes me into the house, and we all collapse in Juleane's foyer, panting hard. I cup my hands over my stomach, wincing as my body protests its rough treatment. Demetra isn't going to be happy with me—nor is my baby. Outside, in the distance, another volley of gunfire ricochets through the air.

"What happened?" Teofila is asking. Rhia's emerged from the bedroom, ghostly and pale in a dressing robe.

"Euan announced that he's going to conscript people into the army," Juleane says, still gasping for breath. "People started protesting—and then—then—"

"He ordered the guards to shoot on the crowd," I say flatly. I'm numb with horror and yet, somehow, terribly unsurprised.

Alistar's nodding. "I got close to the gates. I saw what happened—"

"You did? You're lucky you didn't get shot!" I exclaim.

He gives me a fierce grin. "I was never in their line of sight. I saw Euan give the order. The guards hesitated. They're Ereni, most of them, with a Paladisan commander. Euan had to order them three times, and then he threatened to shoot *them*. The Paladisan captain fired first."

"I suppose that bastard Grenou did, too," I say darkly.

"I don't know, but I—"

A loud pounding on the door interrupts him. We all go very still. Without a word, Alistar and I flatten ourselves against the wall, and Rhia and Teofila shrink back into a doorway. Demetra, who's emerged to see what's the matter, halts just out of sight. The pounding comes again. Juleane wipes her mouth with the back of one hand, then steps forward to answer. Victoire widens her stance in the short hallway and picks up a heavy candelabra.

Juleane opens the door a crack. "Yes?"

"You need to get out of the city." It's a man's urgent voice, robbed of its usual poise. "They're at the temple arresting High Priest Granpier. They'll be here in a matter of an hour. Do you have her?"

"Granpier?" I say with growing horror. I move forward, gently nudging Juleane out of the way. "I'm here, Philippe. Though you shouldn't be—it's too dangerous. Come in."

He does. "Thank all the gods." His eyes are enormous, almost black with fear. "I had to take the risk, and damn Rambaud and my mother if I get caught. There are at least fifty people dead in Royal Square. Perhaps more. Euan's ordered men to simply be rounded up off the street for this damned army of his—"

"I suppose Rambaud's supporters are safe from that, at least," I say bitterly.

Philippe's gaze hardens. "No. Even those of us who have paid him lip service have lost everything. I will be marching on Ida along with the sons of every noble and commoner in Eren and Caeris."

"What?" I gasp.

"We're nothing but clay to him. Bodies he can use. Euan Dromahair doesn't give a damn about this country," Philippe spits, "or the people who handed it over to him, or those who celebrated his return because cursed Ruadan Valtai told them he was the savior of this kingdom for twenty years. We're beneath him, Sophy—all of us. We're muscle, and he's going to strip us to reclaim Ida and Paladis."

"But the Paladisan army is far superior to any force we have," Juleane objects. "Not to mention the people of Paladis threw their support behind Leontius."

"I know." Philippe digs the heels of his hands into his eyes. "Those abominable Saranons—Augustus and Phaedra—insist they have people loyal to them still within the empire, and that if they can raise an army here, their friends will help them overthrow their brother. In the meantime, they've sent for some even *closer* friends to join them here in Eren." His mouth curves bitterly. "They'll be rewarding them with houses and land. Guess who they'll take those from?"

Slowly, I say, "Did Rambaud know this?"

"Believe me, Lord Aristide is as surprised as the rest of us. And possibly more devastated than anyone," Philippe says sardonically.

"As is my dear mother. It seems their plans haven't quite worked out the way they intended."

Juleane folds her arms. "Yet it's the common people who suffer the most for it, as always."

Philippe's chin tilts in acknowledgment. "We all stand to lose everything we gained, not only the Caerisians"—his gaze cuts to me—"but even what we had under the Eyrlais. We'll have even less than we did under King Antoine."

"In the meantime," I say, "people are dying in the city streets. If they resist, I assume they'll be shot."

He doesn't need to answer.

My fingers curl into fists. My father is going to pay for this. I'm not going to let my people suffer, even if I can no longer truly call them my people. Even if I never again sit on the throne.

But—I glance at the others standing uncertainly behind us— right now the people who matter most to me are in danger. We don't have a plan, and we don't have support. If we don't take care of ourselves, we'll be in no position to help anyone else. I turn to the others. "Is there somewhere we can go? Somewhere to gather people, outside the city, to start fighting?"

Teofila and Juleane exchange a look. "It's not practical," Juleane begins, "not to house so many . . ."

"People survived in the caves when Paladis invaded," Teofila says. "Some of our people are already there."

"You mean the Spring Caves," I say in sudden comprehension. "But . . ." People fled there, of course, and have continued to do so in the centuries since. Yet I also suspect that many of them died there.

Victoire is nodding. "When the Paladisans invaded, the Ereni hid in those caves and attacked them by night."

"How will we survive there?" I ask. "Without food, supplies—"

"The caves *are* supplied," Juleane says, with another look at Teofila. "We stockpiled them."

I stare between the two of them. Slowly, I say, "You mentioned this when Rambaud staged his coup. When did you do it?"

"The day you and the Butcher went to Montclair," Teofila admits. "We didn't want to frighten you by suggesting we might need an escape from the city. So Juleane and I arranged it ourselves. Word is already out—some people have taken shelter there already. You know Annis, the maid from Barrody who was meant to accompany me to Baedon? She's overseeing the site."

"Is it wise to leave the city?" Alistar asks. "Doesn't that mean we're ceding the ground to Euan and Rambaud?"

"It's barely beyond the walls," Teofila says. "It's the perfect place to gather people from Laon and the country as well."

Philippe is nodding. "You should go. Euan doesn't know the caves exist, and he's arresting everyone associated with Sophy in the city, hoping he'll find her."

"A reasonable theory," Juleane says drily.

Philippe backs toward the door. "I should go."

"You could come with us," I tell him.

He shakes his head. "I want to help the people here and in the palace, if I can. And I'm more use to you if I can smuggle information out. In the chaos, I doubt I've been tracked."

I look at him and sigh. No doubt his mother has reclaimed control of the spies who were once hers—or if she hasn't, she will. And my father is not gentle. Philippe is playing a dangerous game, and he knows it. "Be careful."

He touches his fingertips to his heart, and then he's gone.

We move quickly. Juleane throws her most important possessions into a small trunk, and Demetra makes me sit for a few minutes with my feet up, drinking a fresh decoction of herbs, while she helps Rhia get dressed. There's little else to gather. As we go out, Juleane gives the house a final, swift look, like a goodbye. I touch her shoulder; the note pulsing from her is lower and deeper than I have ever heard it. She gives me a tiny nod, though her lips are tight.

The streets have quieted, though some small groups, like us, are on the move. The houses sit eerily silent, and I feel eyes on us from the windows as we pass. In the distance, a trumpet blares. We break up into groups of two and three, to attract less attention. At least we're moving more slowly, and Demetra's new decoction is dulling most of my lingering aches. Somehow I end up walking beside Victoire along the riverfront, in the wide lane behind the warehouses.

"We'll send out the news," she says quietly. "Tell people where we're hiding. Rally them to us."

We walk up a low incline, and I glimpse the open sky at the edge of the city buildings. It's quiet here; hard to believe that behind us in Laon fifty or more lie dead on the cobblestones before the royal palace. Shop fronts stand quiet as we pass. I stare at them, my mind and heart worn. Numb. "Why would they rally to us, Victoire? We failed them the first time."

"We were at war with the whole world, practically," she points out. "Now we have Emperor Leontius's help. Elanna and Jahan are coming home."

"El's land magic can't do everything. Rambaud would still have worked against us, even if she had been there." I pause. This is hard to admit. "In some ways, he's right, you know. We claimed equal representation but really we gave the most power to Caeris and Caerisians. Two parliaments would have divided the country further. We might have made things better, but not better enough."

Victoire glances at me. "I've never heard you talk like that."

My eyes smart. "Well, I'm learning. I don't know why the people of Eren and Caeris would want me on the throne again. I'm not sure *I* would want me."

"You wouldn't gun people down in the street," she points out.

"Faint praise."

"And you wouldn't send them off to a war they have little chance of surviving."

"No . . ."

She sighs. "The gods know you're not perfect, Sophy Dunbarron. But none of us are. You at least are willing to see how you could do better, and that's a damned sight more than most. The people didn't cast you off the throne, Rambaud did. I think if you talked to people—if you told them what you told me—they'd be willing to give you a second chance. Or at least consider it."

"I don't have an army, at least not here in Eren," I object, ignoring the warmth that's spread through me. Victoire Madoc is giving me her support? "Rambaud's claimed it. I don't even have any *assurances* . . ."

"The people are enough of an army," Victoire says. "You can fight without firing a single weapon, if you're brave enough." She glances at me. "Oh. You've thought of something, haven't you?"

"I've no idea if it will work." My thoughts are racing ahead; I grip my hands together, as if they can anchor me in the here and now. It's not a move I would ordinarily make without the support of the people. But if I do it to win the people—to save our kingdom . . .

Quietly, I say, "But I think we can try."

CHAPTER TWENTY-FIVE

The Spring Caves lie as silent as I remember, the low dark openings on the ridge facing the city eerie and slumberous. Teofila leads the way into the cave entrance, while Demetra helps Rhia take a seat on a nearby boulder. I breathe in the cool, dark, watery scent—and then my nose catches something else. The thread of smoke.

Light flickers on the cave roof beyond the springs. A tight humming silence rings through the cave, as if the people in the stone chambers beyond have abruptly stopped speaking.

Juleane gives a low hoot like an owl.

A moment later, a woman emerges from behind the statue of the goddess, bearing a raised lantern. She's an Ereni countrywoman, judging by her black bell-sleeved dress and simple red-and-white apron. When she sees us, she brightens. "They're here!" she calls over her shoulder.

A familiar rosy-cheeked girl comes out behind her. "Annis!" I exclaim.

She rushes over and throws her arms around me. "Oh, Queen Sophy! I knew they would get you out."

"Well, we know the truth about my father now," I say grimly. I look at the Ereni woman. "I don't believe we've met. I'm Sophy Dunbarron."

"I'm Brigitte Paquet," she says, "Your Majesty."

"Just Sophy," I say firmly. "I no longer have a crown, and even if I did, I prefer to be the first among equals, not *Your Majesty*."

Her eyes have widened, and so have Annis's. But then she starts to smile. "Yes, Your M—Sophy."

There's another movement in the cave. *"Sophy!"*

I almost scream. "Fiona! Isley—Moyra—Kenna—" For it's my maid and all of my former guards, rushing out from the cave tunnel, sweeping me into enthusiastic hugs. They look a bit gaunt, perhaps, but otherwise unharmed.

"What are you *doing* here?" I demand. "Did Teofila—"

"She told us of this place," Fiona says, nodding. "When Rambaud's people claimed the palace, Isley found me. We sneaked out, along with all the other Caerisian staff we could find."

"We acted quickly enough," Isley says. "They weren't looking for us yet—they thought we were too ill to know what had happened."

I swallow at the thought of what *would* have happened had the mountain women remained at the palace. I somehow doubt Grenou would have treated them with any sort of respect.

The Caerisians have seen Rhia, Alistar, and Teofila now, and they sweep over to greet them. Rhia hangs on to each one of them for a long moment, though it seems to me she clings longest to Isley. My normally unflappable friend is wordless with shock at the sight of them, her face white.

I turn to Brigitte, who is looking amused. "You Caerisians," she says. "There's always such enthusiasm."

"We care a great deal for one another." I look at her. I can hear a thread of sound weaving through her, the texture of magic under her skin. Unlike the other women, she's a sorceress. "How did you come to be here?"

The corner of her mouth tucks in. "I went to light the fire in my hearth one morning, a few months ago," she says. "I was struggling with the tinder, and then I felt the strangest thing. Heat, like a flood, brighter than anything I have ever felt. I stared down at my own hand and watched a *spark* leap from my fingers and light the dry wood."

Familiarity tugs at my mind. "I've heard this story before . . . Did your brother-in-law come to the city with this news?"

"Poor Franck," Brigitte says, but her tone is more ironic than sympathetic. "He doesn't know what to make of women, especially when we change so suddenly. He urged my husband to divorce me. My good man refused, but . . ." She sighs. "When the Duke of Essez seized the capital, it seemed safer to come here."

"I'm glad you did," Teofila says, putting an arm around Brigitte's shoulders and hugging her.

Brigitte gives a sad smile.

"There was another woman," I say, growing more suspicious. "Someone who was locked in her house—"

"Eugenie." Brigitte nods grimly. "She's here, too."

So Juleane lied to me. It takes me a moment to digest this fact; I turn to Teofila. "Juleane told me they all refused to leave their homes!"

"She . . . prevaricated." Teofila nods at the minister of commerce, who is behind us, talking to Demetra and Rhia. "She didn't want these women's locations to become public knowledge. So she arranged for Eugenie to be brought to a place of safety, then here when Rambaud took power."

I glance at Juleane, who meets my eyes with an even glance before turning back to explain something to Demetra. It stings that she lied to my face—though in some ways, I can see that she may have been right. I would have tried to meet the problem head-on, whereas her way of handling the matter kept these women safe and protected.

"I was so worried," I say to Brigitte. "I'm so glad to see you're all safe."

"We are. But come," she says, gesturing me forward. "Come meet the rest of us."

I follow her past the goddess statue. The tunnel opening is cunningly hidden behind a wall of sheer rock, the entrance so narrow my shoulders brush stone. But once we snake through the tunnel, the ceiling lifts and the cave is painted in warm orange light.

Women—for they are mostly women, with a few men and a number of children—rise from their tasks. There must be forty people here, all of them Ereni. A warm fire funnels smoke up through a small hole in the cave ceiling, and the walls are stacked with supplies—blankets, sacks of grain, bundled candles. This, Brigitte informs me, is merely a fraction of the supplies Teofila and Juleane have stockpiled. More caves branch out from this one, burrowing deeper into the ridge. People sleep in those, she tells me, because they are easier to guard.

I stop beside everyone in the cave, introducing myself, though they all seem to know who I am. "There are so many of you," I marvel to Eugenie, the woman who was locked in her house. Apparently she sees spirits.

She looks entirely surprised. "But this is nothing. Magic is awakening in half the people I know, and none of them listened when I insisted they come with me here."

I stare from her to Brigitte. *"Half?"*

They both nod.

"It's even higher in Caeris," Annis informs me, but then she snickers. "Though some of that could be wishful thinking."

Of course, I reflect ruefully, Caerisians *want* to be latent sorcerers, and the Ereni are only admitting to their newfound abilities under duress. The cave practically vibrates with magic.

"Would there be room for more people, if they came?" I wonder.

"Oh, yes," Brigitte says. "There are dozens of caves. Legend has it half of Laon hid here when the Paladisans invaded."

"The Paladisans claim they died here," I say softly.

"No, they didn't." Her voice is firm. "They stayed here, and they fought. And eventually, they won."

I look at them, this circle of women standing around me. "Then that is what we will do. If you'll have me—not as your leader, but as one among the rest of you. I didn't spend my early years in Duke Ruadan's household, you know. My mother was a Caerisian rebel, and a commoner at that. We spent our lives on the run. Once we even took shelter in a cave much like this one." I pause. "So I am just like the rest of you. A commoner at heart and . . . a sorceress."

There's a silence. Then Annis says, "You're a sorceress?"

I finger the bone flute in my pocket. Its hum steadies me, and I nod. "It seems I am. I'm still trying to understand my abilities."

"We all are," Brigitte says wryly.

Eugenie is looking at me. "I think you're being too modest," she says at last. "Maybe the Duke of Essez has seized power, along with that Euan Dromahair, but you're still the queen of Caeris. I wager you have a plan."

I glance over my shoulder; Juleane and Teofila have gathered behind me, along with Alistar, Rhia, Demetra, and Victoire. Fiona and the mountain women are behind them. They're all listening. Waiting.

I draw in a breath. These caves seem an unlikely place to launch a rebellion from. Yet, I remind myself, Ruadan began his campaign against the crown while sequestered at Cerid Aven. Great things can begin in the smallest and quietest of places.

And we are not small or quiet people.

"Before I was betrayed by Lord Gavin and captured, we had begun to make a plan in Caeris," I say. "It involved negotiating with our neighbors in Baedon and Tinan, as well as Paladis. Trapping and isolating Euan, Rambaud, and the Saranons, much the same way we were trapped."

Juleane nods. "Baedon and Tinan will be more hesitant, now that Leontius is on the throne."

"But if we trap them, we make them desperate," Brigitte points out. "It's hard to say what a desperate person will do."

"It seems to me that's a risk we have to take," Victoire says.

I glance at Teofila and Alistar. "Did Ingram Knoll send that message to Count Hilarion, before I was captured? Do we know if he made contact with him, and if Hilarion talked to King Alfred?"

In answer, Juleane reaches into her pocket. "This came yester-day morning, from the warden of the mountains."

I unfurl the small, crumpled note.

On Ard, outside Longlais. Alfred will arrive tomorrow. I shall proceed unless you advise differently.

"With you captured, we thought Ingram Knoll might negotiate with Alfred himself," Teofila explains. "It would have been more leverage to get you out, had we needed it."

"Now I can meet him myself." I look around at the group. "If that's the choice of the majority?"

Eugenie laughs a little. "Do you Caerisians do *all* business by popular acclamation?"

"Only the most important," I say with a quick grin.

The other Ereni are conferring among themselves, and now Bri-gitte says, "If Sophy is willing to take the risk, we approve of the idea."

"I am." I nod. "From what I understand, King Alfred is a bit of an opportunist—but he's also pragmatic. I think he'll hear us out—and he'll be interested to know what Euan's plans really are." The king of Tinan is perhaps twenty-five years my senior, having inher-ited the throne from his grandfather. His kingdom is fiercely inde-pendent; if Euan Dromahair is proposing to conscript Ereni into an army, there's a good chance Alfred will see it as a threat to his own lands.

The others are murmuring agreement.

"I can shift the land," Rhia says. "If we leave in the morning, we can arrive on the border in a few hours."

"That's perfect." I smile at her. It's good to see she's getting some spirit back.

Teofila looks at me. "There is Baedon, as well."

I nod, even though the back of my neck immediately tenses at the thought of sending her away, through the dangers of a hostile Eren. "Are you still willing to go?"

"Of course I am," she says quietly. "You know that."

"I'll go with you," Annis says immediately. "I gave you my word!"

Unexpectedly, one of the Ereni women steps forward. "I'll go, too. I can help you commandeer a ship. My son captains his own merchant vessel; I'm sure I can persuade him to sail. With the Paladisans' arrival, there's bound to be some chaos in the harbor. No one will notice us slip out."

We all smile at one another, with the surety of a plan in place.

"Now, our northern people," I say. "Has anyone established contact with Caeris? With Hugh?"

Teofila smiles a little. "I've been in touch with him by mirror. He's readying a force to bring south."

"Perhaps with the folds in the land, we can bring them here without Rambaud or Euan being any the wiser," I say.

She nods. "I'll contact him before I go."

The thought of her leaving still makes my chest ache, but this time I feel more prepared to let her go. We need to attempt everything we can.

"There's another matter," Alistar says unexpectedly. He's been whispering to Victoire and now faces us. "Euan and the Saranons are a foreign power. We can force them out. But Rambaud and his followers belong here—they're Ereni, and they're the reason we're in this mess in the first place."

"We can't just march on Laon the way we did before," I agree. "What's your idea?"

He looks around at us. "I'm convinced that someone close to Rambaud has magic. I just have to find out who. When I was tailing Ciril, I saw a lot of Rambaud. Believe me, he's no longer campaigning on hatred and distrust of sorcery. He might have been at first, but now . . ." He sends me an apologetic glance. "Unfortunately he's found other ways to attack Sophy—slander, namely, and xenophobia surrounding the refugees. He has said very little about sorcery one way or another in the time I've spent watching him."

"I wonder . . ." I think back to my encounters with Rambaud. He was carrying a witch stone when Ciril was paraded through the streets, but otherwise, have I seen him working against sorcerers? Grenou has, certainly, along with Lord Devalle. But perhaps not Rambaud himself.

"Magic is awakening throughout Eren and Caeris," Demetra says. "It's in your stone circles and humming through the land itself. People who've never had magic have discovered that they do. Perhaps it's the same for someone close to Rambaud."

"There's a house he's been visiting outside the city," Alistar says. "I'm convinced the truth is there, if I can get in and find it out. I'll go and see what I can discover."

I nod slowly. "If you can do it safely . . ."

"I can," he promises. He grins at me, then, as if it's only the two of us in the room. "You can't lose me that easily, Sophy Dunbarron."

Some of the others laugh, though kindly, and I feel myself blushing. Maybe, when all this is over, I can marry Alistar Connell after all. Not one of these people has reproached me for carrying a child out of wedlock, nor made me feel small for the way Alistar looks at me.

"Very well," I say, shaking off these idle thoughts of the future. "Hugh will bring the Caerisians here. Alistar, you'll see what information you can get about Rambaud. Teofila will go to Baedon . . ."

"And we'll spread word through the city and countryside," Victoire says, gesturing to Juleane and the other women. "We'll make sure everyone knows this is the place to rally. By the time you return from the border, anyone interested in resistance will know where to find us, and that we're going to act now, before Euan Dromahair has a chance to take this regime further."

"Elanna will be back soon, too," Teofila adds. "Along with Jahan. Make sure the people know they're rallying not only to us, but to the *Caveadear*."

A ragged chorus of applause runs through the chamber. My heart lifts.

"Euan Dromahair isn't going to give up easily," Juleane says. "Neither will the Saranons. This is their last resort—they have no other home. They'll fight to keep it. And Rambaud has staked his career—and his life on this coup. He won't go down without a struggle."

"Then we'll have to make sure we're all willing to fight as hard, and as cleverly," I say. "Because this is our home, too, and we're not giving it up without a fight, either."

CHAPTER TWENTY-SIX

Rhia's waiting for me outside the cave in the morning, her breath fogging in the cool spring dawn. I can't ride a horse with my pregnant belly, so we've decided that we'll walk the folds in the land, all the way to the Ard. My lingering cramps have finally eased enough to make this possible—thanks to additional decoctions from Demetra—though I can only imagine that the long day will cause my aches to worsen again. I hope I don't pay too severely for it, though Demetra gave me a vial of the honey-herb mixture to help mitigate the worst of the symptoms. I pause for a moment to look out over the panorama of the just-waking city. Over the jumble of roofs, the Hill of the Imperishable rises, looking mountainous in the flat light. Teofila and the others departed late yesterday, and I find myself wondering whether they made it to the port town where the merchant ship is moored.

"Ready?" Rhia asks.

I nod. Alistar's already gone, too, out on his Rambaud mission. The others are preparing to disperse.

"It's this way."

We cross over the height of the hill, and the familiar twinge washes over us. A shift in the land. We're walking now across a pasture, and a few minutes later crossing a marshy area beneath two hills. Rhia checks our location against a map, one she herself has been developing over the last few months. "Three more shifts will take us near my father."

"Do you know that for certain?" I ask, curious how accurate her map is. My feet have already begun to swell.

"My best guess, but it's good enough. Come on."

As we walk down the hill, the land shifts again—this time to an open farm field. In the distance, a farmer rises, hoe in hand, to stare at us. "Who goes there?"

I wave at him, and we move off the field, onto the nearby road. Rhia peers both ways. "I think it's down here . . ."

The next shift brings us to a line of standing stones on the out-skirts of a small town—evidently a place Rhia recognizes, for she nods with satisfaction. We cross a narrow stone bridge, heading away from the town. It cuts away through a tangle of hazel to a larger body of water. We're almost to the Ard.

Ahead, the road turns to skirt a small patch of forest. There's a flash of metal among the trees—the mountain lords' weapons. Rhia lets out an identifying whistle.

Two Hounds are waiting for us in the trees, on their small camp's outskirts. They greet us solemnly, with a kiss to either cheek, and guide us past the small, temporary camp to the gentle riverbank, where stones make a rocky ford. Rhia's father, Ingram Knoll, is waiting for us there, along with a small party of Hounds. In the middle of the river there is a small island, made up mostly of grass and some shrubs. On the bank beyond it, I glimpse movement. The Tinani are approaching.

"Queen Sophy." Ingram Knoll looks worn, his bright cloak mud-stained, but he still offers a smile. "It seems we managed our trick."

I smile in return. "Indeed."

He's turned to his daughter now, though. Rhia throws her arms around him. They rock back and forth, whispering words I can't quite catch.

I clear my throat and look away across the river, past the small, grassy island. Even when Ruadan was alive, I would never have embraced him like that, with such abandon and relief. An edge of formality always separated us; someday, we both knew, I might be his queen. And my blood father . . .

I focus on the figures occupying the Tinani bank. It doesn't look like a large party, though it's well armed—fifty, perhaps. They're flying the royal flag of Tinan—a hawk on a red background.

"I take it we're to meet on the island," I say when Rhia and Ingram Knoll at last stop whispering to each other. "Neutral ground?"

"Aye," he says. "Count Hilarion sent word this morning. He claims the king's come himself."

"Good," I say, "he's supposed to."

A man on the opposite bank raises his hand in a wave. I can tell from his diminutive stature that it's Hilarion, the Count of Ganz. I wave back, then lift my skirts and plunge into the ford. It's a slow, rocky crossing, and each step builds the ache in my back. "We might have to take a coach home," I say to Rhia.

Finally, my stockings spattered with water, I clamber up onto the island, and our people spread out, planting our flag in the turf. Guardsmen set down two stools in the exact center of the island— one for me and the other, evidently, for King Alfred. The party on the other bank has begun to cross.

I take off my hat and arrange myself on the stool. Even in the plain coat I've borrowed from Juleane, I want to look like myself. I ask Rhia how my hair looks.

She rolls her eyes. "It looks like your hair."

"You are spectacularly unhelpful, do you know that?"

"I try." She smirks. "You look fine, Sophy."

I don't know about that, but I also don't have time to argue. The Tinani are coming onto the island now: their standard-bearer plants their flag on their side of the turf. Count Hilarion shoots me a reassuring smile.

I smile back, but my attention is distracted by another man dismounting from his horse. I've never met Alfred of Tinan, but I've seen his portrait, and it's a decent likeness, except the painters have politely covered up his balding head with hats. He's in his mid-forties, a man of middling height who reportedly keeps himself fit with an hour in the fencing hall each morning. He advances with a commanding air.

"Sophy Dunbarron," he says.

I return his stare. "Alfred Tinanlai."

His eyebrows lift at that, and he looks me up and down. Then, surprisingly, he smiles. "How nice that we can be on a first-name basis." He speaks Ereni with a crisp accent. "Your Lord Hilarion here has insisted I must speak with you—practically dragged me out of Darchon by the back of my coat. I hope it's worth my while."

"I hope this meeting is useful for both of us," I reply, and King Alfred chuckles. He settles on the stool across from me. I remember to take a breath. Our meeting has begun.

"Here is the situation," I say. "I understand why you threw your support behind Rambaud and his followers, but Paladis has been taken over by a new regime—one that supports sorcery. Change is upon us, King Alfred, and the only ones who haven't recognized it are Euan Dromahair and his friends—including Phaedra and Augustus Saranon. I want your reassurance that when they are removed from our kingdom and I resume my place on the throne, we can look to you as an ally. I trust you are a pragmatic man."

"I do pride myself on being such," he replies with a faint smile. "Allying with Eren interests me. Yet I am curious—what possesses a girl such as yourself to fight her own father for a crown?"

I press my lips together. I have to think for a moment before I can respond.

"When a father is without honor," I say at last, "a daughter must do her duty."

"Without honor? Indeed?"

I hesitate. Telling the truth seems horrible, yet I can't think of a suitable evasion. "I could tell you how he's levying Ereni and Caerisians to fight in his army, with a plan to retake Ida. Maybe I'd persuade you if I told you how he fired on a crowd of his own people who had done nothing but come to honor him. But on top of all this, the truth is that this is a man who assaulted my mother. I am not the child of a love affair, you see. I am the child of rape. And I will not condone a man who would do such to sit on the throne of Eren."

Alfred of Tinan presses a finger against his lips. He looks thoughtful—haunted, I might almost say. The sound of him has quieted.

"You are right to take a stand," he says at last, still troubled. "Such things should never be condoned." Alfred pauses, then looks at me. "You've given me a truth, and I feel I owe you one in turn. Shortly before our marriage, my wife suffered an assault similar to that of your mother's. It is not common knowledge, and she did not tell me the truth until years into our marriage. But what happened to her does not define her. It has shaped the way she sees the world, perhaps, but it has not hindered her ability to love, nor her intelligence and wit." Ruefully, he says, "I would have brought her with me, had I known. She makes a more formidable political opponent than I do, in truth."

"I find that hard to imagine," I say through the lump in my throat. "Thank you for telling me. It . . ." I think of my mother, and all the unanswered questions that press on my mind. "It does comfort me."

He gives me a thoughtful look. "Then I will continue to speak frankly. I did not come here intending to ally with you. I confess I was merely curious what you might have to say. You have had some decisive defeats, yet you seem convinced you may still win. It is . . . interesting."

Or stupid. I wince. "I don't suffer any illusions that the people might want me to reclaim the throne. I'm doing this for our futures." I touch my stomach. "For *my* future."

"Given the reports I've heard of King Euan, you may stand a chance. But . . ." He looks at me. "I have for some time now pledged my help to the Ereni who oppose you. Rambaud is my friend. I will not back you against him." He pauses. "If you came together, however, I would back you both against Euan."

My brief surge of hope is squashed by the thought of attempting an alliance with Aristide Rambaud—even though he can't be much happier with my father than I am.

"So magic does not concern you?" I ask Alfred, genuinely curious.

"To tell the truth, I always rather liked the old myths." But there's an edge to his voice when he says, "It seems sorcery is in our future, whether we will it or no. I won't lose my kingdom because I was unwilling to change."

"That's wise," I remark.

"We shall see." He stands and extends a hand. "Let me know, Sophy Dunbarron, if you can come to an agreement with my friend Rambaud. I wish you the very best luck."

I clasp his hand, fighting down a sense of disappointment. It's not as if I truly expected him to immediately offer to help us. "And I thank you for meeting."

He nods and turns to go. Count Hilarion comes over to clasp my hand with an all-too-brief greeting, and then they ride away back across the ford.

I turn back to the shallow ford, the water running white between the rocks. Ingram Knoll has already led the bulk of the soldiers back across. Rhia and I trail at the rear. "Maybe we can rent a coach in that town," she says. "You look done in."

"It's just my back. It—"

Noise breaks out in front of us. A man screams.

Gunfire.

Rhia tackles me to the ground. I wrestle with her, fumbling to protect my stomach. The water soaks up my skirts. Ahead, a man falls. Horses stumble, whinnying. Rhia's tumbled off me, her broken arm tangled under her. She's struggling to lever herself back up. I glance frantically back and forth. Alfred's successfully retreated to the far shore. Did he alert our attackers? It seems unlikely.

The land is level, flat, grassy, except for the low-sloping hill overlooking the forest. A plume of gun smoke rises from the crest of the hill. They have us pinned here.

Our soldiers are running for their muskets, but another volley of gunfire brings more of them down. Ingram Knoll is shouting, trying to rally the men. A stampede of horses surges north from the camp into open farmland.

I grab the back of Rhia's coat and help haul her to her feet. She flings herself in front of me as I try to move forward. "Stop!" she gasps. We're just out of firing range. Rhia's right. If we move forward, we run straight into the enemy guns.

Behind us, on the other side of the river, people are shouting. Count Hilarion's urging his horse back across the ford, toward the island.

Gunfire erupts once more. Ingram Knoll is running toward the hill, urging the men to take shelter behind trees and carts and tents to fire back at our enemies. He stands on the edge of the woods, his arms raised.

And the gunfire catches him.

His body jerks. He's thrown backward at an unnatural angle. Cast onto the ground.

Rhia is screaming. Despite her own injunction, she begins to race forward, splashing over the final rocks of the ford. I fling myself after her, snatching for the back of her coat. She stumbles, and I grip her hard, holding her back. She's sobbing, her mouth open, but I'm too stunned for tears. Ingram Knoll, dead? Who's ambushed us—my father's men, or someone else's?

More gunfire erupts on the ridge. I throw Rhia to the ground just as a blast shakes the air where we were standing.

We lie for a moment, stunned. I risk a glance up. Our ambushers are approaching, apparently growing more confident of their victory. They wear Euan Dromahair's colors—gold and white.

I drop back. And then I glimpse her among them. Her face drawn with exhaustion, her robe ragged. It's a temple novice—not Felicité, but one of the others. Does she have magic, too? Somewhere a witch stone is humming. They must have captured her at the temple.

The realization hits me. Euan's forces haven't been anywhere near the Ard, and they only arrested the novices yesterday. If she's a sorcerer, there's only one way they could have gotten here. They're forcing her to help them; she must have tracked us, and somehow helped transport them all the way out here.

Rhia is crawling over to her father's body. Across from us, another soldier falls.

We're not going to defeat them. There might not be many men firing down on us, but we're trapped between them and the river. We can retreat to the island—to Tinan, if King Alfred isn't behind this, if he didn't trick me—but that would give Euan's men possession of the ford.

Ruadan's voice drifts into my mind. *Sometimes a tactical retreat is the closest one can come to victory. At least you'll live to fight another day.*

I gather my legs under me. We'll have to risk the Tinani. "Retreat!" I shout. "To the island!"

I charge back into the water. Now would be a good time to have Elanna's help, or Jahan's—anyone's, really. But they aren't here. The men are covering our retreat, but we're leaving soldiers behind among the tents and the carts—some dead, but more wounded and living. I know what my father's soldiers will do to them.

My feet hit the grass of the island. Hilarion's stopped halfway between it and the opposite bank, his horse pulled around so he can shout back to King Alfred, on the shore. I gather my skirts and run across the island, as fast as the sodden fabric will allow.

"Help us!" I scream to Alfred.

He sits on the opposite bank with a fully armed contingent. Enough men to ride through our camp and turn back my father's soldiers—or at least to make a good effort at it.

His head is turned toward one of his lackeys. I don't even know if he heard me.

I stop, my lungs heaving, beside Hilarion. He looks down at me from the height of his horse, his face grim.

"Is Alfred—?" I pant.

"No. Those must be Euan Dromahair's forces." Hilarion jerks

his chin toward the far shore. "Let's get our people to Tinan. Regroup there."

I glance over my shoulder. The gunfire has mostly ceased. Rhia and the soldiers have reached the island, for the most part. My father's soldiers are approaching down the road. Bodies litter the camp.

Then I see one man lift himself up on his forearms. Look toward us. He starts crawling on his belly toward the river.

He knows what fate awaits him.

I close my eyes. If we retreat into Tinan, I save those who have made it to the island. But I don't save that man. I don't save any of the others who might still be living.

I turn my back on Hilarion—startled, he speaks my name—and I cross back over the island. I pass our men, and Rhia, who all stare at me. I walk back, once more, into the ford, facing the camp. I let my feet anchor on the slick rocks.

I pull the bone flute from my pocket and play a single note. It shears over the water, a noise far bigger than me, and yet somehow less sound than vibration. It gathers wings and beats around the soldiers walking down into camp. It's a hum, not a song. It holds all my desperation. All my hope. All my terror.

I see the moment it sinks into them. Their footsteps slow. Their heads lift.

"Stop," I say.

The word whispers across the water straight to them. An arrow. A plea. A hope.

Some hesitate—but some don't. One lifts his bayonet over a fallen mountain lord—

Every shred of logic tells me to turn tail once more and bolt for the Tinani shore. To save myself, and those I can.

Yet my bones tell me no. My rage propels me forward. I am stalking through the water, the bone flute still at my lips. I feel the power growing in me, feel the movement of the child in my stomach. I am a mother, and these people are my brethren as much as the baby I carry. This is my war.

The soldiers have seen me now. They slow, bayonets raised but not striking those wounded on the ground.

I lift the bone flute and begin to play. The sound is wild, high, sinewy with fury. It pours out of me, inexorable as a rising tide. I release my rage into it. My grief. My guilt. It strikes like a fist across the camp. My father's soldiers have all stopped now, even the Paladisan commander. The others are Ereni. I see it in their faces, in the clothes they wear, in the words they shape in their mouths.

I walk to the center of the camp, past Ingram Knoll's crumpled body, and stop. I'm trembling. With rage and fear.

I widen my stance. Hold out my hands.

"If you kill them," I say, "you are killing our country and our people. You will have to kill me, too. And the child I carry."

One man drops his bayonet. It thuds dully to the ground. He starts to back away. The others are staring from me to their captain, who's watching me with a look of ill-concealed terror.

I look back at him. In Idaean, I say, "The choice is yours."

One of the other soldiers turns with a cry and drives his bayonet into the throat of a wounded Ereni soldier.

The captain whirls around so fast my eye can barely follow the movement, and strikes the soldier across the face. The man staggers back over the legs of the fellow he just killed.

Another points. I glance briefly behind me. People are streaming back into camp from the island. They are all throwing down their weapons. Standing with their hands empty. Rhia takes up position beside her father, tears falling openly down her cheeks.

I turn back to our attackers. The captain looks strangled, and the temple novice hollowed out. Relieved, and afraid.

I hold out my hand to her. She casts a single, frightened look at the captain. He hesitates, and she bolts over to me. She stands at my shoulder, staring defiantly at the men.

"I don't need to fight with weapons." I widen my stance and fix my gaze on the captain and his men. "I won't kill my own people. I will never attack you."

The captain's head jerks back. He's staring at the ford again; I look, too.

It's a river of black and metal now. King Alfred and his men are crossing toward us.

"I won't use a weapon against you," I say to the captain. "But I doubt Alfred of Tinan has any such compunction."

His nostrils quiver. My heart thumps; I squeeze my hands into fists. I won't relinquish this rage. I won't stand down, no matter what they do to us. Let them know this is how Caerisians fight— not with blades or gunpowder, but with all their hearts and blood and bone. This is how *mothers* fight. A mother doesn't strike her children. She shows them what real mettle is made of.

The captain lifts his hand and brings it sharply down. He mutters something.

"What?" an aide asks.

"Retreat," he says, already backing away. "Retreat!"

RHIA'S KNEELING ON the hard ground beside her father, her hand cupping his face. Her shoulders shake. I look around at the other men fallen to the ground—wounded, most of them. One is struggling to rise. He took a wound to the shoulder; red blood stains his coat. I go over and help him up.

"My . . . queen," he murmurs.

"Where's the physician?" I call. There isn't one, it seems. A man is being sent over from the Tinani camp, but he's only just coming up from the river.

Rhia looks over at me from her father's body, a few feet away. "He's gone." Her eyes are shining with tears.

The temple novice crouches beside the soldier, motioning me to go to Rhia. But Rhia just shakes her head and gestures me away. "No," she chokes out, "you're going to tell me it'll be all right. It's not all right. It never will be."

I want to protest; I want to shout that I'm afraid and upset, too. It's hard to believe such a vigorous, powerful man could have been cut down in a coward's ambush. Yet he has been, and now our world has tilted again. Who will be the warden of the mountains now?

I walk away unsteadily, toward King Alfred, who has dismounted and is standing on the turf. He looks at me soberly.

"That was brave," he says, "and foolish. Don't you think it's better for a queen to survive than to die making a futile stand?"

A smile wobbles onto my lips. "It worked."

"I suppose it did." He runs a hand over his balding pate. "What will you do now?"

"We'll go find our people." If sorcerers are being made to track us down, perhaps I'm too late. Perhaps they already found the Spring Caves, and our friends. I close my hands into fists. "See who's left, I mean. And fight."

He gives me a shrewd look. "Perhaps we could hold the ford for you."

Despite everything, I feel the unexpected urge to laugh. "I mean this in the best way, King Alfred, but I think my people would feel more comfortable if you retreated into Tinan. I'm grateful, though, that you put your muscle behind me."

He gestures to the destruction around us. "I am sorry for your losses. Perhaps you will allow us to bring our medics and help your men clean up, instead?"

"Thank you. I—" I think of Victoire, Juleane, the women in the caves, and panic sweeps under my breastbone. "I must go see no one else has been attacked."

He nods. "I'll work with your men—Hounds, is that what they're called?"

I feel my lips quirk. Softly, I say, "And mountain lords."

"I'll be happy to give them a hand. Although"—he lifts an eyebrow—"I hope it's a decision I don't come to regret."

News of what happened will reach my father quickly. We need to act before Euan turns on Alfred. "I will do everything in my power to ensure you don't," I say. "But I'm not a god."

"Neither am I, alas." He gives me one last nod. Then he turns back to his men, calling for them to help carry our wounded to safety in Tinan, and arrange for the burial of the dead.

Ferdan, Ingram Knoll's second in command, moves past me to help Alfred, his face carved with sweat and grief.

I grab his arm and whisper to him, "Make sure all of the Tinani cross back over the river. We don't want King Alfred to start feeling too comfortable in Eren."

He manages the ghost of a smile. "No indeed, my lady."

I watch Rhia, who is reluctantly helping some others put Ingram Knoll's body in a cart. "We need to go," I tell Ferdan. "But if you're feeling bold, once things are settled here, bring a party to me at the Spring Caves outside Laon."

He nods and clasps my hand. "We'll be there. Your Majesty."

I go to Rhia. Touch her shoulder. She looks at me, her eyes red. "We need to go back," I say. "I'm sorry. I know you want to remain with him a little longer. But we need to find the others. Make sure . . ."

"We need to *fight*," she says fiercely. "We need to tell those bastards they can't control us. And they won't keep us down."

CHAPTER TWENTY-SEVEN

Even though we leave immediately, even before Ingram Knoll is put in the ground, I can't release the feeling that time is sliding away through my fingers. It's hard to comprehend that my father is apparently seizing sorcerers and forcing them to work for him. I can't stop feeling we're too late.

I find myself whispering to Alistar, trying to sense him over the long distance between us. But when I speak his name, all I feel is a high, choking fear in my throat. His or mine, I can't tell. It galvanizes me, though at the same time my body is begging for rest. Worry chases through me every time my aching lower back twinges. My feet are sore and swollen, my legs thick and heavy, my mouth incessantly dry. Though I drained the vial Demetra gave me, it hasn't helped much. I put my hands on my stomach, hoping for the reassuring sensation of feeling the baby move. Finally, there is the faintest quiver.

"We're coming," I whisper to Alistar, and this time his awareness brushes against mine. White, breathless fear—panic—as if he's been running. A flare of pain. It's there, and gone.

I gasp aloud, and Rhia swings toward me. "I think Alistar's in trouble," I tell her.

She frowns. She's walking as if she aches as well, cradling her arm. "We're almost back to the Spring Caves," she says. "This is the final shift."

I nod. The shift ripples through the air, and I step quickly into it.

Perhaps Alistar is back at the cave, or perhaps there's been news of him. I hope to all the gods the others are all right. Rhia hurries after me.

The magic tugs us through, and we step past thornbushes onto the narrow path leading to the Spring Caves.

Three horses stand outside it.

I freeze, grabbing Rhia's arm. She's already drawn back, reaching for her daggers. We creep slowly closer. I listen, but I don't hear danger, exactly. There is the tumultuous not-quite-sound, the humming, of many people gathered inside the cave. I move closer yet, clinging to the shelter of the thornbushes that guard the side of the path.

A figure walks around the back of a horse, and I startle. It's small, slight—a boy in a too-large coat, carrying a curry brush. He's got a flop of dark hair and a narrow, wary face. A faint, periodic tremor shakes his shoulders, but he's patting the horses with tender hands.

A man's voice murmurs from the cave entrance. I crane forward and glimpse him. He's come out, saying something to the boy. The horses block everything but his loose black hat.

He's asked the boy a question. The boy looks upset.

"I don't want to go in," he says. "I don't want them to see me!"

It takes my ears a moment to translate the words. Because he's speaking Idaean.

Idaean . . .

Behind me, Rhia crouches, her daggers outstretched.

The man steps between the horses, with a soft pat to each beast's nose. He's tall, his skin a deep olive, his gray eyes sharp in an aquiline face. He's wearing a completely unnecessary scarf and a much-too-heavy coat. "You don't have to," he says soothingly to the boy. "We only—"

I jump up. *"Jahan!"* I whisper-shout his name.

Rhia startles backward—"Korakides?" she says wonderingly—but I don't wait. I'm racing around the thornbushes, tripping over the brambles, whispering his name again because it sounds so damned good.

"Jahan!"

"Sophy!" He runs over, crushing me into a swift hug. I stagger a little, an ache running through my thighs and lower back. Jahan releases me, still gripping my elbows, and I feel myself beaming at him.

"It's so damned good to see you," I say.

He pats my shoulders as though I'm one of the horses. "You look like you've just crawled on your stomach through the forest." His gaze moves past me. "Rhia?"

Rhia's come around behind me. "How did you get here? Is everyone safe?" she demands, the questions I should have been asking.

Jahan glances back at the boy, who's watching us with narrowed eyes. "We came into a harbor near Roquelle last night. We were told by the contact who found us that you weren't in the city, but we didn't know where you'd gone, so my brother . . ." He shakes his head, as if it's too much to explain. "My brother is a better sorcerer than I am. He sensed where you were. We arrived not long ago." He tosses over his shoulder, in Idaean, "You've been seeing to those horses for more than an hour now."

The boy gives the faintest smile.

"His name is Lathiel," Jahan tells us.

Our war-torn kingdom seems no place for a boy who looks no older than twelve, but I refrain from saying so. "My father's conscripted sorcerers didn't find you?"

Jahan's gaze grows keen. "Lathiel sensed something. We set up a misdirect over the entire cave system. He insisted." He snorts. "Then Juleane and Victoire insisted we remove it so your supporters can find us. Lathiel's been keeping an eye out." He smiles at his brother, who regards him with an adoration approaching worship. "And you were meeting with Alfred of Tinan?"

"Yes," I say briefly. "When my father's people found us."

"They killed my father," Rhia says baldly.

Jahan looks shocked. "All the gods, Rhia, I'm so sorry—"

"They'll pay. Don't fear."

Jahan glances at me, and I shake my head. This is Rhia's way of dealing with her grief. "Where's El?" For a moment, I'm overwhelmed by the terrible fear that something's happened to her, too.

But Jahan merely gestures toward the cave. "She's in there, making plans."

My head jerks up. "Making plans?" I echo.

Jahan looks at me as if I'm being particularly dense. "For the liberation of Eren and Caeris."

I want to laugh. Of course she is. The *Caveadear* doesn't dally. Grinning, I stride up to the cave entrance and through to the narrow tunnel. Voices rumble in the cavernous space beyond. I glance at Jahan, feeling my eyes narrow. "That sounds like more than just our original supporters."

"Juleane and Victoire had just arrived with a number of new supporters when we got here," he says. "El thought they might as well get straight to work."

We enter. Demetra, standing near the entrance, sees us enter and comes over purposefully with a cup of water. I drink it down gratefully—though a nagging thirst still tugs at my throat—and turn to the cave. Victoire and Juleane have indeed been busy—and efficient. The cave is so tightly packed that the slender, chestnut-haired woman at its center doesn't even notice us come in. Elanna stands with her hands on her hips, pushing back her salt-stained greatcoat, her sharp chin lifted and her gold-brown eyes defiant. Victoire, beside her, is glowing with joy.

Surrounding her are people who must have fled from the city, their clothes more sharply cut, their eyes warier. But there are also, clearly, country people—presumably from the villages outside Laon, with dirt on their shoes and determination in their eyes. Juleane watches, arms folded, with a look of approval.

"The people don't want Euan Dromahair in power!" El is saying with the fiery enthusiasm that usually gets everyone behind her.

"So we will summon the forests of Eren once more. They will surround the palace and terrify them into submission. We will emerge and demand surrender."

She says it as if it's that simple. As if winning peace with our fractious people will be that easy.

"No, we won't," I say with unvarnished irritation.

There's startled movement in the crowd around me; everyone shifts so they can see who just spoke out against the *Caveadear*. Beside me, Jahan rubs his chin, looking rueful.

Elanna has seen me now, and the wariness in her face splits into a grin. She throws herself through the crowd and flings her arms around me. "Sophy! You made it back!"

I hug her. Her slighter body is still too thin, the angles sharp against me. I pull back to look into her face. Her eyes are drawn with weariness, but she's still smiling at me, and I hug her again. I might find her maddening sometimes, but it's so damned good to see her. "You look exhausted," I tell her. "Have you been eating?"

"I was held captive, if you'll recall," she says with asperity—but a haunted look flashes through her eyes. Softly, she says, "I'm so glad to be back, Sophy. And it's such a relief you're all right."

I smile. "*I'm* relieved neither Euan Dromahair nor Aristide Rambaud found you while we were gone."

She shakes her head, then looks at me more closely—at my stomach, which I haven't troubled to conceal. I'm still wearing Juleane's maid's dress, and its skirt rounds snugly over my belly. Her lips part.

I hurry to speak before she can, for the verdant green sound pulsing from her is threaded with angry sparks. "I suppose no one had a chance to tell you yet. I'm with child!"

"*With child,*" she echoes. Her gaze skims my body, up and down, as if she can't quite believe it's real.

"The symbol of Eren and Caeris's future," I say, though the words sound hollow even to me.

But Elanna doesn't seem to hear. She's looking at my stomach again, and I can see the counters ticking over in her mind. "Sophy," she says, her voice dangerously level, "you must be several months along by now. When are you expecting the child?"

"Let's talk about this later." I can feel people watching us; my shoulders tense. The last thing I want is for El to scold me publicly for lying to her—by omission, anyway—over the course of the last five months.

Her lips purse, but she nods. "We do have more pressing matters at hand." It's hard not to hear that as an indictment of my choice to get pregnant; the stinging anger is still resonating from her. "We have a city and a country to reclaim. Did you say my magic won't help us win?"

I wince a little, but I don't back down. "Yes, I did. Surrounding the palace with a walking forest will not get us a miraculous surrender." I look at her. "It will help, but it won't be enough. The situation is too complicated for magic to unravel so easily."

Her eyes narrow. "It seems to me the power of the land helped us the first time."

Someone in the crowd murmurs. With an effort, I swallow down my exasperation. Elanna only wants her power to help—like all of us. "The magic of the land will be helpful, of course," I say, as graciously as I can. "But a grand display of sorcery isn't going to erase the divisions within Eren and Caeris that led to this disaster in the first place. It's not going to make Rambaud and his followers any less disgruntled, and it's certainly not going to win them over to our side."

"Send the blackguards back to exile in Tinan!" someone in the crowd says.

"This is the blackguards' home," I reply patiently, "as much as it is ours. If we send them back to Tinan, we remain at war with Tinan. If we make an effort to talk across the divisions that separate us, perhaps we can actually win peace." I raise an eyebrow. "Rambaud hasn't brought up anything but troubles that were already simmering under the surface—the old distrust of magic, of course, but also political division. How many of you Ereni were pleased with the tripartite division of rule we imposed upon you?"

None of them answer. Elanna folds her arms, and I look away from her quickly. I don't want to focus on her look of disappointment.

Unexpectedly, Victoire speaks up. "Sophy's right—it *is* a problem. One many of us have been reluctant to discuss, even among ourselves."

I nod, though I'm shocked she's siding with me against Elanna. "These are real problems, and we need solutions," I say, "not simply magic that strikes awe and fear into the population. Magic is magnificent, of course. But we already know it isn't enough."

"So what do you plan to do about it, Lady Sophy?" Juleane asks.

"I've just returned from a meeting with the king of Tinan." I draw in a deep breath. "The meeting went well, but we were tracked. It seems Euan and the Saranons are *using* the sorcerers they've captured. We lost . . ." I look at El, and my voice cracks. "We lost Ingram Knoll."

All the spirit drains out of her face. "No," she whispers.

"But Rambaud promised to hunt us down," Brigitte says. "He would never ally with sorcerers . . . not overtly, at least."

"Maybe Euan and the Saranons have different plans," I say. "I *hope* they have different plans. If they are fracturing, it means we might have an opportunity. I want to meet with Aristide Rambaud once Alistar returns from his reconnaissance."

"You think you should bargain with the man who threw you off your throne?" Elanna says flatly. "The man who staged a coup and killed the Butcher? Why would he want anything to do with you, Sophy? You're putting yourself in incredible danger—"

"I was there when Euan arrived," I interrupt. "I was in the Diamond Salon when Euan told the Ereni nobles his plan to build an army to reclaim Paladis, and to conquer Caeris as well. I saw their faces." I pause. "I saw how Euan treated them."

Unexpectedly, Jahan speaks up. "He's not exactly the most personable man. He treated the Ereni like servants, I expect?"

I nod, relieved Jahan's met him and understands. "The Ereni

brought him here so they could claim their power back. But I don't think Euan even intends to remain in Eren and Caeris; all he wants is the crown. They want to use us to retake Ida, nothing more."

"So you will talk to Duke Aristide," Elanna says, in a familiar tone. She'll have met him before, of course. "But what do we do about Euan Dromahair, and the Saranons, and the sorcerers they are apparently using? They've executed people in the square—they tried to kill *you*, Sophy. Are you planning to have a diplomatic meeting with them, too?"

It's impossible to miss the thread of criticism in her voice. Beside me, Jahan has gone very still. He's giving Elanna a warning look.

"What," she says, "will you do with your father?"

My jaw clenches. I shouldn't be so thrown by her challenging words, I tell myself, when I spoke much the same to her. But at least when I contradicted her, I had a real solution. I wasn't just trying to point out her flaws. At last, I say, "I don't know. Perhaps that's where your magic comes in—where *everyone's* magic comes in. Perhaps we can capture them and send them back to Paladis for justice."

She lifts an eyebrow. "I'm not sure how easily Phaedra or Augustus Saranon will fall into any trap we set."

I open my mouth to retort. I'm going to demand, *Do you have a better idea?* But Juleane claps her hands, preventing me. "The queen and the *Caveadear* have a plan. Let us drink to that." She shoots a meaningful gaze at Victoire, who fishes two bottles of whiskey from a nearby crate and passes them around. While everyone is distracted by the drinks, Juleane pulls Elanna toward me.

"You two," she says in an undertone, "get out of here and talk. I don't know what this tiff is, but *neither* of you is helping matters."

I don't want to be alone with Elanna. "But everyone needs to see us—"

"No, they don't. Go talk it out." She lifts an eyebrow. "Now."

Behind us, Jahan steps away from the tunnel exit without comment. I leave first, seething, El on my heels. As soon as we're outside the caves, she rounds on me, her hair flying loose from its knot.

"What's gotten into you, Sophy? Do you think because I was captured I deserve to be rebuked in public?"

I blink. Rebuked? Elanna Valtai can't possibly feel foolish. Everyone adores her, and sometimes it seems that they always have.

"Maybe you shouldn't try to make things so simple, then," I say. "Of course your magic will help, but this is a complex situation."

To my astonishment, her chin bunches and a sheen of tears silvers her eyes. "I know that," she says in a tight, tart tone. "I've seen the divisions between Ereni and Caerisians as well as you have. I've *lived* them. But perhaps it doesn't matter, because everyone else is one or the other. Perhaps my only real value to you is my sorcery."

"Of course not," I begin, exasperation and sympathy warring in me.

She interrupts. "Well, if it is, then perhaps I should leave you to it! Because my sorcery still isn't all it was, and maybe it never will be again. I can't make a mountain range walk down on Laon. Maybe all that power I had came from releasing the old bonds and waking the land. I'll never be that person again—not a goddess walking on earth."

My jealousy, and my frustration, are shrinking down into sad, flat things. I say, feeling awkward, "No one expects that of you, El."

"Of course they do!" she exclaims. "That's what the *Caveadear* does! I can still do small things. I'm sure," she adds rather bitterly, "I can manage an army of walking trees, if you'd like. It might take some effort, but I can do it."

Rhia's slipped out of the cave and is standing behind El, watching us. I pretend I don't notice her.

"That's not what I meant," I say, fumbling with the words. "People respect you as a leader, you know. It was your plan that won our first rebellion. It's just—it's not enough, now, to simply use force to win."

"I grew up in Eren. I know how deep the divisions go." Her gaze cuts away from me. "I should have guessed about Rambaud. If I hadn't been captured . . ."

"It's not your fault that you were. *I* shouldn't have let it happen."

She holds up her hand for silence. "No, Sophy. I *did* know. I saw how they looked at you, the Ereni, particularly the nobles. I thought it didn't matter because—because I was there. I thought it would heal over time. I was so wrong."

"We all hoped it would," I say quietly.

"You both need to stop feeling sorry for yourselves," Rhia announces suddenly. She steps beside us, making a circle. "It's not your fault, either of you. El, you didn't mean to get captured. And Sophy, you didn't mean to lose your throne in a coup."

I wince, and El glances at me with a little grimace.

"El, you shouldn't have tramped in here and stepped on Sophy's toes by assuming we didn't have a plan already. Sophy, you shouldn't have embarrassed El in front of everyone. So." Rhia looks between us. "Are you done?"

El sighs. "I am."

"And so am I," I say, managing a smile at her.

She returns the smile, but there's a frown between her brows. "Why didn't you tell me you're pregnant?"

All the gods. "I wasn't sure . . ."

"You're a terrible liar, Sophy Dunbarron." El's temper is flaring up again. "What are you, four months along? Five? You must have known months ago, and you kept it from me."

"She kept it from everyone," Rhia volunteers.

El puts her hands on her hips, staring me down. "What did you think I'd do if I knew?"

"You'd have thought I was irresponsible." I can't quite meet her eyes. "Worse than that, probably."

"It *is* irresponsible—not to tell anyone!" She huffs a sigh. "And then I come back and look a fool for not knowing—and that makes you look bad, too. In the future, when a serious political scandal is brewing, we *tell each other*. All right?"

"Yes." I grimace. "For what it's worth, I'm sorry."

She shakes her head. "I suppose with Rambaud and Euan Dromahair seizing power, a child born out of wedlock is the least of our concerns. It must be Alistar's?"

"Well . . ." I begin, and Elanna exchanges a speaking glance with Rhia.

"Where *is* Alistar?" El asks. "And where's my mother?"

"Alistar's gone to spy on Rambaud." I think of the pulse of distress and pain I felt from him earlier, and bite my lip. "And Teofila's in Baedon—or she should be soon. It wasn't my idea," I say quickly, when El's jaw tightens. "She volunteered to go."

"I'm certain she did." Elanna gives her head a quick shake. Awkwardly, she says, "I'm glad at least one of us was here with her."

My lips twitch. "She's been practicing magic."

Elanna's mouth opens. "She *has*?"

"She was certain you were alive." And maybe, I realize, Teofila *did* know, in the same way I sensed Alistar's panic when I called to him. "She's convinced if she gave birth to a sorceress, she should be able to do magic herself. She's made the mirrors work—"

"I have to talk to her!" El exclaims. "I could have talked to her all along!" Then she catches herself. "I'm sure we have more important things to do, of course—"

"No, go talk to her." I draw in a breath. "I need to look for Alistar—I'm afraid something's happened to him. In the meantime, El, after you talk to Teofila, you can start letting everyone know you're back. A lot of people still think you're dead. And once I track Alistar down . . ." And meet with Rambaud, if I can. ". . . we'll make a plan for how to deal with my father."

"Sophy . . ." El starts toward me, catches my elbow. "Do you want me to come with you?"

I hesitate. Part of me does, and yet the other part still needs some space away from her. "You should stay here," I say at last. "So the people at least have one of us, should anything happen to me."

She studies my face, and then she gives me a brief, hard hug. I hug her back.

"I'm glad you're here," I whisper. "I really am."

"I know," she whispers back. "And I'm glad you're here, and you're safe. I really am, Soph."

CHAPTER TWENTY-EIGHT

Rhia tags after me as I make my way toward the crest of the ridge. "You're tired," I tell her. "You're grieving. You're *wounded*. You need to rest."

"Resting won't bring my father back," she points out, as stubborn as a bull. "Besides, *you're* pregnant."

I open my mouth to protest, even though she has a fair point, but just then Victoire comes up the path from the cave. "There you are! El said you were haring off on some secret mission, all noble and self-sacrificing."

"I . . ." I look from Victoire's flushed, stubborn face to Rhia's equally obstinate one. Absurdly, I feel like smiling. It feels so damned good to have friends. "All right, then. I'll show you what we're going to do." I tell myself Alistar wouldn't have gotten caught, but the panic that mirrored itself in my body is too powerful to ignore. He's careful—but is he careful enough?

I take the bone flute and walk up on the path, Rhia and Victoire trailing me. The city hums behind us, a knot of colors and emotion so intertwined at first it seems like nothing more than noise. But I think of how Demetra said that everyone has a note they hum at.

If Alistar were a song . . .

I put the bone flute to my lips. A soft, low note. I think of him. Of the gentleness with which he holds me. Of the way his hair droops after he's pomaded it into spikes. Of his smile. His bold, flashing anger, and his tenderness.

"Sophy," Victoire begins, but I keep on playing. The song rises to a high note, skirls down low and dangerous, then back up, wild and free. I play until I forget that I'm controlling my breath. Until the music is simply pouring out of me in skeins of sound, weaving an almost tangible impression on the night air—an afterimage like the memory of his presence. Until he seems so real I think I can smell him, feel his warmth heating me. The baby flutters in my belly.

But something isn't right. Beneath the shining threads of him, there's a web of grasping darkness. It's clawing up through him, reaching for his heart.

I lower the flute. I can't let myself panic; I have to keep calm, hold on to the music. "Guide me to you," I whisper through numb lips.

He—the Alistar I've made of sound and air—ripples. *Moves.* As if he's no longer the recollection of a person, but a current twining through the countryside. A silver thread that arrows from his heart to mine.

I tuck the flute away and pull on my gloves, still feeling the shivering spread of dark threads inside him. "Let's go."

The silver thread leads us north, over the ridge, away from the caves and the city. As the last lights dwindle behind us, rain begins to fall, a thin drizzle wetting my face. The silver current pulls me forward. We tramp through the muddy dark, past silent farms, through another darkened town. The land around here is soft and fertile, nourished by the river and the rain.

Finally, as my lower back begins to ache, the silver current pulls me sideways. I almost walk straight into a hedge. Rhia pulls me free, and she and Victoire start to giggle, and soon I'm laughing, too, the three of us sodden and desperate in the dark.

A few paces ahead, there's a gap in the hedge. We blunder through, sliding in cow pies through a farm field, and stumbling over the sudden rocks of a brook. The silver thread tugs me through a copse of trees, dense and forbidding in the night. I'm well and truly lost now, and my ankles have begun to ache.

But then Rhia points to it—a farmhouse, little more than a

smear in the night. A ghost through the dark trees. Closer to, it appears deserted. Boards cover two windows; another is shattered. The place has an air of gloom and neglect.

I'd pass it by, except the current doesn't pour on beyond it. It eddies around the house, anxious as a tide.

The baby kicks.

I approach the door, though Rhia shoulders me aside and steps in first. It's pitch black within. Victoire fumbles for her candle, and Rhia for her tinderbox.

I call softly, "Alistar?"

A thin mumble comes from the back of the house. My heart thumps.

I move toward the sound, placing my feet cautiously. The weathered floorboards creak, and the mumble comes again. "S . . . soph?"

"Alistar! I'm here."

Light flares behind me—just enough for me to make him out. He's mashed up against the far wall, in a moldering bed. I run across the final distance, throwing myself onto my knees beside him. He's tucked himself under a moth-eaten blanket, and he's shivering. Hardly any sound resonates from him. The darkness I felt from a distance has wound itself through him, tangling the essence that is Alistar. Squeezing it out. My magic was right; something is wrong. Worse than wrong.

Swallowing my fear, I reach for his hand. It's cold—so cold and clammy to the touch. Dread creeps through my belly.

"Alistar . . ." I crouch closer. "What happened?"

He's breathing hot little puffs of breath against my cheek. "How'd you—find me? I heard—music."

"I played your song. I let it lead me to you."

A small smile cracks his lips. "That's my . . . Soph."

The floorboards creak; Victoire and Rhia are standing behind me now, looking down at him. Even in the warm lantern-light, his skin seems too pale. Dark circles mark his eyes. He seems to have stripped off his coat, or lost it. His shirt is filthy, gray with mud and dirt, as if he crawled here.

I reach toward him, and he flinches. His hand closes over my wrist, but it's weak, his fingers slack. "I found . . . Rambaud. I *found* him. Sophy. It's not—he didn't *buy* . . . a sorcerer. It's—a stone—he has."

"A witch stone?" I guess.

Alistar shakes his head. "Yes—no. More powerful. Older, maybe. In their family. The girl found it. He told—supporters. Not that it was magic—but that—she discovered it."

My heartbeat is thudding dully at the back of my mouth, but I clear my throat and say, "What girl?"

"His—his daughter. Land must have—woken magic—in her. She woke—the stone."

I put my other hand over his, then touch his forehead. It, too, is freezing, covered in a thin cold sweat. "They hurt you."

"Outran them." He flashes a grin. "Except—that one—gun."

The hair rises on the back of my neck. I reach for the moth-eaten blanket. He just blinks, breathing fast, almost panting. "My Soph," he says.

I lift the blanket back, and press a hand to my mouth. I've found his coat. It's wrapped around his left leg, tightly. Dark blood has seeped through it. The darkness I sense swallowing him, made real.

An arm steadies my back. Victoire has knelt down beside me. Without a word, she reaches past my shaking hands. "Alistar, I'm going to take this off." He doesn't reply; simply looks at her, with a bemused almost-smile.

Rhia takes up station by his head, holding the lantern high. "If you die, so help me, Connell, I'll never forgive you."

"I'll live . . . just to spite you . . . Knoll."

Victoire tugs the coat gently from Alistar's thigh. He didn't do a very good job of wrapping it, but the blood is sticky and it's slow to come free. Alistar hisses in pain, and the dark threads tangle tighter around him. The coat pulls loose at last. Rhia brings the lantern lower. I shudder, and Victoire squeezes my arm. The wound is larger than my fist. Either the bullet or Alistar tore his trouser away, revealing deep-purple bruises marring his skin. Dried blood cakes the wound, except for a thin, fresh crimson trickle caused by the coat's removal. I look closer and wish I hadn't. The wound gapes, revealing his raw pink flesh, and deep within, the white, splintered gleam of bone.

"It's all right," Victoire says in a high brittle voice. None of us believe it, but we don't contradict her. "I—I feel like Demetra would check your pulse."

I'm still holding Alistar's hand. I press my fingertips to his wrist and send Victoire a panicked glance. I can't feel anything.

She leans over, feeling up along the inside of his elbow, her lip caught in her teeth. My heart's skirling. A wound like this—and we can hardly feel his pulse—and his skin is so cold . . . with the dark threads winding through him . . . I inhale. There's no odor to the wound, at least. Not yet.

I don't know if we can move him. I don't know how on earth we'll get him back to Laon in time to save him, much less to Demetra.

Victoire is feeling at Alistar's neck. She turns to me. "His pulse is very fast," she whispers.

"Soph!" Alistar exclaims, as if he's just remembered something. His eyes are wild. Staring.

"I'm here." Tears threaten to start, but I swallow them viciously back. I press my cheek to his hand. He turns his head, blinking at me. Cold pricks my neck. There's so much confusion in his eyes.

"Rambaud," he says.

I close my eyes. "Alistar, your life is more important than Aristide damned Rambaud!"

"No!" He's flailing now, trying to sit up. We all push him back down. Rhia's lantern clips him in the head—lightly, but enough to confuse him. He blinks owlishly at us, regains focus. He grabs my sleeve, the sound of his own self valiantly pushing aside the dark threads. "Soph. You have—you have to go. Rambaud's house. Across the field. He's—he's there tonight. Girl will—be asleep. His window faces—woodshed. No guards at back." A faint smile. "Watch the dogs."

I shake my head. "I'm not leaving you."

"You have to go!" he practically shouts, and I startle back. "Bargain with him! Tonight!"

I glance at Victoire, who stares back, wide-eyed. "Alistar, if I leave you—"

His fingers dig into my sleeve. Weakly but inexorably, he pulls me closer. "Make it *for* something, Soph," he whispers. His gaze is clear, lucid. Pleading. He says again, "Make it *for* something."

I swallow hard.

"I'll stay with him," Victoire says, suddenly firm. "I can bandage the wound. You can't go alone, Sophy—you'll need Rhia's help."

"But—" I protest.

"Go!" Alistar says, gesturing toward the door.

I rise, tugging Victoire after me, and pull her into a huddle a few paces from the bed. "We should get him back to the city," I whisper fiercely. "Rambaud can wait."

"Soph, he's right. This is your chance. You have the bargaining chip you need, and you can get to Rambaud directly. You need to go." Victoire glances over her shoulder at Alistar and Rhia, who are arguing weakly. "He's still cogent. I don't know if anything can be done for that wound, but I promise you, I will keep him alive until you get back. I swear it, Sophy."

Rhia turns to us, lantern swinging. "Are you ready, Dunbarron?"

I close my eyes. Those long afternoons with Ruadan come back to me; his instructions always to put the good of the people first. Even above my own heart. Even when it matters the most.

I blow a breath out through my mouth. "Very well."

I cross back to the bed, leaning over Alistar. I kiss his clammy forehead and lift his cold hands to my cheeks. "I love you," I tell him. "And when this is all over, I *will* marry you, at Cerid Aven in the summer, and we will raise this child together. I swear it, Alistar Connell."

He blinks at me. His smile is sweet, and vacant. The pulse of him is fading. "Love it when . . . you're all . . . riled up . . ."

I kiss his hands, then set them down. I cover his chest with the moth-eaten blanket, and he sighs, settling like a child beneath my touch. I turn away before my heart can shatter.

"Keep him alive," I order Victoire. And I stride from the farmhouse, Rhia at my heels, without looking back.

OUTSIDE THE FARMHOUSE, I pause. Rain is still falling. A frog chirrups from a pond. We seem far from anywhere.

Rhia stops beside me. "I grant you Connell's injured, but usually he's better with directions than that."

"We don't need directions." I pull out the bone flute again and play a high, clear note. This time, I build the image of Aristide Rambaud in my mind, from his long gathered-back hair to the smirk in the corner of his mouth. So many things I loathe, packed into one man. But though the notes leap and dance, and I see him clear in my mind's eye, the silver thread won't settle. It pulses into existence and vanishes.

"His daughter's doing?" Rhia wonders.

I curse as the thread dissolves again. There's no difference between this and the song I played for Alistar. I've conjured their images, my memories of them, my feelings—

My feelings. When I summoned the thread for Alistar, it came out of love and it guided me out of love.

But I hate Aristide Rambaud. Hate is what I've been pouring into this song.

My nostrils flare. There's no love in me to pour into that bastard! But I have to find something—only real compassion, a true sense of understanding, will be enough to create the thread. Yet all I can see are the ways in which he has obstructed and hurt me, all the small, selfish acts—

No, they're not selfish, I realize. Rambaud doesn't seek glory for himself; he hasn't placed the crown on his own head. He didn't seize power for the love of it. Maybe he's been afraid, like the rest of us, of what Tinan and Baedon and Paladis would do if they allied against us. Maybe he's been worried that Caeris would hold dominion over Eren, just the way Eren always did over Caeris. Maybe he hasn't been fighting to protect his own interests so much as to preserve the future.

Because Rambaud has a family. He has a daughter, and he loves her. Maybe he loves her with the same raging love I feel for my own child. The kind of love that drives you beyond reason, that propels you to do whatever you must, or think you must, for their sake.

I put the bone flute to my lips, and I play again. This is the song of a man hated by many, but still with a father's heart. A man who tried to turn the tide against the people who'd claimed his country, only to find that his own child had succumbed to magic like a plague. A man who, for all that he might have turned on the girl, still loves her. A man who will do everything he can to keep her safe.

The thread builds. It's weaker than Alistar's, a wisp rather than a river, but it's enough.

I tramp forward, past the trees. The silver wisp leads us through a fallow farm field, overgrown with brambles, and past a low, rundown wall. The muddy ground threatens to yield underfoot. My hair trails soggy onto the back of my neck, and my skirt is growing heavy with moisture, and we've left Alistar behind. I'm angry—angry at Rambaud, angry at the world. Rhia strides beside me, silent.

We cross another sodden field, and another, and another. We've been walking for nearly an hour now, yet still the wisp tugs me on.

Through the haze of rain, ahead, a house finally appears, surrounded by a scattering of outbuildings. We draw to a stop behind what seems, from its fresh-cut odor, to be the woodshed. Rain drips into my face. The house is tall, two stories of stone draped in creeping ivy. Not a mansion, but large enough. The upper floor has an open balcony in the Paladisan style, just visible through the drizzle.

Somewhere on the other side of the house, a dog barks. I go very still. Another answers.

They fall silent. The rain patters. Rhia turns her face toward me.

"Get a rope," I whisper to her. "There must be one in the woodshed."

She's cross and wet. "And what will you do, O majestic one?"

"I'll sing."

"Sing."

"To the dogs."

I don't dare to use the bone flute, which would wake a human, and I don't want to sing aloud for the same reason. So I brace myself against the back of the shed and hum. I hum a soothing song, a memory of a long night by the fire with a full belly and tired limbs, after a long romp in the forest, surrounded now by friends. At some point, Rhia moves past me, slipping into the woodshed. I keep humming.

It's easier to sing for the dogs than it was for Rambaud—though harder to tell if it's working. No more barks, at least, puncture the night.

Rhia emerges from the woodshed. I follow her, still humming, over to the back of the house. She's tied something heavy—a chunk of wood—to the end of the rope, so when she hurls it over the edge of the balcony, it catches and holds.

"If someone comes, you run," she orders me. Then she climbs up first, awkward with her sling, a shadow in the dark.

She tugs the rope three times when she's finished. I start after her. The rope burns my palms, and I'm heavier than I've ever been. I'm sweating too much to hum. At last my palm strikes the balustrade, and Rhia grips my coat with her good hand, pulling me over the edge.

We peer through the nearest window, into Aristide Rambaud's

bedchamber. It's dim and silent through the pattering rain. Rhia tries the handle of the glass Paladisan door. It turns easily.

She shakes her head. "The fool."

She steps inside, and I ease in after her. The room lies still. A banked fire glows in the hearth. Across the room, the bulky shape of a bed is tucked into an alcove. Rambaud's soft, sleeping breaths are the only thing disturbing the silence.

Rhia's good arm moves, and her dagger flashes in the dim glow of the firelight. She crosses to the bed with soft, deliberate steps. I follow, claiming a candle from the mantel and lighting it.

When I turn back to them, Rhia is standing above Rambaud, her dagger kissing his throat. She nods to me. I approach. We both look down at him. He's sleeping with abandon, one arm thrown open, the soft hum of magic pulsing from the curve of his elbow. Rhia's right. He is a fool.

With careful fingers, I reach past his elbow, where the pillow lifts. The magic deepens, spitting at me. The smooth edge of a stone meets my fingers; I grip it and pull it quickly free. Rambaud sleeps on, undisturbed.

I look down at the stone. It's smooth, polished; a smoky gray like clouds banded together. It hums, but far less cruelly than any witch stone. I listen to the tone of it, fierce as steel. Perhaps it's enchanted to protect Rambaud—or any bearer—from magical attack.

It's not prepared, however, to deal with simply being stolen by non-magical means. I balance it thoughtfully in my hand and clear my throat.

There's a soft cessation of breath. Then Rambaud opens his eyes.

"If you call out, I'll slit your throat," Rhia murmurs.

Rambaud's eyes flick toward me. I raise an eyebrow, and he swallows, gingerly, his throat vulnerable against Rhia's blade.

"I have your stone," I say. "If you think it might save you."

Slowly, he lifts one hand, and then, turning onto his back, the other. He lies there like a dog with his belly exposed. For the barest scrap of a moment, I almost pity him.

"Get up." I point at the carpet beside his bed; it occurs to me that he could have a dagger hidden under his pillow.

Slowly, Rhia's blade never leaving his throat, Rambaud climbs out of bed. He stands there, shivering, in a nightshirt, his legs bare. "Perhaps," he says with some dignity, "I could have my dressing robe?"

"Would you have been so humane, when we were your captives?" I ask.

"I am not Euan Dromahair!" Then, with more composure, he says, "It seems to me I treated you with as much courtesy as possible, under the circumstances."

Though he can't know it, his outburst reassures me. I find the dressing robe draped over a stool next to the bed and check its pockets and seams for a blade. Nothing. I hand it to him, and he slowly tugs it over his shoulders and belts it, Rhia never releasing her dagger from his neck.

"I don't want it to be said that I deprive my allies of their dignity," I remark. "Regardless of how they've treated me and my friends."

Rambaud eyes me. "And to what exactly do I owe the pleasure of your company?"

"We're here to talk." I park myself on the upholstered stool; it feels unspeakably good to sit down. "I apologize for the less-than-civilized method of entry, but we're starved for choice."

I nod at Rhia to ease the pressure of the dagger, though she still keeps the tip kissing the back of Rambaud's neck. He twitches inadvertently.

"So," I say, and his gaze moves back to me. I palm the stone, just for the pleasure of seeing his eyes narrow. "How are you enjoying my father's company?"

Rambaud lifts an eyebrow. "I'm glad I don't have to claim him as family."

"He's not exactly charming," I agree. "Augustus and Phaedra Saranon don't seem like particularly pleasant company, either. I'm not sure you've done a good job choosing your associates."

He gives a faint nod of acknowledgment. "Perhaps I should not have answered the letter."

The letter? I look at him more closely. "You mean they contacted *you?*"

He actually laughs. "I may be bold, but I'm not that bold, Lady Sophy. I'm afraid contacting your father—much less the Saranon siblings—did not occur to me. My own plans were much more modest."

"Philippe," I say, and he nods.

"Of course, as you know, Philippe fancies himself something of a radical. His mother tried to put a stop to that, though in fairness it can't be said she did so with any care or discretion. I thought, given the opportunity to marry you, he might take the chance to put some of his rebel sentiments to work."

"And that's what you would have wanted, in a king?" I say skeptically.

Rambaud eases one shoulder up in a slight shrug. "After that initial attempt at rebellion, he's remained loyal to his family, even if his mother gives him no reason to be. I was gambling that we'd get our needs met, too, if we applied the right kind of pressure. But he refused to wed. He has particular standards, does Manceau."

"I'm aware." I tilt my head. "You can't tell me you weren't planning to overthrow me, though."

"There are more ways than one to win power over a queen," Rambaud says mildly. "I prefer subtleties myself, but some of my allies beg to differ."

My mind has stuck on a particular point. "If the Saranons contacted you—"

"Phaedra Saranon," he says, and adds with disdain, "I am fairly sure such maneuvers are out of the scope of Augustus's rather limited intelligence."

"Why on earth would Phaedra Saranon want to ally with you?"

He shrugs—incrementally, since Rhia's dagger is still pressing against his neck. "Presumably so I'd remove you from your throne, and Eren would be loyal once more to Paladis. Except she lost her bid for power in Ida, of course, and instead announced she was coming here *with* Euan Dromahair."

"Interesting." Something nags at me, but I can't quite put my finger on it. Perhaps it's Phaedra's apparent fascination with sorcery. I wonder if she's the one who employed that temple novice to find us, not my father. "I admit I was expecting them to attack our sorcerers, not conscript them into fighting for them."

Rambaud's eyebrows pinch together. "It was . . . unexpected."

I look at him. "What will you do once they learn magic has awakened in your daughter? That she has woken whatever sorcery lies in this object?" I hold up the stone; it pulses in my hand. "Will you let them use her, too?"

He jerks forward. But Rhia follows just as fast with her dagger, and Rambaud hisses in pain. He stills. Touches his fingers to the back of his neck. They come away stained bright red, with two drops of blood.

"Just a sting," Rhia coos. "Since you couldn't be troubled to stop Euan Dromahair from having me flogged in a public square."

Rambaud's jaw clenches visibly. But he sits very still. Roughly, he says, "That stone's been in my family for generations—since sorcery was first driven from these lands. They won't discover the truth."

"Won't they?" I raise an eyebrow. "Yet my friends managed to, and we've spent less time with you than they have. What will they do with her, that you're so afraid to trust your own allies?"

"She's only a girl." Rambaud closes his eyes. "She has no part in these machinations."

"I doubt Phaedra Saranon would feel the same way."

He looks at me. "What would you do with sorcerers, *Queen* Sophy? The people fear magic—"

"The people fear what they've been made to fear. For instance, when some people fake assassination attempts by sorcerers. Or," I add, even more sharply, "when they murder sorcerer refugees to frighten the queen."

He has the grace to look abashed.

"Magic's awakening throughout Eren and Caeris," I go on. "Undoubtedly it will lead to fear and distrust at first, in some parts, but eventually people will be forced to make peace with the fact that their mothers and sons have power they don't understand. And unlike Phaedra Saranon," I add, "I will never use sorcerers to bolster my army, unless they choose to join."

"What will you do instead?" he asks, skeptical.

"I'll educate them." When he stares, I explain, "Most sorcerers don't even know how to use their own power. Educating them will make them more skilled and controlled, and less alarming."

"I don't know about that," he says drily. "A sorcerer in full possession of his power sounds fairly terrifying to those without."

I lean forward. "Not if laws are put in place regulating the practice."

"Laws." Rambaud looks interested now, though he's trying to conceal it. "Even governing the *Caveadear*?"

Elanna might rage at me for it, but I nod. "Naturally. Now that she's back in Eren, she'll be the one who oversees such measures."

"So she's back," he says thoughtfully.

"People will start remembering why they love magic now," I say. "It helps when you're presented with a legend come to life."

His eyes narrow, but I think he's amused.

"Then there is the matter of our government." I look at him. "I understand the Caerisian system leaves something to be desired— and I sympathize, though we do have opportunity within our governance for discussion rather than blatant propaganda."

"Your Ruadan employed the technique so well," he says comfortably. "I was merely imitating him."

"Mmm. I am certainly open to revisiting the old laws and customs, and making them more equitable for both Ereni and Caerisians." I raise my eyebrows. "Somehow I doubt Euan Dromahair—not to mention the Saranons—are much interested in anything but a top-down monarchy. They'll be bringing their friends from Ida here, won't they? They'll give away your lands and titles to Idaeans who despise you. They're not interested in you, not really, even though you handed them Eren on a silver platter. They'll conscript your children to be their soldiers, or their sorcerers. Your wealth and lineage won't be enough to protect you anymore."

Rambaud's head has lowered. For a long moment, he's silent.

I wait, though it makes my shoulders tense. He might laugh at me. He might summon his guards—the same ones who shot Alistar.

But when he finally looks up at me, he's frowning. "Veronique Manceau has told me that Euan and the Saranons must be removed. The other nobles talk of returning to Tinan, except their sons are being conscripted into Euan's army. We're trapped," he says bleakly.

"Not necessarily," I say. "They might have brought some Paladisan soldiers, but they are the commanders. Most of the army is Ereni, or Caerisian. Like us."

"They have sorcerers."

"So do we." I lean forward on my elbows. "Aristide Rambaud, if you ally with us, you will have the power of the entire land at your back. You will have Elanna Valtai, and Jahan Korakides, and the common people in whom magic is awakening. You'll have me."

His gaze meets mine. "So you *are* a sorceress."

"A modest one, but I am. There," I say, "you have my secret."

Now he's the one who leans forward, and this time Rhia doesn't chase him with her dagger. "And the future? What will you do with your child? Whom will you marry?"

"I'll give my child a queen's education." I bite down hard on my irritation that he's decided to bring my choice into this conversation. If he wants to bargain over an unborn baby, so be it. "But she won't be my heir unless the people elect her."

"And your consort?" he says.

"I won't marry Philippe Manceau," I begin, even though it's equally accurate to say that Philippe won't marry *me*.

There's a glint in Rambaud's eyes I don't like. "The Ereni won't accept Alistar Connell as their king."

"It is not for the people of Eren—or you—to say who I'll marry." I pause, and Rambaud's eyebrow lifts. I draw in a shaky breath. "Alistar Connell is at this moment lying in a farmhouse with a mortal wound—one inflicted by your lackeys, I might add. I gave him my word that I would wed him if—when—he survived. Would you deny a dying man the right to wed the woman he loves?"

"Of course not," Rambaud says, though beneath his swift denial I can see his mind working, sifting through the few facts I have given him. Already he'll be calculating what the likelihood is of Alistar's survival—and realizing that if he dies, I'll be free to marry. I shudder at the callous thought. Alistar hasn't even drawn his final breath and here we are, bickering over him like a slab of meat.

"I pledged myself to Alistar," I say. "And I do not back down on my promises."

Rambaud studies me, long and thoughtful, as if he is really seeing me for the first time. At last he says, "I can see that, Lady Sophy. An offer of legislation on sorcery, but a refusal to marry anyone but the man you love. A plan to overthrow your own father and his supporters. You are full of surprises, Sophy Dunbarron."

I smile, though my free hand is clenched so tight my fingernails dig into my palms. "I just want to help my country."

He sighs. "I suppose this means we will have arguments over land rights, and whether peasants own their own plots . . ."

"And all of the things that you and the Ereni nobles so strenuously objected to. Yes." I lift my chin. "But it can be a discussion. A compromise. It doesn't have to end in a bloody coup."

"That may not please all my friends," he begins.

I force myself not to roll my eyes. It seems just like Rambaud to turn our desperate situation into an opportunity to dicker over the details of future legislative changes.

But before he can speak again, there's a tap on the door. We all freeze.

The door creaks open. "Papa?"

A girl slips into the room on soft feet. She's no more than ten, with long straight brown hair tangled over the shoulders of her robe, and dark, wide eyes. She looks from us to her father. Rhia's shifted slightly, concealing the dagger.

I glance at Rambaud, but he doesn't look back. He's watching his daughter. The sudden hum of love and fear that pulses from him is so strong I wince.

The girl whispers, "Who are these people, Papa?"

Now Rambaud glances at me. He says, "They're our friends, Claudette."

Rhia lowers her dagger, though she still keeps it tucked within her palm. I hold my breath.

Rambaud opens his arms, and the girl runs into them. She peers owlishly from me to Rhia. "It's the middle of the night."

"Hello, Claudette." I lean forward, holding out my hand. She clasps it cautiously, and I smile at her. "My name is Sophy. I have magic, just like you."

Claudette hauls in a deep breath. "Papa said I wasn't to tell about it!"

I wink at her. "You can tell me. We're alike."

Uncertainly, she nods. She turns to her father and whispers loudly, "I've never met another witch before."

I hold the stone out to her. "You enchanted this."

"No," she says shyly, taking it back. "There was magic in it already. I just let it out."

I smile and watch Rambaud.

He looks back at me, then sets Claudette on his knee. "Dear girl, our guests are being much too modest. This is Sophy Dunbarron. The queen of Eren and Caeris."

CHAPTER TWENTY-NINE

Dawn is lifting the sky as Rhia and I cross back through the fields toward the farmhouse. I feel fierce, sharpened like the edge of a blade. We succeeded in turning Rambaud—at least, I hope we did—and he not only pledged me his support but promised to speak with the other Ereni nobles as well. Now it's time to take Alistar back to the city, to a doctor, to safety. We've only been gone a few hours, and I'd know if he'd grown worse—or at least, I'm almost certain I would. When I reach for him, the dark threads binding him seem the same. Under the fresh, bright morning, it seems impossible anything could truly be wrong. Even the derelict farmhouse seems sturdier in the growing light, something that could be transformed by a few hammers.

But underneath the earth, the softest groan tickles the edges of my hearing. I pause, blinking. Am I starting to hear the land the same way Elanna does?

The sound doesn't come again and, with a wordless prayer, I step inside the farmhouse. A putrid odor greets me. Just behind me, Rhia inhales and gags. Victoire starts up from Alistar's beside, holding her hands out, as if to keep us back.

A low, desperate hammering starts in my chest. I can feel all my hope, all my certainty, pouring away through my feet, into the earth. Alistar is lying still on the bed, wrapped in soundless darkness like a shroud.

"Is he . . ." I begin.

"He's hanging on. Barely." Tears brighten Victoire's eyes. "I think he's been waiting for you to come back before he . . . he . . ."

I move past her. I seem to feel my heartbeat in each footstep. Alistar sprawls on the bed, his eyelids twitching. The odor is stronger here. I have to cover my mouth. When I crouch beside him, I can already feel the heat pouring off his skin. He's sweaty. Tenuous.

"The wound got worse." Victoire's followed me. "I'm sorry. I'm so sorry. We could try to take him back to Laon in time, but . . ." She pulls the blanket back, gently, and I glimpse the wound, now red and swollen. An angry red streak arrows up his thigh. Victoire lets the blanket drop, but not before I glimpse an ugly, thick green discharge seeping from the wound. I bite my lip hard against the urge to retch.

I turn back to Alistar. I touch his cheek. His lips are parted. Chapped. His breath is coming faster even than before, in quick heaving breaths with long pauses in between. The sound of him has faded, so faint it is little more than an echo.

"Alistar," I whisper, but he doesn't answer. There's no indication that he hears my voice, that he knows I'm here, that I came back for him.

I fumble for his wrist, but again the pulse is too faint for me to find. There has to be some way to breathe the life back into him. What use is my magic if I can't save him? It will be like Finn all over again, like my mother, like Ruadan. Another death I am powerless to stop.

"Sophy." Rhia's hand is on my shoulder. A high, desperate noise has escaped my throat. I must not scream. I must not panic, though hot tears are seeping into my mouth.

He's not dead yet.

I grip his hand tight in mine. Heat burns in his palm, but the tips of his fingers are growing cold. I don't know what to do. I don't know how to keep his life from slipping away, carried on a tide I can't control.

There is one thing I can do. I wipe away my tears. A good brave man like Alistar doesn't deserve to be wept into his grave. He deserves to be loved until the breath leaves his body. And beyond.

I clutch the bone flute in my pocket, but it can't help us now. I tell him, "I'm here. It's Sophy. Sophy, and your daughter." The baby stirs, a tremor in my stomach. "We made it to Rambaud. You were right about him. I did it, Alistar. I talked him into negotiating with us." I pause, wetting my lips, adjusting my grip on his hand. "But you don't want to hear about that. Instead, I want to tell you how much I love you. How much your child loves you. I wish you would stay here. I wish you would open your eyes, and you would be alive, and we could raise this baby together. I want it. I want our family more than I have ever wanted anything. I'd give up my crown. I'd live with you in the woods and bake bannocks over the fire." My voice thickens. "But if you have to go now, then you must. I—I can't keep you here. I just have to tell you I wish—I wish so much that you would stay, and hold my hand when this baby is born, and see her take her first steps—"

Tears are falling down my cheeks now, whether I will them or no, and my voice has gone raw. Yet I keep talking.

"If you leave me, *promise* you'll watch over us—if that is what happens when souls cross over." My throat is swollen; I rest my face against his shoulder. The baby twitches. I feel the warmth of her, growing and growing in my womb, and I whisper, "Alistar Connell, if you leave me and this child, so help me, I will never forgive you. When it's my time, I'll follow you into the Good Land and hunt you down and—and I'll make you pay."

The shirt beneath me is soaked through with my tears, but what does it matter now? I can't tell if the warmth between our hands belongs to both of us still, or if Alistar's has burned away. I don't want to know. I don't know how I can bear losing him. I don't know what I'll do with this emptiness where my heart should be. I want to scream. I need to go out into the woods and scream into the trees so only the great silence in the forest hears me, and maybe the gods if they're listening. I want to tell Alistar that I'll raise our daughter with twice as much love, enough for both of us, but I can't say the words.

"Don't leave me," I whisper. I want to tell him that I've loved him for so long, so much longer than I even admitted to myself, since our second, or third, or fourth kiss in that cold hallway with the snow falling outside. He asked for a good-luck kiss, and I said I didn't have much luck but maybe the kiss could help both of us. He leaned into me and said, "Sophy Dunbarron, you give me the most fearsome feeling in my chest." I laughed and asked whether that was a good thing or a bad one, and he said he didn't quite know yet.

Neither do I, Alistar. Neither do I.

I want to tell him everything, but I can feel the stillness coming into his body beneath me. Hear one last ragged breath, and then nothing.

His body is soundless now, as the green-brown humming that is Alistar tugs loose from his blood and bones. It's so tremulous, so tentative. So fragile.

The baby kicks. Heat burns up through my chest. I'm reaching for it, instinctively, for the last whisper of Alistar's soul, as if I can capture it with my mind. But it's slipped beyond the confines of his silent body now, out into the open world. It's vanishing away from me.

I don't know how to stop it.

I was wrong. I can't scream. I sit instead, numb in the spreading coldness of my grief. The world was never supposed to take this man from me.

Something is humming against my thigh. Its insistent frequency tugs at the edge of my mind.

I close my burning eyes. There is nothing I can do for him. No way for me to keep him here. I can do only one thing: Send him into the spirit world with my lament. A Caerisian farewell.

I tug the bone flute from my pocket and bring it up to my lips. My fingers move, leaden, over the flute's holes; I have to force the breath into my lungs. But I play. I play the memory of him. I play the song that brought me here, the song of Alistar himself, crafting the shape and smell of him from the weight of sound. I play a bright, leaping melody that subsides into low, soft notes. I weave the music around the shell of his body, a lament carrying the tears I cannot shed, the yearning and pain so tangled like threads around my heart. Beyond me, deep within the land, I'm aware of a deep, powerful groaning, a counterpoint to my song.

I reimagine the imprint of his body and his soul, even though it's gone. I play my helpless longing for him to return, and the bitter knowledge that he has left too soon.

I play until I can no longer feel my fingers, until my very teeth are humming. On the other side of his body, Rhia and Victoire whisper, and still I play. I squeeze my eyes shut. My cheeks are damp with tears, and somehow these are in the music, too, the shape of my grief. I can't stop playing. Not even for Eren and Caeris.

But I know I have to stop. He's gone. I have to release this song, and I have to leave him here. Bury him and go. And when all this' is over, I'll find my way back here, and I'll build a marker to him, so that anyone who comes to this farm knows a man came here once, a good man, who left the world too soon.

". . . Not possible," Victoire hisses.

"But he *is,*" Rhia says.

I lower the bone flute. Numbness aches through my hands, my arms and back. I should take Alistar's cold hands and cross them over his chest. I should put the bone flute back in my pocket. I should get up and be queen.

Ruadan would expect it of me. My mother would. Finn would. If I don't, they all died for nothing.

"I love you," I whisper to Alistar Connell, or to the cooling shell of him. I shove the bone flute deep into my pocket, though fresh tears seep down my face, and it feels as if I'm ripping the seams off my own body. I gently lift his hand to lay it on his chest. I'll cross his other hand over it, and soon, if this cruel world will give me time, I'll pick a posy to put between his fingers, or on his grave.

His fingers, which tighten on mine.

I feel myself freeze. It must have been my imagination. His soul is gone. I felt it leave.

But . . .

A faint blush of sound ripples through him. So slight I wonder if I imagined it.

I lift my eyes. Victoire and Rhia are both staring at Alistar. They've been crying, but they aren't now. Victoire's face holds a kind of awestruck wonder. And Rhia . . .

"Sophy," she says, and she turns to me, terror and joy chasing each other across her face. "Sophy, he's breathing again."

HE'S BREATHING, BUT he doesn't wake. His fingers do not tighten on mine again. The wound is still weeping greenish pus.

But his pulse has evened, though it's still too fast. The sound of him remains faint, flickering, yet it's there. Somehow my music summoned him back.

I stay with him while Rhia and Victoire run in search of something, anything, we can use to carry him back to the city. "Talk to him, sing to him, do something, Sophy," Victoire says. "Keep him alive!"

Is it me or the bone flute that breathed life back into Alistar? Was it my longing for him to return—the way I crafted the shape of him through music? I don't know, but my jaw aches from playing, so instead I speak to him. I talk and talk. I remind him of our picnics together, of the way he'd bring me music and play the tin whistle while I sang. I remind him of the music we made together, of how I'd coax him to sing despite his self-consciousness, and we'd both laugh when his voice cracked on a note. Finally, I simply sing to him.

His breathing deepens. The sweat seems to be lessening on his brow, and the sound of him has steadied.

This is magic so powerful, my mind can't comprehend it. So I just keep singing. I sing as Rhia and Victoire return with a cockeyed stretcher made from pine boughs and a few old boards. We lift him onto it, and it holds, and I sing. I sing the old folksongs from Caeris, about the maiden with the owl's eyes, who flew through the mountains at night when she should have been lying with her husband. I sing about the sorcerer who turned himself into a tree as an experiment, and was forgotten for a century until a woman found him, a woman who'd had her heart broken, who had seen too much of the world, and when she looked at the tree she saw the man inside it and the tree cracked open to spill him out. I sing about the princess who left Caeris one dawn and returned ten years later with a book full of all the knowledge in the world, and a heart too wide to settle.

Outside the land is humming—a strange, deep groan that mingles with my singing. I sing, though my throat is growing raw, while Victoire and I carry Alistar out of the farmhouse. Rhia forges ahead to make sure we're unseen. The morning has advanced; the dew has dried from the grass.

We begin to move through the forest, and the soft moan in the earth begins to deepen. I stagger as we step onto the path. Alistar rocks in the litter. The very earth shakes. A deep, persistent moan rises from the ground beneath our feet, trembling through every tree, every blade of grass.

"Do you hear that?" Victoire gasps.

"Yes." It's not only me, then.

Rhia comes running back through the trees, her face stark. "Is it an earthquake? We need to take shelter!"

"No," I say involuntarily. There's another sound twining through the moaning, aching earth. A vast green sound, a sound that belongs not just to this still forest in Eren but to all the mountains and meadows, the rivers and stones, that together make up our entire land. It is the earth's voice, and a woman's. "It sounds like Elanna."

They both stare at me. The earth is still twitching under our feet, as if a great shiver is running through it, like a horse trying to fling off a fly. Around us the tree branches have begun to sway. The wind roars through, sudden and powerful. A great *crack* echoes through the woods.

"Run!" Rhia and I scream simultaneously. She grabs one side of the litter with her good hand and we all charge into motion, lurching as fast as we can over the buckling earth. The voice around us is rising to a deep bellow, a pitch that sets my teeth on edge. Just behind me, a great branch crashes down in the place we just passed. The trees are whipping into a frenzy.

We run, awkward between the litter and the protesting ground. "What's she doing?" Rhia pants. "Bringing the whole place down?"

I just shake my head. If El has indulged in some mad, impulsive act of magic . . . Yet a voice in the back of my head reminds me how difficult sorcery has been for her. The land is drained, exhausted— or it's supposed to be.

This doesn't feel like drained magic. This feels . . . desperate.

"The road!" Victoire cries out. We lumber over the ditch and onto the firm track. The wind hurls itself along the corridor between the trees, so forceful we have to bend double. Alistar mutters but doesn't come alert. We lumber on, no longer caring whether we're seen. No one in their right mind is on this road, anyway. The trembling in the ground vibrates up through the soles of my feet. My whole body is shaking now in rhythm with the earth. Still that unholy cry continues, pouring out of no human mouth.

Finally we glimpse the ridge where the Spring Caves lie. The wind gusts harder, sending us all stumbling as we climb, but we hang on, practically horizontal on the steep path. As we reach the top, the wind bellows again. There's a clatter below in the city. Roof tiles fly off the terraced houses below us, crashing down in the street. Victoire cries out.

"Sophy!" Elanna's run out from the cave to help us. I'm astonished to see her; I imagined her marooned on the height of the ridge, directing some magical feat of the land. She has to shout over the roaring wind. "Let's bring him inside!"

The four of us heave Alistar into the cool cave. It's marginally quieter within the stone walls, though the earth is still groaning. Victoire and I set Alistar's litter down, then drop to the ground, both of us gasping for breath.

"What happened?" El demands. She's staring down at Alistar.

"Rambaud's guards shot him." I shake my head, still panting. "What are you doing to the land?"

"It's not me." She looks at me grimly. "I didn't do anything."

"But—" I exchange a blank stare with Victoire and Rhia. "—it must be your doing."

"It's *not,*" she insists. "The land's all strange. I can feel it. Yet some parts are almost *dark.* I don't know who's doing this, or what they've done."

A deeper thread of worry twines down my spine.

El has crouched beside the litter, her hand on Alistar's arm. He doesn't stir. "Jahan may be able to help him, though it'll be difficult to draw on magic." She looks up at me. "Did you meet with Rambaud?"

"I did. He seems to have agreed to help us."

"Good." She calls over her shoulder for Jahan, then turns urgently back to us. "Hugh and the Caerisians arrived a short while ago; we were able to hide their coming from the spies in the city, as far as we know." She presses her lips together. "There's been word from Laon. Your fa—Euan made a decree. They've rounded up people who evaded the conscription. They're to be executed at noon."

I suck in a breath, and hear Victoire do the same. "Is there any chance—"

"Perhaps, if we act fast enough." She pauses. "They're also going to execute a man convicted of espionage. A traitor to the nation."

"Who?" I whisper.

She meets my eyes. "The minister of public works. Philippe Manceau."

Philippe. My stomach flips over; I'm gripping Alistar's arm, I realize, far too fiercely for a man who has taken such an injury.

"He should be able to flee," I say. "He knows all the routes out of the palace—he has spies—he knows—"

I'm babbling, and I force myself to stop.

"He knew the risk he took," Victoire whispers, but her hands are clapped to her lips, and she's gone white. Perhaps she and Philippe took some time to get acquainted after we escaped the warehouse. Her concern seems too great for a reluctant ally.

I close my eyes. Maybe my arrangement with Rambaud was for nothing; perhaps we will lose everything here and now. I suppose it's even possible that he never truly meant to ally with me—yet somehow I don't believe he was lying.

Footsteps scrape behind us. It's Jahan, with his younger brother on his heels. He drops down beside Elanna, putting his hand to Alistar's throat, checking his pulse. "What happened?"

"He took a shot to the leg," I say numbly. I can't stop thinking of Philippe and the others waiting in some cell for my father's orders. We need to act fast enough to stop them.

We must hope Rambaud is on the other side to help us.

". . . Sophy played him back to life with that flute," Victoire is saying to Elanna and Jahan. "I swear it. He was gone, and—and then—"

I look up to see them all staring at me. A flush rises in my cheeks.

El and Jahan exchange a glance. "The land's awakening the magic in you, Sophy," she says softly. "Why didn't you tell me?"

"It's no good," I say, almost angry. "I can't heal him."

"But you kept him alive," Jahan says. He's frowning a little as he studies Alistar. "I've knit together bone and skin. This is farther gone than most things I've done, but I'll try."

He leans forward, and I feel it *humming* out of him—his magic, like a sure current, wrapping around Alistar, pouring into the wound, into Alistar's inflamed, infected skin. As we watch, Alistar's skin becomes less flushed, the area around his wound paler, no longer so deeply reddened. The green pus softens into a clear fluid. The very sound of him grows stronger. He takes a slow, deep breath.

Then Jahan pitches forward with a grunt. I hurry to him. He looks up at me, a hand at his ribs, as though he has a stitch in his side. "It's taking a lot out of me," he says ruefully. "It's been a long month, and the magic here . . . it's harder to use than I remember. Did you really bring him back from *death*?"

"He was gone," Rhia says. "He'd stopped breathing."

"I couldn't feel his pulse," Victoire confirms.

"His soul had gone." The words choke my throat. Elanna grips my hand and squeezes it hard.

"Maybe that's why I can't quite heal him completely," Jahan says. "It feels as if something's not quite right."

My blood runs cold. "Something's wrong?"

"All the parts of him seem to be there, and working. But the spark that puts it all together—call it his soul—it's as if it hasn't engaged yet. It's there, but it's . . . slow."

I draw in a hard breath, feeling the hum of Alistar's resonance. Jahan's right—it's there, hovering inside him, yet it doesn't seem to have fully animated him yet. Is this my doing—the consequence of summoning Alistar's soul back from wherever it had gone? What if he doesn't come back; what if he can't? Perhaps in trying to save him I've only made things worse.

Jahan pats Alistar's wrist and manages a smile at me. "He *will* heal, Sophy. He'll wake. It's only a matter of time."

"Are you certain?" I whisper.

The corner of his mouth tucks in and I can tell, from the eddying sound of him, that no, he isn't. But he looks at me firmly. "Nothing's ever certain. But we're going to hope."

There's movement behind Elanna: people are emerging from the caves—Juleane, Hugh. I stand up, and Hugh holds out his arms, and I rush to hug him like a girl. "Thank goodness," I say through a choked throat. "You made it here."

"We weren't about to let you down." He smiles at me, though there's a grief caught in his eyes. "Teofila made it to Baedon—she spoke to me by mirror last night."

"Good," I say, relieved. Perhaps she tried to speak to me as well, but I was so busy searching for Alistar, and then confronting Rambaud, that I didn't hear the whisper of her voice.

In the crowd behind Alistar, there is Lord Aefric and Alistar's sister, Oonagh, a female doctor I know named Sorcha Kerr, and more Caerisians yet. I see Fiona and my mountain women. Behind them come the Ereni—Brigitte and Eugenie, and more. So many of them, all crowding out into the main cave. There must be a hundred. Two hundred—maybe even three.

Yet are we enough? Is my plan with Rambaud secure enough? Will he speak to the palace guards, to the Ereni nobles, and convince them?

I'll have to trust him. We have little other choice.

The ground quivers, and we all stumble. I look at El. Her face is pinched. Strained. She must feel the land aching in her own body. Realization hits me. "Rambaud said Phaedra contacted him—and she seems to be interested in sorcery. She asked me about it when I was imprisoned in the palace."

El's shaking her head; she looks dizzy. "If it goes on much longer, the land—" She stares at me, her eyes wide. "It feels as if it could break apart."

I stare from her to the gathered crowd, wetting my lips. Philippe and the others are depending on us to save them—and Rambaud is depending on me to arrive so he can enact his part of the plan.

But Elanna doesn't look as if she can hold on much longer. The tendons are standing out in her neck. The land is thrumming through her, green and aching, its beat so strong her body is rocking with it. It looks as if not only the land is going to break apart, but she, too.

She gasps, cries out. "It's cracking—all the way up to Barrody—the whole land!"

Jahan and I both reach for her, instinctively, at the same moment. I *hear* it roaring through her—the buckling, raging land. I hear not only the earth here in Laon. It's as if there's a shining, blackening line running from the ground at our feet all the way north, arrowing into Barrody, past it, up into the rugged teeth of the Tail Ridge, all the way to the northern sea. The land is pulling, puckering, *shifting*. It's loosening from its moorings, like two great planes dragging apart—and ready to crash back into each other.

I open my eyes, staring speechless at Jahan. If the land pulls apart like this, if it buckles—this is a greater catastrophe than a few people facing possible execution in Royal Square. If we don't find a way to stop this, we could *all* die.

Between us, El is shaking, shrinking into herself, whispering unheard words. Jahan tucks her against his chest, holding her tight. He's murmuring something to her, but whatever it is, it's not enough.

I grip her hand. "El. Who's doing this? Where do we go?"

She stares at me, her golden eyes enormous and blank. "The Hill," she whispers.

"The Hill of the Imperishable?"

But El's eyes have fixed at a point beyond me with an uncomprehending horror. She cries out, and Jahan hugs her tighter. His hands are wrapped over her chest, and one of hers comes up to tentatively curl around his forearm. I notice that a bit of twine has been wrapped around both of their ring fingers. So they're planning to marry.

I know what we must do. It must be Phaedra Saranon on the Hill—doing what, I don't know. But I am going to find her.

I turn to the crowd. "It's time for us to move," I shout over the groaning of the earth. "I want you all to march into Laon—knock on doors, shout for more people to join you. I want the city, the entire kingdom, to rise up and demand Euan Dromahair and the Saranons depart forever!"

There's a ragged cheer, but most people look more afraid than bold.

"No one's going to come out in this mad weather," Juleane protests.

"We're going to stop it." I look fiercely at Elanna and Jahan. Her eyes are closed now; she seems entirely unaware of her surroundings. But he nods back at me. "We'll go to the Hill of the Imperishable, but you must go into the city as soon as the land calms." *If* the land calms, I think, but don't say. "Gather everyone you can into Royal Square. Make them ready to take the palace!"

"What if they fire on us?" Brigitte demands. "They massacred the crowd two days ago!"

"That's why we're marching on them again," I say. "Hundreds of us—thousands, if they'll hear the call."

"Thousands?" Victoire echoes. "But there are only a few hundred of us, Sophy."

"I know." I reach into my pocket and pull out the bone flute. "I'll call them. I don't know who will answer my song, but I will play it for them. For all of Eren and Caeris."

They're listening now, all of them, looking from the bone flute to me.

"You *are* a sorceress," Jahan murmurs.

"We'll march without weapons," I tell them. "We will march with the power of our magic, and the power of our hearts. Our sorcerers will break their guns, and our allies inside the palace gates will let us in. We will show that we're not afraid of Euan Dromahair, or Phaedra and Augustus Saranon." I look around at their brave, frightened faces, and I press my hands to my stomach. "I don't want my child to grow up in a world where men and women slaughter each other for crowns. I want her to grow up knowing her mother fought *like a mother*—with the potent weapon of her love."

There's a moment of silence. Then Juleane Brazeur puts her fist to her heart, and so does Hugh. Then Brigitte and Eugenie and Annis. Fiona and the mountain women. Rhia and Victoire. I echo the gesture; my heart feels too wide. Soon we are all standing in the cave with our fists to our hearts and the earth roaring about us like a living thing.

I take up the bone flute and play a note. With deliberation, I build a swift, interlocking melody. I weave the song around us in pulses and curls, a wall of sound that envelops the cave and the hill, creating an island of sanctuary in the bellowing land. The roaring of the wind softens, until I hear it only in the distance, beyond the cave entrance. We are cupped in the cool protection of the cave. Safe, until we step outside.

I lower the flute. My limbs are trembling, and a hot sweat has run down between my breasts. It took effort, fighting the land with each note, but now that the protection has been created, I plant my legs, aware of my own power.

"Plan your approach to the city," I tell them, for now they'll be safe in here, "and we will join you as soon as we can."

If we can.

Juleane and Victoire immediately set to work, organizing everyone by streets and sectors. "We need to get to Philippe before they take his life," I hear Victoire saying to Juleane, "even if he knows the risk he took." I allow myself a smile, though part of me feels I'm letting them down by not joining them.

Well, we will soon enough.

I turn to Jahan and El. The protection I wove around the cave seems to have helped—she's breathing more deeply, though her eyes are still closed. She's still tucked into Jahan's arm.

"Let's go," I begin, but he shakes his head.

"Let me see that."

I hand him the bone flute. He studies it, his eyes narrowing slightly, then hands it to his younger brother. Lathiel's lips purse, and he says something to Jahan in a language I don't know. It must be their native Britemnosi. Jahan replies, and Lathiel says something emphatically.

"It's powerful," Jahan says, handing the bone flute to me. "It must be tied to some source of magic, yet it carries the magic with it."

I think of the spring outside Barrody Castle, and the woman I followed there. I think of the magic that runs like seams through our land, the thin veil between past and present, the wavering division between history and myth. But I simply tuck the flute into my pocket and nod. "I think so." I glance at Lathiel, then say to Jahan in Ereni, so the boy can't understand, "Is he coming?"

"No." Jahan turns to his brother, explaining something in swift Britemnosi. Lathiel looks mutinous.

I start toward the cave entrance, but Demetra is crouching there beside Alistar. She gestures for me to kneel beside her. "I've been trying to work on him," she says softly. "He's coming to."

I lean over Alistar and draw in a breath.

His eyes have opened. He blinks once, twice. Then he looks up at me, his eyes creased with confusion, as if he's woken in a foreign land. "Where did they go?" he says. Even his voice sounds strange—not his own.

A shiver runs up my spine. Perhaps Jahan was right that something is missing, though the sound of him seems to fully inhabit his body now. I find I can't look at Demetra, even though she's reached over and clasped her hand atop mine. "Who?"

"The light people." He frowns at me, as if he can't quite place my name, and the shiver bursts all over my body. I summoned his soul back—I kept him in his body on the journey here—but for the first time, I wonder not whether I should have done it, but what I brought him back from. "They were singing."

"No, Alistar." My voice breaks. "*I* was singing."

"Oh." Comprehension spreads across his face, and I feel a pulse of relief. Surely, now, he'll be all right. But then he says, "You're the one who brought me back here. I wanted to stay, but I had to follow your song." He scowls. "They *said* so."

He sounds like a child. I don't know what to say, or even whether I dare to touch him. Tentatively, I put my free hand over his. He looks blankly down at it.

I'm blinking hard. I pull away and move to rise. I can't bear this.

Alistar says, "Sophy."

I whirl, but he's still got that confused look on his face. Doubtfully, he says, "That's your name?"

"Yes," I whisper, "it is."

He looks at Demetra, now. "I feel strange."

"You've suffered an injury. You need to stay here and rest." Demetra glances at me, firm and reassuring. "I'll keep an eye on him. You go."

I look one last time at Alistar, and swallow. But I don't have time to fear for him, or for what I've done.

I rise. Jahan and Elanna are waiting for me in the cave entrance. Her eyes are open, and she's shuddering.

"Can you walk?" I ask her, worried.

She manages a nod. "I'll walk, Sophy," she says in a small, hard voice. "I'll run if I have to. I'm not letting these bastards tear apart my land."

I glance at Jahan. "Lathiel promised to stay here with the others," he says. "He'll march with them and break the guards' guns when they arrive at the palace."

Rhia comes over and gives Lathiel a nod. "I'll keep an eye on him."

"Good." I tuck the bone flute away and push up my sleeves. "Let's go."

CHAPTER THIRTY

We emerge from the cave, and the wind nearly flattens us. The sky is churning from boiling black clouds, to staring blue, and back again. The earth buckles, nearly pitching me to my knees, and I throw my arms instinctively around my stomach, as if that can protect the child.

There's a deafening crash. I look up. An old oak tree at the top of the ridge thunders to the ground, split into two ragged pieces.

"Run!" I scream, and we all pelt forward just in time. The logs slide past where we were standing, slipping down the hill as if they're running downstream.

What is Phaedra doing? Assuming, of course, that it *is* her. Yet who else could it be? Euan hasn't demonstrated much interest in sorcery—or anything aside from cruelty. Across the rooftops, the Hill of the Imperishable leans up, as tranquil as a cloud.

The earth bunches and buckles again, and we begin to run, the three of us, Jahan and I holding El up on either side. We plunge down into the city. The streets are empty. A crack snakes through the cobblestones before us, coming to a stop at our feet. We press on all the same. The wind tosses shutters off the sides of houses, and more tiles from rooftops. The earth is groaning and Elanna is groaning, too, or maybe it's the sound of the land pouring through her. It seems long, too long, through the streets, past the palace, to the city's southwestern edge where the Hill of the Imperishable rises.

We reach the last street, and stagger between the final houses onto the narrow, heathered path. The baby kicks hard in my womb. A flight of birds has scattered up from the oaks and elms. The tree branches fling about like arms, swinging at us, breaking off and crashing to the ground. Behind us, there's an enormous shudder as the soil flees from underneath a house and the entire building collapses into a pile of rubble.

El sways. "Run!" I shout, and we do, Jahan and I half lifting her between us. The path rises, curving onto the little ridge that leads up to the Hill of the Imperishable. At the crown of the Hill, the ragged stones rise from the earth like quartzite specters.

The roaring land eases as we approach—perhaps because the Hill is the eye of this particular storm. Yet the sound of the stones themselves is utterly changed. Ordinarily their magic creates a kind of melody, but now the music is fractured. Shards of song scratch down the pathways of my mind. The broken pieces make no unified music. Instead they jar against one another, fragments of a disagreeing, shattered whole.

"No," El whispers. Tears are falling down her cheeks.

I don't know how anyone can tolerate being inside the noise. And at first, I think the circle is empty, that Phaedra has fled. Perhaps she was never here. The stones quiver in the ground, but the altar stone sits pristine. The grass and bracken lie apparently untouched. Everything appears abandoned.

But then Jahan grabs my arm. He pulls me to a stop just before the entrance stones. "Someone's in there," he breathes. "They're using persuasion."

I pause and listen. A girl's thin whisper trembles over the apparently empty stones. *There is nothing here.*

My ear catches a crisp wooden clack. Like beads knocking together.

Felicité. They took *Felicité.*

Rage pours into my head. I step into the circle, my hands fisted. I reach for the power of the stones, for the heart of the magic. Demetra told me that sound has power—and so do words.

"Enough," I say.

Felicité's thin magic evaporates—and there they are, gathered around the altar stone, with a pair of Paladisan guards behind them, bayonets at the ready. Felicité, kneeling on the ground to the right, her hands bound before her. Her hair is wild and her hollowed face has gone beyond tears to a fear so profound she appears numb.

To the left—I draw in a breath—is Ciril. He's bowed forward, dressed in the same filthy garments he was wearing when they dragged him through the streets. If Felicité is numb, his anger is like the earth's—rising and falling, barely contained. Yet he doesn't move. His hands, too, are bound.

And between them, of course, is Phaedra. She stands over the altar in a fragile white gown, its skirt stained with a crimson smear of blood. Her own, or someone else's? I can't tell from here. The sound of her is sharp as a diamond, and as strong.

Behind the group stands an additional ring of people—a dozen of them—sorcerers, to judge by their humming energy, and the dull fear in their eyes. Threads of power run, trembling and raw, from the earth to them, and then to Ciril and Felicité.

El is gripping my hand, as if it's the anchor keeping her in the present. I hang on tight.

On the altar stone, spattered with a few drops of blood, sits a cup. It is wide-bellied, silver, an old-fashioned style with two round, ringed handles.

And it is humming. Humming, like the bone flute in my pocket, but with a far more powerful song. So loud it's almost a roar, like water. It's a current of magic, pouring into the chalice.

I gasp aloud as I realize what they're doing. They're funneling magic into the chalice—not just from this stone circle, but from all of Eren and Caeris. Somehow, Phaedra has persuaded these sorcerers to draw upon the magic that runs through the entire land—*all* of it.

She's creating a source of power that she can use—or rather, force a sorcerer to use, since even now she doesn't appear to have magic herself. When I was captive in the palace, she told me that whoever controls magic controls the future, though not in so many words. At the time, I didn't guess that this could possibly be what she meant.

We've been seen. The guards start to move, but there's a sharp whine in my ears. Their guns crack. Jahan gasps as if breaking the weapons physically pained him—and it must, with the magic being drained away into the cup. Ciril and Felicité both sag, the magic tugging at them, too. Two of the sorcerers behind Phaedra stagger to their knees.

The guards throw down the broken guns and pull out their sabers.

"Phaedra," I say, and her head lifts. I gather all the power I can project into my voice. *"Stop."*

But the magic is slithering like a fish out of my control, and Phaedra simply gives us a strained smile. She looks weary, as if the draining of the land is draining her, too.

"Hello, Sophy," she says conversationally. Her gaze cuts to the side, and her lip curls. "Korakides."

Behind me, I can feel El's energy seeping down into the earth. Trying to hold it. Soothe it. But it keeps bucking out of her grasp.

"Phaedra, you're going to lose," I say. "Ciril and Felicité aren't powerful enough to funnel that much magic. You're going to kill them both."

Jahan is the only thing holding Elanna upright. "And you'll destroy the land!"

"How fascinating," Phaedra drawls. "I never thought of that, of course."

The back of my neck pricks at the sarcasm in her voice. My mind is circling back to that conversation with Rambaud—to his claim that Phaedra was the one who contacted *him*. Even before she lost her bid for the imperial throne, Phaedra Saranon wanted Eren and Caeris. It wasn't only for political gain, or for our resources, I finally realize. No, she wanted our magic.

The earth is quivering again, and now it buckles beneath us, throwing us all forward. El crashes to her knees, digging her fingers into the earth. Jahan stands protectively over her.

Over the altar stone, Ciril has locked his eyes on Felicité. He seems to be trying to communicate something to her, without words. Her eyes have widened.

I step forward, staggering as the earth quivers. Phaedra starts to look at the sorcerers, and I say quickly, "So you came here to make this—this cup? You came here to put all of Eren's magic into it, so you could use it in Paladis?"

"You're less of a fool than I thought, Bastard Queen," she remarks, with a faint smile. Yet her eyes look so tired.

I wet my lips. Ciril is mouthing something at Felicité now. The magic hums through the earth, from the other sorcerers, even from the guards and Phaedra, pouring into the two of them, a current so powerful it will eventually destroy their bodies. They must both know it.

"I know what you want," I tell Phaedra Saranon, and her gaze jerks back to me.

"Do you?" she says, ironic. Yet there's something avid in her face as well. She wants to hear me say it—she wants to hear it spoken aloud.

"You want to be seen," I say. "You want to be recognized for what you've done. Augustus is younger than you, yet if you had taken the imperial throne, the crown would have gone to you *and* him. But you're the one who allied with Euan and with Rambaud. You arranged to come here. This was all *your* idea—and this sorcery, too. And when you go back to Ida with that chalice, with all that power, everyone will know it."

"Yes," she breathes.

To her right, Felicité has closed her eyes. A thin tear escapes from her eyelashes.

"But there's one thing I don't quite see," I add. "How you'll control the sorcerers who do your work for you, since you aren't a sorceress yourself."

"Oh, that's simple," Phaedra says. She's a little flushed—with pleasure, thinking of the future. "Blackmail is a marvelous tool. It works on sorcerers just as well as on ordinary mortals." She smiles. "It will work on you. Guards! Seize Korakides and the steward of the land."

"No!" I exclaim.

But before the guards can advance, Ciril bellows, "Let go!"

Felicité is shaking her head, sobbing in earnest now. The other sorcerers simply look confused, exhausted.

"I have no one," Ciril says. "You have them all. This whole land."

And I finally understand. I lunge forward—

Felicité lets go. The magic she was gathering, channeling into the cup, dissipates.

The other sorcerers, understanding, abruptly release their threads of power, too.

It funnels now into Ciril—*all* of it, all the power of Eren and Caeris. A stream of white light so brilliant I could almost touch it. He disappears within its glow.

He's screaming.

"No!" I pelt forward, but the earth buckles again. Phaedra's cast backward, and the guards are knocked off balance. I'm thrown onto my knees. Behind me, Elanna collapses to the ground, motionless, Jahan gripping her arm.

Ciril is still screaming—and then he stops. The white light keeps pouring in, but he's folding in upon himself. He sags to the side, onto the ground. For another moment, the roaring current pours in and his shoulders heave.

Then he stops moving. The light dissipates to the faintest glow, and then to nothing.

I don't need to touch my trembling hands to him to know he's dead. The sheer force of magic killed him. Felicité is sobbing. The other sorcerers are calling to one another.

On the other side of the altar stone, Phaedra scrambles to her feet. The land is buckling wildly now, as if Ciril's death only made it worse. I can't even look at Elanna behind me, but the sound of magic running between her and the land has faded to the slightest thread. Jahan is frantically saying her name.

"Phaedra, stop!" I cry.

The Saranon princess has snatched the chalice from the altar stone. She clutches it to her chest. The tone of her is tired. Angry. But she meets my eyes.

"We took Laon," I lie. "We took Augustus, and Euan. There's nothing more here for you. No way to return to Paladis. I'm not afraid of your guards." I hold out my hand. "Give me that cup, and I'll let you live."

For a moment, she hesitates. The land rages around us, and the thread of Elanna's power pulses so dimly—too dimly. Phaedra's gaze flickers from me to El.

Then she whispers, "No."

And she wrenches the lid off the cup. Setting it on the table, she plunges her hands into its shallow bowl. The magic roars, a raging current, eager to escape its confines. It pours, sparking, white gold, into her hands, races up her arms. The sound of her is frantic, grasping. She's summoning the magic. Inviting it. It surges into her face, pouring in shining rivulets down her body. She looks like one of the beings Alistar saw on the other side.

But Phaedra Saranon isn't a sorcerer.

The magic pours into her, and it *erupts*.

I throw myself over Felicité, knocking us both to the ground, just in time. Fire lashes over my head. Phaedra is screaming, writhing. The land is bellowing. The magic races like white fire. The power floods over the earth, between the stones, trembling into our bodies.

I push myself upright. The guards have fled, and the land is buckling, heaving. I crawl behind the altar stone, and my gorge heaves at the wreckage of Phaedra Saranon. There's little left of her, in the charred mass, except a hank of white cloth. She seems to have burned up entirely.

The chalice has tumbled a short distance away, just in front of one of the other sorcerers, who stares at it. I pick it up, and its power thrums in my hands, in my very blood and bone, so potent I shudder. It's pouring out of the cup now—through me, back into the land. I am the conduit for this song, but I'm afraid if I hold on to it much longer, I'll be nothing more than an empty husk, like Ciril.

So I do the only thing I can think of. I sing.

I sing to the chalice, to the land of Eren and Caeris. It is a wordless song, the simplest tone moving up and down. I don't have El's ability to move the land, or to see through its eyes. But I feel the air spin and condense. I hear the land's distress begin to wane. The wind ebbs; there is a sudden hush. The roar of the land softens to a soft, low keening.

At last, I set aside the chalice. I rub my blistered palms.

Felicité sits up on the other side of the altar. "S-sophy?"

"It's all right," I say, though my lips are numb from singing, and so is my mind. "It will be all right."

But she shakes her head. Points with a trembling finger.

I turn. Elanna.

She's collapsed on the other side of the circle, unmoving, her hair tumbled about her. I stumble over to her, crouching beside Jahan. He's shaking his head, breathing in short gasps to keep himself from sobbing. "She's gone, Sophy. She . . ."

That can't be. The *Caveadear* can't die, not like this. Not when I stopped Phaedra!

"Stay here," I whisper to her. "Stay."

I reach for her soul, the way I reached for Alistar's. I imagine I am cupping it in my grasp, the way I'm holding her hands. Her fingers have gone cold, and the faint, damp heat is fleeing from her palms. Her breath has stilled. The spark of her is tugging free, spectral in the air.

I draw in my breath, and I sing. I gather up the melody of the land, the quaking of dew in the morning sun, the swift, secretive movements of the animals. I sing the density of mountains and the enigma of forests and the flowing veins of rivers. I sing the woman who can contain all this vastness within herself.

Yet somehow it's still not enough—her soul is still sparking away from me, insisting on its freedom. Somewhere beyond my closed eyes, a choked noise escapes Jahan's throat. Elanna's palms have grown cold in my grasp.

I need to think, but panic has begun to tear at my throat. I won't lose Elanna—I can't. And yet . . .

It strikes me then. I breathe in. I sang the land, and her magic, but I didn't sing *her*. Elanna Valtai is more than the steward of the land—she is a woman, too, as human as I. And for too long, I have resented her. Ever since I was a child, because I always believed Teofila loved her more than me. I always wanted a mother of my very own.

But Teofila, of course, is mother to us both. The very land is a mother to us.

I gather myself, and I sing of Elanna. The girl who survived. A girl who had, in many ways, more fortitude than I ever gave her credit for. A woman who has grown into the power of the land, yes, but also of herself.

I sing her whole, and the spark that is her soul hesitates. I keep singing and, tentatively, it begins to settle back into a shroud about her body, as if it recognizes the shape I have made for it.

Elanna's pulse flickers against my palms.

"She's back, Soph," Jahan whispers.

My head bows. My throat's gone raw, but Elanna is still coming back into herself. I reach for the words that will bring her fully home.

"From the mountains beyond the moon, nursed by dragons, Wildegarde came," I whisper, *"her hair crowned with the pale light of stars. Where she placed her foot, the earth trembled. When she raised her hands, mountains moved."*

Elanna's eyelids flicker. Her lips part, moving ever so faintly along with the words.

"She came to the court of Queen Aline. The queen did not know what to make of such a woman, her hands and legs covered in leaves as a tree is, her face a woman's countenance. She said, 'Who

are you? Why have you come?' and Wildegarde answered, 'I am the breath of the mountains, the whisper of the waters, the swift passing of a bird, the hollows within the hills. I have come for you. I have come so we can make a song together.' "

Jahan leans closer, kneeling on El's opposite side. I look up, give him a small nod. It's time for his final healing.

He puts his hands over mine. Over El's.

The current of magic pours through him—slow, yet steady. Not as powerful as it was even yesterday, but it comes. Through me. Into Elanna. Her mouth moves.

I whisper more of the poem. *"Where Wildegarde passed, the land grew fertile. Flowers sprang up at her feet, and springs flowed from where she had stepped. She brought all the bounty of the earth to life, and Queen Aline treasured her for it. 'For together,' the queen said, 'we may bring new life to the world.'* " I murmur, "And they did, El. They did, and so will we."

Her fingers twitch in mine.

Jahan bends over us, his brow furrowed. The magic hums and hums. I sense it whispering through Elanna's body, persuading muscle and organs and skin back to pulsing life. Slow, so slow. Yet steady.

"Come back, El," I whisper. "Come back."

Her eyelids flutter. And open. The faintest smile tugs at her mouth. "Is that a command?"

"Yes, it is." I press my face against her arm to blunt the sting of tears in my eyes. "From your sister."

CHAPTER THIRTY-ONE

We limp together down the path from the stone circle—Jahan supporting El as her steps grow stronger, and me with my arm around Felicité. The girl's shoulders have not stopped shaking. "I shouldn't have let him die," she's whispering. "I knew it's what would happen, and I—I—I wanted to live. I wanted to live so badly."

Of course, the other sorcerers did the same thing, too. We've left them with the guards, under orders to keep them safe until we have time to learn their names and help them return to their families.

"Ciril told you to do it." I tighten my arm around her, though my own aching back longs for support. "He gave you permission. It's what he wanted, Felicité. You did nothing wrong."

"But I—I killed a man!"

"You let him die the way he wanted," I insist, as much to comfort her as anything else.

"He said he had nothing else to live for, but that I did. He said I should be the one who lived." She covers her mouth with a shaking hand. "High Priest Granpier will never condone it. Except I don't even know if he . . ."

So this is what Phaedra meant by her blackmail, I suppose. "Phaedra told you she'd kill him if you didn't do it, didn't she?"

"I should never have agreed," Felicité whispers. "But how could I let him die?"

"You did the right thing," I tell her, again. Phaedra would have killed Granpier, too. She seemed keen to make her point.

"Except now that man Ciril is dead!"

I glance over and see Jahan's grimace of sympathy. "How did Phaedra persuade Ciril to do it?" he asks.

"She didn't only say she'd murder Granpier," Felicité says wearily. "She said she'd massacre half the city. Kill those taken captive, then go into people's homes. She'd have Ciril take the blame for all of it." In a shaky voice, she adds, "Anyone who thinks that poor, brave Ciril Thorley was a murderer should know that he—he *saved their lives*. He gave himself for this kingdom."

I squeeze her tighter as we walk. "Felicité, did he ever tell you why? Why he attacked Rambaud—why he would sacrifice himself now?"

She turns her face up, startled, then wipes her cheeks. "He told me, when we were captive together. He lived as a blacksmith in Darchon; he had a good business, a wife, three children. He even had a grandchild. They had magic, all of them, but it was a small thing. It wasn't until after the *Caveadear* woke the land that it started growing into something more—and then the Tinani crown began to crack down on sorcery."

"The emperor of Paladis sent witch hunters," I say. "Ciril's children . . ."

"Yes, but King Alfred sent out his own army as well. Not all the sorcerers were rounded up by witch hunters; there were too many people accused, it was a massive panic. Ciril came home one day to find soldiers rounding up his wife, their children, the grandchild—all of them. He flew out of control and tried to attack them by magic—he wounded at least two men. But the soldiers retaliated. They killed his entire family, right there in the street."

My blood runs cold. "Did Ciril escape?"

Felicité nods. "He summoned lightning and set fire to the entire block of houses, and he ran. He made for Eren, because he'd heard that we were welcoming refugees. On the way, he fell in with another sorcerer, a man from the southern reaches of the Ismae." She swallows hard. "But they were pursued, though Ciril didn't know it. One evening where they camped, Ciril went off to catch a fish while the other man made a fire. He heard shouting and came running back, but it was too late. His friend was already dead. An entire squadron of soldiers surrounded their campsite, and Ciril hid in the shrubs. He listened to them, while they . . ." Felicité chokes and whispers, "They cut off his friend's hands and feet. They drove nails through his . . . his . . ."

I grip her hand. Quietly, I say, "I know."

She looks at me. "He heard the men talk about their employer. Aristide Rambaud, the Duke of Essez."

Of course. I release a breath. After all this, I finally have proof against Rambaud—and now I need him as my ally. Well, I'll do what I have to, and if we win, Rambaud will be made to suffer the consequences of his actions.

"Ciril was sick with himself for all of it," Felicité whispers. "He blamed himself for everything. He said he shouldn't have sought revenge on Rambaud; he should have gone to you and told you the truth."

"But he wanted vengeance himself." It's something I can understand. I sigh, rubbing my hand over my mouth. "He was a hero in the end, Felicité. We'll see he's remembered that way."

As long, I think, as the rest of our plan works.

It sounds like it's begun. A new roar is building in the air—the echo of people's voices in Royal Square. As we approach the top of the street, I glimpse the square at the bottom of the low hill. It's crowded with a river of people, pressed shoulder-to-shoulder. More are flooding in from the other streets. Even the tightness in my chest, and the exhaustion in my legs, eases at the sight of them. Jahan utters a startled laugh, and Elanna lifts her head with new strength.

"They're here for you," she says to me.

I look at her. "For *us*."

A smile touches her lips. She doesn't disagree.

As we approach, we're sighted by the crowd. "The queen! The

Caveadear!" The people are shouting, then part for us to pass through to the scaffold surmounting the fountain, where three nooses hang. I draw in a breath—I am unbearably thirsty—and we plunge into the crowd.

People bellow around us, shouting, stomping. Their rage, their fear, their boldness sweeps over me, lifting me up almost like a physical thing. We're swept up onto the scaffold where Rhia is waiting with Victoire, Juleane, and Hugh. "She's all right?" Rhia whispers, nodding to El.

"She will be." I glance around the people flooding the square. "Philippe? The others?"

"They had just brought them to the scaffold. We got here just in time." Rhia nods. "There he is."

Indeed, Philippe is below us in the crowd that presses against the palace gates. He's mussed and dirty but leading a chant, his fist in the air. "Euan Dromahair! Euan Dromahair!"

They want him to come out. They want him to see us, and run.

Through the wrought-iron gates, I glimpse the plumed helmets of the royal guard. They're holding their bayonets at the ready. Lathiel worms out of the crowd behind us. "I broke the guns," he says in an aggrieved voice, "but they haven't set them down."

"Probably because of him," I say, pointing. Even at this distance, I can make out the man in the shining gold helmet who's walking through the guards' ranks.

"Augustus," Jahan says, like a curse.

The chanting in the crowd dies down; even Philippe has stopped agitating the others. Everyone turns quiet—so quiet that we hear, on the other side of the gates, Augustus's exhortation to the guards.

"I don't care if you can't fire! Open the gates and spear them through!"

A rustle echoes through the crowd. I know people are staring up at me, wondering whether they should run.

But I'm staring at the palace guards on the other side of the gate. Men who, except for the few Paladisan commanders, are Ereni, even Caerisian. They are our people, and Rambaud promised to speak with them. I know their names, their families, their histories. Yet now, under Augustus's pressure, they're wavering. I hear the thready, uncertain sound of them. The tremor of their fear.

I claim Rhia's water flask and take a drink, soothing my parched throat. Readying myself. Then I step away from Rhia, from Felicité. I stand on the edge of the scaffold where they were going to execute Philippe and the others, and I draw in a breath.

I begin to sing.

I sing a song of Eren, for Eren. A song of mothers and fathers, brothers and sisters, standing out here in the square with their hearts breaking for the men inside the palace gates. I pour into it all my strength and determination, all my hope and even my fear. I let my heart dictate the song.

My eyes are closed; I'm feeling the power of the words, the music, within myself. But then I hear them—more voices, joining mine. A woman, a man, a child. Everyone in the square is beginning to sing. More of them, and more, the weaving of our voices spreading over the palace, over the city, over all of Eren and Caeris. Everyone inventing their own words, but the melody the same.

We sing, and the earth quivers. The fountain below the scaffold trembles, and water erupts from its spigots, seeping over the edge of the fountain and onto the cobblestones, wetting people's shoes and stockings. The sky grays over, clouds floating over brilliant patches of blue. The finest mist begins to fall. It's as if the land is demanding freedom, too.

A cry rises from the other side of the gate. *"Silence them!"* Augustus Saranon roars.

But the soldiers have heard us. Our song is, after all, their song.

First one man turns, in a blur of steel. Then another, and another. They put their backs to the gates and turn on Augustus Saranon and his Paladisan commanders. A shout goes up, but I can no longer distinguish who's who.

Then there's movement at the gates—Philippe and the others. The gates swing back, and the crowd surges in, into the palace courtyard, a flood that swamps Augustus Saranon and his commanders. I'm moving with it, the others on my heels, sweeping into the courtyard.

My father hasn't emerged.

Augustus and the Paladisans have been cornered—trapped in the inner court, beneath the royal balcony. The prince's gold helmet shines; he's hiding behind the bulk of his men, forcing them to be brave for him. I start to maneuver toward them, but then a movement in the colonnade catches my eye. Aristide Rambaud is leaning from a doorway, beckoning me in.

My pulse pounds in my hands. I glance for Elanna, but she's already seen Rambaud and my reaction. She gives me a quick nod; she seems steadier on her feet now. "I'll keep Augustus alive, if I can," she says, pushing away before I can protest. She calls, "Let him live!" and some of the Ereni guards groan in disappointment.

I work my way toward Rambaud. Rhia's following me. "I'm not letting you in there alone."

I don't have a chance to respond; we've reached the colonnade, and Rambaud drags me inside, then slams the door behind Rhia. I wait for him to make some derisive remark, but he just nods toward the east wing. "They gave an order to slaughter the prisoners. Hurry!"

"But we've taken Laon," Rhia protests. "There's no reason to kill them—"

"That hardly matters to Euan Dromahair. Or," Rambaud adds bitterly, "my former ally Grenou."

Grenou. My hands tighten into fists. I might have known.

"We have a few minutes before they carry out the order," Rambaud says, hurrying us up the steps to the east wing. "I slipped out when Euan was giving the command. Come."

He pushes open the door to the upper floor, and we emerge—

Face-to-face with two guards. Both are so startled they simply stare.

"Alain!" I exclaim. "Sebastien!"

"Queen Sophy," Alain says. He clasps my hands in obvious relief. "Did you take the city?"

"We did, but we need to free the prisoners from these cells, and fast. Help us?"

He and Sebastien both nod, and Alain wrestles out a ring of keys, striding quickly down the hallway to the first door. Rambaud casts me an ironic glance. "Here I thought we would have to use some persuasion by force. I seem to have misjudged you yet again."

"The guards and I have always gotten along well enough," I tell him. "It's only Grenou who—"

But I stop, because Alain's gotten the door open, and he turns to us with a high-pitched sound of rage. "There are *children* in here."

Children? I rush forward, pressing into the cramped room. I don't know whose children they are, but they must belong to an Ereni sorcerer—that, or they have displayed magic themselves. The three small figures are watching me from behind a single pallet bed. I drop to my knees, holding out my hands. "It's all right," I whisper. "You're safe. We're taking you out of here."

One child steps forward, and then the others. The smallest throws her arms around my neck. I pick her up, and she fits her warm, quivering body against me, locking her legs around my hip. She smells of prison and fear, and my heart pounds with renewed hatred for my father. The other children are older, too wary to touch me, but they approach as I gesture them back into the hall.

And stop short.

"There Her Majesty is." It's Captain Grenou, his voice heavy with irony. He's standing at the end of the hallway, flanked by a company of ten guards. Alain and Sebastien have fallen back, their weapons raised, protecting Rambaud, who stands exposed at the opposite end of the hall.

Two doors stand open between me and Grenou. I don't see Rhia.

Grenou isn't watching me, though. His gaze has fixed on Rambaud, and his tone has changed. Quietly, he says, "I didn't expect this of you."

"I could say the same in turn," Rambaud replies flatly.

"Grenou," I interrupt, and he swings toward me, "this

building—the entire city—is surrounded inside and out. You're trapped here. If you kill us and these prisoners, all the people in Laon will know. They'll see you die."

His eyebrows lift. "You think I'm going to kill you?"

"Yes. Or you can join me." I meet his eyes, but I see only anger there. Revulsion. "You can join all of your people rather than fight against them."

He takes a single step forward. "Join the Bastard Queen? The woman who deposed the Eyrlais, and stole my promotion to captain of the royal guard?"

I stare. That's why he hates me?

"Perhaps I would," he says softly. "If you hadn't made me serve under that mountain bitch. But you did."

Raising his bayonet, he steps forward—

And a figure lunges from the cell door beside him. Even with a broken arm, Rhia's aim is deadly accurate. She knocks aside Grenou's arm and steps within it, slashing her dagger straight across his neck.

He looks extremely startled before he falls.

The other guards stand frozen as she wrenches the blade free. "Anyone else care to insult me?"

I press the child's face against my shoulder so she doesn't see the blood. Weariness hugs my very bones, but I can't pretend to be sorry Rhia made this choice. Quietly, I say, "Alain, Sebastien, open the other doors, if you would." The guards have lowered their bayonets; they seem to be arguing among themselves, looking from Alain and Sebastien to Rhia, Rambaud, and me.

The prisoners are emerging from their cells now—including High Priest Granpier. His robe is rumpled, his hair tousled, but he appears otherwise unharmed. He rushes to me. "Sophy! Thank all the gods."

"I'm glad we found you." I embrace him with my free arm, then see Rambaud watching us. I make a quick decision. I hand the child over to Granpier, and say to him and Rhia, "Look after the prisoners, would you?"

"Of course," he begins, hefting the girl easily.

Rhia steps over, suspicious. "What are you—"

"Granpier and the prisoners need your help," I tell her firmly. I look at Rambaud. "But I have an appointment. With Euan Dromahair."

EUAN DROMAHAIR HAS not been watching the proceedings in the square. He doesn't seem to have heard the crowd banging down the doors of the palace, or Elanna shouting for the Paladisan guards to surrender along with Augustus. Instead we find him in the Diamond Salon, seated in a velvet chair before the fireplace. He's drinking sherry from a small, cut-glass cup. His guards watch us warily from the sides of the room.

He doesn't even turn when we enter.

"Father." The name sticks in my throat, but I fist my hands and wait, though fierce aches knead my legs. I'm tired down to the pit of my stomach.

He looks around at that. A wordless, pulsing rage hums off him. He stares past me at Rambaud, who stands with his hands curling into fists.

"You," Euan Dromahair says, but not to me. He's looking at Rambaud. "You brought *this* here?"

This. Me.

"We made a mistake," Rambaud says with great politesse. "We have realized *you* are the pretender to the throne."

Now Euan Dromahair does get to his feet. He's dropped the sherry glass; it crashes to the floor, and his shoes crush it to dust.

"*This* is your queen?"

Rambaud simply nods assent.

"I've come to offer you a bargain, Father," I say, and Euan's pale, angry eyes whip to me. "We've claimed Laon—and all of Eren and Caeris. The city and the kingdom are ours. Phaedra Saranon is dead, and so is Captain Grenou. The palace guards turned on Augustus Saranon; he's a captive now. It won't be long before the people break through the doors of the palace. Before they arrive here, in this chamber, and demand your surrender or your life."

He just stares at me.

I meet his gaze. "But you are my father, much though we both wish it were otherwise. So I'm here to make you an offer. You can walk out there at my side and face the people. I will tell them that we've reached an arrangement, and you're going into retirement in a lovely house beside the sea. And you will. You'll want for nothing. Food—comfort—everything will be yours. You will live there undisturbed for the rest of your days."

Euan's head tilts, as if he's considering my words. He says, "You would give me a house on the sea."

"A lovely house, with servants"—though he would only interact with them through a barred door—"and everything you could want."

"I have a house on the sea," Euan Dromahair says, and my stomach sinks. "I have servants. I have everything I want."

I stare at him. "If you don't cooperate, you're going to be killed."

Without answer, he strides over to the nearest guard and seizes the bayonet from the man's startled hands. With a smooth, practiced gesture, he puts it to his shoulder and sets his finger to the trigger.

I draw in a slow breath. He's mad—he must be. The song he makes is low, dangerous.

"I am the king of Eren and Caeris. And you are just like your mother. Nothing more than a whore."

My mouth snaps shut.

He fires.

But not at me. He fires at Aristide Rambaud—and the duke drops to one knee. Blood slips, red, between his fingers.

Euan looks at me. He smiles. *Smiles.* "I'm the king now," he says. He grabs a bayonet from another guard, who lets him have it.

Behind me, the door bursts open. I risk a glance over my shoulder. People are scattering into the room—Elanna, Jahan, Rhia, Victoire, all our followers. Rambaud's already kneeling on the ground, the life sweating out of him. If we don't act now, Claudette will lose her father. And if I don't act, someone else is in danger of losing their life to my father.

So I reach for Euan Dromahair—with my mind. I reach for the humming life that makes him up, the tremulous gray wisp that animates his body. His soul. I whisper the words, powerful enough to pull him apart: "Damn you."

My father's gaze has gone wide. He drops the musket; it barks when it hits the floor, spewing out a shot that sprays into the plaster of the wall. Euan stretches out his arms. Balancing himself. He's dizzy. The sound of him has turned thin and stretched. The gray wisp is fighting me, struggling to stay inside him. It's trying to claw its way back into his head.

I dig the bone flute from my pocket and play a note. High, piercing. Disruptive.

All the glass in the room shatters. People cry out. The force of the magic knocks me to my knees, but I play the note again. And again.

Euan Dromahair stumbles. He's losing his balance—losing the fight to keep the wisp of soul in his body. My music is pulling it out, demanding it release. I play it again. My magic might not be great, but it is enough. It is enough to save the people I love.

I am enough to save the people I love.

The fragile wisp is tugging free, and a wave of dizziness sweeps through me. I stumble, lowering the flute from my lips. Something hot and bright and tremulous is rushing through me. I'm panting. I open my eyes. My father has fallen to the floor, his arms splayed over his head like a felled tree. The wisp still clings to him, faint but there.

I put the flute back to my lips—and stop. If I play my father's soul out of his body, he will be the first person I have killed. One of the only people, besides Grenou and Phaedra, who have lost their lives to this coup. And I will have his blood on my hands. He's my father, after all, even if I wish to all the gods he weren't.

But I don't want to bring back the man who tried to steal my throne; who has hurt, so thoughtlessly, so many people. I don't want to bring him back the way he was.

Maybe there is another way to do it.

So I put the flute to my lips and I play a new tune, ignoring the pang in my lower back, and three small kicks from the baby, and the noise of the people behind me in the chamber. I play while Euan Dromahair's soul slowly sinks back into his body, but I don't play him back into the fullness of who he once was. No, I weave the song of a man whose anger has been burned out of him. A man who doesn't demand kingship or bodies or power. I play into being whatever parts of my father remain when the cruelty has been removed—and the rest I force out.

His soul is gathering a humming density now, and I know I can let him go. I can play another song. One that isn't for him.

It's the song of a woman who set afire every room she entered. Whose flame burned so brightly people wanted to possess it; who could not be dimmed even when her rebellion was lost, but who ran for her life across Caeris until she was consumed by a conflagration she could not stop. And I play for her daughter, who ran at her side through the wilds of Caeris; the girl whom Teofila taught to trust again, and to sing. The girl who fell in love with a bold Caerisian boy, though she pretended it was only a dalliance. The woman who claimed her father's crown, and who lost it. Who asked the people to follow her one last time.

The song of my mother, and me. The women who, though he tried, he could never dim nor drown out.

And as I draw to the end of the music, another thread slips inside. It's the yellow, vibrant pulse of a child not yet born. The anticipation of a life yet to come.

I lower the flute. The throb of the song lingers in the room, in my blood. I look down at my father, whose eyes have opened ever so slightly. He's watching me, confused. Uncomprehending. Perhaps drawing him to the edge of death snapped something within him—or perhaps when I drew the old anger and cruelty from him, it left little behind. Surely this can't be all there is to him without it. I can't have taken that much from him. He looks shrunken, defused, lying there on the floor.

Rhia has snatched the bayonet away from him, and I startle as a man moves past me. He kneels beside Euan Dromahair and ties his hands behind his back before my father even thinks to move.

"Alistar," I whisper. Did Demetra bring him here?

He turns his head. Smiles at me. "Sophy Dunbarron."

I take a step forward on my aching feet. "You remembered."

"How could I forget you?" He rises to his feet, holding out his hands, while Rhia stands guard over my father. The sound of him resonates into the room, as full and strong as it has ever been; the sound that is most like home. "I am beginning to remember more, but it's your name I recalled first."

I look into his face. He looks as he always has, the shadow of a beard on his cheeks, the creases around his eyes from his easy laughter, the quirk of his black eyebrows. Yet there's a shard of something different in his eyes. Something I haven't seen; a world I've only imagined.

I reach out and touch my hand to his cheek. He turns it over and kisses my palm.

I become aware of people moving around us. Rhia is barking an order, and Elanna has come to stand behind me, saying, "The queen will answer your demands in due course. Be patient!" Jahan is kneeling over Rambaud, healing the wound he took to the gut, Lathiel at his side.

And there is a voice whispering into my mind—a woman's voice, all the way from Baedon. *Sophy,* Teofila says. *Sophy!*

Alistar, meanwhile, is looking up, above my left shoulder. The faintest frown tucks his brows together. "Your music must have drawn them, Sophy."

The back of my neck prickles. "Drawn who?"

"The ancestors," he says, and then he looks at me, flashing a smile. "Don't worry, Soph. They're only here to watch."

So he's seeing the spirits of the dead now. I find myself starting to laugh. Now the ministers really won't like my marrying him. But for Alistar Connell, I am willing to face down an outraged Ereni or two. I take his hand.

Behind me, Elanna is saying, "You can speak to *me*—the *Caveadear*. The queen is *busy*."

I look into Alistar's eyes. They've creased; he's starting to laugh.

I'm smiling. "You look more yourself."

"I don't *feel* myself. I . . ." He closes his eyes briefly. "I feel *bigger*."

We both do, I think. We both stand here, carrying the traces of the bone flute song. We are both more than we have ever been.

"Alistar Connell." I take both his hands. "I have something to say to you."

The gleam in his eyes turns wicked, and suddenly there is the Alistar I love, himself once more. "Are you proposing to me?"

"Yes," I say, "and no." I lean close, breathing in his scent, his slightly bemused smile. "I promised you marriage, Alistar Connell, and I want it more than anything. Because I've finally realized that as the queen of Eren and Caeris, I'm the one who makes the rules. I don't have to marry for duty or advantage. I can choose to marry for love, and I do. I choose you. Will you have me?"

He's smiling now. "I will always have you, Sophy Dunbarron."

"But I'm also asking for something more than marriage. Something even bigger." I look into his eyes, with their new, unfathomable gleam. "I want to know if you're willing to be the father of my child. I want to know if you'll raise her by my side, if you'll stand by me when she's born, if you'll coach her through her first steps and her first words."

His lips open, but I hold him tighter, forestalling him. Fiercely, I say, "I want our daughter to grow up knowing she has a father who will love her."

"I will always love her," Alistar promises. His eyes are gleaming bright.

"And you will always be there for her," I press. "Even when it's been a long night, or some duty is demanding you be elsewhere, if she needs you—"

"I swear I'll be there. For her, and—" He leans closer still, pressing his forehead to mine. "—for you. I accept your proposal of marriage, and your proposal of fatherhood, Sophy Dunbarron. I always will."

I'm smiling so hard I can't speak. So I simply take our joined hands and lower them to my stomach. There's a soft flutter, so subtle I'm not even sure Alistar can feel it. But then he looks at me. I know we're both grinning like fools. I know my head aches and so does my back, and the baby needs me to rest. I know I have a room of Ereni and Caerisians to quell, and a kingdom to tend to, and a surrogate mother growing more and more irritated by the fact that I haven't answered her summons.

But just for this moment, I draw Alistar Connell's face down to mine, and I let the world go on around us.

BUT FINALLY THE world can't be left alone any longer. I turn from Alistar to the ruined salon, drawing in a tired breath. Rambaud is sitting up from the floor, looking pale, with Jahan and Demetra both supporting him. Elanna passes me a hand mirror, all the while not breaking from her steady argument with Philippe's mother, Veronique, over possible changes to the process of receiving a noble title.

I shelter the small mirror between Alistar's body and my own, and look down. It's Teofila's careworn face that reflects back at me from the mirror, of course; she must finally have summoned Elanna when I didn't answer. She's somewhere bright and warm. The wide veranda behind her is filled with sun.

"We took the palace," I tell her.

That was quick work. She returns my smile. *And El—? You're together . . .*

"She's fine, and so is Jahan." Or they will be. I glance at Elanna, as tenacious as ever in her too-large greatcoat, her hair spilling loose from its knot. I don't know how much Phaedra's ploy damaged her, not to mention the land itself. But for now, it's enough to tell Teofila that she's whole. Safe. "We all are."

Teofila's intent gaze has marked my hesitation, but she doesn't press. *We made our way here with little incident, and I've met with Queen Sylvestra. She's a bit more, shall we say, querulous than I remembered, but she's willing to consider an alliance. Though she has certain demands . . .*

"Does she, now?" I'm amused despite myself.

She insists that if sorcery is the way of the future, she needs her own court sorcerer. Teofila casts her gaze heavenward. *She wishes us to send someone to her.*

"Well, tell her she'll have to wait for a volunteer."

I'll do my best, though I doubt she'll like that.

I look into her face, so full of the strength that raised me from girlhood; the strength that lost, and regained, Elanna twice. I say, "Did you find your family?"

A soft smile touches her lips. There's love in it, and regret. *I did. My parents have grown old, and my brother's children do not know me. But we are here, together, for now.* She looks at me. *Tell me, is Hugh—?*

"He's here." Alistar nudges me and points. Hugh himself is wading through the crowd toward us, his gaze preoccupied. I say, "I'll let you talk to him yourself."

Hugh approaches, and I push the mirror into his hands. He looks down, befuddled, and then he sees Teofila. The lines of his face, which a moment ago looked so tired to me, soften with hope and relief. "There you are," he says softly, as if he's already forgotten my presence, and Alistar's, and indeed the rest of the room.

I let myself look at them for a moment—Teofila caught in the small mirror, and Hugh cupping it before his own face. My heart pinches. I press Hugh's shoulder. "Tell her to come home soon."

He nods without taking his eyes off the mirror.

"Sophy!"

It's Rhia at my other side, tired and impatient. "They want you outside. People are gathering in the inner courtyard. They want you to make a speech."

Philippe's mother, Veronique, leans out of her conversation with Elanna. "You must promise them you'll give the Ereni more power in government! That was your bargain with us, and we'll hold you to it."

"Naturally," I say, glancing at Rambaud. He's listening to our conversation, even though his whole body appears tight with pain. He gives the smallest nod. I know I will have to take him to task for his murder of the sorcerer refugee, Ciril's friend—but that will be an unpleasant job for another day. I turn back to Countess Veronique. Behind her, I glimpse Lord Devalle. He's hovering in the doorway, as if he doesn't quite dare to come in. I pitch my words to reach him as well as her. "More but *equal* power. You have my word on it."

I move past her before she can protest further, sweeping El, Alistar, and Rhia along with me.

But before I reach the door, Devalle holds up his hand. "Your Majesty," he says, and bows.

I wait, but he says nothing more. When he straightens, there's a kind of fear in his eyes, and I know that even if I've promised to give more power to the Ereni people, I am the one who really wields it, right now.

"Devalle," I say at last, "we have not exactly been friends. But I believe in second chances, for the people of Eren and Caeris are giving me one. I would like to give you one, as well."

He looks entirely surprised, and bows again. "I am deeply grateful, Your Majesty."

I really should correct him on the honorific. But just this once, I decide, I'll let him keep calling me *Your Majesty*.

I move past him into the corridor. It's quieter here—people have scattered to the inner courtyard, to await my arrival on the balcony. The palace shows signs of the catastrophic magic Phaedra attempted: A long crack runs through the parquet floor, and the paintings hang askew on the walls.

"There's rubble in the streets," Elanna says, following my line of thought. She looks exhausted, her eyes dark. "I can't even tell the scale of it yet, only that it runs from here to Barrody and perhaps even Dalriada. It's as if she tried to tear up the foundation of the earth."

Ours is a magical land, so I suppose in a way, Phaedra did. I halt our little party in the corridor, looking more closely at El. "Are you . . . ?"

"Oh, Sophy," she says, and instinctively I hug her. She speaks into my shoulder. "I don't know. I don't feel numb, the way I did when my magic was blocked. But my head aches. My *mind* aches. When I feel out into the land, it hurts. The land is in pain."

I can feel this, inside her, the green ribbon of her magic frayed thin, stripped with pulses of red pain. I hum a little, and she presses her face into my coat. "It will heal," I promise her. "And in the meantime, the people need their *Caveadear.*"

She smiles at that, though faintly. There's movement in the corridor behind us; Jahan and his brother Lathiel emerge from the Diamond Salon, catching us up. Jahan takes one look at El and puts his arm around her shoulders. She hugs him back but doesn't crumble. She looks at me and nods. "Are we ready?"

"One more thing." I turn to Rhia, who's chewing on her lower lip. "We no longer have a warden of the mountains."

Rhia's eyes widen. "Not me," she says automatically.

Elanna folds her arms. "Why not you?"

"You could at least put your name forward," Alistar points out. "It doesn't mean they'll elect you. I don't know why people would want a mad Knoll any—"

I smack his arm, and he stops, looking pleased with himself. "Rhia," I say, "the tripartite rule might have suited Caeris, but it doesn't suit Eren *and* Caeris—as Rambaud and his followers made abundantly clear. I think we'll have to split the warden's duties between more than one person. It would be a new position we're creating, one that's never been done before. You could be the one who fills it."

Rhia looks shifty. "*If* I'm elected."

"Yes," Jahan says drily, "that will be a key step."

We all look at her, and Rhia looks back. She swallows. "I suppose—well, if I have to—I'll think about it."

"That's all we're asking." I wink at Elanna, who grins.

Rhia sees it—and now that the pressure is off her, predictably erupts. "It's so typical of you southerners! You can't leave a Knoll to simply fulfill her duty as the head of the queen's bodyguard. It's always *improvement,* and can we do *better,* not are we doing well enough *now* . . ."

She stumps off ahead of us down the corridor, and Jahan whispers, "How much do you bet she'll do it?"

Alistar shakes his head, but he's laughing. "Never bet against a Knoll."

"She lost her father," El says, more soberly. "It'll help her work through her grief."

"You mean it'll keep her busy growling at people," Alistar says, and Jahan snorts.

But El's gaze has caught mine, and I hear the flare of grief within her. I know we're both thinking about fathers, and loss. Neither of us says anything. It's enough to know that someone else shares this, and has seen it in me.

We move on, to the balcony at last. My ministers are there, or some of them—Victoire, Juleane, High Priest Granpier.

And Philippe. I reach out a hand to him, and he clasps it. He's dirty from prison, his hair wild, and he looks now like the rebel he once pretended to be, that night he and I slipped into Rambaud's party. Perhaps the rebel he wanted to be, before his mother stopped him.

"Philippe Manceau," I say, "I am glad you're my friend."

He smiles. "I'm glad to be your friend, Sophy Dunbarron."

"I hope you'll continue to be my minister of public works." I glance at Victoire, who is waiting beside the balustrade, her gaze flickering toward us, and though she's obviously trying not to appear interested, the quivering sound of her tells me differently. "Perhaps you and Victoire could work together."

"I'd like that," he says, and I hear a giddy resonance pulse from him, even as the tips of his ears turn red.

I hide a smile and turn to the others, embracing Victoire, Juleane, Granpier. My feet are swollen, and my back throbs. My body—the baby—demand rest, yet at the same time I feel vibrant, almost electrified. Below us in the courtyard, voices are roaring, "The queen! The queen!" and "Justice! Equality!" and someone, quite unexpectedly, is singing a ballad. Each one of them possesses a song, a tone that weaves and dives among the others, a kind of madness that turns to melody. It's the song of this land; the soul of her people. It is our true power, both theirs and mine.

I step out to the end of the balcony, to speak to my people.

EPILOGUE

We're here at last. Alistar opens the door of the coach, and the smell of spring blossoms inside. He climbs out first, onto the gravel drive of Cerid Aven, turning back so I can pass Mag to him. She's slept the last few hours and she doesn't even wake now, but settles against Alistar's shoulder, the pale mauve of her eyelids moving in a dream. Her small hands float free. She lays against her father, utterly trusting.

I step out after him, into a din of noise. People are disembarking from the carriages behind us, and the guards are leading their horses over to the stables. I hear Rhia giving a stern lecture to Isley, whom she appointed as captain of the queen's guard in her stead.

I peer back down the drive. "He isn't here yet."

"They broke that axle back in Portmason," Alistar says, reassuringly. "It's probably still giving them trouble."

I shake my head. "I *told* Rambaud we shouldn't put him in that gold carriage. It's not meant for a cross-country expedition."

"Oh, well." Alistar grins at me and bounces Mag gently in his arms. She goes on sleeping, entirely oblivious. "Leontius is an emperor. I suppose we can wait for him."

I find myself returning his smile. To tell the truth, it's something of a relief to be so far ahead of the emperor of Paladis, who arrived last week for his first state visit to our newly renamed kingdom, Ard-Terre—named for the river Ard that unites both Eren and

Caeris. Not that I don't enjoy Leontius's company—I do, very much—but, if possible, people insist on showing him even more deference than they do me. It gets exhausting. Lees, who is the mildest of people, prefers quiet and talk of gardening.

Perhaps here he can get it. Cerid Aven is large—large enough to comfortably house not only my retinue but an imperial one as well. And Elanna is just the person to discuss gardening with.

She's come out to the front step now, a slender figure before the great house. "Sophy! Alistar!" Then she's pelting toward us, embracing first me and then, more carefully, Alistar and the baby. She's dressed for the occasion in a fetching yellow gown, though there are grass stains on her knees.

I seize her arm. "Let's go in," I whisper, "quickly, before anyone else follows!"

We race into the house, dodging footmen and guards and the housekeeper. The inside, however, is just as much a hubbub as outside. Demetra and the other refugees are gathered in the foyer, a circle of earnest faces. They wave to me but don't approach.

"They're practicing some sorcery to welcome Leontius," Elanna explains. "An illusion meant to look like fireworks, but without the racket that frightens the dogs and wild creatures."

We slip past the refugees, and the house staff straightening the vases of flowers and the ice buckets holding champagne. Back behind the stairs is a salon I remember well, transformed now with rows of chairs and a lectern at the front. New books crowd the walls.

"This will be the main lecture hall," Elanna says, spreading her arms. "What do you think?"

"I love it, El." I beam at her. "You've done marvelous work."

She smiles. She and Jahan have been busy these last few months, transforming Cerid Aven into a school for sorcery. Some of the refugees have volunteered to work as tutors, and Rhia's aunt Granya Knoll has come down from the mountains with masses of books.

"We may have to expand," El says seriously. "More people keep signing up every day!"

There's a noise at the other side of the room: Jahan comes in. "There you are!" He embraces me and pats Alistar on the back— gently, on account of the sleeping Mag.

"How's married life?" Alistar asks them with a twinkle.

El and Jahan look at each other, and they both begin to grin. "Well," Jahan says, "El invited every sorcerer she knows to join us in our house . . ."

"But I told Jahan I'd have another house built for us," Elanna says with satisfaction. "A little one, by the Sentry Rock, just for ourselves."

"But we might ask the same of you," Jahan points out. "How is it to be wed?"

Alistar and I exchange a glance, and I start laughing while he makes a face. "I might not have agreed if Sophy had mentioned there would be *royal duties* involved. Lists, letters, functions, people always demanding you help them or just send a *little message* to the queen . . ."

"I promise you'll learn to love it," I tease him.

"I don't know, Sophy," he says with mock seriousness. "That may be one promise you aren't able to keep."

I just smile. He doesn't dislike it as much as he professes— though when the Ereni ministers predictably made their protests, I thought he might change his mind. So we slipped away early one morning to the temple to Aera and had High Priest Granpier bind the cloth around our hands in secret, just like lovers in a story. When the ministers found out a few hours later, it was too late; we were already wed. We salved their damaged pride by throwing a party for the entire city.

"Whenever I find myself growing irritated, I think of the looks on the ministers' faces when they found out we'd married without their supervision," Alistar tells Elanna and Jahan. "It was marvelous."

The door squeaks, and a boy slips into the room. Lathiel's grown taller since I last saw him, but he seems as diffident as ever behind his flop of dark hair. He looks shyly at us, then addresses his brother and sister-in-law. "Is Rayka here?"

"He's coming with Emperor Leontius," I answer, and look at Jahan. "Some friends of yours have come as well—Pantoleon and Tullea?"

A smile transforms Jahan's face. "They came!"

But Lathiel has gone still, and even though he's filled out and grown tall, the faintest tremor runs through him. He whispers to Jahan, "Not Father?"

"No," Jahan says firmly. "Never Father. I wrote him back and forbade it. Though"—he glances at El—"one day we'll have to return to Britemnos and settle affairs there. But you won't have to go with us, Lathiel. You never have to see him again."

Lathiel lets out a breath of release.

Jahan moves as if to ruffle his hair, then holds himself back. He smiles instead. "Let's show everyone the other lecture halls, shall we?"

They move out, Alistar following with the still-sleeping Mag, but Elanna catches me back. Her brow is knit with slight concern. "Is Alistar . . . ?"

"He's better," I say. "Though sometimes he sees people no one else does. It unnerves the ministers no end."

El raises a brow. "Who's to say those people aren't really there?"

I look at her. She seems so at ease here, and the sound of her has steadied, green and vibrant once again. It's strange to think I envied her so long, this woman who is more comfortable out in the green land than with people. "How are your headaches?" I ask.

"They're better." One corner of her mouth tucks down. Quietly, she says, "I don't think I'll ever be able to do what I once did again. Well, perhaps an army of walking trees on a *particularly* special occasion. The land is recovering, and the magic of it . . ." She looks at me. "I think its magic has spread instead into the people who are receptive to it."

"I think so, too." I shake my head; it's extraordinary how many would-be sorcerers have come forward in the year since we defeated Euan. "Perhaps it's for the best that you can't. With this school, everyone would want you to do extraordinary displays of magic!"

"That might be," she says wryly. Then, with a smile, "Teofila came, didn't she? And Hugh?"

I nod. "They were farther back in the line. I expect they've unloaded by now."

"But I suppose Victoire and Philippe remained in Laon."

"With the two of them managing the south while I'm gone, I'll hardly have anything to do when I return," I say with a laugh. But El looks regretful; she misses her friend. I add, "I'll make sure Victoire comes north soon."

"Tell her to bring Philippe. I want to see the two of them together." El gives a wicked grin, then glances toward the door. "I do want to see Mother and Hugh before the formalities begin. Do you mind if I . . . ?"

"Go find them." I grin at her. "You don't need to show me around."

She disappears through the door, and I'm left alone in the sudden silence of the large lecture hall. I walk past the chairs, tapping their backs with my fingertips. Ruadan used to host parties in this salon. It's the room where I first met Finn, when he told us of Euan.

Strange to think of it, and of my father, who is ensconced in his pleasant seaside prison. Not behind bars, because that is no longer necessary. I put a hand to my throat. The guilt won't leave me, no matter how many times I remind myself of Euan's cruelty, no matter how often I tell myself that this is the cost I must bear. He is still my father, and I took away his mind. He is simple as a child—simpler, perhaps, for he shows only the dullest curiosity. His nurses tell me that he appreciates clear days, and the sound of the sea. He can watch butterflies chasing in the garden for hours. The nurses don't fear him, for he can scarcely dress himself. He can form only the most basic words.

Perhaps it is what he deserved, but I did this to him. And I must live with that.

Leontius told me that he had also exiled his brother Augustus, whom we shipped back to Paladis after our victory. Unlike Euan, he is guarded—watched at all hours of the day and night. Leontius's eyes met mine when he told me, and I saw in them the echo of my own guilt. They are our family, whatever they have done.

With an effort, I shake off the thought and open the glass doors into the garden. I step through into the clean, bright air of Caeris. It's quiet here, and the sun beats down over the young spring plants. I turn my face up to its warmth. I've learned to make Laon and Barrody comfortable, but this is home. There is the Valtai Stone, under its shelter; there, an old oak I used to climb; there, a swing on which someday we'll push our daughter.

And there, standing on the other side of the gardens, is Alistar, holding her.

I make my way over to them, putting my arms around Alistar's back and nestling my chin onto his shoulder. We lean together like that for a long moment, drinking in the sunlight, the quiet, the growing plants. The child still sleeping in his arms.

Then he says softly, "I thought I heard her." He nods toward the far end of the garden, where there is a tangle of rosebushes and early-spring flowers, and birds trilling.

"I don't see anyone," I say, but I'm careful to keep my tone light. Gentle. We've gotten used to this by now.

"A woman's walking there. She's singing. It's a lullaby, I think. The one you always sing to Mag." Softly, he says, "She has golden hair. She's wearing an old coat with patched elbows. She's tall, bright-eyed. Bold."

My throat closes. "Does she look like a rebel queen?" I ask when I can speak.

Alistar studies her, this woman I cannot see. Then, as if he can see the true question in my heart, he says, "She looks content."

I close my eyes. Sometimes I envy him the sight; sometimes I think it would comfort me to see them again—Finn, Ruadan, Ingram Knoll. My mother. Even the Butcher. Yet perhaps it is enough that Alistar sees. That he tells me, so tenderly.

He's turned to face me. "Look," he murmurs.

I look down, and he passes our daughter into my arms. I hug her weight and warmth against my chest. Her small pink fingers are fluttering, as if in time to music.

For a moment, I hear it, too. The whisper of a woman's voice, carried on the wind. The skirl of music, a breath of hope on the breeze. Here, and gone. My chest aches, and at the same time I'm smiling. I look down into the garden, and for the barest instant I think I glimpse the movement of a long blue coat. The fall of golden hair.

Then it is gone and I am standing here with the baby I named for her, and the man I love wrapping us both in his arms, and my heart is so full.

I am ready to be brave, Mother.

Our child opens her eyes. The sky reflects in them, a deep and infinite blue.

ACKNOWLEDGMENTS

I'm so grateful to everyone who has had a part in the making of this book. So much gratitude to my wonderful editor, Anne Groell, for encouraging me to write a series with multiple narrators and for championing Sophy. Many thanks as well to my equally wonderful agent, Hannah Bowman, for support, guidance, and feedback on pregnancy issues!

Thank you to the fantastic team at Del Rey Books for all their hard work, particularly Isabella Biedenharn in publicity, and to the art department for gracing these books with gorgeous covers, and to Diane Hobbing for the lovely interior design. I'm also grateful to Sam Bradbury and everyone at Hodder in the UK. Thank you also to the team at Liza Dawson Associates.

Particular thanks to Peggy and Linda for advising me on several medical matters. (Any errors are mine!)

I'm grateful to everyone who supports me in daily and writing life, especially my parents, Nancy, my sister Eowyn, and my soul sisters Licia and Martha (and Joel!). Thank you to Julia for writing meetups and non-writing adventures! Thank you to Denise, Peggy (again!), Bernie, Deb, Jim, Mel, Sarah, Katlyn, Pam, the staff of the Discovery Center, and everyone who has helped celebrate several years of books.

Last—but far from least—I'm grateful to the readers. Thank you.

ABOUT THE AUTHOR

CALLIE BATES is the author of *The Waking Land, The Memory of Fire,* and *The Soul of Power.* She is also a harpist, certified harp therapist, sometimes artist, and nature nerd. When she's not creating, she's hitting the trails or streets and exploring new places. She lives in the Upper Midwest.

calliebates.com
Facebook.com/calliebywords
Twitter: @calliebywords

ABOUT THE TYPE

This book was set in Sabon, a typeface designed by the well-known German typographer Jan Tschichold (1902–74). Sabon's design is based upon the original letter forms of sixteenth-century French type designer Claude Garamond and was created specifically to be used for three sources: foundry type for hand composition, Linotype, and Monotype. Tschichold named his typeface for the famous Frankfurt typefounder Jacques Sabon (c. 1520–80).